Call of the Lapwing

Marjorie P. Dunn

*To Bob with love
and thanks for everything*

CALL OF THE LAPWING

Marjorie Dunn

By the same author

For the Love of Children

CHILDREN'S BOOKS:
Flambo the Dragon
The Wild Rocking Horses of Whirlow
Mr Fisher's Ducks
Horace Returns to Dore

HISTORICAL NOVELS:
The T'alli Stone
The Reluctant Traveller
Abe's Legacy
The Maggie Kelly

© **Marjorie P. Dunn 2007**

Published by The Hallamshire Press
The Hallamshire Press is an imprint of
Hallamshire Publications Limited

Printed in Great Britain by
The Cromwell Press, Trowbridge, Wiltshire.

British Library Cataloguing in Publication Data:
 A catalogue record for this book is available from the British Library

ISBN 978-1-874718-67-3

Prologue

Abe's Legacy

When Edward Morton inherited the old farm and land from his late employer, Abe Bagshaw, the Will had a clause that Edward must marry within a year of receiving the legacy and ultimately sire a child from the marriage. The terms of the Will reflected Abe's determination that Edward's nephews should not inherit the farm on Edward's demise due to their feckless irresponsibility. Should Edward not comply with Abe's intentions the farm and land would eventually be gifted to the parish of Bradfield.

Edward was an intelligent but shy man and very reluctantly advertised for a potential bride in the local Sheffield newspapers. He was successful and brought Hannah Hardy and her young daughter Lizzie to live in the farm's nearby cottage. However, on the eleventh of March 1864, before they could wed, the Dale Dyke Dam burst. The torrent of water raced down through Bradfield and on to the town of Sheffield destroying Abe's old farm and many other buildings as it went. At least 240 people lost their lives that night and many animals also.

As a result of this calamity Edward was forced to move into the small cottage with Mrs Hardy and Lizzie and eventually they did marry. Sadly, after several happy years, Hannah died and a distraught Edward was left to bring up his stepdaughter alone.

Peter, the youngest of Edward's nephews, left home to better himself in the Army and occasionally visited his uncle and his new family with the result that Lizzie became infatuated with him. He, though, wished to marry Clara Burton, a nurse. However when Clara met Edward they fell in love and a disappointed Peter went to India with his regiment while Lizzie concealed her unhappiness at his going. She knew that her stepfather never would have agreed to her marrying Peter anyway due to the unreasonable terms of the Will.

Lizzie always kept a diary yet it had a gap of ten years, from Peter's departure until his return. What happened in the intervening time is a mystery.

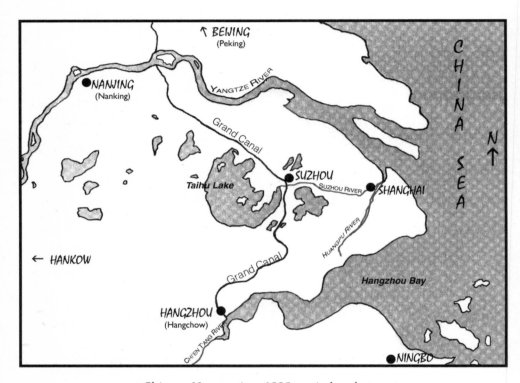

Chinese Names circa 1885 are in brackets

England 1985

Mimi had travelled halfway round the world to reach England, and there, somewhere beneath her almost destroyed now by neglect and time, lay her goal. She had only viewed the farm on an early, fading photograph; now her dream of seeing it for real was about to be fulfilled.

Within a secluded valley, surrounded by wild moors and rolling hills her Great Great Aunt Lizzie had roamed as a young girl. There had been family stories of a disastrous flood, of a peculiar legacy and a marriage of convenience. Then, for some unknown reason, there had been a gap in Lizzie's diaries of nine or ten years; this was inexplicable and had always aroused Mimi's curiosity. She'd spent many hours reflecting on the photograph, the other diaries and Great Great Aunt Lizzie's later letters, almost willing that an explanation would lift itself from the papers, but it never did.

Mimi's desire to find out more had increased, and she had vowed that one day she would holiday in England and visit her ancestral home to see the farm for herself. This ambition was a comfort in times of despondency, and she knew that one day she would be compelled to seek the answers she craved by treading those same paths taken a century before by her Great Great Aunt. Eventually she wrote to England, to the local newspaper in the nearest town of Sheffield, a mere nine miles from the farm in Bradfield, asking if anyone knew the history of the family. One reply thrilled her, and for some time she had been corresponding with Mark Weston, a keen family historian who was willing to help. It was he who had discovered yet another of Lizzie's diaries in the Archives Department of Sheffield's Central Library; one which Mimi guessed must have existed but had no idea where it was or why it should be separate from those already in her possession. Mark had tediously copied it for her so that she could enjoy another period of Lizzie's existence so long ago.

Life had been difficult for Mimi since her painful divorce two years earlier. She had survived financially and mentally by earning extra money selling her writings and saving for her trip to England. It was that one dream, to visit the farm, which kept her sanity. She had held garage-sales, buying and selling anything worthwhile, until at last she had sufficient money spare to fulfil her dream. She had worked hard and started to write an account of Lizzie's story, encouraged by her publisher who felt he had a market for such a book. It was then that Mark Weston advised her that what was left of the long-neglected farm was to be demolished and, to the amazement and concern of her parents, she decided to leave for England as soon as possible. She was determined to explore all avenues that might lead her closer to her heroine.

After a tedious flight across the Atlantic, Mimi was greeted at Gatwick Airport by a pleasant young man who she instantly recognised from the photograph he'd provided. Strangely, she had not thought much about the man behind the portrait, their easy correspondence although friendly had not warranted it. Smiling hesitantly, she reached out and shook his hand, and did wonder why she had not asked more questions about him during the months in which they'd exchanged letters. Had she been selfish in her eagerness to seek information about Lizzie's life? She knew only that he was two years her senior, (she was twenty-eight) and that he lived a quiet, single life-style, as she did now. He appeared to be quite reserved and she wondered if their conversations might be a little strained, but this turned out not to be the case.

Mark Weston was, to her great relief, pleasant, articulate and far from stuffy. He was taller than she'd imagined he would be, for those Englishmen she'd previously met were neither athletic in build nor as outspoken as many Americans. Only later did she discover that he'd been equally apprehensive over their meeting.

At seven-thirty in the morning, after a long flight that had been constantly disturbed by a noisy passenger, Mimi was tired. Consequently she found that once settled in the front seat of Mark's car she dozed fitfully, occasionally jolting her head against the near-side window until Mark offered her a spare jacket to lean against.

She wasn't sure how far they'd travelled when the car came to a halt. Waking and looking around her, she desperately attempted to understand where she was, before once again sinking into oblivion.

'Wake up!' Mark said softly, gently nudging her shoulder. 'A cup of coffee will do you good!' He opened the door, came round to her side and courteously helped her out. Such gentlemanly behaviour at another time might have amused her, but not today. Normally she was a good traveller but now she was surprised by a slight nausea that caused her to momentarily lean against the car. The English coffee that accompanied the in-flight breakfast still lay heavy in her stomach, and this was no doubt the cause of her queasiness. 'I'm sorry,' Mimi apologised, 'it was such a wearisome flight.'

'I've never flown,' he replied, 'but friends who have did warn me that you might be exhausted.'

Regaining her equilibrium, she asked, 'How long do you think it will be before they pull down what is left of the farm?'

'They've already started clearing the outbuildings,' Mark informed her with a note of regret in his voice. 'The sooner we get out there the better!' He looked keenly at her and commented, 'You look quite pale; are you sure you're fit to carry on?' Mimi gave a weak smile, and asked if they could take a walk in the fresh air.

The morning was quite chilly but a few minutes sufficed to revive her and soon she felt able to resume their journey. A piece of barley sugar Mark proffered helped, and they set off again. What Mimi had seen of England so far did not much impress her. The long asphalt carriageways like the highways back home were noisy and boring: the small fields on either side, although richly green, continued mile after mile and gradually became uninteresting. The quaint towns and villages they by-passed no doubt had their mysteries, but where were the beautiful hills and valleys for which England was so renowned? Where were the thatched-roofed cottages and stone walls?

For some hours, Mimi dozed on and off until Mark announced that they were only about twenty miles from where she was to stay with his sister and her family on the outskirts of Mark's own city of Sheffield. She feared he might think her very rude, for whenever she woke she suffered the dazed confusion that only the dog-tired, long-haul traveller can appreciate. However, once Mark turned off the motorway she was able to concentrate more—until the strangest of sights met her eyes.

'No!' she exclaimed shaking her head, 'I haven't had an intoxicating drink all day and my new glasses aren't broken!' She sat bolt upright to see if the leaning, twisted church spire piercing the sky in front of them really existed or was she hallucinating?

Mark laughed at her obvious amazement, explaining that Chesterfield's church spire was not a mirage. It had been built twisted to a continental design deliberately, but the lead sheathing had responded to the contrasting weather conditions causing the whole thing to lean. She was not to be alarmed, he assured her, it would probably remain standing long after they were both dead and buried, God willing! Hesitating then, as if unsure of himself, Mark added, 'They do say that the spire will straighten the first time a virgin gets married inside the Church'. Then he flushed with embarrassment, wondering if he should have been so forward. She smiled. English humour was noticeably different to American, but she appreciated his attempt to entertain her. She was more amused by his almost shy attitude than anything else. 'I thought we'd take the scenic route through Cordwell valley,' he suggested, almost as atonement for the joke, then concentrated on negotiating his way through the town.

To Mimi's delight, the landscape changed dramatically within a couple of miles as they drove along much smaller country roads. This was more like her expectations! They passed through small hamlets and lush valleys on the way to Mark's sister's home. In spite of the winding journey Mimi was now feeling more like her old self and she marvelled at the magnificent banks of pink and purple rhododendrons which completely covered the hillsides of the last deep valley out of which they climbed. The narrow twisting road rose steeply, the view opening out suddenly and Mimi felt that they were on top of the world. The landscape was now bare of trees but incredibly beautiful in its simplicity. They were surrounded by wild, rugged moorland and in the distance between the far hills she could see the spread of a city. Mimi took a sharp breath at the vista and leaned forward with interest.

'We'll pull in here for a minute,' Mark said, steering the car into a convenient lay-by.

For the first time since leaving home Mimi wondered if she had been wise to put her life into the hands of a stranger. They were almost at their destination, so why stop now?

Mark gestured before him towards the view, which in that moment of caution she'd forgotten. 'I thought you might find the city impressive from this place.' There, beyond the moorland, beyond the hamlets, and beyond the deep cleft in the trees in the distance, lay the city which was obviously his pride and joy. 'That's Sheffield,' he said proudly, 'like Rome it's set on seven hills, with five small rivers between them.'

'It's is a lot smaller than I imagined,' Mimi replied.

'It's very deceptive. The city's tentacles spread for miles between the hills but the trees make it a very pleasant place to be.'

Later Mimi discovered that had she entered the city from the north, through an area of factories and demolition sites, she would not have been so impressed. However, from their present position, the sun enhanced the spring green of the surrounding fields.

For the first time since landing she felt a surge of excitement. 'It's wonderful,' she cried, feeling guilty over having suspected Mark of devious intentions in stopping the car so near their destination.

'I thought you'd like the view. It's hard to imagine that thirty years ago all you would have seen from here was a cloud of industrial fog hanging over the city, you wouldn't have been able to see any buildings at all!'

Her eyes wandered enquiringly over the scene. It was unlike all she'd imagined. 'Can we see Bradfield from here?' she asked hopefully.

'Only in a helicopter, if then,' Mark replied with a chuckle; 'the village lies six or seven valleys away to the left. If the weather's good tomorrow I'll take you there but now I think that we should move on, or Eileen will be getting worried. We can almost see her house from here.' He started the engine and drove towards the valley below. 'My parents used to cycle down this hill when I was a child,' he confided, 'I rode in a sidecar fastened to a tandem; apparently I had a paper windmill which spun round on a pin whilst I sang to myself. That was before Eileen was born,' he added.

It was pleasant sharing his memories and Mimi was grateful that he kept talking. She had always been self-conscious and afraid of long gaps in conversation with strangers and, as a result, either kept silent or chattered incessantly.

Finding that Mimi seemed to enjoy his reminiscences, Mark relaxed. 'I hope you won't mind,' he said, 'but I've taken a few days off work to show you a bit of the area, as well as help you sort out Lizzie's story. I've made appointments and booked micro-film readers in the Archives, and even ordered a few documents to start you off.' All hesitancy had left him; he was an efficient family historian on the trail of a good mystery. Mimi liked the change in him, and felt she was on familiar ground.

'That's very kind of you,' she replied, 'I just hope you won't regret spending so much time with me.'

He smiled as they drove on. 'I've enjoyed the research I've done so far and would like to see it through if I can. You'll be pleased to know that I've also ordered Lizzie's diary for you to see tomorrow.'

Mimi was thrilled by this. 'I can't wait to handle it and read her actual writing myself. I know you copied it out for me, but to be able to hold the real thing, smell it and go through it will be wonderful.' Mark laughed at her childlike enthusiasm and this caused her to blush. She was grateful to him, but how was she going to repay him for his kindness when it had taken most of her savings simply to fly to Britain? She decided then and there to take the bull by the horns and said, 'Look, I'm very grateful for all you've done but I'll be frank, I don't have much money to pay for all this. I'm quite prepared to do the research and live quietly while I'm here; I can pay your sister what we agreed, but I'm afraid there's not a lot spare for anything else.'

Mark chuckled. 'You've paid me for doing the research I've done so far and what I've planned now won't cost much, just a drop of petrol here and there.' After a pause he asked, 'Did you bring that sturdy pair of shoes that I mentioned? They'll save you pounds.'

She was puzzled by this and looked at him in some amazement, 'What do you mean?' she asked.

'Well, there are some wonderful places to see around about here and walking is something we Sheffielders are noted for. It's also cheaper to walk.'

'Walk!' Mimi exclaimed as if struck by thunder. She, who thought nothing of driving two blocks for some simple shopping! Shaking her head in disbelief, she replied lamely, 'I can't walk far.'

Seeing her dismay he laughed out loud. 'You'll learn, or you'll not see much of Lizzie's landscape.'

Rounding several sharp bends, each one revealing more of the delightful countryside, their road narrowed as they entered a village.

'This is Totley,' he informed her, 'it is part of Sheffield, but still very rural.' Two minutes later he turned off the main road and entered a pleasant avenue lined on both sides with houses, each one having its own garden enclosed by a wall with a gate leading off the pavement.

'Here we are, Eileen's at last!' Mimi climbed out of the car feeling quite stiff, and desperate to use the toilet after such a long last section of their journey. 'This is Mimi Holden, Eileen!' Mark said to his sister, a pleasant homely figure who was shorter than her brother, but had the same rich dark auburn hair.

Shaking Eileen's hand Mimi said, 'It's so nice to meet you, but would you mind if I used your bathroom straight away?' It was hardly a great introduction but she feared the worst if delayed much longer.

Maybe, by having to take Mimi upstairs the ice was broken for Eileen, as she smiled before leaving her saying, 'I'm so pleased someone else has the same problem as I do when travelling. I'm always being teased about it.'

By the time Mimi rejoined her hostess, she found that refreshments were on offer. 'Do you take tea or coffee?' Eileen asked, and once her coffee had been served, Mimi faced a barrage of questions.

'Is it really windy in Chicago? Do you watch the Chicago Bears? Have you met the 'Refrigerator'?' The answer to all three was no, although Mimi had once seen the Bear's famous player when shopping in the local Mall. 'The truth is I don't actually live in Chicago,' Mimi finally admitted, needing to dispel the illusion they seemed to have created about her.

'Oh, what a pity,' Eileen's husband John sighed. Mimi couldn't be sure whether he was referring to the 'Refrigerator' or where she lived.

'They say Chicago is quite beautiful!' Eileen added, as if also disappointed.

Mimi smiled. 'Oh it is, on the lakeside and in the affluent parts, but it has some poor, rundown areas too. I live out of town about half-an-hour's drive away, in a suburb called Elmhurst.'

Mark rose to leave. 'I'm sorry to have to go, Mimi,' he said, 'I'll call in later—I suspect you'll be glad to get some rest now. If you're asleep when I get back I'll not disturb you, and will pick you up at half-past nine tomorrow morning, if that's ok? I made an appointment at the Archives Department for ten-thirty so that you can see Lizzie's diary before we go out to Bradfield. It might give you a feel for the place, mind you it all depends on the weather as to when we go there, so bring those walking shoes, it might be muddy! We daren't leave it too long or the builders might destroy what remains of the farm.' As he prepared to leave, Mimi shook his hand and thanked him for the trouble he'd taken to fetch her from Gatwick Airport, and for arranging everything so efficiently.

After he'd gone, Eileen showed Mimi to the small upstairs back bedroom which she was to use during the two weeks before returning home. She gratefully dumped her belongings, slipped into a pair of pyjamas and climbed into the bed where, within minutes she was oblivious to all about her.

She slept through Mark's return later in the day, but rose in time to enjoy a couple of hours chatting amiably to her hosts, whilst their two young sons hovered nearby playing with their Action Men; Mimi was a novelty to them with her strange accent. Not wanting to outstay her welcome, she made her excuses and retired so as to prepare for the excitement of the following day. Accordingly, when Mark arrived promptly the next morning he found her ready and eager to be off.

With Lizzie's diary ordered in advance they were able to have immediate access to the faded document and Mimi's hand trembled as she held the brown paper parcel for the first time. As she untied the thin ribbon she marvelled that it had survived at all! Mimi tried to imagine Lizzie sitting in her room expressing her inner thoughts onto the paper.

The leather binding of the book was fading and shedding its surface, the leaves inside when carefully separated were brown and fragile to the touch and the writing difficult to read. This was why Mark had not been able to photocopy it but had painstakingly copied every word by hand.

She placed the book gently on the desk and supported its front cover on a velvet covered support as she carefully turned the pages. These were Lizzie's own thoughts, her own hand written memories; Mimi was quite emotionally moved now, even though she had previously read Mark's transcriptions. Why had her Great Great Aunt been so unhappy in later diaries; had she regretted some action in her life? Why were there some pages so meticulously stitched together at the end of the diary: had she made some mistakes and decided to prevent anyone seeing them? Would anyone ever be able to find out now?

Whilst Mimi was examining Lizzie's journal, Mark obtained a few other Bradfield Parish records concerning the farm for her to view, some of these he'd already sent photocopies of, but he thought she might like to see the originals. She was thrilled.

After a couple of hours Mark suggested that it was time they left. He'd been keeping an eye on the weather and, although it was still windy and cool, the rain had at least ceased. 'Will it stay fine, do you think?' Mimi asked hopefully, in a whisper so as not to disturb the other researchers. 'Can we go to the farm?'

Mark smiled wryly. 'In England everything depends on the weather,' he explained as he collected together the material they had been using and returned it to the desk. 'What did you think of the diary?' he asked, although he could guess the answer from having seen her rapt concentration.

'It must have taken you hours and hours to copy out every entry for me— I really don't know how to thank you enough!'

'I gave a copy of the transcript to Archives, that way it will prevent wear and tear on the diary. You really have been privileged to actually hold it, I don't think they'd let everyone do so. Now, of course, anyone else will just get the transcript.' He waited for her to gather her pencil and belongings. 'Shall we go, then? Eileen gave me some sandwiches and a flask of coffee to have when we get to the farm; it's such a lovely area to have our lunch.'

Once they were clear of the city, their route wound in and out of first one valley and then another. 'This is the path the flood took back in 1864,' Mark explained, 'it happened several months after Lizzie went to live at the farm, when she was only about six years old. The dam burst one night in foul weather and swept through the valleys, taking houses, animals and people with it. Two hundred and forty people died that night and countless more were maimed, or made homeless. But then you read the book I sent. I have a better one I can lend you to read whilst you're here.'

'Yes, please, I'd like that,' she replied. Mimi was beginning to enjoy hearing Mark tell her the history of the area and, having entered the city from the high plateau the previous day, she could now more appreciate the layout of the land. 'So many hills,' she said, 'it's quite flat prairie land where I live in Illinois, totally different and the fields are so green here.'

'But you also have dramatic scenery in America; the Grand Canyon, huge rivers, giant trees and forests,' Mark exclaimed. 'I've always wanted to go to the Rockies and New York.'

She chuckled at his remark. 'America is so vast that you can travel for days in one direction before reaching a different terrain. Few Americans have ever been more than a couple of States beyond the one they live in, and not many have seen the Rockies, except on film. In contrast, things seem so compact over here.'

'Old fashioned you mean, and congested, making us small minded.' His voice was more resigned than critical.

'You have to think big in the States because of its size. Don't decry England, everyone wants to visit here and then come again once they've been.' She tried to reassure him that small wasn't necessarily a bad thing.

They had long since left behind the congestion of traffic and were now in lush green countryside. 'I'll bring you out this way again.' Mark offered, 'so that you can see some of the places Lizzie wrote about. Today, after we've been to the farm, I'll drop you off at Eileen's with some reading matter, and then take you for a meal, if you like. I've got to show you an old English pub.'

'I'd like that!' she replied, thinking he was quite an ambassador for his country.

Their road dropped down towards a quiet little village and shortly Mark pulled in beside a wall surrounding a large field. 'I can imagine cricket being played here,' Mimi said, wondering how pleasant that might be to watch.

'Come Sunday in good weather they do,' he replied. 'We'll eat here before going up to the farm, and there's a loo over there if you need it!' he added with a grin, pointing towards a small stone-built building.

Mimi giggled and didn't argue as she was hungry. It felt good to be looked after so well and she considered herself very lucky, for without Mark it would have taken forever to find her way about.

'There are a couple of books in the bag on the back seat, one with photos showing the aftermath of the flood,' Mark explained as he ate. 'I'll take you up to the site of the old dam later in the week—then you'll need those shoes you've brought!'

As it had rained earlier in the day the grass was too wet to sit on, but Mimi felt comfortable anyway sitting in the car eating the lunch Eileen had prepared, and watching the sun glistening on the wet field. Conversation flowed between them as if they had known each other for years, until Mark noticed the attention she began to give the small building he'd mentioned earlier. As if anticipating her reluctance to leave the car, he said, 'It's quite primitive in there, but what can you expect? Hundreds of walkers begin their outings from here, or finish here, as once you're in the hills you have to make do with any shelter you can find as a toilet.'

'It sounds a bit wild out there,' Mimi retorted, wondering how far he intended walking her, but she let the matter drop and quietly finished her lunch.

As they eventually drove on, she began to feel sleepy, and yawned. 'I was right,' Mark remarked, 'by the time we get back to Eileen's you'll need a rest before going out again. The country air is noted for making one sleepy. However, here's the gate leading down to the farm.' He pulled in behind a white van. 'There must be someone else looking round,' he said. 'We'll have to walk from here I'm afraid.'

A twinge of excitement ran through Mimi at the prospect of seeing where Lizzie had lived, but as the lane seemed not to lead to anything in particular she was intrigued. Mark closed the gate behind them and they walked on. The lane soon became a rough track but there were still no buildings to be seen. 'I had hoped that the builders might have made a wider track by now but they can't have started yet. That's good, because you ought to see everything as undisturbed as possible.'

The damp air enhanced the sweet smell of the grass around them as they walked down the hill, heightening the sense of exhilaration in Mimi's already excited mind. The lane soon turned sharply, and there ahead they could see the remains of a ruined stone building obviously ravaged by years of neglect.

So there it was, or what was left of it! For years she had dreamed of coming here, and felt that she almost knew the place from Lizzie's description of the farm in the diaries. During Mimi's lowest moments within the past few months, she had read and re-read Mark's transcript, so that when he'd discovered the old place was to be sold and rebuilt she was deeply disturbed. This had been totally unexpected and was the final spur, driving her to work even harder in order to be able to come over before it was too late.

As they approached the ivy-covered ruins Mimi marvelled that anyone could possibly neglect a building in such a wonderful setting. All around her she could recognise the very things Lizzie had described or had drawn; the distant hills, a wall enclosing the small garden, the heady perfume of grass and foliage. 'Oh dear,' she whispered softly, 'why would anyone allow a place to go to wrack and ruin like this. It's scandalous!'

'It's often not economical to keep very old buildings going when their use is over,' Mark replied with a sigh. 'The valley has no industry, and not too many people want to live in such isolation either.'

'But someone *is* going to rebuild it!' Mimi was unfairly a bit peeved, not with Mark but that someone should do this to a place of history.

'Yes, I know, but for many years it hasn't been fashionable to do so. People are just starting to discover the advantages of restoring old and neglected properties. It takes money to do it, although sometimes one can get a grant for such work.'

'Why was it abandoned in the first place?'

'According to the deeds and local gossip,' Mark patiently explained, 'once the old lady—presumably Clara, Lizzie's stepmother—had died, her son who was a Doctor didn't want the farm, and sold it to the parish council. They couldn't afford to repair it in those days, and now someone has offered a good price for the land and ruins, and not before time.'

Mimi thought of the ghost towns in some of America's Western States where, once their usefulness was over they had simply been abandoned to the elements. She felt sorry for her sharpness and apologised.

'Good morning, can I help you?' A voice called out, causing them to jump. They turned and saw a man in dungarees coming towards them from the direction of a small wood. Mimi was apprehensive in case they were trespassing, but Mark seemed quite unperturbed.

'Why, yes!' Mark replied eagerly, quickly explaining who they were and why they were there.

'Well, you can't do much harm,' the man said, looking at the dilapidated ruin. 'Feel free to look around, but take care as it's none too safe. I'll be down there by the original farm ruins, I'm trying to see what can be salvaged for rebuilding the cottage here. If you need me just come down.'

'We'd like to take a few photos, if you don't mind,' Mark asked. 'Are you going to restore this place as it was?'

The man shook his head. 'No, it wasn't an out of the ordinary sort of building, just a cottage with an 1860's extension. The barns nearby which collapsed years ago were built from the left-overs from the old place. Take photos by all means!'

'It's a shame you're not rebuilding the original farm,' Mimi commented, 'now that would be great!'

'Nobody knows what it looked like. I understand that after the flood the damage was so severe that the owner extended the labourer's cottage here to live in himself. I was hoping to find a few architectural pieces but I'm not too hopeful. We'll use what is left as backfill and levelling.' With that he said goodbye and retraced his steps down the footpath to the copse.

Mark and Mimi approached what was left of the crumbling cottage; the cobbled yard was still there but was mostly overgrown with grass and moss, whilst the outbuildings had almost disappeared except for mounds of rubble covered with weeds. 'Someone must have pinched practically all the stones from these too,' Mark pointed out. 'Let's concentrate on what's left of the cottage.'

Mimi had come a long way for precisely this and wasn't sure what she'd expected to find. The remains of the main building lay behind a low wall surrounding what had obviously been a small garden. The two of them walked carefully along the uneven path towards a gaping hole in the side wall of the cottage where the front door had once been. Mimi had an eerie feeling as she entered the shell of the building; could Lizzie's spirit be watching them from somewhere, she wondered? There remained part of an old fireplace, the glass had long since gone from what was left of the rotten window frames, high in the walls were the holes where beams had been housed before they collapsed bringing the ceilings and all above down with them. The floor was covered with debris and rubble, making an entry very dangerous.

'Disappointed?' Mark asked. 'You've come a long way to see this, but I did warn you.'

'I am a little,' she had to admit, 'although it does have an atmosphere all of its own.' They took several photographs, some with Mimi in various poses at the old doorway or by the stone fireplace. Then Mark left her alone for a while, so that she could close her eyes and imagine what the place would have been like furnished and occupied. That so little was left of what had been a happy home saddened her—perhaps she had expected too much? After a time Mimi rejoined Mark who was sitting on the wall enjoying the view.

He was very patient and helpful, admitting that in doing the research he himself had become quite attached to Lizzie and the house. As they left the derelict area and walked back towards the car, Mimi could see in her mind's eye, Clara and Peter waving goodbye from their carriage as they left on the last day of their visit so long ago, this was the point at which the diary had ended. Mark must have instinctively been aware of her feelings for he walked quietly in front, leaving her to contemplate on all they had seen.

She tried to analyse her feelings and was strangely near to tears. Something had happened to sour Lizzie's life and it was impossible for Mimi to understand how or why a once lively young girl had become a withdrawn and unhappy woman.

According to the old diaries, Lizzie had been half in love with her dashing soldier cousin, Peter; he on the other hand, had been in love with Clara who had nursed him in hospital. However, on meeting Lizzie's widowed stepfather, Edward, Clara had fallen in love with him instead and they had eventually married. Now this would seemingly have opened up the way for Lizzie and Peter to get together, but when Edward inherited the old farm from his employer, Abe, it was on condition that none of Edward's blood relatives ever gained possession of the farm. Therefore, if Lizzie had married Edward's nephew Peter, she would have forfeited her inheritance. So Lizzie had lost her love, she went to London and became a nurse, whilst Peter went to India with the Army.

The day on which Clara and Peter left the farm and waved good-bye, here in the lane, must have been an emotional one for Lizzie, and it was from this point that there was a large gap in her diaries.

'You're deep in thought!' Mark said, breaking her concentration as they drove home. 'Is it something I've said?'

She could tell by his smile that he was not offended by her lack of conversation and, clearing her throat, answered. 'It might sound silly to you but, coming up the lane from the farm, I felt a sadness which is hard to describe, and it set me thinking about all the things I've read later in the diary which you haven't seen.' She looked at Mark's profile as he drove along, his genuine interest lifting her spirits. 'There is a ten-year gap in her writings as you know, which is hard to fill. Do you think if we keep digging we'll be able to discover more? Would you continue to help? I would appreciate it if you did.'

'I don't mind at all, I'm enjoying putting the pieces together!'

'Without your efforts none of this would have been possible,' Mimi said, thanking him, 'it has been quite exciting, like doing a jigsaw.'

Mark laughed, 'I like jigsaws. However, next time we come out here I'll show you the family grave in the churchyard. We can also go into the church where Edward married Lizzie's mother, Hannah, and then his second wife, Clara'

The fresh air had taken its toll and it wasn't long after Mark had returned her to Eileen's in the late afternoon, that she nodded off instead of reading the books which he'd given her.

In the meantime, the builder whom they'd met earlier in the day continued to rummage amongst piles of rubble that had so far revealed nothing of importance. Although much of the stone could be re-used, saving time and money, Reg Barker was a little disappointed. As he suspected, anything of consequence had gone years before but, as the building contractor, he was being paid to look and that's what he was doing. The foundations of the old farm covered a larger area than he'd expected, and these lay beneath weeds and small bushes which sprouted happily through the stones. It must have been some house, he thought, and marvelled at the power of the floodwater that had caused such destruction. He decided that the following morning he would bring a couple of lads from the yard with him and set them to piling up stones of any use. This made good sense and would save having to haul lorry-loads of back-fill all the way from Sheffield.

By the time he'd finished surveying the ground and walked back up the lane to his van, Mark and Mimi had long since left for home. Reg was used to the curiosity of the public but anticipated no vandalism out here in a remote valley; in fact he'd been rather pleased to get the job in the first place, especially for the summer months. What it would be like to work here in the winter, however, was another matter, but he hoped to have the shell of the house completed by then. Fastening the drive gate behind him he drove off, whistling contentedly and looking forward to getting the project started.

Mimi woke with a start when Eileen knocked on her door. 'May I come in?' she asked, and entered at Mimi's invitation, 'I thought I'd better wake you before

Mark comes in half an hour,' she went on, 'it seemed a pity to disturb you, I hope you don't mind?'

'It's a good job you did, Eileen, because I need to wash and get changed. Besides, the dreams I've had were disturbing.' She looked guiltily at the book lying open on the bed. 'I haven't read much,' she confessed, 'I hope Mark won't be disappointed.'

'I don't know what he sees in this family history lark,' his sister remarked, 'still, it keeps him happy and earns him a little extra money. He likes solving mysteries, anyway, does Mark!'

Hunger was overtaking Mimi's tiredness at this stage and she quickly got off the bed. 'Aren't you interested at all?' she asked.

'Not me, I hear about it ad nauseam from Mark, that's enough,' Eileen grumbled, 'whether I want to or not. I sometimes wonder if he thinks more about the dead than the living. It's time he got married and put his energies into a family of his own.'

This was touching on a subject about which Mimi was hardly an expert, and she didn't want to get involved. 'Perhaps he's content with his lot,' she replied, thinking of the perils of marriage from her own experience. 'It isn't that easy living with someone unless you have a lot in common and have a great desire to make it work.'

Eileen shook her head. 'I suppose I'm lucky— but this isn't getting you ready is it? I'd best leave you to get on.' At that she left and Mimi hastened to prepare herself for the evening which turned out to be one of pleasant conversation and good food.

As they ate, Mark told her a little of his life, about where he lived, also of his job as a laboratory technician in the local teaching hospital. He wasn't well paid but by being careful he'd been able to buy a small apartment which he was gradually improving. The extra money he earned doing family history research for other people added the few luxuries he had. This made Mimi feel awkward at accepting such a lot of help from him, until she began to learn just how much he enjoyed searching through old records. It was probably a good substitute for some more expensive hobby he might have had. This rang a pertinent bell when she thought about the yacht her ex-husband had bought when they were hard up.

'Eileen thinks you should find a wife and raise a family of your own,' she commented without thinking. 'Oops, I'm sorry,' she added quickly, realising that she should perhaps have kept her mouth shut, 'Eileen meant well and I should not have repeated what she said.'

'Its no more than she tells me to my face,' he grumbled, 'she thinks it's her duty to see me settled. I just let her ramble on, it keeps her happy!'

Once the meal was over they began to discuss plans for the following day. 'I'd like to show you a bit of Derbyshire tomorrow,' he said, 'there are lovely views and some picturesque villages. Also there's Chatsworth House which you must see after coming so far. The day after, we can go back out to

Bradfield if you like. You may as well shop and do more research when I'm at work, besides, I think you'll have had enough of me in a couple of days.'

She didn't think she would have had enough of his company as, after all, what could she do for a further two weeks on her own in a strange country with little money to spare? The thought of being alone for such a long time unsettled her, and she began to wonder what she was doing so far from home, eating out with a stranger.

'You look glum!' Mark remarked when she didn't reply immediately.

Startled by his interruption to her thoughts, Mimi asked, without thinking, 'What am I doing here? I've been scrimping and saving for months in order to make the journey just to look at a ruined building when I really could have spent the money on more important things.' There were tears lurking beneath the surface which she fought to hide.

Mark recognised the signs but he didn't comment lest he upset her more, saying simply, 'It's just jet lag by the sound of it. You'll be alright when you've had another sleep. I've never had the opportunity to fly so I don't really know what it feels like, but some of my colleagues have suffered for several days after such a trip. Perhaps I've pushed you too hard today in my eagerness to show you everything. Would you like tomorrow by yourself to get acclimatised?'

'No!' she heard herself cry, maybe a little too strongly. 'No, I don't really want to be on my own. In fact without your help and company I'd be alone in a hotel, out on a limb not knowing what to do!'

'Perhaps you placed too much emphasis on coming here, and the act of saving up gave you a goal to reach. I know from your letters that you've had a rough time, but you're here now so let's make the most of the opportunity. An early night and a trip into Derbyshire tomorrow will do you good.'

'Thank you for being so understanding,' she said with a slight smile, 'I'll be OK. It's just that I suddenly thought, what the hell am I doing here, away from everything and everyone I know, just to be by myself! But I do realise that all those miles, and the ocean between me and normality, plus lack of sleep is bound to have an effect.' She was glad Mark didn't question her further or she might have bored him to death, and as they drove home she endeavoured to shake off her momentary downheartedness. She went straight to bed after a few words with Eileen, but sleep wouldn't come. Instead, she read several chapters of Mark's book on the flood which helped her to appreciate more why she had come, and what she sought. No more gloom, no more self-indulgent pity she warned herself! Only ten more days to go and she would be winging her way home to Chicago, hopefully with all her questions answered.

She woke the following morning in a different frame of mind, her sense of adventure had returned and she felt quite bright whilst dressing suitably for a day in the country.

Mark made no comment over her behaviour the night before and just checked to see if she had the right footwear for the outing. They retraced the journey they'd made on the day of her arrival; back up the hill to Owler Bar to where the view of Sheffield had so entranced her. However, this time instead of stopping they went straight on towards the open moors. Mimi glanced from side to side absorbing the beauty all around; she intended missing nothing. It was wild and rugged, and set her imagination on fire. 'I could write about this place,' she cried fervently, 'it's almost as the Brontë sisters described it in their books.'

'There's history and legend everywhere you go in Derbyshire,' Mark explained, 'and so much to see and do.' He spoke with pride, 'Charlotte Brontë came to Derbyshire before she wrote the book "Jane Eyre", you know, and was inspired to draw on what she saw. I'll show you some of the places she visited and wrote about before you go home, if you like?'

This appealed to Mimi. 'Yes, please!' she cried with enthusiasm, but then modestly added, 'I also write a little you know, when I'm inspired, and this place certainly does that.'

They continued their journey down Baslow Hill until they reached the village nestling in the valley bottom. 'Out you get!' he ordered as he parked the car. 'This is Baslow. We'll walk through the park to Chatsworth, and then climb to what is called the Hunting Tower.' He hoisted his battered rucksack containing the sandwiches and a flask and led the way, Mimi followed as meekly as a lamb wondering what she had let herself in for!

Whilst Mark and Mimi were walking through the kissing-gate to enter Chatsworth Park, Reg Barker back at the farm set about putting two strong lads to work clearing up the old site. He planned to bring in a dumper truck soon with which to transfer the selected materials to a spot nearer the proposed new development.

The ground had dried after the rain of recent days and a pleasant breeze blew down the valley as they worked. Reg was deep in thought when Bob, the eldest youth, gave a sharp cry and let the stone he was lifting fall to the ground with a thud, narrowly missing his foot as it did so.

'What is it?' Reg called to the youth, thinking he was larking about.

'Come over here quick, Mr Barker!' Bob called back with such a strange voice that Reg stopped what he was doing and ran across to him.

'What is it, Lad?' he asked, hoping this wasn't going to be the first of many interruptions. The boy's face was pale and his eyes held a peculiar look in them. 'You look as though you've seen a ghost,' Reg suggested flippantly.

'I think I have, Boss,' Bob gulped, and plonked himself down on a pile of stones.

'Don't be daft!' Reg answered sharply. 'What have you dragged me over here for? You've not been mucking about have you?' Bob wasn't the brightest of lads yet he worked well when he wasn't daydreaming. Reg had got him on a work experience scheme and decided to keep him on after it had finished. However, there was obviously something disturbing him and Reg was puzzled.

'Look down there,' Bob spluttered, pointing a finger towards a hole in the ground where he'd been working. 'There's some old steps!' He turned to one side as if frightened and said no more. By this time the other boy, Les, had joined them, intrigued by the conversation and wanting to know more. He peered down the steps but was none the wiser for his efforts.

'Stand back then,' Reg ordered, and pushed Les to one side.

'There's some old bones there Mr Barker! There's a body!' Bob burst out, finding his voice again.

'It'll be animals, a dead sheep or fox, you'll see. Nothing to worry about,' Reg reassured him and climbed down a couple of steps to see more closely what had disturbed the lad. Moving the stone which Bob had nearly dropped on his toe to one side, he recoiled with shock at what he saw. 'Good God!' he gasped, struggling to maintain his balance. 'It's a skull!' He took another look, then brushed the dirt from his hands as if fearful at what they may have touched. He thought for a moment, trying to gather his wits together. 'We'll have to fetch the police,' he said grimly. 'We can't do any more work here lads, not till they've been, we've no choice.' He was shaken and realised that it must have been an even greater shock to the youngster. So, softening his tone, he turned and said, 'Let's get away from here, we'll finish for the day and I'll drop you off home once we've been to the Police Station. They'll not let us touch anything again until they've thoroughly examined everything anyway.'

Bob couldn't take his eyes from the hole where the bones were and stood petrified.

'What's it doing there?' Les asked. Not yet having been confronted with the grisly remains, he was more curious than shocked.

'Something fishy I shouldn't wonder,' Reg replied, shaking his head. 'You don't get piles of rocks on top of you for nothing.'

'A murder!' Les suggested excitedly, 'Just wait until I tell me dad.'

'You'll do no such thing—not until the Police say you can.' Reg warned, but suspected his words were probably falling on deaf ears. 'Just keep it to yourself until tomorrow,' he cautioned, 'or the Police won't like it!' Reg cursed his luck as he led the youths back to his van. He'd known of jobs being held up for months after human remains had been found on building sites. His one consolation was that he could still work on the newer property whilst the investigation was going on here. How long had the body been there? And who was it? He was just glad that he didn't have the job of uncovering the rest of the body—but it put paid to clearing the rest of the stones near it for some time.

Glancing through the mirror as he drove off towards town he saw two glum faces in the back of the van and wondered how long it would be before shock turned to excitement for the young lads. Within days they would be shouting their experience and their find from the rooftops!

Meanwhile in the heart of Derbyshire, Mark and Mimi, unaware of the drama unfolding in Bradfield, had entered the tranquil parkland of the Chatsworth Estate and were beginning the climb leading to the Hunting Tower perched high above them.

'Wow!' Mimi gasped, as she struggled to regulate her breathing when finally they emerged from the trees having reached their goal. 'What a view!' The vista stretching out before her had certainly been worth the effort to see and she stood in awe of it. 'It's like looking down on a model world,' she exclaimed enthusiastically, her face still flushed from her exertions.

'I thought you'd appreciate this, if not the walk,' Mark teased, aware that physical exercise was not one of Mimi's habits.

'We just don't walk like this at home,' she said, 'but I am enjoying it, and yes, it was worth it,' she agreed. She didn't complain that she had a blister coming on her foot or that her calves ached, as that might have seemed ungrateful. Instead, she sat on the old iron cannon directed towards the valley below and sipped the coffee Mark offered her, trying to blot out the thought that they had yet to descend the slippery steps, which would probably exacerbate her problems.

'I'll take you down the easier way,' Mark said, noting the way she was gently rubbing her calves and realising he might have been a bit too adventurous for her.

'You mean that there is an easier way up?' Mimi cried in disbelief.

'Well, yes, but it is longer,' Mark replied, defending his decision and suspecting that Mimi might throw something at him for what he'd done. He grinned. 'Besides, it was more fun that way.'

Mimi simply refused to answer; instead she carried on savouring the sandwich she was holding.

Thinking it wise to change the subject, Mark said, 'I'll tell you what, if you can walk to that small village down there I will go back and collect the car, it will only take me half an hour. There's a tea-shop in the village and something in the graveyard which I think you might find interesting. The village itself was re-located in the 1890s. It used to be across the road from where it is now, but was demolished to improve the view from the big house.'

'How could they be allowed to pull down the ancient village and move it such a short distance?' Mimi was irritated at the thought of someone spoiling something so old.

'Simply because the Duke wanted an uninterrupted and unspoilt picture of the park from his window, I suppose.'

'What a waste!' she declared strongly. 'You English don't appreciate what you've got.'

'I agree, but the new village has a style of its own—wait until you get there!'

Taking the estate road down to the park Mimi began to limp and wished she'd practised walking more before she left home. 'We won't have to go further will we? You'll end up carrying me if we do!'

Mark laughed. 'No, but I think it would be better to come another day if you want to go round Chatsworth House and the gardens. There are long corridors and many steps so you won't do it justice in your present state!' They walked over the fine stone-arched bridge that crossed the river, then climbed a small bank at the other side of which lay the village of Edensor. 'You can walk for weeks around here, there are so many footpaths in Derbyshire. I often come out with a walking group on Sundays.' Pointing towards a single isolated cottage he remarked, 'That's the only house left from the old village.'

Seeing the small house which was neatly enclosed by a wall, Mimi said, 'You seem to know something about almost every stone, how did you learn all this?'

'I pick things up from books and when talking to other walkers. If possible we rarely use the same path twice in a year. I love rambling no matter what the weather is like, snow, rain, wind or sunshine. Some days we cover twelve to fifteen miles.'

'You must be mad!'

By now they had crossed the main road and entered the village. 'It's built in an Italian style, rather attractive in its own way. Look, there's the tea-shop I mentioned, go and get a drink and a sit down. I'll be back as soon as I can, then I'll show you the churchyard. There's someone special buried there!'

'Who, some Duke or other?' Mimi asked.

'No, you'll see later—go and rest, I'll not be long.'

True to his word, Mark returned with the car in less than half an hour and found Mimi waiting expectantly outside the shop. 'I'm glad you're back,' she said, 'what would I have done if you'd abandoned me?'

Laughing, he led her to the top section of the graveyard and stopped before one grave in particular, 'Read the inscription,' he said, as he stepped to one side.

'It's Kathleen Kennedy—President Kennedy's sister!' Mimi exclaimed. 'What's she doing here?'

'She married one of the tenth Duke's sons but he was killed in the war, only four months after they were married. Then she was killed four years later in a plane crash.'

'What a tragic family,' Mimi said sadly, 'I had no idea there was an English connection at all.' As they left the graveside Mimi realised that the blister on her foot was getting more painful with every step. 'I can't walk much further,' she lamented, 'can we go back to the car?'

'As long as I can have a cuppa in the tea-shop first,' he agreed.

After breakfast the next day a refreshed Mimi awaited Mark's arrival with a light heart, the blisters although plastered up and still hurting did not spoil her anticipation of revisiting Bradfield. However, it came as a shock when they found the lane down to the farm blocked off and guarded by police. It had been their intention to make a quick visit and then go looking for the places Lizzie had written about.

'There must have been an accident!' Mark suggested, trying to explain away the unusual activity as they drew up behind several police vehicles.

'Move on please, Sir,' a police constable ordered as Mark wound down his window.

'Has there been an accident, officer? We were here only a couple of days ago, so what's happened?' Mark was worried, thinking that one of the workmen might have been injured in the ruins.

The constable eyed Mark keenly. 'You mean you were down at the old ruin recently? The one beyond the cottage?'

'No, we only took photos of the cottage before that too disappears altogether. My friend here has come from America to see where her family lived. There seemed nothing amiss then, so what's up?'

'I think you'd better remain here, Sir, if you don't mind, while I contact someone.' He motioned to Mark to switch off the engine, then unclipped his hand-held radio and spoke to someone, referring to details which Mark could make no sense of.

'I wonder what he wants with us?' Mimi asked quietly as she and Mark watched the man who was in earnest conversation. 'Why would they want to detain us if it's simply an accident?'

Mark shrugged his shoulders. 'It's something serious by the look of it, so I do hope they won't keep us too long.'

The constable who had wandered out of earshot came nearer. 'You're to stay here Sir; my officer is coming to speak to you. He shouldn't be more than five minutes.'

Knowing that they were guilty of no more than having explored the ruins, Mark and Mimi sat chatting, trying to guess why they were being delayed. Eventually another policeman appeared in the lane. 'Thank you for waiting,' he said on approaching the car, 'but I don't think you can be of much help, as things go!'

'What's the mystery all about, Officer? Has there been an accident?' Mark was getting a little impatient by this time, wanting to get on with their plans for the day.

'We're releasing the news to the Press now so you might as well know. We've found a body under the old ruins.' Mimi gasped and her face drained of colour. 'It's been there many years,' he went on, 'so I don't think you'll be able to assist us. You can go now, but please leave your names and addresses, and thanks for waiting.'

'Oh!' Mark exclaimed, much like a punctured balloon.

'We won't know until forensics have done their job but I'd say the body's been there at least fifty years, so there's no need for you to worry at all.'

It was some time before Mimi could bring herself to speak as they drove back towards the village. She was deep in thought and somewhat shocked to think that something evil may have taken place in such beautiful surroundings. 'Who could it be?' she whispered.

Mark shook his head. 'It's no good guessing, but it's shaken me up a bit as well. We'll go to Bradfield and see the church; I don't feel like driving far at the moment.'

'Let's have a cup of coffee first,' Mimi suggested, reaching for the flask. 'I feel quite chilled with shock at the thought that we might have been near the body the other day.'

After a walk round the village Mark took Mimi into the church which, although interesting felt quite cold and before long they decided, under the circumstances, to stay outside in the warm sunshine. It didn't take long to find the grave where Edward and both his wives were buried. 'What a lovely place to end your days,' Mimi said as she looked across the valley.

'Mmm, I bet it wasn't such a good view in 1864 after the flood had rampaged through it.' Mark was still disturbed by what had happened at the farm. 'Look, let's take the old Mortimer Road towards the Strines. You can imagine Lizzie riding out that way, then we'll find a pub for a drink and a bite to eat.'

It wasn't difficult for Mimi to imagine Lizzie, her hair flying in the wind, galloping out onto the moors. 'It would only have been track then, I suppose, not a proper road? I can see why she loved it so much, but not why she left for good.'

'It can be raw up here in winter and very isolated, perhaps she found London more interesting.' Mark replied. The long straight road suddenly descended and then, after a steeply rising double bend, it continued upwards. Seeing the isolated pub, Mark drew into its car park. 'Let's take a break,' he said, 'I could murder half a pint.'

They entered the pub and found a table in a corner by the window. 'I'd enjoy a hot drink, if they do one,' Mimi asked, 'will they mind?'

'I'm sorry if this has spoilt your holiday,' Mark said once he'd managed to obtain the drinks. 'It's a pretty kettle of fish, isn't it? There could be something nasty involved.'

'Do you think it's a murder or someone who was accidentally trapped in the ruins? A hobo maybe, hiding from bad weather?'

'We can only guess until we know the truth—it will certainly be in the local paper. I'll buy a copy tonight and if it's not in then it should be tomorrow.'

In spite of the bright sunny weather, no matter where they went or what they did, the rest of the day was overshadowed by their experience at the farm. Always at the back of Mimi's mind was the question, who could it be and why was it there? She was preoccupied and as a result was not the best of company. Was this the reason why the farm had been abandoned, had Edward and Clara's son not gone away at all? Mark had said that the son had left in the 1930s, but a dark shadow began to form in Mimi's mind.

'Look,' Mark said abruptly. 'Why don't we give all this a break tomorrow and take a trip to York? The place will be swarming with tourists but it's full of history.'

Without hesitation Mimi agreed. 'Yes, that sounds good to me. I don't fancy being alone or doing any more research right now. I'd be glad of your company.' If she stayed at Eileen's on her own she would probably think about the farm all day. She knew no-one other than Mark and Eileen's family and didn't want to disturb their usual routines.

That night Mimi slept fitfully, her thoughts constantly turning to the body under the ruins, so that when Mark arrived next morning with a newspaper she felt compelled to tell him her conclusions. 'I think I know who was buried up there,' she blurted out, the moment he entered the house.

Mark raised his eyebrows and looked at her in amazement. 'How can you— you've never known anyone over here!' His tone was dismissive.

At this Mimi felt a little foolish, perhaps she'd let her imagination get the better of her. 'Has the newspaper got an explanation?' she asked meekly as Mark handed the paper to her and turned to include Eileen. 'They say they won't know exactly for some time but suspect the body has been there for years.'

'Fifty years, the officer said!'

'He only guessed, he had no facts to confirm that.'

Mimi soon found and quickly read the article. There seemed to be no urgency in solving the mystery, it had apparently happened a long time ago and the police were busy endeavouring to find more evidence. 'It was just an idea I had because of something you said, but I guess it was silly of me,' she explained.

'What was your idea?' Eileen asked, not at all put off by her brother's unwillingness to consider Mimi's suspicions.

'I just wondered why Edward's son disappeared in the 1930s, leaving the farm to go to Parish tenants. Could he have had an accident whilst working at the ruins and no-one realised where he was? The time would have been about right.'

Mark's attention was caught by this and he pondered for a moment. 'I suppose it's worth thinking about, but look, if he'd had an accident he wouldn't have been in a position to cover himself with stones and rubble, would he!'

'He might have been killed by someone!' Eileen interrupted, 'Maybe Mimi has a point, Mark. You ought at least to tell the police about this, what harm can it do?'

'It will cause them a lot of paper work and we'll never get to York,' Mark grumbled, causing Mimi a twinge of conscience. 'We'll just have to go to York another day.'

At his stubbornness Eileen's patience was running out. 'No, that's silly! Just tell the police your theory, it won't take long, why should it? You're not connected with the blooming thing, and you weren't even born fifty years ago.'

'Just forget it,' Mimi said quietly, 'I wish now that I'd kept my mouth shut.'

'No,' Eileen broke in, 'You've obviously thought a lot about this, Mimi, you could be right. Your mind isn't cluttered with other events hereabouts, so it all seems logical to you.' She turned to her brother. 'Have a bit of patience Mark, Mimi's not stupid.'

'I'm causing a lot of bother,' Mimi cried. 'Please let's leave things as they are.'

'Hold on a sec;' Mark interrupted, 'everything has happened so suddenly, I've had no time to think. I know I've probably been a mite hasty but you have to admit this isn't something that happens every day, is it? Let's just calm down.'

In spite of everything, Mimi was still convinced that she was right to consider the possibility that William Morton's disappearance and the body were connected. 'I don't mind missing York, if necessary,' she said. 'Especially if it means doing the right thing.'

'I do,' Mark said bluntly, 'I was looking forward to going.'

Eileen smiled to herself, she knew her brother well. He was not a man who liked his plans set adrift by outside circumstances. Well, for once he would just have to compromise. 'I don't think you have any choice,' she insisted, supporting Mimi's argument. 'You have to go to the police.'

'Alright, alright!' Mark ruefully conceded. He was not pleased, although common sense told him he was probably being stubborn. 'Let's get off and do it now; but we're going to York afterwards, no matter what.' He picked up the paper, 'We may be back much later than planned, so don't panic,' he told his sister very pointedly. 'Don't go reporting us missing to the police.'

Eileen wisely ignored his sarcasm and, turning to Mimi, she winked knowingly. Mimi, who was now seeing this as something other than her fault, turned away and smiled too, waiting for brother and sister to sort themselves out.

Arriving at the Police Station, Mark asked, 'Do you want to tell them of your idea or would you like me to do it?'

Mimi shook her head; she was determined not to let him make her feel more guilty of spoiling his day than she was already. 'I'll explain, then they will simply think I'm a stupid interfering foreigner, won't they!'

'Miss Marple!' Mark muttered under his breath.

'I know who Miss Marple is,' Mimi quipped, having caught the remark, 'and she was usually right!' With that she opened the car door and got out. Mark followed suit and led the way into the station.

At the desk, Mimi faced the officer with some hesitancy; he appeared more interested in the papers in front of him than in their arrival. She on the other hand, having let her fancies run away with her, now felt foolish.

'Well, Miss. Can I help you?' the Desk Sergeant asked politely, and waited for her to begin.

'It's about the body they've found!'

'Oh, which one?' The man asked as if corpses were discovered every day.

'Is there more than one?' Mark chipped in innocently, discretely concealing his amusement at Mimi's determination.

'Two yesterday as a matter of fact!'

'We may have a clue as to the identity of the one found at the farm in Bradfield,' Mimi informed him. 'We think it could be a man called William Morton. He seems to have disappeared about 1930 and the farm was then let out to tenants until finally it became derelict.'

'I see, well, I'll have to fetch the Inspector—if you'd like to sit down a minute?'

'I hope it doesn't take all day,' Mark said when the man left. He had been keeping an eye on the clock whilst Mimi had been speaking. 'We could still get to York for lunch if we leave soon.'

In spite of everything and the possible disruption of her holiday, Mimi was intrigued to find herself in a police precinct and felt quite safe, having heard so much about British Justice (and having read many Agatha Christie novels). Shortly the man returned with his superior who invited them into a small interview room where they sat for several minutes exchanging pleasantries, the officer seeming more interested in Chicago than why they were there.

'Now, you say you may be able to help us regarding our investigation,' he said, finally changing the subject. 'In what way?'

Mark sat back and relaxed as Mimi put forward her theory, hoping she wouldn't get sidetracked and thus prolong their stay.

'My forebears lived at the farm for many years, from the mid-1860s onwards, and the last known survivor to inherit the property left in the 1930s. His name was Doctor William Morton. Eventually the house was tenanted out by the Parish but later was abandoned and became a ruin. Nobody knows what happened to William and, as I understand it, the body that has been found has been there for at least fifty years. Is it possible that Dr Morton could have had an accident and died, or possibly even have been killed?' Mimi paused for breath, awaiting some comment from the Inspector.

He smiled kindly at her. 'I appreciate your concern,' he said 'but I'm afraid the body has been there much longer than that judging by some of the clothing. I'll certainly make a note of what you say, and if you leave your name and address we'll contact you again if we need to.' He rose to indicate the interview was at an end, thanking them for taking the trouble to call.

'Well, that was a bit inconclusive,' Mark commented once they were back in the car. 'At least it didn't long and we can get away, though it looks as if your theory's shot to pieces doesn't it?'

'Not necessarily,' Mimi persisted, 'I've seen pictures mis-dated because of the clothing worn by poorer people long after they've gone out of fashion!'

In spite of her excitement at seeing York's many historical sights, Mimi's mind was never very far from the gruesome discovery in Bradfield, and as they sat eating fish and chips in a restaurant near the Minster, she speculated on other possibilities. 'If it was William Morton, how did nobody realise that he was missing? We don't even know whether he had a family of his own; there's some research still to be done.'

Mark refused to comment, instead he suggested that as there was so much still to see in York they should waste no more time, but simply get on with it. As a result they were quite worn out by five o'clock when the museums and shops began to close. 'We're going to get caught up in the traffic now,' he remarked as they negotiated a one-way traffic system to cross the river and leave the ancient city.

'I don't know how you cope with such narrow, winding streets,' Mimi said with admiration when once they were on the open road and able to increase their speed. 'I like York, thanks for bringing me. We've had a good day after all.'

'I'm glad you found it interesting, we've certainly covered a lot of ground, but there is so much more to see. At least I've given you a feel of what's there.' Mark was glad Mimi had enjoyed herself and had to admit that he wouldn't have wanted to have been there without her company. 'Look,' he said, 'I finish work at lunchtime tomorrow, for the weekend. Why don't you go to the Archives department and do some research and I'll come straight from work to meet you?'

'Sounds good to me!' Mimi replied, pleased that he still wanted to put up with her company. Then, as the miles went by she began to doze, her head nodding until it finally came to rest on Mark's shoulder, soon she was oblivious to everything around her.

On Saturday morning, Mimi sat once more in the Archives with Lizzie's diary before her, wondering what other documents might reveal more of Lizzie's life. Without Mark's help she was at a loss as to where to start and, as it was still only eleven o'clock, what was she to do until he came in two hours time?

As she toyed with the diary which the Librarian had approved her handling, she pondered on the stitched up set of pages near the back. Lizzie had been meticulous in recording her history right up to the point where Peter left the farm, bent on travelling to India, and began again when he returned nine years later. Why the gap? Why the stitches? Mimi, always curious over anomalies, tried to lift the edges of the pages with the greatest of care to see what, if anything, lay between them. She could just make out a few letters purposefully made in ink, and her inquisitiveness grew. She glanced round nervously, making sure she could not be overlooked by other readers and slowly, but deliberately, began to work free the knots and stitching of the discoloured cotton thread that Lizzie had used.

At last, after some time, the individual sheets opened to her touch: she had done no damage and was able to relax. It certainly was Lizzie's writing, but not as neatly formed as elsewhere. Perhaps she may have been ashamed of it and decided to hide it? Mimi began to read more intently, and soon forgot everything around her.

Bradfield 1876
Lizzie Hardy's Diary

The carriage trundled slowly up the lane away from the farm, and the two figures remaining in the yard watched, their thoughts as diverse as they were unified. Edward, although not yet ready to relinquish the pleasantness of the last few days spent with his departing guests, broke the silence.

'Well, Lizzie,' he said, turning to his stepdaughter, 'I'd better catch up on the work I've neglected this week.' He sighed involuntarily. 'I must go up on the moors later to fetch the sheep down into the lower fields; many of the ewes are nearly ready to lamb.'

Lizzie nodded in agreement though her thoughts were less optimistic than her stepfather's. 'I noticed that yesterday when riding up there with Peter. The weather doesn't look too good either,' she added, her voice flat, reflecting the void that Peter and Clara's departure had left.

Edward agreed, 'If we get a fall of snow before I get the flock down safely we'll be in trouble.' The fluttering nerves in Lizzie's stomach returned and a slow ache there made her ready to weep with emptiness. Edward looked closely at her. 'Will you be alright here on your own?' he quizzed, mindful that the visit had meant so much to her, and that the farm was a lonely place. 'You could come with me if you like,' he suggested. 'This will probably be the last season that Bella's up to it, she's getting too old for hill-work now, so I've asked Bill Taylor over at Stannington to rear a good pup for me in readiness.'

'Oh, I'll be alright,' Lizzie assured him, fondly. 'You've enough to think about without worrying about me. I might take a ride while I'm able, for if the weather does break it might be the last chance I'll have for some time—if I am indeed going to London.'

Sensing a possible revival of her spirits in this last remark, Edward smiled. 'Be sure not to go too far, just in case, and stick to the road,' he cautioned. He knew Lizzie was a good rider but he worried that her judgement might be impaired by the excitement of the past week. She had certainly not been herself of late and was inclined to be impetuous at the best of times.

A graceful lapwing twisted and tumbled above them, calling plaintively as it swooped down towards the valley floor, its black tipped wings loudly flapping as the carriage carrying Clara and Peter took them towards the village of Bradfield and their long journey home to Aldershot. The trees were still in their winter mantle and the hedgerows bare of growth as the bird hovered in the sky, seeming to watch the moving carriage on the ground below. As the vehicle eventually disappeared into the distance, with a final swoop the bird called 'pee-wit' and glided out of sight, leaving a clear empty sky, with the story in the valley still to unfold.

Later in the morning Edward set out for the moors with Bella at his side, leaving Lizzie moping about the yard with a heavy heart. He was relieved that his nephew was going to India with the Army; this would at least take him far enough away from Lizzie whose attachment, although seemingly lessened, would fade more by the time he finally returned to England. All Edward's hopes were now pinned on the certainty that Clara would return and marry him, whilst Lizzie, out of frustration and boredom seemed determined to train as a nurse in London. He realised that with Clara becoming Lizzie's stepmother, this would not alone make up for the realisation that Peter could never be anything other than her cousin. Nursing and London seemed now to be a good compromise in the situation and he was willing to help wherever he could.

Eventually, once Edward had departed, Lizzie took a grip of her fluctuating emotions and resolved to devote what remained of her time wisely. Today she would ride, then tomorrow she intended writing a long letter to Clara, reminding her of the promise she'd made to find a position for her in a hospital in London.

Saddling and mounting the chestnut mare, Lizzie left the stable and rode sedately, pensively at first, and with little joy at the thought of riding alone. Then, as the rhythm took hold she rode as fast as she dared along the moorland road. The decision to ride had indeed been a good one; the wind blew hard against her face, sweeping her hair out in an unrestrained stream. Few people trod this isolated track anymore, not since the construction of the firmer, alternative route, so she was able to forget decorum and, with complete abandonment, she rode simply with the intention of blotting out her despondency. She trusted the horse, it had been her one true companion since her mother's death years before, but as time went by she knew the limitations age was bringing to her faithful friend.

In this state of mind she was not aware of the watching figure half concealed in the trees by the side of the track, nor could she see the look of triumph on the man's face.

It was Nathan, out for revenge and seeking to teach his brother Peter a lesson that he'd never forget. He wasn't used to being beaten in a fight, let alone by a younger sibling. Bruised and battered, Nathan had rested a few days before setting out to settle the score, and now, having walked for miles and after filling his belly with ale at the Strines Inn, he was in no mood to forgive or to forget. He lurched out suddenly from the shelter of the trees, frightening the horse with his raised stick.

Lizzie realised too late that someone was there! The man's unexpected appearance and the shying of her horse were sufficient to unnerve her and she clung valiantly to the pommel and the horse's mane. As the mare reared higher she finally recognised Nathan, fear and alarm driving all colour from her face, and she screamed. She could not disguise the revulsion as she spat his name, 'Nathan!'

Seeing her scorn and fear served only to heighten Nathan's jubilation. Here was the very woman he and Peter had fought over, Peter defending the good name of his cousin, his brother taking delight in demeaning anything the more successful brother held dear.

'Yes, Miss high and mighty!' Nathan snarled, his voice as ugly as his mood. 'So, Peter lets you ride alone, does he? The young fool!' He made to seize the reins, lunging like the drunkard he was.

'Take your hand away! You're drunk!' Lizzie shouted with disdain, trying to control her fears. 'Peter has gone back where he belongs, away from you!' With the horse now under control her voice became sharp and mocking.

Nathan was taken aback at this news and was angry and disappointed to hear that his intended victim had gone away. 'My time will come,' he growled. 'No-one beats me and gets away with it!' He spat the words, the muscles in his throat expanding with anger.

'Peter's a man!' Lizzie scoffed, 'unlike you. He's going to India while you loaf about, fighting and drinking!' With that she turned the horse suddenly, breaking free of his hold on the rein. His long arm reached out menacingly to re-capture the reins before she could spur the horse on, and instinctively, she whipped him sharply across the face with her crop, before galloping away out of his reach.

'You bitch!' he yelled after her, inflamed by the pain of his cheek. 'I'll not forget that either.'

His tirade of abuse grew fainter as Lizzie distanced herself from him, but she was well aware that Nathan was not a man to be ignored and that she had made an enemy of him, one to be feared. Lizzie vowed never to ride out alone that way again. She rode on a mile or so before daring to slow the horse to a trot, but she was badly shaken by the encounter and in no fit state to return to the farm where her father would question her appearance. She was glad now that Peter had been forced to return to Aldershot, thus preventing an inevitable further confrontation with Nathan. Whatever had caused the fight between them must have been greater than she had been told, and Peter's Army career would certainly have been in jeopardy had his senior officer at the barracks learned of the incident.

Lizzie's infatuation with Peter had gradually reduced when she realised that he saw her merely as his lively, companionable cousin, but she'd concealed her bitter disappointment well. Then had come the unexpected revelation that Clara, Peter's real love and friend had thoughts only for Edward, Lizzie's stepfather. As a result, Peter was now leaving for India with his regiment, sad and disillusioned, and without him Lizzie realised she must make the most of what life had to offer.

Glancing backwards to reassure herself that Nathan wasn't following, Lizzie attempted to steady her trembling hands. 'Good girl, Nancy,' she called affectionately to the sweating animal beneath her, and leaning forward patted its sleek moist neck in appreciation. In this mood she ignored the lane which led down to the farm and continued along the road towards the village, trotting up the hill to the churchyard where her mother lay in an ivy-covered grave. She dismounted by the lychgate, tethered Nancy to a post and walked slowly to the graveside. There had been many times when she'd come here alone, not particularly in sorrow or pain, but simply to draw comfort and strength from the peace the visit gave her, as it did now after the confrontation with Nathan.

After a while she rose and glanced out over the valley, recalling how it had looked, ravaged and spoilt, twelve years before when the dam wall burst and the valley had been flooded. Several months before this Edward had brought her and her mother Hannah from the slums of Sheffield to keep house for him when he lived in the original old farm. In the devastation wreaked by the floodwater the farmhouse had been lost, forcing Edward to move in with them in their small cottage higher up the hill. Fortunately no-one at the farm had lost their life, but many had died in the tragedy which extended well beyond to the town of Sheffield, nine miles away.

Once their lives had resumed, an agreement had been reached between Edward and her mother, and so they married. Their existence became extremely pleasant, that was until, eventually, sickness took Hannah from them. After that, Edward had taken good care of Lizzie, spoiling her perhaps, yet treating her as his own daughter.

Bending to pull aside the Ivy to reveal her mother's name, Lizzie whispered, 'I'll make you proud of me one day, Mother, you'll see. I'm going away, though it will break my heart to leave all this, and you, but I must!' she hesitated, a feeling of guilt and disloyalty creeping over her, 'I have to find fulfilment, Mother!' She looked around her once more, breaking the spell. By speaking out loud she had opened her heart and gained some relief, but now she felt vulnerable and afraid. Lizzie turned and hurried to where her horse tugged restlessly against the rope, causing the woodwork to creak.

The ride earlier had been spoilt for her and the peace she'd sought was destroyed. She dare not tell Edward of the encounter with Nathan, or that he had intended to confront Peter, lest he too became embroiled in the affair.

Suddenly a voice disturbed her and she swung round to find Mrs Fox passing on her way home further up the hill. 'Hullo, Miss Lizzie, have the young people gone?' Mrs Fox came from the village twice a week to help at the farmhouse. There was optimism in her voice, knowing that her workload would be greatly reduced once the visitors had left.

Concealing her nervousness, Lizzie smiled weakly. 'Yes, Peter and Clara will be on the train and half way home by now.' Then, as an afterthought she added, 'Oh, Clara asked me to tell you how very much she appreciated all that you have done for her during her stay.'

Mrs Fox returned the smile. 'She's a nice lady, Miss,' she replied. 'You'll miss their company, I don't doubt!' Lizzie nodded soberly in agreement. 'Well, I'll be along tomorrow to do some cleaning.' With that the older woman turned away, intending to feed her husband before putting her feet up.

Slowly Lizzie rode back to the farm where there was no sign of life. Even Jack the farmhand was nowhere to be seen, so she took Nancy into the stable herself and began to release the girth strap. 'I may as well take care of you this time,' she said softly, placing her cheek against the animal's soft, silky neck. 'I shall miss you too,' she whispered with a catch in her voice. Nancy whinnied, and skittered on the stone floor. 'You sense my feelings, I know you do!' Lizzie murmured. 'But they'll take good care of you, and I will be back now and then. It won't be forever.'

The mare, however, became even more restless, until her behaviour began to disturb Lizzie who wondered if the horse had sustained an injury during their frantic escape from Nathan. 'Keep still, girl!' She ordered firmly, running an eye down the nearest leg, looking for signs of trouble. Nancy's eyes rolled, and she pulled her head up, snatching the reins from Lizzie who was trying to avoid the horse's hooves.

Such strange behaviour baffled her. Then, when a muffled sound came from behind, she half-turned but before she had time to find out what was happening a hand was clamped firmly over her mouth: it was horrible and sweating. The fear she'd sensed in Nancy suddenly welled up within her.

'Keep quiet!' a voice hissed roughly against her ear.

Lizzie struggled, frantically trying to escape the strong arm that was pinning her own to her side. The man swore and his drunken breath made her gasp— she knew the voice belonged to Nathan. She tried in vain to scream but could only moan helplessly. 'Shut up!' Nathan threatened, pressing his hand even harder across her mouth and pulling her away from the rearing horse. Lizzie was powerless to release herself, or to stop him from dragging her into the adjacent stall where she stumbled against the ironwork of the byre crying out with pain.

'I'll teach you to mock me, you bitch!' he growled. His eyes were wild, his face flushed with anger and drink, and there was a vivid weal across his cheek which had been made by her crop earlier.

'What do you want?' she begged. 'Father will be here in a minute!' Nathan grinned evilly and she screamed, hoping that Jack wouldn't be too far away and would come to her aid.

Nathan snarled at her. 'Shut your mouth! He's not here, I've been watching and waiting.' He moved closer. 'There's no one about and if you scream again I'll choke the life out of you!'

There was no doubt in Lizzie's mind that if provoked he was quite capable of doing just that. She sobbed, deeply frightened and desperately searched her mind for a way of calming him. 'You frightened me earlier, jumping out like that,' she pleaded, looking down to avoid his eyes. 'I've done you no harm.' He was looming over her now, and she raised her eyes to find out why he didn't answer her. She saw the bruising on his face and winced, knowing it was her fault and that he intended to make her suffer for the injury. There were other marks too, recent ones probably made during the fight with Peter. She couldn't conceal the contempt in her eyes.

'You proud, stuck up little bitch, you struck me!' he shouted. 'You and Peter, and your fine ways, you think I'm nothing.' He was beginning to lose his self-control. 'You think he's a man—I'll teach you what a real man's made of!' He spat the words at her, then lunged forward, a nasty leer on his face, and threw her into a corner from where it was impossible to escape.

Driven by fear, Nancy threw up her head and bolted from the stable galloping out across the yard in such frenzy that Edward's old horse Mattie and the other animals close by were disturbed and alarmed by the commotion.

Inside the stable, Lizzie cowered, hoping that common sense would prevail and Nathan would regain his self-control. 'Please!' she cried. 'Your quarrel's not with me. Go home!'

'Go home?' he barked. 'Go home?' He gave a hateful snort. 'I came to get Peter and he's gone away—leaving you behind. I'm not going home without some revenge. I'll make sure he'll never look at you again!' He raised his arm as if to strike her and Lizzie covered her face, expecting a blow that would disfigure her. Instead he reached down and pulled her savagely to her feet, dragging her towards him by her jacket and wrenching the buttons off it as he did so. Lizzie looked round desperately, seeking some means of escape, anything would be better than being maimed by a maniac. She fought, lashing out with her feet to ward him off, beating him with her fist. The fresh blows made him angrier and he pushed her backwards against the wall, pinning her there with his chest. She was no match for his strength and slowly he began to overpower her.

What could she do? Suddenly he began to lift her riding skirt with his free hand. Lizzie froze. He wasn't going to beat her at all, he intended to molest her! His hand fumbled with her undergarments and the shock brought her to life. With the one hand she had free, and with what strength she had left, she seized a handful of his hair and pulled hard. This only served to increase his fury and his hand hurt her as he forced it even higher, his fingers searching and probing. In that instant Lizzie felt that she would rather die than let him have the satisfaction of forcing himself upon her. She looked round wildly, seeking help—anything to stop him!

Nathan mistook this moment of distraction as weakness and pressed his mouth hard against hers. Lizzie shuddered and bit his lip so hard that he grunted with pain. He drew back, momentarily releasing her and turned sufficiently for her to push him off balance. She would have fled then if he hadn't still retained his grip on her skirt, preventing her from getting away.

Suddenly, almost within reach, she saw a shoeing hammer on the ledge where Jack must have left it: all she needed was a chance to seize it. Thinking quickly, she yelled towards the doorway, 'Jack! Thank God you're here!'

Nathan spun round in alarm releasing Lizzie who reached out and grabbed the hammer just as he realised she had tricked him. He lunged for her again. With a strength born only from fear, she lashed out striking him violently on the side of his head and he crashed against the side of the stall.

The shock of what she had done appalled her, but as he lifted his head and came at her again, she swung at him hitting him full on his forehead, then watched in horror as he slid to the floor.

The thud as he fell sickened her and she watched him twitching and moaning: he held his head and tried to get up to reach her. He knelt between her and freedom and with an hysterical scream Lizzie aimed the hammer directly at his head and smashed it down.

In the dreadful silence that followed, Lizzie could only stand and stare at the horrific sight before her, his ashen face, his crumpled body, the terrible gash on his temple and the blood seeping out. She knew that she must have killed him. He was dead! What was she to do? Hurried footsteps from the yard outside warned her that someone was coming, and that it was in fact too late to do anything. The hammer slipped from her hand and she leaned weakly against the wall, shocked and sobbing.

Jack rushed into the stable, brought there after seeing the still saddled Nancy galloping up the lane, and then hearing the terrible screams coming from the direction of the stable.

'What's up, Miss Lizzie?' he cried, taken aback by the distraught figure in front of him. Then he saw the ghastly sight of Nathan's body. 'Miss Lizzie!' he gasped, his voice reflecting the horror of what he saw. 'What happened?' Stunned by the realisation of what she'd done, Lizzie stared at him with terrified eyes. 'What's happened?' he asked again, seeing her disturbed clothing and dishevelled hair. 'He didn't...?' His voice dropped, he was reluctant to speak of what might have taken place.

'No! No!' Lizzie cried hysterically, understanding his suspicions. 'He tried...!' She was shaking and bewildered, so much had happened so quickly. Suddenly overcome by it all she began to sob again uncontrollably.

Jack stood watching, struggling to understand what had occurred. He looked around and, seeing a stool said gently but firmly, 'Here, Miss, sit on this,' and helped her onto it. He'd never had to deal with a matter as serious as this before and didn't know what to do. He felt foolish and repeated, 'What happened?'

Lizzie shuddered, trying to compose herself, and fought to control the turmoil in her spinning mind, so that the explanation when it came was in short bursts. 'It was horrid!' She pointed at Nathan, her tone flat, cold, even. 'I was putting Nancy away when he... he came from behind and put his hand over my mouth. He said he would kill me if I screamed! He meant it, I know he did!' She covered her face with her hands to wipe out the memory. 'Then he started to touch me!'

'Who is he? Do you know him?' Jack asked, going over to the body and closing the now staring, lifeless eyes.

'It's Peter's brother—the one he had a fight with.'

Understanding dawned in Jack's eyes. 'So that's what happened to Master Peter. But what's *he* doing here now?'

Conversation was beginning to calm Lizzie, she looked at Nathan, secretly glad that he was dead and could harm her no more. 'I met Nathan when I was out riding earlier—he was coming to get even with Peter! He was drunk and horrible. We had a quarrel, and when he found out that Peter had gone home he became worse. He seized Nancy's reins, so I hit him across the face with my crop, then fled. When I returned from the village he was here waiting for me.'

Jack had been listening intently to her explanation, trying at the same time to find an answer to the situation. He was a simple-minded man who hated violence and trouble. He had taken care of Lizzie since she came to the valley at the age of six, and had in fact taught her a great deal about the countryside, he was devoted to her and was appalled at what had taken place.

'What am I going to do, Jack?' Lizzie begged, interrupting his thoughts.

He shook his head. 'I don't know, Miss,' he replied bluntly. 'What will Master Edward think?'

'Oh, Jack!' Lizzie wailed. 'He'll think I encouraged him here. They'll all blame me because I hit him. If the truth comes out about his fight with Peter, the Army will know the real reason why he couldn't go back to the barracks earlier, that it wasn't through a fall from his horse that his face was bruised, but that he'd been fighting with his brother.'

Jack gasped. 'Even worse than that, Miss Lizzie, will they think that you're merely covering up for Peter? Could they think Peter killed him?'

'But he left several hours ago?' Lizzie replied with relief.

'A few hours will make no difference Miss. They might say he did it earlier, before he left. By the time the law gets here he'll be cold and they won't know how long he's been dead.'

Lizzie looked round wildly. 'Can't we bury him before father gets back?' she begged.

Jack was startled by this suggestion, 'Master Edward will know someone's been digging wherever we put him. Besides, I couldn't dig a hole big enough in this stony ground that quickly.' Even though he wanted to help her, Jack dismissed any thought of hiding the body nearby. He shook his head. 'It can't be done; you'll have to tell the truth! Now tidy yourself up Miss, you look awful. The Master'll know something's up if he sees you like this!'

'Oh! Jack' she protested. 'Nathan attacked me! They'll wonder why I hit him so hard if his quarrel was with his brother. They might still think I'm covering up for Peter, or even for Father! What reason would I have had otherwise to hit him, they must see what he did!'

Confusion showed clearly on Jack's face at her reasoning. 'Then we'd best wait until the Master gets back before we fetch the Law,' he suggested. The situation was more than he could cope with and the more he thought about it, the more bewildered he became. 'Master might be hours yet, then it'll be too dark to go to town.' He walked to the open stable door and looked out across the yard, his mind reeling with the enormity of it all.

Thinking that he was going to leave her, Lizzie got up and hurried to him, pleading, 'Can't we drag him into the cart and dump him somewhere on the moors?'

Turning to face her, Jack shook his head. 'It's too risky, Miss. Anyone could see us at any time. Then it would look like murder—and I'll be your accomplice.'

Lizzie began to shake. 'Do you think they really would believe me, if I tell them exactly what happened?' she cried, her eyes filling with tears.

Jack's face was glum. 'I don't know!' he said doubtfully, 'Why did you hit him so hard? I wouldn't have thought you had the strength.'

'He was horrid, Jack! I was frightened that if he got up again he would...' She stopped, unwilling to put into words the awful crime Nathan was intent on. Nevertheless, deep down, she knew that in those final blows she had fully intended to end his hateful life, to kill him, and this knowledge she would have to live with forever. Her eyes hardened and her face set with determination. 'I'm going to hide him, Jack!' she said without any emotion at all. 'He was the evil one, not me.' She looked straight at him yet hardly seeing him. 'You go away, Jack, I'll not involve you. If they catch me, neither you, Father, or Peter will be involved.'

'They'll suffer anyway if you get caught!' Jack muttered. 'It will kill Mr Edward; he's so fond of you.'

'Go, Jack!' Lizzie commanded, edging him roughly to the door. 'What you don't know won't harm you!'

Jack stared at Lizzie's resolute face for several seconds without moving, the veins in his neck throbbing, then he came back into the stable. 'I'll not let you do it alone, Miss,' he said firmly. 'Let's get him into the cart and cover him up. You start tidying up in case the Master returns, and I'll harness old Mattie.'

The relief on Lizzie's face, however, soon turned to doubt. 'Where will we put him if not on the moors? He must never be found; not near the farm at least.'

'We'll worry about that as we go,' Jack replied, his face grim and anxious. 'First thing is to move him out of the Master's way.'

Once Jack had gone, Lizzie was alone with Nathan's body. She looked at his bloodied head sadly, asking herself why he couldn't have put his differences with Peter aside and stayed away, instead he'd ruined everything. He was dead, about to be hidden away, and she had to live, haunted forever and marred by a secret she could only share with Jack. Wherever she went, whatever she did, the dreadful knowledge of his corpse would allow her no peace. She had to get away as soon as Clara could be persuaded to find a place for her in London. This beautiful valley which she loved so much seemed to have a spirit of destruction about it from the very time Edward had brought them to it, away from the slums of Sheffield. Within months of their arrival the dam had burst, later on rinderpest had decimated many animals adding further troubles for the farming community. After that catastrophe her mother had died, and now, once more, fate had taken a hand. Perhaps if she left the valley all would be well, but Edward and Clara must never know of her pain and guilt if they were to find lasting happiness here.

Tidying herself up as best she could, Lizzie then wiped the blood from the hammer onto Nathan's jacket. She covered up any signs of there having been a struggle, but could not remove the blood from her skirt without soaking it through, and time was running out. It was now important to get rid of Nathan for she had removed all the evidence of their struggle, and could not show proof of the assault or her innocence.

At last the cart rumbled across the yard, reminding her that her own horse had bolted up the lane and was wandering free. There were so many factors to consider and tend to before Edward returned, and so little time in which to do it, she must keep control of herself and not betray the fears she had.

Jack carefully backed the cart close to the stable, attempting to shield what was happening from the outside world. Lizzie's hands were still shaking, her confidence in what they were doing ebbing at the thought of moving Nathan. 'What a mess this is, Jack,' she half sobbed, 'where are we going to put him?'

'I've been thinking, Miss,' Jack responded, sounding far more positive than he felt. 'You know the ruins of the old farm; we could remove some of the stones and drop him in the cellar. With a bit of luck the Master won't go down that way until after lambing, by which time the weeds will have started growing over the stones again.'

'But someone will see us and wonder what we're up to. Father might be back soon!' Lizzie warned, dismissing the idea.

'Tonight. Tom and I will do it after dark, but you must keep the Master busy.' Lizzie gasped, her eyes widened with fear. 'It's the only way,' Jack protested. 'You and I can't do it alone. I can't dig a grave in this ground by myself without being found out. Even if we took him on the moors we couldn't get him far enough away from the road to hide him for long.' Jack sighed. He was resigned to the fact that having gone this far he was already implicated in the affair to the degree that he was not now entirely blameless. Lizzie had cleared away too much of the evidence and Nathan's injuries certainly didn't look like an accident.

Lizzie was nervous. 'I...I don't like involving your son Tom,' she said with a great deal of apprehension. 'Besides, he might tell someone.'

Jack shook his head. 'Once he knows the story and knows I could be in for it, he'll help. Anyway, once he's helped he'll be as guilty as me. You can trust him. Now, you help me get this wretch into the cart and cover him up with some sacks. I'll take him and drop him under the trees where he'll be out of view 'til dark. Then you leave the rest to me! Think about your side of it for when the Master gets back. I'll know nothing about anything if he asks.'

Lifting the heavy body was no easy task; Nathan was well built and weighed more than she realised. Lizzie had no desire to touch him, but he was more than Jack could lift alone. 'Come on, Miss,' he gasped, 'lift his legs or we'll not manage it.'

A feeling of nausea swept over Lizzie but she did as he ordered, and, standing between Nathan's legs she gripped beneath his knees, staggering under their heavy weight. Her efforts seemed in vain. 'A bit higher, Miss, and push,' Jack gasped. 'Higher!' was all he could say.

Somehow she managed to raise the legs, and between them they pushed and pulled the corpse into the cart. Weakened, she leant miserably against the wall, all fight gone, sobbing uncontrollably.

'I've got to go, Miss,' Jack said sternly. 'Now you think how you're going to explain your torn clothes and that bruise on your neck to Mr Edward. I'll bring the cart back as soon as I can.' With some trepidation he led the horse away in the direction of the old ruins and a small copse of trees. This terrible business could ruin them all if he was spotted now. He'd known something bad had happened when Nancy went charging madly up the lane, and by the time he'd reached the farm gate he was further alarmed by Lizzie's screams. His loyalty was as much to his master as it was to Lizzie. Ever since Edward had taken on the farm after the death of old Abe he had been a kind and fair employer to Jack and his family, more so than many other farmers in the district. Edward had been a solitary man until he'd brought Lizzie and her mother to the valley to housekeep for him and Jack had witnessed a slow change in his master as little Lizzie gradually crept into his heart. This had brought her mother Hannah and Edward together in the end.

Hannah's early death, however, turned Edward back in on himself, and out of concern for Lizzie he'd eventually sent her off to school, away from the loneliness of the farm. She had only been back a few months and now this had to happen! Such thoughts strengthened Jack's resolve to help Lizzie, and soon he was able to back the cart into the hedge, where, after removing the animal from the shafts, he tipped Nathan's body unceremoniously into the ditch and concealed it. This wasn't an easy task as it was early spring and there was not much brushwood about. Though there was little reason for people to pass near the old ruin these days, Jack still made doubly sure that nothing could be seen if they did. He was careful not to make things more difficult for himself later when it was dark as he would need to shield the light of his lamp from prying eyes, lest the unusual activity roused distant neighbour's curiosity.

Jack was a God-fearing man and took no pleasure in what he was doing; in fact his conscience prompted him to think God would punish him sooner or later. Glancing towards the pile of old stones that had tumbled over the cellar in the ruins, he tried to determine what difficulties he and Tom might face later that night if there was no moon. He knew the layout of the cellar and rubble well, having used much of the fallen stone to repair other walls nearby; all that remained today was sufficient to ensure that no-one ever fell into it.

Meanwhile up on the moors, Edward was of course unaware of the terrible happenings below and continued gathering his pregnant ewes together. The bad weather had held off, giving him a little time to spare, so he allowed himself the luxury of a few moments to contemplate his future with Clara, who he was missing already. In this mood he was in no hurry to return to the farm where he knew he'd be just as lonely as ever, in spite of Lizzie's company. Thank God Clara loved him, for when Lizzie went to London his life without her would be unbearable.

When Jack finally returned to the house Lizzie was inside trying to appear as if nothing untoward had happened. Her face, however, told a different tale. She was pale and bruised, her hands still trembling as she nervously rehearsed an alibi whilst striving to recall anything she might have overlooked.

Fortunately Nancy had trotted quietly back into the yard unaided, and Jack fed and watered her before putting her into the stable for the night. Lizzie was now in clean clothing and her riding habit had been sponged to remove the bloodstains. The bruise on her neck, however, could not be hidden, nor could the rents in her jacket be mended in time. After a discussion with Jack, a story was agreed: Lizzie had been thrown from Nancy who'd stumbled in a rabbit hole and, although shaken, she and the horse weren't seriously harmed in any way. Later, after tea, Lizzie was to engage Edward in a game of chess for an hour, thus allowing Jack time to hide Nathan. Edward usually sat and read for a while after dinner anyway, but he'd always enjoyed a game with his stepdaughter and tonight this would hopefully prove to be the case. Whether Lizzie could steady her thoughts and concentrate on the game was an entirely different matter, but try she must.

With his work done, Edward returned home just as the light was beginning to fade. The rich smell of cooking drifted across the yard as he tied Bella to the chain on her kennel and fed her, reminding him that he'd eaten very little himself that day.

The paleness of Lizzie's face warned him that something was wrong, and as he sat at the table his eyes caught sight of the bluish mark on her neck. He looked at her keenly. 'Is there something amiss?' he asked, 'What's happened?'

'It was foolish of me,' Lizzie began, avoiding his eyes, 'but I took Nancy over the fields where the ground was soft and she caught her right foreleg in a rabbit-hole, and stumbled. I fell off and banged myself on the branch of a tree as I hit the ground.' Edward caught his breath and put his knife down on the table. 'I'm alright,' she hastened to assure him, 'just shaken and with a bruise or two. I should have kept to the road.'

Edward was puzzled; it was so unlike Lizzie to be careless in the handling of her horse, in fact she had never fallen off before. 'Are you sure there's nothing broken?' he asked, half rising from his seat.

'Of course, we're both alright or I wouldn't be sitting here eating, would I?' Lizzie reassured him more sharply than intended.

Suspecting that she was probably still in shock, Edward ignored this and relaxed back onto the chair, knowing that things could have been much worse. 'I'll go and check Nancy after tea,' he offered.

Lizzie was about to protest but bit the words back just in time. Keeping her voice as steady as possible she looked straight at him. 'There's no need, Father,' she said calmly, 'I've checked her thoroughly and she's better off than I am.'

'Oh, Lizzie!' Edward cried with relief. 'You do worry me sometimes, you're so impetuous. One day you'll do some real damage.'

'Stop worrying,' she chided, 'and tell me about the sheep: are they ready? You've been on the moors longer than normal—perhaps it is I that should have worried?'

He knew Lizzie was trying to change the subject and as she seemed to have come to no real harm he let the matter drop. 'I think I'll start bringing the sheep down tomorrow. What will you do?'

'I'll write to Clara, then I have some mending to do.'

His eyes softened at the mention of Clara. 'I must write to her myself,' he said, his voice quieter, almost pensive. 'If I do it tonight we can post them together.'

'What a good idea,' Lizzie hastened to agree, glad to see him distracted. 'Would you like a game of chess after dinner?' she asked casually, her heart racing anxiously in case he should decline. She felt trapped in an ugly type of charade, a game which was unfortunately all too real, especially when it meant deceiving her father.

In order to placate her, Edward agreed to a game and set the board up, although he would have much preferred to sit quietly, pleasantly contemplating the future. Was it only last night that he and Clara had kissed in the kitchen, unaware that Lizzie happened to be passing the open door at that very moment? He smiled inwardly, warmed by the memory, and wondered what she must have thought of the pair of them. Later as he toyed with a pawn he looked up to find Lizzie gloomily staring at a chess piece. She was strangely withdrawn tonight, and seeming to hardly enjoy the game and this realisation quickly brought him to the present, and he played his man.

'Brighten up!' he said, trying to encourage her. 'You're winning so far!'

Startled, as if returning from another world, Lizzie reddened. 'I'm sorry,' she apologised. 'I was miles away!' This was a lie, for she was only too aware that her thoughts were much nearer home, down by the old ruin with Jack and Tom.

'It's probably the memory of the fall,' Edward conceded. 'Are you sure you're not hurt?'

She shook her head, trying to concentrate. 'No! Really I'm not; I'm just a little stiff, and of course I'm missing Clara and Peter,' she admitted quite truthfully. 'It was a surprise to find that you and Clara felt that way about each other,' Lizzie said bluntly, yet not unkindly, having accepted that his and Clara's kiss obviously meant more than something casual. 'Are you going to marry Clara?'

The change of subject took him by surprise. 'You wouldn't mind then?' he asked, sounding her out.

'No, of course not, why ever should I?' She replied truthfully this time, and smiling at him said, 'You couldn't do any better than to marry Clara.'

'It doesn't mean that I've forgotten your mother,' he said softly, his eyes holding hers as if seeking her reaction, 'but it's lonely here without her, and Clara and I seem to get on so well.'

Under different circumstances Lizzie would have been delighted that her stepfather had found happiness again, but the events of the day had marred everything. She patted his arm, 'I really don't mind, I just hope she won't find it too lonely here, Aldershot is so alive and interesting.'

Relief showed on his face. 'It means a lot to me that you don't mind,' he confessed. 'I worried that you might be hurt to find my affections awoken again. As for her being lonely, I'll make sure she's not.'

His so obvious need of her approval touched Lizzie deeply, renewing her determination to protect him from the mess she was in. Fortunately the game went on for over an hour, mainly due to Edward's happy inclination to talk about his plans and their departed visitors, thus relieving her of any further need to stall or prevaricate over her actions.

When the game was over he reluctantly got up, intending to check on the animals before they settled down for the night, as was his custom. At this, Lizzie quickly went upstairs to light the lamp in the window of her bedroom, this being the prearranged signal to Jack that Edward was about to leave the house.

Two days passed uneventfully except for Edward's gradual movement of sheep nearer to the farm. Otherwise nothing much transpired to alleviate Lizzie's constant struggle with both her conscience and a feeling of dire apprehension. She was tempted to walk past the ruins and check for herself that nothing untoward could be seen. Instead, she had to content herself with Jack's reassurance that all had been accomplished satisfactorily.

It therefore came as a shock when she heard unfamiliar voices in the yard and found two policemen in conversation with her stepfather.

'Not that I know of,' she heard her father say, 'I've not set eyes on him since his mother's funeral, last week. He's not welcome here I'm afraid,' he continued.

'We've traced him to the Strines Inn where he was last seen in a drunken state heading in the Bradfield direction. He was apparently agitated and in a bad temper.' The elder of the two men then informed Edward. 'It appears he was muttering something about looking for his brother. We understand he's staying here?'

It was too late for Lizzie to draw back without drawing attention to herself, lest this be seen as an uncharacteristic reluctance to speak to strangers. Steeling her nerves she went hesitatingly towards her father who beckoned her to him.

'You've not seen your cousin Nathan lately have you Lizzie?' he asked.

She shook her head. 'No, why?' Her voice was quiet and surprisingly steady.

'Apparently he's disappeared. It seems as though he was looking for Peter.' Edward turned to the policeman and asked, 'What time did you say he was at the Strines?'

'Lunch time,' the younger man replied. 'Or at least shortly after.'

Edward thought for a moment. 'Well, Peter left with Miss Burton that morning for Aldershot so he couldn't have seen him. I was up on the moors in the afternoon and saw no-one either. Did you see him anywhere, Lizzie, on your ride?'

Unused to lying to her father, Lizzie looked slowly down at Bella as if thinking, and made to pat her. 'No, I'm afraid not!' she replied calmly, but her heart was beating wildly.

'Strange, where he's got to,' the older man intervened, accepting her word without hesitation. 'His father says it's unlike him to stay away for so long without letting him know. We'd better set up a search of the moors. The drunken fool's probably fallen and injured himself. If you've any ideas where he might be or you should see him, let us know.'

'Do you need any help?' Edward offered reluctantly, having scant regard for Nathan and little time to waste. He could quite easily have told the officers that Nathan was involved with the pugilists who often met at the Bell Hagg Inn, but for Peter's sake he held his tongue. He remarked instead, 'It's lambing time and I'm busy, but I could let you have a man to help in a search as it'll be like looking for a needle in a haystack up on the moors.'

The senior of the two policemen shook his head. 'He won't have gone far in his state, but if we do need a man I'll send word.' After a further short exchange the two men departed, heading for the village.

'The drunken lout!' Edward said in disgust when the men were out of earshot. 'It's a damn good job Peter did leave early in the day or there might well have been another brawl between them.' He turned and went to continue his business in the barn without even looking at Lizzie; his nephews foolish behaviour did not surprise him unduly and he hoped the fool would keep away from the farm indefinitely.

Lizzie swallowed hard, grateful that he had not seemed to expect a reply from her. Had he done so, or questioned her, she might well have broken down and been tempted to confess all.

For a week the moors were searched without success, and more enquiries were made until Lizzie became edgy and withdrawn. Finally the police gave up in the expectation that Nathan would eventually return and explain his irresponsible behaviour, or that a gamekeeper would one day come upon his mortal remains. To Lizzie's great relief, at least Peter was in the clear. There was no other reason for anyone to connect Nathan's disappearance with the farm and Lizzie began to hope she would never be found out.

In spite of Edward's lack of concern for Nathan he felt it his duty to send a message of concern to his brother-in-law, saying that he had written to Peter informing him of the situation. At least Nathan's mother, Edward's sister, was no longer alive to suffer further distress, and Peter, being the decent chap he was, would naturally be concerned at his erring brother's disappearance. Edward assured him that everything had been done to find Nathan and that the absence of a body was encouraging. He also warned Peter not to speak too freely about the fight he'd had with his brother, in case his adjutant became suspicious over the unexpected leave he'd been forced to take whilst the bruises healed.

No word passed Lizzie's lips about Nathan, she merely nodded in agreement at Edward's opinions, yet the memory of what she'd done never left her, and she shuddered when she mentally relived the incident. She had little appetite, and in consequence grew thinner, causing Edward so much anxiety that he decided to seek Clara's advice, writing to ask if she could hasten her search to find Lizzie a place at a hospital in London as soon as possible.

Fortunately, within weeks, Lizzie was informed that a position had been found for her to train as a nurse at St Thomas's Hospital. Thus it was with very mixed feelings that she parted from her father and set off with a heavy heart to an uncertain future in an embryo profession for women.

Here the entries in the diary ceased and nothing further was written for nine long years.

Sheffield 1985

When Mimi had finished reading the stitched-up section of Lizzie's diary, she sat spellbound by its contents. Surely Lizzie must have realised that one day someone would unpick the stitches and read it; was that her intention or had it simply been a way of unburdening herself of the guilt she so obviously felt? What was Mimi to do now that she knew the body was Nathan's? She didn't know whether to be pleased by her detective work or to cry over Lizzie's awful experience. Should she simply close the diary, hand it back and hope that no one would blame her for the vandalism, or be honest and own up? In doing the former she would never be able to share her secret with Mark or include it in the book she was writing about Lizzie. In a turmoil of indecision, she sat staring at the open pages in a quandary, not knowing what to do. If she did own up to Mark, she knew he would be very angry at her actions and the rest of her vacation would probably be ruined.

When Mark eventually arrived to collect her, she was oblivious to his presence until he spoke. 'You look engrossed, Mimi,' he said looking over her shoulder.

Taken by surprise the decision seemed to be taken out of her hands. 'Oh, Mark!' she cried, 'You must read this! Dinner can wait.'

Not realising how serious the situation was, Mark simply looked bemused. 'It's a good job I've had a snack then, aren't you hungry?'

'I can wait, it's far more important that you read this section of Lizzie's diary. I can go out and find a sandwich whilst you are reading—it really is important you do so!' Mimi's tone was so strange that he felt compelled to read it in order to satisfy her.

'Alright,' he laughed. 'You go and get something to eat, it will save time later.' He was puzzled by her nervousness and curious to see just what had brought this about. After she'd gone he looked closely at the pages and realised they had been unpicked. He gave no further thought as to when and why this had been done, or who might have done it, instead he made himself comfortable and started to read.

Nearly an hour later Mimi returned and stood hesitantly by his side. 'What do you think?' she asked. 'Isn't it a tragic story? Poor Lizzie! No wonder her later diaries are so mysterious at times.'

'It really is incredible,' Mark replied, still stunned by what he'd read. 'What made someone unpick these stitches in the first place?'

Mimi's face reddened. 'They didn't, Mark,' she admitted with a sheepish voice, 'I did it!'

'You did what?' He's voice was so loud that several heads turned and looked disapprovingly at him. Aware of this he hissed, 'How do you mean you did it? Did an assistant say that you could?' He was angry, and Mimi knew he had every right to be so, but suddenly she felt trapped and as guilty as Lizzie.

'No,' she replied with a sob in her voice. 'I didn't ask, and I know I shouldn't have done it. I'm sorry, but I haven't really damaged anything, I was very careful.' She sat down in dismay. 'I'm so sorry, something came over me— what shall I do?'

'God knows!' he said, still angry. 'I have to work here regularly and the atmosphere will be terrible when they discover what you've done, and that's not all, now we know whose the body is we'll have to tell the police. It's a crime to conceal evidence!'

'Can't we just keep it to ourselves? Can't we simply return it without saying anything?'

'No! The next time they get it out they'll know who borrowed it last. You'll have gone back home and I shall be blamed.'

'Can't you say you didn't know and blame it on me?'

Mark was irritated by this and looked hard at her. 'I'm not a liar, Mimi, and I don't intend becoming one!' His words hit home and he saw the mortification on her face.

'I'm sorry,' she said again. 'I just don't know what to do. I can't explain, I felt a compulsion to do it. You don't think Lizzie's spirit had something to do with it, do you?'

He looked at her as though she was mad, 'You don't really believe all that kind of stuff do you?' he said disparagingly but, watching her face, he realised that she probably did. He sighed. 'Well we've got to tell them. Now you've opened the pages someone, someday, is going to read that part. You'd better apologise and face up to the consequences.'

'But what will people think of Lizzie?' Mimi could have wept for her, 'Will they try to understand?'

'I don't think they'll care after a hundred years, just so long as the police can clear up the case. The poor unfortunate woman spoilt her life by covering up what she'd done when there was every chance they might have believed her story if she hadn't panicked.'

'It would have spoilt all their lives; Edward's, Clara's and Peter's,' Mimi grieved, 'If they had found her guilty, would she have been hanged?'

Mark was not a heartless man and he could see that Mimi was as distressed by the discovery as she was ashamed of what she'd done. After all, apart from unpicking the threads on a few pages of a diary that had been entrusted to them by the Archivist, she herself had committed no crime. 'What does it matter now? By speculating you're upsetting no-one but yourself. On the other hand, I do research here and rely on their co-operation.' His anger had subsided now but he was still disappointed in Mimi, whom he'd warmed to over the past few days. 'I might never have thought anything about it—or could have suggested to the Archivist that the diary section should be undone, but I'd never deface an original document.'

Mimi flushed, 'I don't make a habit of it!' Her American voice rose, causing heads to turn again in the usually quiet room.

'Keep your voice down,' Mark whispered. 'Everyone is watching us.' He was beginning to wish that Mimi and her problems would go away. Nevertheless, the damage had to be admitted, especially as he was probably the only person who had shown interest in the diary since its deposit in the archives in the first place. 'You're as foolish as Lizzie,' he muttered 'if she'd been honest in the beginning none of this would have happened.' He saw Mimi's face fall and suspected that she might be near to tears. 'I'm sorry,' he said quietly. 'I didn't mean to be heavy handed but what you've done is a serious matter.' He fell silent then, at a loss as to what to do or say next; he could hardly go to the desk and blame Mimi, yet he didn't want them to think he'd been so stupid.

Pushing back her chair, Mimi rose and walked slowly towards the large desk behind which a serious faced young woman sat checking documents which had already been returned to her. She looked at Mimi's pale face with slight annoyance. 'You must be quiet in here,' she said. 'People are trying to work.'

The coldness of the woman's tone took Mimi aback. Already having upset Mark, and now being confronted by such sternness, it quite unnerved her and she swallowed hard. 'I've done something I shouldn't,' she stammered with such anguish that the librarians face flushed with embarrassment.

It had been a tiresome day in the Archives so far, with constant requests for documents which seemed harder than usual to find, especially whilst the department was short staffed. Oh, no, not another problem, she thought, bewildered by the distraught face before her. 'What is it then, Madam?' she asked impatiently.

'I've broken open the stitching of this diary,' Mimi whispered so that no one else could hear.

'Oh, dear, let me look—these things do happen, but you have to take great care when handling old documents, you know,' the Archivist said, endeavouring to make the point without distressing Mimi any further. She took the diary and upon examining it, noticed immediately that Mimi had intentionally unpicked the sealed pages. 'Just what did you think you were doing?' she exclaimed in disbelief.

Mark had been watching all this from the table and, feeling ashamed of his rudeness he rose, deciding that the deed was done and should be sorted out diplomatically as soon as possible. By the time he reached the desk, Mimi was incapable of explaining her actions. 'I'm sorry,' he said quickly, 'but this lady didn't realise that the stitching was so important, and simply thought that nobody had bothered to open it. I'm not excusing her but she doesn't understand the rules here,' Mark persisted. It was a feeble excuse and he knew it, but he couldn't stand by and see Mimi humiliated any further.

'I'll have to tell the head Archivist,' the woman muttered severely. 'Unfortunately he's away today. I've never heard of such behaviour—if everybody did this sort of thing there would be nothing left for future historians to view.'

'I really am sorry,' Mimi replied contritely. 'It's not Mark's fault, he knew nothing about it, and I did untie it very carefully.'

'These pages could be very important,' Mark interrupted, 'Mrs Holden's ancestor actually wrote the diary.'

'It doesn't matter; this diary has been entrusted to us and as such should be treated as a public document.' The tension was rising again and a dozen pairs of eyes were watching them, some of the other readers almost enjoying the spectacle.

'I know that,' Mark insisted, aware that the archivist was not noted for her patience at the best of times, 'but this particular section of the diary holds a clue to the murder case out at Bradfield.'

At this the archivist raised her eyebrows. 'If that is true, then the police should be informed immediately and they can come and see it for themselves! We help the police and the press whenever they require it.' She glared at them both with disdain, 'You should know better, Mr Weston,' she said immediately.

'I really am very sorry,' Mimi broke in, 'I was very careful—what can I do except to promise not to break the rules again?'

'Huh!' muttered the woman, and Mark could swear he heard her grumble 'Americans' quietly under her breath.

Taking Mimi's arm Mark led her away. 'Gather up your things, I think we'd better go.' He waited for her to do so and caught the sympathetic eye of another historian whom he knew.

'That'll give the old bat something to chew on for the rest of the day,' the man whispered as Mark passed, then out loud he said, 'Bye!'

It was a very subdued young woman who left the large building in which they'd been studying. Mimi didn't know what to say and felt very uncomfortable. After several attempts she gave up, wishing that this holiday which she'd so looked forward to would soon be over.

'I'm hungry,' Mark stated suddenly. 'I feel as though I've done battle with a Trojan.' Mimi smiled uneasily. 'I suppose they could sue us for vandalism!' he concluded.

'I didn't actually damage it, I was very careful about that,' Mimi insisted.

'No, I know that,' he agreed, then chuckled. 'It's a wonder old bossy boots hasn't unpicked the stitches herself before now. However, it does shed a different light on Lizzie's life, doesn't it?' They were now outside Lyn's Pantry on Surrey Street. 'Let's go and have a real cup of coffee and a bite to eat,' Mark suggested, 'then we'll decide what to do.'

Once seated in the basement of the café, in a corner and out of earshot of other patrons, Mark took the initiative to melt the ice a little more. 'Look,' he said, 'I'm afraid I was a little hard on you in there, but I'm not used to being affected by other people's actions. I live on my own and find it difficult to cope with trouble not of my making.'

Mimi nodded, 'I quite understand, it wasn't your fault, and believe me I won't do anything like that again. It was pure instinct, an almost uncontrollable urge.' A smile creased Mark's face, the first for quite a while. Seeing this she responded, 'You think I'm mad, don't you?'

For a moment his face betrayed none of his feelings. 'Look, I don't believe in ghosts,' he finally admitted, 'but in a way I'm glad you've uncovered the truth. Now we can see the full picture. It's quite a story, but what happened in the end? I suppose Lizzie went to America because we know you're descended from her?'

'No, she didn't!' A far away look crossed Mimi's face as she recalled Lizzie's story.

Looking at her solemn, earnest face, Mark softened. 'Many family historians seem to get strange feelings of being led on in their research. Mormons are a bit like that.'

'I know,' Mimi smiled, 'I am one!'

Mark's jaw dropped, he'd never considered this possibility.

Seeing the surprised expression on his face, Mimi laughed, 'I haven't suddenly got two heads, have I?'

'But you drink coffee,' he gasped, looking at her as if seeing her for the first time.

'I'm afraid I'm not a very good one,' Mimi admitted, 'but I still do my genealogy. Have you never met a Mormon before?'

Mark was embarrassed, 'Well...' he hesitated, 'I've passed the time of day with one or two in the Library, that's all.'

He was clearly surprised at her revelation. 'I won't bite, you know,' she reassured him not knowing what to make of his reaction.

Why the news should intrigue him so much was mystery to Mark. During the past week he'd enjoyed Mimi's company and looked forward to showing her around, but today with so much happening, he felt surprised by a feeling of uncertainty.

'So what did happen to Lizzie in the end?' he asked again, as he finished his coffee, preparing to leave.

'I'm not going to tell you the rest. You see, from the diaries and letters we have in America and the photocopies you sent, I've written a biography about Lizzie's life. I've brought a copy of it for you to read, so I won't spoil it for you by telling you what happened. After today's discovery, however, I do have some alterations to make but it will make a much more interesting story. We knew nothing of her early years until I contacted you, and now thank goodness we know everything.'

'I don't!'

'No, but you will when you've read the manuscript. I really brought it over because I wanted your comments. I thought you might be kind enough to correct any of my mistakes regarding this area. I respect your knowledge and judgement.'

'I'll look forward to reading it,' he admitted, 'but now we'd better go to the Police Station before I drop you off at Eileen's.'

The thought of returning so early to his sister's home depressed Mimi who wanted to spend more time with Mark to discuss her writings. 'Have you something important to do later on?' she asked, barely concealing her disappointment.

'Not now, I wanted to take you to Bakewell, but it's a bit late and the shops will be closing by the time we get there. It's always a bit noisy at the weekend at Eileen's with the kids about. What will you do?'

'I really don't know. It would have been nice to go with you, and it's all my fault we've wasted so much time,' she sighed. 'So much has happened today that I must admit to feeling quite shaken, and rather strange at being so many miles from home. Perhaps it was a mistake to come by myself. Without your company what would I have done? More than likely I'd be stuck in a hotel room now, passing the time reading or watching TV.'

It was obvious that she was depressed and Mark wondered if he dare suggest taking her back to his flat, plain and simple though it was. At least they would be comfortable there. 'You're homesick, that's all. I'd take you home with me but I'm afraid the flat's not very fancy, though it is clean and tidy.'

A faint smile flickered across Mimi's face. 'I don't mind all', she said, then with a more sombre look she continued, 'I would enjoy going back with you— right now I could cry at the mess I've made, and Lizzie has really got under my skin. I can feel the pain and the hopelessness she must have felt. What with that and the trouble I've caused, I'm beginning to I wish I'd never left Chicago in the first place.'

They were now approaching his car, parked nearby. 'Well, we'd better change all that,' he said emphatically. 'It's a long way to come, half way round the world and then be miserable.'

'Now you make me sound ungrateful,' Mimi groaned, 'after all you've done for me. I shouldn't have told you how I feel.'

'I'm glad you did, I've enjoyed helping you, and your company. It hasn't been all that bad, has it?'

Mimi knew he was disappointed at her reaction, which only made her feel worse. She admitted she was being selfish and full of self-pity, so resolved to brighten up. 'I've looked forward to coming for so long that it's ridiculous to feel this way, I'm usually a very positive person.' Once in his car again she felt more relaxed. 'Strange, isn't it?' she went on, 'of all the things we've done over the past week I feel secure in here, as if I've come home.'

'Perhaps it's not as strange as you think,' Mark said, glancing at his side mirror before moving off. He concentrated on the traffic and then pulled out before speaking again. 'Your visit so far has been a whirlwind of events. I just wanted to show you as much of Sheffield as I could, in case you never came again.'

'It's a lovely thought, please don't think I haven't enjoyed myself, Mark,' she hastened to reassure him, 'I've had a wonderful time. This finding of a body and then reading Lizzie's account of Nathan's death has made everything seem unreal somehow. I felt quite sick in the Library thinking about her—and knowing that I shouldn't have interfered.'

The drive down to West Bar Police Station was only a short distance, but the tea-time traffic was already increasing. 'You could do with wider highways like those we have back home,' Lizzie said seeing Mark's frustration.

'It's worse during the week. I usually avoid town at this time of day,' he replied, as he finally turned into the visitor's car park at the station. Inside the building a duty officer soon located the detective dealing with the case. To Mark's annoyance the officer announced quite casually that they already had the new information, as it had been reported by a member of staff at the library. 'Investigations are continuing, and we'll be in touch if the need arises,' he said, and waited for them to leave.

'That bloody woman!' Mark exploded once they were back in the car. 'She must have phoned the police immediately we left just to take credit for submitting the information.' Mimi laughed at his outburst. 'I'm surprised you find it funny.' he grumbled. His face was flushed and his mouth grim with annoyance, causing Mimi laugh again. Seeing her point of view he calmed down. 'Sorry,' he apologised. 'At least you'll be able to tell them at home that your visit was far from boring.'

'I feel better already,' Mimi assured him. 'I'm quite looking forward to relaxing at your place and letting you find out what eventually happened to Lizzie.' She sat back, allowing Mark to concentrate as he drove off, wondering what he would think of her rendition of Lizzie's life-story. 'Have you anything special you can do whilst I'm updating some parts of the manuscript before you read it? I know roughly which sections need doing, and perhaps you can read between the lines, now that you know the truth. I will of course need to revise some of it later, so you won't be able to read the full manuscript today anyway, as part of it is at Eileen's.'

'Do you want me to fetch the remainder? Will Eileen be able to put her hands on it? I can also do some shopping at Sainsbury's and call in on a friend—would that give you plenty of time?'

'Great, but it won't be perfect you know, not at this stage.' She was nervous now, wondering what his opinions would be.

Later in the evening after several hours of deep concentration Mimi felt satisfied with her adjustments and, when Mark returned, she passed the sheets to him before relaxing thankfully on the sofa as he began to read what happened to Lizzie when she began her diary again, nine years later.

London 1884

Waiting nervously for Peter who was to arrive at Waterloo Station, Lizzie had a near compulsion to avoid this meeting with him. What would he look like now, after nine years of service with his regiment in India? He'd never taken leave to come home to England in all that time, and the only letters she'd seen were those he'd written to Edward. These were always full of manly adventures, political intrigue and complaints about the heat, dust and poor food, hardly sentiments to encourage correspondence between himself and his younger cousin.

This had relieved Lizzie of the need to write to him. How could she, without invoking the disturbing image of Nathan's dead, ashen face, that same image which had been the cause of her many nightmares. Bathed in sweat she would wake disorientated, not to be relieved by the approaching dawn but to realise yet again that she was doomed to live in perpetual torment—and that it was of her own making. Nathan's features still haunted her by day and night; he sought her out at unexpected moments, giving her no peace.

Then, out of the blue, Peter's letter had arrived from India. He was to take a new posting, and wanted her to meet him on his return to London. It would have been impossible, even churlish of her to have refused for they had parted good friends, and he knew nothing of her dilemma.

She bit her lip anxiously and smoothed the folds of her uniform cape, wondering if she would even recognise Peter amongst the seething, bustling crowd as they approached. Indeed, would he recognise her after all these years, years in which she'd immersed herself in nursing in order to ease her conscience? She had changed of course; she was older, but not noticeably in her own eyes, for she never allowed herself to do more than quickly tend her hair before a mirror in fear of what she might see there. Her eyes rarely met their mirror image.

Lizzie was not aware of the striking figure she made standing there, apparently so competent and self-possessed. It was this very air of detachment that singled her out. The taught lines of her face were almost classical; her eyes calm yet somehow forbidding. She was tall and had grown stronger with the hard physical work of nursing, and with her hair tied sleekly back into a chignon under her cap, she drew appreciative glances from passers-by. If aware of such attention, Lizzie gave the credit to her uniform. People respected it and so they should, for it represented a fine company of women, dedicated to the care of the sick or injured.

Thus, standing apart, low in self-esteem and spirit she waited. Then she saw him moving, head and shoulders above the crowd, and he seemed not to have changed at all. He looked very smart in his uniform, his shako making him even taller, and she involuntarily raised a gloved hand to attract his attention. Surprised, he checked to see if the wave was really intended for him. She smiled wryly, waved again and he came towards her with a porter behind struggling with his bags and trunk.

Lizzie was struck by his saluting her formally, and then as he swept off his shako and placed it on the crook of his arm she realised that this was indeed Peter. He was broader than she remembered, his hair bleached fairer by the sun and his face bronzed, but otherwise little had altered.

'Lizzie?' he gasped, peering at her. 'Well, I never would have recognised you!' He looked keenly down at her face, shocked inwardly at what he saw there, for the bright lively eyes which he remembered were sombre and distant. Where was the vibrant young cousin he'd teased so much?'

'You haven't changed much, Peter,' she smiled as she took stock of him, 'I would have known you anywhere—even in uniform.'

He was tired after the long train journey from Southampton and taken aback to find himself talking to someone who seemed almost a stranger. Her words of welcome were sincere enough but the warmth they'd shared all those years ago was lacking. 'Let's get away from the crowd,' he offered, thinking to establish some kind of rapport and suggested that they went to a refreshment room where they might find seats and space to stack his possessions.

'You look smart in your uniform, Lizzie,' he remarked once they were seated. 'Do you like working in London, amongst so many people?'

'Very much,' she replied. 'I miss the fields and open sky, of course, but there are parks and heathland where I walk on my days off.'

He observed a hint of isolation in her reply. 'Do you walk alone? Have you no escort?' he asked.

Choosing to ignore the question, she said, 'I never thought I could stay away from the valley for so long but it grows easier as the years go by.'

He smiled the same infectious smile she remembered so well. 'I thought you would have been married by now, Lizzie. Is there no man in your life— Edward never said?'

She shook her head. 'I have no time for such things.'

He spoke without thinking and laughed softly. 'Watch it Lizzie! You'll be in danger of becoming an old maid.'

'I am that already at twenty-six,' she quipped back, beginning to relax a little.

'That's more like the old Lizzie,' Peter chuckled. 'I thought I'd lost the girl I used to know.' As soon as he uttered the words he saw a change in her eyes and wondered what had happened to cause this moment of discomfort in her. 'Thanks for meeting me,' he said warmly. 'I've lost touch with so many people after all these years, and in any case I had to come to London before going on home. I'm going up north next week, and will stay with your father and Clara for a few nights before going to Bamford.' He paused, a puzzled look appearing on his face. 'I wonder what did happen to our Nathan?' he said pensively. 'We never got on but he was my brother, fights and all. In spite of everything he was a home-bird, surely our last quarrel wouldn't have driven him away?'

Lizzie was gripping the handle of her cup so tightly that her fingers were almost numb. 'It's strange isn't it,' she forced herself to agree, and deliberately knocked the half-empty cup over. 'Oh dear,' she cried, springing up to avoid the tea running onto her skirt. 'That was clumsy.'

'I'll see to it!' Peter said and standing also, beckoned to the waitress who'd served them, 'Can you mop this up, please?' he asked, before turning to see if Lizzie would like a replacement cup of tea. Noting her pallor he put this down to the unfortunate mishap and did not return to the subject of Nathan again. Once the mess was cleared up and order restored, he asked, 'Where are you living in London?'

'I am very fortunate,' she replied, relieved that he'd not pursued his earlier line of questioning. 'I have a couple of rooms in a house in Kennington belonging to one of the hospital doctors. It was all due to Clara's influence of course, and now that I am established there I have the freedom of some other parts of the house, even the garden, which gives me pleasure.' Pausing she then asked, 'Where will you stay? I'm afraid it's not possible for me to offer you accommodation, under the circumstances.'

'Don't fret yourself,' Peter assured her, 'I've been recommended to a couple of small hotels in London which should be adequate enough for a short stay. Cheap and clean, that's all I need, but I trust you will accompany me about town when you're free?'

Lizzie hadn't contemplated much beyond their first meeting and her eyes widened. 'Why, of course,' she agreed, not wanting to disappoint him. 'I don't have too many hours off duty as I choose to work extra if I am needed, but it can be arranged.'

'Good, then we must have dinner and go to a theatre one night if you know of a production worth seeing.' He noticed that Lizzie had finished her second cup of tea and had looked at her watch once or twice. 'Are you short of time? Do you need to go now?' he asked.

'I have only an hour to spare, then I must return to the hospital, but I will be free tomorrow evening if that suits you?' She gave him a card with her address on.

'Splendid! I'll call with a cab to collect you if you'll tell me what time you'll be ready. I'm not familiar with that area, is it a pleasant place in which to walk?'

'It's safe if that's what you mean,' Lizzie reassured him. 'Come to the house early so that I can introduce you to Dr McCreary and his wife, they will appreciate knowing that I am in good hands, particularly as you are also a friend of Clara's.'

Peter was pleased by these arrangements. 'It sounds as though Clara excelled herself on your behalf,' he said. 'Edward doesn't know how lucky he was to have stolen her from me.' There was a twinkle in his eye at the last remark, and no sign of bitterness. 'Are they truly happy?'

For the first time since their reunion, Lizzie felt comfortable in his company. 'Yes, it was quite a surprise about Father and Clara but they are very well suited to each other. I think you knew at the bottom of your heart that you and she were not so attached for it to cause you anger. You were, after all, determined to go to India and she in turn did not want to leave England.'

Peter grinned. 'Clara was too good for me, Lizzie, and not really in love with me at all, but to lose her to my uncle, well, that did hurt a little. Don't repeat that, of course!'

They both now began to relax and the old banter they once exchanged returned to their conversation, so much so that when next they looked at the time Lizzie realised she would be late getting back to the hospital. 'I must go— I'm late already,' she cried, rising quickly.

'Let me get a cab and drop you off,' Peter intervened, 'after all it's my fault you're here.' He rummaged in his pocket, 'I've a small gift for you,' he said, handing her a packet. 'It's a little bit of India, nothing much, but I have no-one else to buy for! I'll go and get a cab, wait here.' He dashed outside leaving Lizzie bewildered and looking at the small parcel in her hand.

'Thank you!' she called after him, but her cry was lost in the hubbub around her.

In spite of her curiosity over the contents of the package she placed it unopened in her reticule for safety, intending to open it in the cab, and waited anxiously for Peter to return. He did so almost immediately with a porter, and together they wove their way through the throng as quickly as was possible in case the waiting cabbie took a better fare and left them to find another conveyance.

Once seated, Lizzie repeated her thanks and with trembling fingers opened the gift.

'It's just something I thought you might like,' Peter explained as she untied the ribbon and wrapping, thus revealing a small tortoiseshell box.

'You are too kind,' Lizzie said, 'I really don't deserve it—I haven't written to you in all these years.' She opened the box in which lay a small oval brooch of fine filigree silver. 'It's beautiful!' she exclaimed, embarrassed by his generosity, yet pleased by his thoughtfulness. 'I will wear it tomorrow. Thank you so much.'

Peter laughed at her obvious delight with the gift that had been a last minute inspiration, a gesture of goodwill, and now he was pleased he'd thought of it. 'In all the years I visited the farm I never did buy you anything even when you were a child. That will make up for my youthful negligence.'

'I never expected you to bring gifts; I just enjoyed your visits. Mother looked forward to spoiling you and after she died your calling to see us was a link with her. Edward is a good stepfather but I was lonely without my mother, so your visits were special times for us.' She fell silent, the effect of her memories together with the jogging of the carriage were both making her feel slightly uncomfortable, so she was glad when eventually the hospital came into view.

'Here, by the lodge gates—drop me here please,' she called to the cab driver. 'You keep the cab, Peter, it will save you having to find another. I live just off the road up there,' she said, once Peter had alighted and handed her down.

He watched her pass through the gate before climbing back into the cab, his mind spinning with the strange encounter he'd had with her.

At six-o'clock the following evening, Peter looked in his dressing mirror, smoothed his hair with his hand and grinned. 'Not bad!' he said to himself. 'Not after nine years in the drying heat of India!' He was, however, more nervous at meeting his cousin this time, though goodness knows why! He had been prepared to find Lizzie a chatty, self-willed and lively girl; instead he was intrigued by her cool self-possession. She wasn't bad looking though, which pleased him. He'd fancied she'd been half in love with him at seventeen, and had teased her unmercifully. She'd been a pretty little thing then, one whom he could quite easily have taken advantage of; indeed he might have done if he hadn't already been in love with Clara. Would Clara, too, have changed so dramatically if they'd married and he'd gone off to India without her? He had yet to meet her face to face after she'd written to him to say that she was going to marry Edward. He wondered now, after seeing Lizzie, how many men had married and served overseas, only to return home to find themselves wedded to a stranger. It was a solemn thought, one that left him grateful still to have his freedom intact. His occasional dallying with the daughters of other officers had never left him anything but glad when the affair was over and done with. He had a few regrets but, at thirty-five, the urge to travel was not what it had been, his career in the Army had gone as far as it ever would and a decision had to be made. Should he settle for continuing Army routines or begin to cultivate some business interest for when he chose to resign? He wasn't one for making great personal decisions; the Army had been both his mentor and guardian, wet-nursing him through all his adult life. He was good at his job, men followed him without question, but the emotional side of his character was like a blank sheet. He was in fact too lazy and selfish to want the trappings of marriage or the responsibility of civilian life, yet the future alone was bleak.

Not that Peter wasn't ready for a relationship, but it needed to be a simple one, the Army was his life and a wife meant excess baggage. Even Clara had realised that. Now here he was after weeks at sea, hoping to have a little fun with Lizzie, feeling somehow that she had the upper hand. 'Get a grip of yourself, man!' he grinned at himself in the mirror. 'She's only your cousin for God's sake.'

Lizzie on the other hand was extremely worried. She had little in her wardrobe to recommend her, for when not in uniform she chose to wear plain, severely cut gowns which she hoped would make her inconspicuous. However, in her desire not to attract the attentions of men she little realised that the simplicity of her dress and figure actually caused more than one pair of eyes to linger in her direction. Tonight in order to brighten her image a little she chose the best she could and added the little brooch he'd bought her, and hoped for the best.

Peter ordered the cabbie to wait and walked briskly up the steps where he knocked on the door promptly at six-thirty and, when ushered into the hall, he saw Lizzie standing on the landing waiting for him. As she descended the stairs he had a strange feeling that she was watching him guardedly, yet her greeting was warm enough, and she proudly introduced him to the good Doctor and his wife.

'I'm pleased to meet you,' Peter said, shaking their hands, 'and very grateful for the care you're taking of my cousin here.'

'We have become very fond of her,' the Doctor replied warmly, bringing a flush to Lizzie's cheeks.

So the old Lizzie still lurks behind the facade, Peter thought to himself with satisfaction as he saw her blush. 'I do believe we have another mutual acquaintance,' he went on, trying to allay Lizzie's embarrassment, 'Clara Burton, now Mrs Morton? I also think you and I met briefly at the Cottage Hospital in Aldershot some years ago when she introduced us.'

'More than likely. Clara is the daughter of my late friend Dr Burton, whom I met when we were both at the Crimea. I understand you have just returned from India?'

'That's right sir, I landed at Southampton three days ago.'

'Who were you with out there?'

'The King's Royal Rifle Corps.'

'I suppose you're being sent to the Sudan with the Expeditionary Force then?' the Doctor asked with an involuntary sigh, 'I really don't know what Gordon was thinking about, not withdrawing when he had the chance.'

'Now then you two,' chided the Doctor's wife, Jane. 'If you two want to talk business then Peter must come again, when he's not taking Lizzie out.' She had a motherly figure, and like her husband was grey haired. She was also obviously used to holding her own in the house because the Doctor immediately agreed with her comments.

'Forgive me. Yes, do come again. I'm interested in tropical medicine these days but not too keen on field work, I'm afraid. I leave that to the younger men. If you can spare the time I'm usually free in the late afternoon. We have a telephone now so you can call to make sure I'm available—Lizzie will give you the number. Now off you go,' he said to her with a fatherly smile. 'Enjoy yourself for a change.'

As they took their leave and left the house Peter remarked, 'You've done well there, my lady, but what did he mean 'enjoy yourself for a change'?'

Lizzie laughed. 'I do go out, mainly to the Mission Church which Dr McCreary thinks is an admirable thing to do but considers it to be a dreadfully dull existence for a young woman.'

'You go to the Chapel?' Peter gasped. 'That's not the Lizzie I remember.'

'It's been nine years since we met, Peter, and a lot has happened in that time,' she laughed. 'You don't really know much about me now at all.' Her laughter had a hard ring to it which disturbed him. 'I find great comfort at the Mission,' she went on, 'particularly in helping others.'

'But you do that all day long, nursing! It certainly is time you enjoyed yourself, and we'll begin tonight or I'll be damned. I've got tickets for the Haymarket Theatre, so let's get a move on—I asked the cab-driver to wait.'

'Haymarket Theatre,' he called as he handed her into the cab.

'I didn't realise you knew Dr McCreary?' Lizzie said once they were seated comfortably inside.

'I didn't until I saw him. When you mentioned Clara I then remembered her introducing him to me. It's some years ago but he's not changed much, he's got the kind of face you don't forget.'

'I'll always remember the first time I went to the theatre,' Lizzie chuckled, 'that was in Aldershot—don't you remember us all going one night?'

'Was that really your first visit?' Peter seemed amused at this.

'And my last!'

'My God, Lizzie, you have led a sheltered life!' Peter exclaimed in amazement. 'You live in London with all these theatres around you and you don't go—you must be mad, I would be there every week!' He sounded like a young boy in his enthusiasm and Lizzie wondered if what she'd heard about the insular life led by the military in India had a grain of truth in it after all.

'How long are you staying in Town?' Lizzie asked, changing the subject. 'Are you coming back here when you've been home, or have you to go back to Aldershot?'

'I've not been to Aldershot since I first left for India. I should have gone to Cyprus with the men but I had a home leave coming up and needed to sort out some business in London. Now we are expecting to join an expeditionary force to go and help Gordon in the Sudan.'

'War, war and more wars,' Lizzie remonstrated. 'As if there aren't enough dead and wounded already. We seem to be fighting everywhere, losing thousands of good men in the process.' Her voice was heated but her opinions were well considered.

'You seem well informed, Lizzie, I didn't think you'd be interested in politics.'

62

'When it brings suffering, I am. I always remember listening to you and Father talking about the Crimea and the Ashanti expedition when you came to the farm. Your descriptions were so realistic that I've never forgotten them. The Doctors at the hospital talk constantly of politics, of war and the frustrations of combating the foreign diseases some men bring back. So you see I am well informed whether I want to be or not.'

Peter's admiration for Lizzie was returning, as after his initial meeting with her he had begun to despair at the dullness of her existence. 'Look, why don't you come up north with me,' he asked, prompted by the memories she had invoked. 'We could go riding on the moors and it would be like old times again.'

Lizzie froze at the suggestion and was glad to be protected by the darkness inside the cab. 'Oh, I can't,' she protested firmly, 'we are very busy now, besides you don't need me with you. My father will lend you a horse and you can ride over to Bamford to see your people.'

'What a pity,' he replied, unaware of the fear and trepidation she always felt during her infrequent visits home. 'And a shame,' he continued, accepting her reason without question. 'We could have had a good time.' He fell silent then, wondering what his own reception would be after so long away.

Lizzie too said no more, and was grateful when the cab drew up before the doors of the theatre. She knew, however, that she would have to go home sometime in the near future, to tell them of her plans for later that year.

Once inside, amongst other theatre-goers, they both relaxed, thrilled by the atmosphere and eager anticipation of those near them. As the orchestra played a lively prelude, Lizzie leaned towards Peter. 'Thank you for bringing me,' she said. 'It's a long time since I have felt so much excitement.'

Peter turned and studied her face. 'How's that, Lizzie?' he asked. 'Why have you allowed yourself to become so isolated? You were such a lively girl; surely London has much to offer?'

Startled at his directness, Lizzie searched for a suitable reply. 'I suppose you're right,' she finally admitted, realising also that she would have to watch her words carefully in future, for it wouldn't take much, or long, to arouse his curiosity and for the truth be forced out of her. 'Oh, Peter! If only you knew,' she cried inwardly. 'You would never understand. How could you?' No matter what provocation there had been, his brother was dead, and she had dumped his body in an unmarked grave leaving his family bewildered and bereft. As the years had passed she had found it harder to accept just why she had panicked and hidden the body, thus compounding the deed, so that now she would never be able to prove her innocence. The crime was done, however, and no good could come from its disclosure at this time.

The orchestra continued to play as the curtain lifted and the lights went down, alleviating the need to converse further until the interval.

'An excellent show so far, don't you think?' Peter asked, when the curtain came down, he was obviously as transported by the production as she seemed to be. 'I've not seen as good a show for years.' He leaned back in his seat, contentedly, 'Now come on, why don't you come home with me next week?' he asked suddenly, as if trying to surprise her into accepting his offer.

'I can't,' she replied, half whispering. 'I told you earlier.'

Not one to be easily thwarted, Peter laughed. 'I don't believe you couldn't come if you really wanted to. I'll pay the fare if that's the problem.' He was getting enthusiastic now; the thought of travelling alone did not please him, nor did filling in time alone on the farm. He turned, smiling fondly at her. 'Come on, be a chum and keep me company,' he cajoled, teasingly.

Lizzie saw in an instant why, as a girl, she had been charmed by him, and wondered how he had managed to stay single all these years. She also realised that he was probably used to having his own way, a trait that did not particularly please her. 'I cannot abandon my responsibilities, just to please you!' she told him firmly. Then added, 'And trying to charm me simply won't work, Peter!'

Laughing at her somewhat petulant outburst, he grinned. 'It used to, Lizzie, I must be slipping!' He looked around. 'Look, let's go and have a drink before the warning bells go,' he offered, helping her from her seat and trying to conceal his disappointment as he did so.

Following him, Lizzie knew that now was not the time to tell him of her future plans: on the other hand, it would make it easier to tell her father and Clara of them if Peter were there to divert Edward's disapproval. So, by the time the third bell rang to summon them back to their seats, she had decided to tell him that she would accompany him after all, but not tell him anything else of her plans tonight.

They left the theatre in a happy frame of mind and boarded the cab Peter had secured for them. Some time elapsed before Lizzie raised the matter, explaining that it would be difficult to get away at such short notice, but that she would try. Peter's jubilation at the news made her reluctant to tell him the real reason behind her acceptance. 'Before we go north,' she said soberly, 'I need to talk to you seriously. Can you come to the house? The matter doesn't lend itself to a discussion in the park and I'm sure Dr McCreary won't mind us using the parlour—we being cousins.'

'You've aroused my curiosity now, Lizzie,' Peter confessed. 'It's nothing terrible is it?' Lizzie shook her head. 'How about me calling tomorrow in the afternoon, after I've dealt with my business in town?'

Nodding, Lizzie agreed. 'I'm sure two o'clock will be convenient, as I'll be back by then.'

Setting Lizzie down at the house, Peter set out to return to his lodgings puzzling as to what it was that she needed to discuss so urgently. He certainly had business to attend to the following day, but would ensure he'd finished by one o'clock, thus leaving ample time to reach the Doctor's by two.

He was looking forward to travelling north and to seeing Edward again. Ever since he'd joined the Army he'd thought of his uncle's farm as his real home. He'd never got on with his own father, and certainly not well with his brother Nathan, so the farm held fonder memories for him. Now, faced with the reality of his first visit for so many years a feeling of foreboding came to him, and he began to ponder once more over Nathan's disappearance. Whilst he was in India it had not seriously worried him, and he'd always presumed and hoped that one day a letter would arrive from Edward, telling him that Nathan had turned up. Time had gone by though and he'd thought less and less about his brother. 'The selfish good-for-nothing,' he thought, letting the family worry all this time without sending a single word of explanation. Where had Nathan gone and with whom? Peter shook his head with some relief; at least this time there would be no confrontation between the two of them.

He returned to his lodgings and then, having poured himself a large brandy, he lowered himself into the only comfortable chair in the room, put his feet on the stool and tried to relax. The contents of his glass soon began to warm him: it was damned cold in England in July compared with India, and no amount of brandy could compensate for the loss of the balmy evenings spent on colonial verandahs. He'd got used to the flies and mosquitoes being kept at bay by the punkah wallahs, but it had been an artificial world, one of tight English communities with their own social rules and habits. As he waited for his fire to heat up he began to doze, only to be disturbed by the slamming of a door somewhere.

The worn seat of the old horsehair chair was beginning to make his buttocks ache so, sighing, he rose stiffly to his feet to prepare himself for bed, wondering as he did so what on earth had changed Lizzie so much? He also pondered briefly on what kind of bedfellow she would make! It was hard to judge. Beneath her neat and almost staid veneer he'd witnessed a glimpse or two of the old Lizzie lurking there. He'd no intention of hurting her of course, he was too fond of her for that, but a little titillation might bring them both a touch of comfort. The affect of the brandy set him thinking of the women who had shared his bed over the years and he finally came to the conclusion that none had been worth the luxury of a deeper attachment. The unexpected changes in Lizzie though, intrigued and puzzled him, so much so that he found himself awaiting their next meeting with a mixture of anticipation and apprehension. With his private business over, the following afternoon found Peter hastening towards Lizzie's address in Walcott Gardens, where he knocked on the door and waited with less confidence than was usual for him.

Having seen his approach from her window, Lizzie opened the door herself and invited him in. She was dressed as for work, with her hair concealed in a chignon as before.

Peter breathed in sharply. She was, again, almost untouchable, impersonal even. Who was this stranger before him? He felt slightly rebuffed, as though their rapport of the previous evening had been merely an illusion brought on by the soft lights and atmosphere of the theatre.

Seeing his hesitation, Lizzie smiled. 'Come in, Peter. I'm afraid I can't keep you long, as I have to go back to the hospital—I have to make up for the time off.' She had planned this meeting to be a short one, as his growing attentions at the theatre could become awkward if she did not soon explain what she intended to do later in the year.

Peter followed Lizzie into the drawing room somewhat subdued, and took the seat she offered. 'What's the mystery?' he queried, aware that she had retreated back into her own secretive world.

'There is none,' Lizzie replied, 'but before we go home I have to tell you of my future plans. These may shock and worry my father and as I have to tell him sooner rather than later, I may as well go with you to do so.' Her face was flushed, whether from embarrassment or sheer determination he wasn't sure, but he had the feeling that her news would not be to his liking either.

Suspecting that he was being used, Peter said a little stiffly, 'I get the impression that whatever your plans are; your mind is made up already.' He paused, then continued, 'You are obviously not seeking my advice but hope to gain my support?'

She smiled wryly. 'I'm sorry if you think that. Please be assured I am not. It was your idea that I accompany you, remember?'

He nodded. 'Well, what can be so dreadful or momentous that you hesitate to tell even me in an open manner?' There was a stern look on his face, and Lizzie knew that he was far from pleased with the situation.

'I intend to go to China soon, as a nursing missionary.' she stated bluntly.

He stared at her, then exclaimed in disbelief, 'Good God, Lizzie!' He spat the words out, then giving her no time to reply, continued, 'Are you mad? You have no idea of foreign places, the dangers, the climate, or the futility of trying to convert idol worshipping savages.' He was very angry.

'How Dare You! How dare you!' Lizzie snapped back at him. 'Have you no respect for people who are different?' She was icy cold with indignation, and determined that he wouldn't make her lose her composure.

Incredulously Peter's eyes widened and he laughed disparagingly. 'Different!' he repeated. 'You can't be serious. Don't forget I've been to such places, West Africa, India—you can't reason with most of the natives. At the end of the day they soon go back to nature, with their strange ideas and customs.' He wasn't giving Lizzie time to retaliate. 'Beneath the surface they remain ready to revert to type when the going gets tough.'

He was almost breathless with the strength of his convictions but Lizzie refused to be deterred by his outburst. She stared at him, hurt by his lack of humanity for those less fortunate than themselves; she had not expected him to oppose her intentions so violently. However she had, over the years, learned to discipline and control her feelings well, particularly when listening to the rantings of ill-informed disbelievers. She stood patiently, waiting for him to calm down, then said quietly, 'It's a pity you feel that way. After all, if I hadn't heard of your adventures when I was a girl, I might never have wanted to travel.' As soon as the words were out she regretted them and felt ashamed, for if Nathan hadn't changed the course of her life things might have been very different. She owed him an explanation. 'The training I've had has given me strong beliefs, Peter, and there is also something within me which gives me no peace, so I have to fulfil my calling to help others.' She could think of nothing else to say and fell silent.

'I would have thought there was sufficient misery and deprivation here in England to keep you occupied for a life-time,' Peter said grimly, 'I think you're simply letting your imagination run amok!'

At this, Lizzie realised that there was nothing to be gained by continuing the argument. 'Please, my mind is made up, and all is arranged. Would it not be better to remain friends? Otherwise it will be impossible for me to travel home with you and I will have to go alone, after you have been there.'

'How can I go without you now, knowing of your plans?' Peter retaliated. 'How could I not mention these to Edward? You leave me no alternative.'

'Then let us beg to differ,' Lizzie suggested, 'after all, you know very little about me. It is nine years since we last met, and much has happened to us in that time—we are not what we were.' She also felt like saying that he had no right to interfere or judge her, but was reluctant to say so and thus risk an open breach in their relationship. Peter's high emotion had now lessened and he shook his head sorrowfully. The day that had dawned so brightly was ruined, overshadowed by anger and disappointment. He could see that Lizzie could not be deterred by anything he might say, yet was sure she was making a big mistake. She might even be putting her life at risk as so many had done before her, out of naivety and a lack of understanding of conditions never experienced here at home. He realised that Lizzie was Lizzie and that, as in the past, shouting at each other would do nothing but strengthen her resolve. It would take patience and tact to divert her from her folly. 'I can see that you are determined,' he admitted, reluctantly striving to appear as calm as she. 'And I apologise for my outburst. You are right. Nine years is a long time and people do change. Perhaps you would tell me more of your plans as we travel, for although I may not agree with you I will at least try to understand.'

With a gracious nod and smile, Lizzie accepted his apology, knowing full well that he would continue to try to dissuade her in the belief that it was his duty to do so. As for her father, she knew he would never acquiesce, although Clara just might. It would therefore be better if no more was said for the time being, as the exchange of angry words had left an atmosphere of discord. Perhaps time would help. 'I'm afraid I have to go out now Peter,' she said gently, but firmly. 'If you would still like me to travel to Bradfield with you, let me know where and when we are to meet.'

Peter eyed her solemnly as he spoke. 'I was thinking that next Tuesday might be the best time, for me at least.' When Lizzie did not demur he went on, 'how about me picking you up from here with your luggage? I'll send you word when I have the exact time—if that suits you?'

Lizzie responded gratefully. 'Yes, please. Tuesday would be fine, and that will give me time to warn Father that we intend to visit.'

She had regained her poise and her manner now, reminding him very much of Clara as she stood there. He decided not to lengthen the parting with trivial conversation, so bade her farewell and made his way down the street in search of a public house, where he intended regaining his own equilibrium as best he could.

Closing the front door behind him, Lizzie lay back against it with some relief. She really had no reason to go out again that day but knowing her news would cause a stir, had made the right decision to keep the visit short. Hopefully, by Tuesday, Peter would have calmed down sufficiently to discuss her plans in a more rational and helpful frame of mind. In turn, she would spend some of the time writing and despatching a letter to her stepfather to inform him of their intended visit. She was disturbed by the thought of returning home, as painful memories were always stirred when she did. This was why her visits were rare even though she knew her long absences hurt and puzzled Edward. Now she was to distress him even more with her news.

That Lizzie could even contemplate going to China astounded Peter, and he was convinced that this was simply a fanciful whim on her part, one which with careful handling he might still change. He was determined to try hard, by relating some of his own experiences to her, in order to save her from the dreadful climate, the dangers of many diseases, and of cultures totally alien to her. China, he had been told by colleagues who had been there, was a country steeped in mythology and opium. Lizzie was no longer a playful, amenable and biddable girl and he would need to proceed very cautiously if he was to make any headway at all.

As a result he took little pleasure in making the necessary arrangements for their journey, instead he took refuge in the hip flask of brandy which he kept in his pocket, and shivered in the cool English summer.

By the time Tuesday arrived Peter was bored with looking at the four walls of his room, fed up with strolling through the parks alone admiring the scenery, and annoyed at paying more than he felt was necessary for poor food. He was relieved when he was able to lift his bags into the cab when it arrived, and instruct the driver to go to Walcott Gardens where Lizzie was waiting.

'Have a good time, dear!' Jane McCreary said as Lizzie stepped into the cab. 'The change will do you good,' she added with motherly concern.

The cabbie whipped his horse along the uneven surface towards Lambeth Bridge and an uncomfortable silence settled over the cousins. Lizzie gazed out of the window while Peter observed his boots, wondering if he would have to endure the same atmosphere for the whole of their coming rail journey. At least at the farm things might revert to normal in Edward's presence. Throughout his travels he'd thought of the farm as unchanging, knowing that it would be there awaiting him and, in times of stress or depression, it had been his anchor, a haven, more so than his real home. Only now did Nathan's disappearance seriously disturb him. He sighed out loud, causing Lizzie to turn.

'Sorry,' he said lamely, trying to throw off his gloom. 'It's been quite a shock, arriving back in England, things have changed so much. This last weekend was a bore and going home is bound to be an ordeal.'

Lizzie was alarmed at his despondency. 'Look,' she offered, 'I know it didn't help, telling you of my intention to go to China in such a manner, but I didn't know how to break the news, even to you. You see I've told no-one yet, apart from Dr McCreary and the people at the Mission....' her voice trailed off and he realised that she too was under considerable strain.

He tried to brighten things up. 'Listen,' he said, 'let's go back nine years and pretend nothing's happened in between—just for the week!'

Appreciating the effort he was making to ease the situation, Lizzie felt guilty. 'It would be nice,' she admitted. 'If only it were possible. As for riding I haven't done any for years, not since...'. She stopped, the colour draining from her face, and was unable to continue.

'Since what?' Peter asked, concerned and a little baffled at the sudden change in her.

'Since the accident. Not since I fell on the day you and Clara left the farm to return to Aldershot. I never rode again after that, then I left for London.' No one had ever questioned her explanation about the bruises on her face; the ones on her body she'd managed to keep hidden from the world.

'Was it such a bad fall?' Peter asked. 'Edward never mentioned it in his letters.'

'His mind might have been pre-occupied with Clara,' Lizzie suggested. 'There were no bones broken and only a few bruises, together with some shock.'

'Poor you!' Peter exclaimed with brotherly affection. 'You should have got straight on again, you know. It's the only way.'

'I have never had the desire to ride again. My long absence from home has broken the bond I had with Nancy, and she's getting old now I'm afraid.'

Peter placed a hand gently on her arm. 'All the better, she'll be quieter as a result. Leave it to me, before we part you'll be riding as though it never happened.'

Taking control was the one thing Peter was good at, and his reassurance touched Lizzie deeply. She blinked a tear away and turned back to the window. If only it were that simple. If only she could tell him the truth, cry on his shoulder and unburden herself. The deception, however, was her cross to bear and she had to do it alone. There was no time to discuss his offer further as the carriage had reached the station approach, and Peter became absorbed in organising their departure.

The ice between them now being broken, the journey by train which followed was much more pleasant than expected, and Lizzie enjoyed listening to Peter's tales as she had done years before. His stories of adventure this time, however, had a different aim in mind. The more he spoke of the hardships (which he embellished of course, for her own future good) the more determined she was to go to China. She wanted hardship; it was her penance for what she'd done to Nathan. Now in her maturity she saw Peter's qualities for what they were, good, bad and indifferent. He was no longer a hero, simply a man whose aspirations were mixed with doubts and fears too. She began to feel much closer to him even as he admitted to some of his weaknesses and, true to his promise, he never mentioned China throughout the entire train journey. He was pleasant, helpful and considerate, and he made her laugh. Perhaps his presence would, after all, make this visit home easier to bear.

Bradfield 1884

Familiar sights came and went,
drawing them ever closer to Sheffield where,
hopefully, her father would meet them off the train. If Edward didn't do so,
Peter would hire a carriage for the nine-mile journey to the farm.

'Wake up, my dear!' Peter said gently, touching her on the arm as they
approached the station.

Lizzie woke with a start and began tending to her appearance. She gazed
pensively through the window, wondering if her father had received her letter
and would find time to come and fetch them.

'It's still a smoky old place,' Peter remarked as the train drew in to the
platform. 'God knows how people live here. Couldn't you find it in your heart
to help these poor folk instead of going to China?' It was the first time he'd
mentioned her plans so as to avoid aggravating her on the journey. Besides,
he wanted to get Edward on his side, to back him up, before he tried harder
to make Lizzie change her mind.

Lizzie ignored him and looked along the platform, scanning the crowd for
her father. 'There! Over there.' she cried, waving her handkerchief frantically,
trying to catch his eye. 'Father!'

'You wait here, I'll go and get him,' Peter offered as he handed her down
from the train. 'Watch the luggage, Lizzie!' She waited as he strode briskly
through the crowd to where her father stood, then saw Peter embrace him as
if he were indeed his father and not his uncle. It is a pity Lizzie thought, that
he wasn't, especially as it looked as if Edward and Clara were not intended to
have children of their own. Edward would have loved a son.

The two men quickly made their way back to Lizzie who immediately
clasped her arms round her father's neck and hugged him tight. She missed
his solid strength so much.

Edward was a little embarrassed by all the fuss and said gruffly, 'It's not
before time that you come home to see us!' The twinkle in his eye however,
belied the reprimand. 'Clara is overjoyed at your coming and has some news
for you.' He appeared very happy and excited and Lizzie sensed he had a
secret which was difficult to keep. Was Clara pregnant again? Three times she
had miscarried; bringing their joy to an abrupt end, but to ask him now would
only cause pain if she had drawn the wrong conclusion. Lizzie let the matter
drop, and linking her arm with his, walked with the two men to where her

father had left the horse and trap. 'I'm glad you didn't bring too much baggage, Lizzie,' he said as he placed their things under the seats. 'I was afraid we might be a little cramped.'

It was a long, bumpy ride, first through the throng of the town traffic, then out along the rutted country lanes to the village, and beyond that to the farm. It was nearly dark when they arrived, and Peter helped Lizzie climb down; she was stiff and cold but thankful that the dusk concealed the yard and stable.

Inside the house Clara had been waiting impatiently, listening all the while for the trap to return. Immediately she heard the clatter of hooves, she hurried into the yard with a lantern in her hand.

Lizzie saw Clara's swollen form and laughed; the secret was hard to conceal. 'So, you've been eating too much I see,' she chided playfully, embracing her stepmother with affection. 'Why didn't you tell me?'

Clara smiled broadly. 'I wanted to make sure everything would be well this time,' she replied. 'If you hadn't come to visit we were going to tell you once I had safely delivered.' Lizzie gently released Clara who then saw Peter hanging back in the shadows. 'It's good to see you again, Peter,' she said, 'when did you get back to England?' She took his arm and led him towards the front door.

Before Peter could answer, Edward took the lantern from Clara saying, 'I'll take it and put the horse away while you make us all a hot drink.' With that he went off whistling happily to himself. It pleased Lizzie to see him so contented; a child would bring him comfort and also compensation for her more prolonged absence in the future.

A wonderful aroma met them as they entered the house and Peter sniffed, 'Oh, what's cooking, Clara?—It's years since I smelt anything so good.'

'It's only stew and dumplings,' she responded with a chuckle. 'I'd no idea how long it would be before you arrived so the pot's been simmering gently for hours. I knew you'd be hungry after your long journey, so all I need do now is drop the dumplings in.'

'I was always hungry, you know that and I've not changed,' Peter laughed. 'But I'd better fetch the bags in and help uncle put the horse away first. I'll not be long.' Peter caught up with Edward and felt a deep sense of well-being steal over him. He was home again. The journey from London had been long and tiring but far more enjoyable than he'd expected under the circumstances, and now he was happy to talk to his uncle. The two men chatted continuously, filling in the gaps that their letters had omitted.

'You go ahead!' Edward insisted once the horse was secure in the stable and the trap put away, 'I'll not be long, and don't forget to clean your boots before you go in or Clara will be after you!'

Peter scraped his boots on the scraper by the door before re-entering the house, but he couldn't see anyone about. The clatter of pots then led him to the kitchen where he saw Clara busy in the pantry, so he coughed gently, in order not to startle her.

'Oh, there you are,' Clara said, looking round. 'Sit down and talk if you like, Lizzie's gone to change. Dinner won't be long!'

Peter looked about him. 'I'll use Edward's chair until he returns,' he ventured, 'I always did like sitting in it.' He immediately felt comfortable, as he had done in the past, in the robust ladder-backed elm chair,. The kitchen hadn't changed much in the intervening years, yet there were many subtle signs of Clara's care and attention. Simple changes which the old housekeeper, to save work, had previously avoided. A gleaming copper kettle sat on the oven top. 'I remember that kettle,' he laughed, 'it's from Aldershot.'

'It looks better here with the glow of the fire on it,' Clara said smiling. 'How did you like India, then?'

'Much as I expected in many ways, an eye-opener in others,' he confessed. 'I'm quite pleased to be back, although I expect to be sent to The Sudan at anytime if the Government think it necessary.'

Clara looked troubled. 'Things haven't gone so well there, have they?' she sighed. 'We get newspapers sent out here so I keep abreast of things. How do you feel about it?'

He shrugged, 'Perhaps I'm getting older and just a little afraid that my luck might run out. I don't believe it's going to be easy though, in spite of what Gordon thinks.'

'You've done your duty in India, Peter. God only knows why we're constantly striving to sort other countries out.'

A loud voice came from the hallway. 'Trade, that's what, as well as greed.' Peter jumped up as the door from the hall opened, heralding his uncle's return. 'Stay there a while, I need to wash,' Edward said, seeing the guilty look on his nephew's face, and laughingly continued, 'you always did sneak into my chair when you thought I wasn't looking!' He looked around. 'Where's Lizzie?'

'Getting changed,' Clara replied. 'Dinner's almost ready, will you call her down?'

'There's no need, I'm here,' Lizzie called out as she entered the large comfortable kitchen. Suddenly life was back to normal, the room a cocoon of warm familiarity and friendship, although she was well aware that it couldn't last, that they would all go their separate ways again before very long. She was amused to see Peter sitting in her father's chair, something he'd never done before in Edward's presence. This had been her fault for letting Peter believe his uncle to be particular about who sat there, and which caused her cousin to jump up whenever Edward could be heard approaching. He'd never been caught out but had once knocked the chair over in his frantic attempt to get up in time. Lizzie had thoroughly enjoyed his guilty scrambling about, whilst her father probably never really cared who sat there.

Eventually during the meal Edward asked Peter of his plans during his stay with them, and inevitably the question of Nathan's disappearance reared its ugly head. No-one seemed to notice the shaking of Lizzie's hands or her total silence on the subject as differing theories were discussed. Had he run off with a woman? Had he died up on the moor and might never be found? Was he in trouble with the Law and hiding far away, or was he keeping them in suspense, only to return some time in the future and laugh at their discomfort?

When finally asked for her opinion, Lizzie merely shrugged her shoulders and mumbled that she supposed he could be anywhere. But she knew he wasn't, didn't she! She knew he was but a stone's throw away, and if his spirit was free to roam it was probably waiting to catch her alone. This had been, and still was, Lizzie's real fear which lengthened her absences from the farm, the fear that one day she would be confronted by his ghost when she least expected it.

As it had been a long and tiring day, Lizzie chose not to spoil the evening by mentioning China, which at the moment seemed a long time ahead. Clara was also showing signs of fatigue and, as a result, they both decided to retire and leave the men to discuss whatever they fancied.

Once alone in her room it wasn't long before Lizzie succumbed to the warmth and comfort of the feather mattress, thus blocking out all worries from her troubled mind.

Rising early, in spite of having stayed up late the previous evening talking to Edward, Peter quickly dressed and went for a long invigorating walk up on to the mist-enshrouded moors. On returning, he found Clara alone once more in the kitchen. 'Did you enjoy your walk?' she asked.

'Yes, although it's a bit fresh up there,' he replied, 'and will take some getting used to after India; anything's better than the flies, dust and smells though.'

'From what I know of our Army in India you all live like lords, with your batmen and servants.'

'You wouldn't have liked it!' He grinned at her in the familiar boyish way she remembered from the past. 'Who'd have thought my bringing you here that time would end like this,' he said. 'I was hoping to propose to you right here, instead you went and fell in love with Edward, then eventually married him!'

'Did it hurt so very much?' Clara asked, returning the smile. 'Your true love was the Army, was it not?'

He chuckled. 'Perhaps you're right, you always were.'

He moved closer and spoke in a low voice, 'But tell me, what has changed Lizzie so much? I know nine years is a long time not to meet, but I sense there's something wrong. Sometimes she's like a stranger to me.'

Clara's face clouded over. 'I really don't know, she doesn't confide in me. She came to stay with me in Aldershot shortly after I went back there, prior to my marrying Edward. I was shocked at the change in her in such a short time.' Clara's voice was low, cautious in case Lizzie should appear. 'Edward couldn't understand it either, and he often wonders if the fall she had from her horse on the day you and I left, might have had a permanent effect on her. Be patient though, you'll find that she does soften after a while. I believe that she is lonelier in London than she admits, even more so than if she had stayed here with us in the country. However, she has become a very good nurse and has a strong will. Why her visits home are so infrequent also puzzles us, and this hurts Edward very much, though he would never admit it.'

Peter watched Clara bustling about, obviously content and happy with her life, and asked, 'Don't you miss the hustle and bustle of a large town? Aren't you lonely here yourself? It's different for me,' he went on, 'I was brought up in the countryside, but it's a long way out for you, you're so isolated here.'

'The village isn't that far away,' Clara laughed. 'Besides, I'm often called upon to see people who are sick and can't afford to go to the Doctor. I've even delivered a few babies, and that helped me to be accepted in the community. No, I like it here and who knows, when our child is born, providing everything goes well, Lizzie might come more often.' The look on Peter's face at this remark puzzled Clara. 'What is it, there's nothing wrong is there?'

'No, no!' he lied uncomfortably, and was ashamed not to be able to share with her the truth about Lizzie's plan to work in China. He shrugged his shoulders. 'My opinions really don't count after all these years, I'm just concerned for her, that's all.'

'She needs a man, someone who can control her.' Clara said sharply, with more feeling than she intended. 'I had hoped that you and she might marry one day, in spite of Abe's Will.'

'I was never that interested in the farm anyway. But uncle made it clear that Lizzie would lose her inheritance if we did marry, so that was that.' He sighed. 'When you have your child, Lizzie loses that right to inherit, so I suppose there wouldn't be a problem anymore.'

Clara had no answer to this and busied herself for a few moments then, turning to him, she asked. 'Why did Abe hate your family so much?'

Peter sighed again. 'My brothers liked their beer and were always fighting. Abe thought that none of them deserved to reap the benefit of his hard work and, as Uncle Edward wasn't married, they would have obtained the farm by default. As for me, I was a mere child. My brothers thought me strange, always reading and dreaming of far away places.'

Clara chuckled. 'If Abe only knew. You've turned out to be a successful and worthwhile man, putting the others to shame. As for Nathan, he deserted your father immediately after your mother's death. Surely her passing didn't disturb him enough to turn his mind?'

'No, not Nathan! But I still don't understand, he must have been in real trouble to have left the area. He was work-shy and selfish through and through, but not sentimental. However, he was my brother, and I am concerned.'

'Would you have married Lizzie if Abe's Will and then Edward hadn't forbidden it?'

'I really don't know to be honest, Clara,' Peter replied with a wry smile. 'I thought I loved you. Lizzie was such a girl then.' He looked keenly at her. 'I didn't encourage her, you know.'

'Nevertheless I think she loved you,' she rebuked him, 'and you preferred India.'

'If you recall, I was already going to India and you didn't want to come with me. I knew Lizzie was attracted to me, but I thought it was simply a fad which she'd grow out of.' He was speaking quietly in case his cousin appeared unexpectedly. 'Where is she anyway?'

'I told her to have a lie-in and that I'd wake her at ten o'clock if she hadn't come down by then. It's well past that now, so I'd better go up. You help yourself to some refreshments while I'm gone.'

Lizzie was aware of Clara's footsteps on the landing before her knock on the door, and quickly closed one of her diaries which lay on the small table before her. 'Come in,' she called, and slid the book beneath a pile of papers out of sight. 'I'm not asleep.'

'Oh, you're dressed!' Clara exclaimed. 'Have you enjoyed the chance to take it easy?'

Lizzie nodded. 'Yes, and I took the opportunity to write a little, and do a mending job which needed urgent attention. I've also sorted out some of my things that I no longer need. Here are several items which no longer fit; do you think they may be of use to someone in the village?'

'I'm sure they will. That's very kind of you.' Clara was puzzled as to the thickness of the thread passing through the large needle in Lizzie's hand but didn't pry as to its use, and her curiosity soon evaporated. 'Peter went for a walk and he's back now asking for you. Shall I go and get you something to eat?'

'Yes, please,' Lizzie agreed as she rose from the chair. 'I'll make up for my laziness later. Is Father out in the fields?'

'Yes, but he shouldn't be long, I know he wants to make the most of you, now that you're here.' She looked wistfully at Lizzie, 'Will you be staying a while this time?'

There was no disguising the hope in Clara's voice and Lizzie turned her face towards the window. 'I'm afraid not, Clara. I'll come straight down now,' she said, whilst busying herself unnecessarily with some books on the table, 'then we can talk.'

With a sense of foreboding, Clara left the room and made her way back to the kitchen where she found that Edward had returned and was in lively discussion with Peter about the troubles in the Sudan.

'Gordon was only sent out to Khartoum with orders to study the situation, write a report and make recommendations,' Edward stated disparagingly.

'I agree, but the Khedive of Egypt waylaid him in Cairo and persuaded the General to accept the Governor-generalship of the Sudan. Without pay at that! And you can't serve two masters.'

Edward laughed in agreement. 'He was still in our pay though and should have simply done what he was told to do, that was to escort the Khartoum garrison and its inhabitants to Suakim. As a result, he's failed to mediate with the Mahdi and ended up under siege. Now you've got to go and rescue him.'

Peter shrugged his shoulders resignedly. 'That's what an army is for, uncle. What annoys me, are those self-opinionated people with idealistic beliefs who think they can fight rebellion and discontent with justice and words instead of weapons. He had neither troops nor money to sustain him.' Peter was used to arguing with Edward; in fact he had often done so in the past, deliberately, just for the sheer challenge of it. Edward was a well-read man in spite of living out of the way in this isolated valley, and Peter valued his level-headed understanding of things.

'You're at it again!' Lizzie's voice made both men turn, Peter's eyes twinklingly challenged the rebuke on her face. 'With whom did you argue in India?' she asked.

Edward looked fondly at his daughter. His nephew's visits had always given him the opportunity to air his views more fervently than he otherwise could, with Clara and Lizzie. Whenever Peter had come to stay, the house had been noisy and untidy, but full of life and this made his absence all the harder to bear.

'Now don't get Lizzie going as well,' Clara remonstrated, 'or we'll never get any work done.' There was sudden silence in the kitchen, as three astonished faces looked towards Clara in mocked amazement, making her blush. 'But don't stop on my account,' she said, concealing a grin.

A lump rose in Lizzie's throat at the companionship she felt in the room, recalling the happiness that had been theirs on that fateful day nine years earlier; a day that ended in such tragedy. She stood, observing each one in turn, with her feelings of love and respect overshadowed by guilt—and the thought of what might have been. She was sallow from the smoke-laden London air, her body thin and taut from the hard work and the gaiety had quite gone from her eyes.

A stillness settled over them. It was Clara who broke the ice. 'What we all need is a good hot drink,' she declared. 'Put the kettle on the stove please, Lizzie.' Obediently, Lizzie did as she was asked; glad to be occupied rather than being in need of sustenance—she had lost her appetite.

The strange atmosphere in the kitchen disturbed and worried Edward the most because he felt powerless to understand Lizzie. The sudden change in her was bewildering but he had the good sense not to pry, for fear that this might make matters worse. Instead he would ask Clara later to make discreet enquiries of Lizzie in case they could help in some way.

As it was, Lizzie broke the spell herself. 'I need to talk to you all together,' her voice was toneless and matter of fact. 'I have something to tell you that is best said now, rather than have it left hanging over me.'

This is it, Peter thought to himself. He'd been dreading the time when Lizzie broke the news—and possibly Edward's heart. As Lizzie sat down, instinctively the others in the room also drew their chairs to the table and sat waiting tensely for her to enlighten them.

'Well get on with it!' Edward said suddenly. 'It's obviously bad news or you wouldn't have kept it to yourself for so long.' He watched Lizzie's pale face flush as she summed up her courage to speak.

'You must all know by now that I'm not the most content or the happiest of people, but lately I have found solace in The Church Missionary Society.' Edward breathed a sigh of relief. 'When I'm not working I go to the Mission where I try to help others.'

Her father relaxed a little. 'I'm not a religious man, Lizzie, but I can see no harm in that, if that's what gives you comfort,' he said, puzzled that she might not think him sympathetic.

'But it's not enough, Father,' Lizzie said emphatically.

Edward's eyebrows lifted, he was not used to her being quite so abrupt with him, and was at a loss as how to deal with her.

'Lizzie's upset, Edward,' Clara said trying to smooth things over, even though she was disappointed with Lizzie for spoiling what could have been such a happy reunion, and she asked, 'What can we do to help, my dear?'

Realising that to hesitate further would only making matters worse, Lizzie decided to be frank, announcing bluntly, 'I'm going to China as a nursing missionary.' She then lowered her eyes as if to avoid their reactions.

'China?' Edward gasped in disbelief and shock at the enormity of her statement. 'Why China?' His voice was almost a whisper.

Lizzie had expected him to ridicule her or, even, forbid her to go, instead his eyes were troubled and his brow furrowed as he repeated his question. 'Why China?'

Realising that Edward's response was having a greater affect on Lizzie than his own had had, Peter for once kept his own council. This was too important a matter to risk making mistakes. If anyone could change Lizzie's mind then Edward, and perhaps Clara, might.

'I just know it is something I feel compelled to do. I seem to lack a full purpose in my life, yet I am trained and capable of helping other people.'

'Can't you do that here, Lizzie? After all there is so much poverty and sickness in England,' Edward said with a catch in his throat.

Intervening, Clara tried to be practical in her approach, hoping to add strength to Edward's plea by stressing the personal risks involved. 'There are dangers and diseases for Europeans out there, my father was involved in tropical medicine and the tales he recalled were often terrifying.'

'I know all that. Peter has gone on at length about it, but I will not change my mind. China is a challenge not just in nursing but in enlightening a people steeped in legends and myths. I would also like to learn more about their use of herbs and natural medicines.' Lizzie looked directly at Clara, 'That part you surely understand, your father had similar interests, and you were a nurse.'

'It also killed him in the end.' Clara's patience was evaporating a little by this time. She had always supported Lizzie but now even she was bewildered by what drove her stepdaughter towards such a future.

'Then so be it if the same should happen to me. I have nothing to live for other than relieving my conscience of its burdens.'

'But you can have nothing to atone for.' Edward protested. 'You imagine too much. My keeping you here, isolated on the farm for so long after your mother died, didn't help. I should have sent you off to school earlier, but I couldn't bear to part with you. However, if you must go, you go with my blessing. I would never forgive myself if we parted in anger.'

Tears welled up in Lizzie at this unexpected support. 'Thank you, Father,' she said huskily, and reached over to press his hand with hers. 'Your support means everything to me.'

Clara swallowed hard to fight back her own tears, for she realised that Edward was only too aware that he could lose Lizzie forever whichever path he took, and knew that in his wisdom he had chosen the best way. She looked fondly at him, hoping that their coming child would give him the pleasure and comfort he rightly deserved.

'Well, Lizzie,' Peter conceded graciously, 'you'll become a traveller at last and will have many tales to tell when we meet again around this table.' He lifted his mug of tea high and held it out. 'To Lizzie,' he offered.

'To Lizzie! To Lizzie!' Edward and Clara chorused in unison.

'Now, how about a ride,' Peter suggested, 'would you mind if we did, uncle?'

'Why not,' Edward agreed, but his heart was heavy and he wanted only to be alone with Clara to sort out the emotional turmoil that Lizzie had created. He was getting too old for complications like this in his life and he realised that, but for Clara, he would soon have no-one.

Lizzie was grateful to Peter for his suggestion. 'I will go riding,' she said, but I'd like to go down the valley towards Sheffield, as I have a couple of calls to make, and it will be some time before I am able to get that way again.'

'Suits me. I'll be ready in an hour, that will give you time to have something to eat whilst I sort tack out for the horses.' Peter was resigned to Lizzie's decision and determined to enjoy his stay to the full. After all, it could be his last visit if things went wrong in the Sudan. 'Tomorrow, though, I must ride over to Bamford to see my father. I'll stay the night, I owe him that much at least.'

'Of course, but remember not to ride the horses too hard today, neither of them are getting any younger, you know,' Edward called out to Peter, who was already leaving the kitchen. 'They're used to a more sedate life now.'

When Peter had gone, Lizzie stood up and went round to Edward who still sat quietly at the table, staring at the mug in his hand. She touched his shoulder gently as if to comfort him, 'I'll be alright, you know,' she whispered softly. 'It's not your fault that I'm like I am. You've been a good father to me, and I've been difficult to handle. I shall write often and, who knows, one day I might settle down to be a dutiful daughter. She embraced him lovingly then looked up at Clara who was watching the episode with an aching heart. 'Look after each other, 'Lizzie urged. 'My thoughts will often be with you.'

There seemed no point in going on and on about the same painful subject. Each of them had their own thoughts and knew that Lizzie's course was set for years to come.

Clara, urged on by her practical good sense, said, 'It's overcast outside, be sure to take a cape in case the weather turns nasty later in the day.'

Edward remained silent but there was no rancour on his face or in his manner, for which Lizzie was grateful. After a while he rose, saying he would go to see if Peter needed help, so leaving the two women alone to talk.

'Will Father be alright?' Lizzie asked, once he'd shut the outside door behind him. 'I'm not doing this to hurt him, you know that.'

'He knows, Lizzie, he's just a very sensitive man underneath, a man who cares greatly for us all. He won't be happy about the risks you are taking but he would never stand in the way of your happiness.'

'But what do you think, Clara? Am I ungrateful or even foolish after the way you've helped me?'

Putting down the tray she was holding, Clara sank heavily onto her chair with a sigh, 'No, but I would have given anything for you to be here with me when my time comes, I have that much faith in you. Can you not delay your departure, at least until we know that I am safely delivered?'

'How long will that be?'

'Six or seven weeks.'

Lizzie hesitated; the planned voyage was still at least three months ahead and she couldn't bring herself to stay at the farm for such a length of time. However, she owed Clara so much and realised how isolated she would feel here in the valley as her time drew near for the birth. She was torn between duty and her fears, nothing else. Finally she decided to compromise. 'I have to go back now, as there are people depending upon me and preparations to be made,' she said. 'But I promise to return for your confinement, there should be sufficient time before I sail.'

'Oh, Lizzie,' Clara cried. 'Will you? Edward and I will be so happy. I know he will appreciate having someone he loves and trusts with him at such a time. He's never been through this kind of thing before, and especially being so much older, he will find it harder to cope.'

Standing there looking at Clara, Lizzie realised how much she missed her own gentle mother. Hannah had been a hard-working, honest woman who'd tried her best to shield her daughter from deprivation and the threat of being evicted by the bailiffs. Unknown to Lizzie, she'd answered Edward's advertisement for a wife, which she'd accepted. Lizzie had only seen the benefits of this move, and there had been many, but she hadn't been aware of the emotional turmoil Edward and Hannah had suffered, until they finally realised the affection they felt for each other.

'Oh, Clara,' she cried as she crossed the room and put her arms gently around her stepmother's swollen figure, embracing her with real affection. 'Of course I'll come and help.'

At this, relief flooded through Clara, but she was disturbed by the conflicting expressions she'd seen on Lizzie's face. 'Hurry up and eat, don't forget Peter's waiting,' she urged, hoping the ride would offer some diversion from the emotional turmoil in her stepdaughter. Lizzie did Clara's bidding and tried to put the memories temporarily to one side, quickly finishing her meal and then going upstairs to dress more suitably for the long ride.

When Edward returned to the kitchen he found Clara weeping quietly in the chair, and soothingly he placed an arm around her shoulders. 'This is all a bit too much for you,' he comforted. 'Hopefully it will soon be over, then we will have a child of our own to care for.' He squeezed her hand tenderly and placed his lips gently in her soft hair. 'You're bound to be nervous, and Lizzie isn't helping, but we'll get through, don't you worry.' But Edward himself was anxious and disturbed, he could hardly be otherwise.

With the day warming up as the early morning mist cleared, Peter and Lizzie cantered at an easy pace towards town, stopping only to water the horses and check the girth on Peter's saddle. 'I think we'd best get something to drink in town when we get there,' he suggested before re-mounting. 'It's hotter than I thought it would be.'

'I suppose you'll soon be looking forward to the heat in Africa, away from the rain and our temperamental English weather?'

'I don't know. If it was just the sun I'd be happy enough, but one gets a little tired of skirmishes and bloodshed. Perhaps I'm getting too old and need roots, somewhere to lay my head if you know what I mean. Travel has its drawbacks—as you will find out for yourself.'

They rode on, passing the endless rows of terraced houses, the Barracks, the Infirmary, and into the town centre, where Lizzie felt strangely out of place astride a horse.

'Where exactly do you want to be?' Peter asked, curbing his mount so that she could rein in beside him.

'I need to buy some quality scissors and a few simple surgical instruments to take to China,' she replied. 'Also a present for Dr McCreary and his wife for being so kind to me.'

After considering his options and having no inclination to shop, Peter decided to let Lizzie go off by herself. 'Look, I need a drink. Why not leave Nancy with me then meet up at the Angel Hotel over there in an hour. I'll get you a drink when you return.'

This pleased Lizzie who was more than happy to shop alone, knowing exactly what she needed and preferring not to be rushed. 'What a good idea. I should be able to get all I want in Norfolk Street; anyway I'll be quicker on my own.'

'Right. That should give us ample time to have a bite to eat before setting off back.' He helped Lizzie down from the saddle. 'Shopping's not for me,' he went on, relieved of the burden of trudging round the town. 'I'll see you later.'

When Lizzie rejoined him as arranged, Peter appeared relaxed and very pleased to see her. 'Did you get everything you wanted?' he asked. 'I've ordered a hot pie each, I know you like them, and thought it would save time if I ordered in advance.'

'Oh yes, thank you.' Lizzie smiled gratefully. 'I'm ready for something to eat, a pie will do nicely.' She joined him at his table where a welcome breeze came through an open window. 'It's hot out there.'

'It's quite pleasant sitting here,' he replied as the landlord put the pies before them. 'I'm looking forward to this.'

They ate in silence for a while in comfortable companionship, this gave Lizzie an opportunity to observe Peter without being too obvious. He was indeed beginning to look older, a few strands of grey hair mingling with the sun-bleached brown, and of course there were wrinkles and creases due to squinting in the blazing sun of India. His skin was bronzed but dry and she felt a twinge of concern, suddenly realising he was no longer the Adonis of old. Time in India had taken its toll.

Peter lifted his head and caught her pensive look. 'Penny for them Lizzie,' he teased, yet his face retained the soberness that his maturity had brought. Without thinking, he then added wistfully, 'Don't go to China, please Lizzie.' This was said as if her going would be a great personal loss to him. However, the moment he spoke he regretted it, suspecting that it might only aggravate her making her all the more determined. She smiled calmly, fondly, refusing to answer. 'You've changed,' he said with a sigh.

Nodding her head, Lizzie finally did reply. 'We've all changed, Peter, life and experience changes us. We're not the same as we were all those years ago and I've not lived a completely sheltered existence in London. I just don't get too involved in social circles I'm afraid.'

'You should be married by now,' he stated bluntly. 'You're still very attractive and should have a house of your own and servants—a family of your own. If only...' He stopped, afraid of going on, knowing he'd probably overstepped the mark already.

'If only what?'

Peter reddened and looked sheepish.

'If only what?' Lizzie persisted.

'Well...Oh, I don't know,' he flustered. 'You seem different somehow, detached—withdrawn, on your way to becoming an old maid...' He bit his lip, annoyed that he'd been rude and probably boorish. 'I'm sorry, Lizzie,' he said apologetically, 'I didn't mean it like that. I've been mixing with a different set of people, and perhaps become a bit of an uncouth idiot out in India. I just remember you as a bubbly, happy girl, that's all.' Instinctively he leaned over and placed a hand protectively over hers, only momentarily, but it caused Lizzie to flinch. He drew back immediately at her reaction. Neither spoke, nor could they eat in the unhappy atmosphere he'd created and he wished he had kept his mouth shut. He'd certainly lost his appetite, and pushed his plate away. 'I'm sorry,' he repeated, 'I wouldn't hurt you for the world.'

'It doesn't matter,' Lizzie said, not unkindly. 'We all say things at times, things which we regret, especially when we don't fully understand the reason behind someone's actions.'

He could not know the turmoil Nathan had wrought in her life, and she acknowledged that what he said was probably not far from the truth. Twice within the last week or so he'd referred to her as 'becoming an old maid' but, though the words did hurt, what she had done with her life was of her own choosing. She had also finished eating and urged him to finish his meal, but he refrained, saying that it was time they went to collect their horses from the stables.

After saddling up he carefully helped Lizzie to mount, making sure she was comfortable and that her purchases were packed and secured safely. Looking up at her he said, 'You, Edward and Clara are the only people I care about, Lizzie, don't let what I said earlier spoil things.' He was trying to tell her that he regretted his outburst. Then, without waiting for a reply, he mounted his horse and rode on, leading the way through the traffic. This allowed Lizzie to reflect on all he had said. By the time they reached the farm she felt drained emotionally and ached physically, the latter being due to her long absence from the saddle.

Though she was subdued during the evening, Edward and Clara suspected nothing untoward and put it down to simple tiredness after her long ride. Lizzie showed Clara the fine, sharp scissors she'd bought, together with a small set of surgical knives, needles and syringes.

'What a gruesome collection,' Edward commented as he looked with interest over Clara's shoulder. 'Do you know how to use them?'

'If necessary, though there is no way of knowing what may be required— so it's best to be prepared.'

'Couldn't you have bought them in London?' Peter intervened, his curiosity also aroused by Edward's remarks.

'Yes, and no. Many of the medical instruments available there are made in Sheffield but marked with the names of London Houses. I wanted to make sure I got the best. I also bought a silver-handled paper knife for Dr McCreary and a small pair of sewing scissors for Jane, to thank them for their hospitality.'

'That's kind of you,' Clara said with approval. 'Knowing them as I do, I'm sure they will be quite touched by your gifts.'

Peter had lost interest, so brought about a change of subject. 'I'm off to Bamford tomorrow, Uncle, if that's alright with you? I'll stay a couple of nights with Father, see if he needs anything and do what I can now that Nathan's not there.'

'Is it definite about you going to the Sudan?' Edward asked. 'I thought the Government hadn't made its mind up.'

Peter shook his head. 'I think they'll have no choice but to go in and rescue General Gordon. He's got himself into a situation from which it is almost impossible to escape.'

Edward sighed, 'The press and public have known this for months and it's a forgone conclusion that some action will now be needed.'

'I agree. I have to report to my Regimental Headquarters in Ireland ready for redeployment when the decision is made. It's a pity, but there it is.'

Edward turned to Lizzie, 'What about you?'

'I shall come up to help Clara in her confinement before going to China.'

Accepting the inevitable but pleased that she would return soon, Edward nodded. 'That's good, Clara needs a woman she can trust at such a time, and I don't like the thought of the local midwife attending to her.'

Lizzie snorted. 'How many babies has that lady delivered in the past twenty years? By now she should know what she's about. Besides, Clara knows what to do.' She smiled at Clara who winked knowingly back as Edward tut-tutted as if doubting her words.

The subject of China did not arise again and Lizzie managed to avoid being alone with Peter for the rest of the evening. When she considered the time was right, she excused herself and went thankfully to bed.

Next morning, however, Peter chewed his lips impatiently as he paced the kitchen floor, looking repeatedly at his pocket watch. 'Is Lizzie still in bed?' he asked Clara, 'It's almost nine o'clock, and she knows I'm going over to Bamford today. I was hoping to talk to her before I went.' He suspected that Lizzie was deliberately avoiding him, but was reluctant to tell Clara of the clumsy remarks made to his cousin at lunch the day before.

'I think yesterday may have exhausted her, Peter,' Clara offered, seeing how agitated he was. 'I've noticed that she's lost weight since she was here last. Let her rest. When you get back she'll be a different person,' she tried to reassure him. 'Have you had enough to eat before you go?'

'I've had plenty, thanks; I think I'll set off. Just tell her... Oh, don't bother!' he muttered irritably. 'Just say I'll be back in time for tea tomorrow instead of the day after, if that's alright with you, Clara?'

Relieved to get him out from under her feet, Clara waited until he'd ridden off before going upstairs to see if Lizzie was stirring. Tapping gently on the door but receiving no answer, she went quietly back downstairs where she spent the next hour deep in thought. Inevitably Peter had changed in the intervening years and Lizzie was slowly becoming a stranger. Sensing that there was a disagreement between the two she was herself not completely comfortable in their combined presence anymore. She couldn't put a finger on what was amiss between them, yet there was certainly a detachment that had never been there before. Should she talk to Edward about it or simply let things take their course? She was deep in thought, and Lizzie's sudden appearance brought Clara back to the present with a jolt. 'Oh; you made me jump Lizzie!' she exclaimed. 'I was miles away.'

'Forgive me,' Lizzie pleaded softly, 'I've been really lazy, haven't I?'

'You must have needed the rest,' Clara conceded, casting her gloomy thoughts to one side. 'Peter delayed a while to see you before he went, but finally gave up.'

'I know,' Lizzie replied as she sat down in Edward's chair. 'I waited until he'd gone then fell asleep again. Was he very angry?'

'He seemed none too pleased but he'll get over it. With so much on his mind about Nathan and his father, he'll no doubt return with more problems than you on his mind. But why do you want to avoid him? Has he upset you in some way?'

'No, but he's not too happy with me at the moment, he even suggested I was on my way to becoming an old maid.' At this remark Clara burst out laughing. 'What's so funny?' Lizzie asked indignantly.

'It's the same old story, when a man's not sure of himself he tries to make you feel insecure too. Are you sure Peter's not getting ideas?'

'What do you mean?'

Clara shrugged her shoulders and suppressed a smile. 'You've a lot to learn my girl. Tell him you think he's an old bachelor past his prime.'

The light-hearted banter between the two women continued as they busied themselves, until Lizzie insisted that Clara put her feet up and rest, while she helped with the chores.

Watching her at work, Clara had difficulty in suppressing her continuing curiosity regarding Lizzie's plans. She'd hoped that after being home for a while her stepdaughter would see things in a different light, yet she knew just how determined Lizzie could be. 'I know,' she exclaimed, 'let's make a special welcome for Peter when he gets back tomorrow, he'll probably need cheering up. I'll get Mrs Fox to make some delicacies and Jack can kill a chicken, if Edward agrees.'

'What a good idea!' Lizzie liked the prospect but the mention of Jack's name alarmed her. Although she'd seen him several times since that terrible day when he had disposed of Nathan's body, it was never without feeling guilty at what he'd done for her.

When Edward had selected a suitably large bird, Jack did what was necessary and brought the prepared chicken into the scullery for hanging as requested. Lizzie made a point of greeting him. He was ageing fast; his grey hair thinning and she wondered if the strain of what had happened so long go had taken its toll on him.

'Thank you, Jack,' she said gently as she took the chicken. 'Your help is always appreciated.' She looked directly at him, trying to let him know by this that she had not forgotten. 'Here,' she whispered, 'it's just a little something to make life less of a burden,' and she pressed a couple of guineas into his hand.

'Why, bless you, Miss Lizzie.' Jack's voice cracked with emotion. 'It's good to see you again—are you staying long?'

'No, Jack,' Lizzie replied softly, shaking her head. 'I can't. Only you can understand why.'

He nodded, 'It's such a shame, Miss but I do see that.' He touched his hat, 'I'd best be on my way now, Miss. Look after yourself.'

'I will, Jack, and God bless you.' As she watched him walk slowly down the path her eyes filled with tears, knowing that the burden he carried on her behalf probably spoiled many of his waking thoughts as well.

When Peter returned late the following afternoon he was in a bad mood, and Edward was reluctant to question him too deeply about his visit. 'Is your father keeping well?' Edward asked, having no great regard for his brother-in-law but feeling sorry for his nephew and trying to lift his spirits.

'He's not as strong these days,' Peter replied, 'and as usual he's drinking too much.'

'It's a wonder he can afford to.' Edward uttered, barely able to contain his disdain at Peter's news.

'He's still fretting over Nathan, wondering when or if he'll return, and angry at him for going off without a word. I didn't disillusion him but I don't think Nathan will ever come back, not after all this time. Something's happened to him, I can sense it—it's a rum affair and no mistake. Apparently he was coming to sort me out that day, got drunk on the way and that was the last time anyone saw him.'

Edward shook his head. 'If you had been here all hell would have been let loose, it's a good job you left with Clara when you did, before he could find you.' As Peter had raised the matter Edward went on. 'What caused the upset in the first place—you never did say?'

'I'd rather not go into details if you don't mind Uncle. Let's just say he was an uncouth lout.' Peter's reluctance to speak out was not through loyalty towards his brother, but more an unwillingness to recall the hatred which had erupted between them once the fight had started. It had begun with Nathan making insulting remarks about Lizzie, and ended in the release of all Peter's pent up resentments over his brother's many spiteful actions towards him over the years. Nathan had teased and bullied him even as a child, thinking him a weakling, but the worm had finally turned and he'd more than held his own, beating Nathan fairly and squarely on that occasion. Both had sustained bruises, but whereas Peter had his satisfaction at last and was willing to let things lie, Nathan apparently had not, and had set out seeking revenge. Knowing this, Peter doubted if he could ever meet his brother with any joy again.

Having the good sense not to prod further, Edward let the matter drop. 'The ladies have made a special effort for you tonight,' he said. 'We're having Christmas dinner early this year. It'll please Clara. But tell me, what do you think about Lizzie's plan to go to China?'

Peter was taken aback at the suddenness of the question, and had little time to gather his thoughts clearly. 'I don't think it's safe or necessary,' he blurted out, 'in fact I think it's ridiculous. I've tried talking to her but it only makes her more determined to go. She's changed so much since last we met that I find it difficult to reason with her.'

Edward shook his head. 'That happened almost overnight—it was as if the fall was more serious than we thought at the time. Shock can leave permanent effects you know. I've done my best to understand, but I don't know what else I can do.'

'You've been a good stepfather Uncle, and Hannah would appreciate what you've done for Lizzie.' Peter paused and reflected on his aunts early death. Sighing, he continued, 'I really was fond of Hannah, you know. She made this place a second home for me. Lizzie seems quite happy about you and Clara, so it couldn't have been your marriage that caused a problem.'

'I'm sure it wasn't,' Edward replied. 'We've both tried, especially Clara.'

'I'll do my best to dissuade her in the time I have before I go to Ireland,' Peter offered, 'but don't expect miracles, I don't want to spoil my friendship with her by getting too heavy on the matter.'

'Do what you can, lad, I'd appreciate it.' With his work done in the barn, Edward shut the doors behind him. 'We'd best go indoors and change for the feast.'

Lizzie had missed Peter's company more than she cared to admit and was surprised how pleased she was at his return. She now waited happily in anticipation of the evening ahead, but hoped that neither Nathan nor China would be mentioned as this could spoil the proceedings.

'How many years have you been with us now, Mrs Fox?' Edward asked her as she placed the plump, crisply roasted chicken on the table.

'Too long,' Mrs Fox replied, trying to work it out. 'Maybe ten, twelve, Mr Edward. Seems I've worn a track between here and the village in that time.' She went to the kitchen then returned with a dish of vegetables in each hand and placed them before Clara.

'Merry Christmas!' she called laughingly.

'What a nice idea, Clara,' Peter said, observing the table which was laden with dishes more suited to Christmas than a midsummer evening. 'It's a long time since I've had such a homely English meal, and it'll probably be the last for a while.'

'I thought you'd considered leaving the Army?' Edward prompted as he passed dishes round. 'One visit to the cold North hasn't persuaded you otherwise has it?'

'It all depends on what happens in the Sudan. I've got to plan my future before I can think of resigning, and my savings won't last forever—I must find something to subsidise my income and keep me from boredom.'

'What sort of position or business are you considering?' Clara enquired.

'Administration work I suppose, I'm not really cut out for anything else. As to which sort of business, well, I have some contacts in London and could sound them out.'

'Horses! You always said you enjoyed working with them, so why not extend that interest?' Edward suggested. 'Perhaps some country estate would be in need of a groom, to start with.'

'I'm a bit old for a stable boy,' Peter chuckled. 'Besides, I'm used to giving orders, not taking them. Seriously though, if I could get a position in the Colonial Office, it would solve a lot of problems for me, housing, travel and so on. I've travelled widely; I know how their overseas Administrators work and have seen their problems at first hand—experience should speak for something.'

'It does sound very much more like your cup of tea,' Clara agreed, 'in fact now you mention it I think it would suite you perfectly.'

'I thought I might also do a bit of snooping whilst in London, to get an idea if there are any possibilities being talked about, I might find something to work towards whilst I'm away.'

Throughout the conversation Lizzie sat listening to Peter and wondered how he would cope without the Army: would he be lost in civilian life? In spite of all they had both achieved, neither of them seemed to have attained a sense of permanence in their lives. Much to her relief, no-one appeared to have noticed that she had expressed no opinion in the matter, or asked for her thoughts.

'It's a great pity,' Edward lamented, then, turning to Lizzie he pleaded, 'can't you stay behind? Do you have to go back so soon?'

'No, I'm sorry Father! I am committed to going back, and there is now much to do if I am to return later to be with Clara.'

Sighing, and reluctantly accepting their decisions, Edward sat back in his chair.

'That was a splendid meal,' Peter said contentedly, placing a hand over the buttons of his brightly coloured waistcoat. 'It's as well I'm not staying long or I would soon need a larger clothes.'

'You'll enjoy some exercise, why not come up on the moors with me, tomorrow? I can spare an hour or two,' Edward offered, 'it'll do you good.'

'I'd like nothing better, Uncle; it would round off my visit nicely.'

The thought of having his nephew to himself for a while lifted Edward's spirits, but he didn't want Lizzie to feel neglected. 'Will you come, Lizzie?' he asked her.

She shook her head. 'No, I'll keep Clara company, and besides, you'll enjoy yourselves much better without me holding you back. My feet aren't used to walking on rough ground any more.'

'Let's have a drink,' Edward said as he pushed his chair back from the table. 'We'll go through into the sitting room—perhaps Clara will play the piano for us.'

The soft glow of the sitting-room fire combined with the effect of the sweet wine mellowed the atmosphere as Clara played softly.

'That's not the same piano you had in Aldershot, is it?' Peter asked Clara when she'd stopped for a while.

'No, I didn't think the old one would stand the journey, so Edward bought this at an auction in Sheffield and had it delivered as a surprise.' She turned back to the keys, 'You remember this tune?' she asked, playing a rousing melody. 'Come on sing. You had a good voice I remember.' Peter coughed and reddened a little. 'Please!' she insisted.

Lizzie listened, enjoying the sound of Peter's deep, lively voice. He sang well, she thought. The lines in his face had softened in the glow of the oil lamp and it was as if time had rolled back showing her the old, easy-going Peter she once knew. Edward sat contentedly in his chair, allowing the music to waft over him, pleased that Lizzie seemed more relaxed for the first time in years.

'Let's sing something we all know,' Peter suggested. 'How about *When Johnny comes marching home?* Come on Lizzie.' Lizzie tried to decline but Peter insisted, dragging her firmly to the piano. Edward, however, was happy to simply hum along without leaving the fireside. Singing made Peter thirsty and after several glasses of wine he became almost boisterous in his enthusiasm, teasing Clara and Lizzie unmercifully.

'Oh, do behave,' Lizzie chided warmly, 'you've had too much to drink.'

'Pooh-pooh, Lizzie,' he responded, giving her a gentle squeeze around the waist, as they stood behind Clara. 'I have not had this much fun in a long time.'

Although she didn't show it, Lizzie was surprised and happy with his attention—even if it was only the wine talking. A little bewildered at her own sense of pleasure, she laughed at him. 'You're drunk, Peter—that's what you are,' and she patted his hand. 'Hopelessly drunk!'

Peter's eyes widened as he peered amused at her colouring face. 'Me!' he laughed, 'You should talk! Anyway what does it matter, it won't be long before we're back in London and facing up to God knows what.'

'Now then you two,' Clara laughed as they bantered above her head. 'How can I play with all that noise going on?'

'I think it's time to calm down,' Edward joined in. 'Clara should be resting but we could have a quiet game of cards.' Without waiting for a reply he reached into a drawer in the desk beside him and took out a pack of cards, 'Come on Peter, bring that table over here.'

The familiarity of Peter's touch caused Lizzie's mind to wander constantly throughout the game of canasta which followed and, in consequence, she lost. 'It's not like you, Lizzie,' Peter cried triumphantly. 'You really are out of practice.'

'And, no doubt, judging by your deft shuffling Peter, you play rather a lot,' Edward rejoined with a wry smile. 'It's certainly a good job we're not playing for money or we'd all be bankrupt in no time.'

Peter dealt another hand. 'I will admit that to pass many a weary hour we do play cards often. However, under those circumstances I don't always win.'

'Then you are taking advantage of us,' Clara complained good-humouredly, as she sorted her hand. 'Come on Lizzie, we can't let him win again.'

Never one to turn down a challenge, Lizzie strove to collect her thoughts, determined to give Peter a run for his money.

'Well!', he exclaimed to her later. 'What's come over you? That's twice you've beaten me in ten minutes.'

She smiled jubilantly at him, her eyes sparkling for the first time since they had met in London. To Edward, who was aware of the battle for supremacy at the table, this was also a delight. To see her so animated, happy even, brought a lump to his throat and, catching Clara's knowing glance, he smiled discretely back. Time, however, was passing, and he had to make the usual rounds of the animals before retiring. 'I'm sorry to spoil the party at such an important stage,' he said, 'but you will have to excuse me whilst I go to check things outside.'

'I'll come with you,' Peter offered, as he gathered the cards.

'Oh! Just as I was beginning to enjoy beating you.' Lizzie cried in dismay, scolding him. 'Any excuse to escape.' The passion in her voice and the flush in her face made them all laugh.

'Yes,' he conceded with a slight bow of his head. 'I hate to admit it but I don't like to be beaten by a woman.' With that he hastened to join Edward who was preparing to leave the room, but not before he playfully poked Lizzie in the ribs.

Outside in the cool of the evening air, Peter shivered. 'You'll need a coat if you're coming with me,' Edward remarked. 'There's an old one of mine in the hall which you can borrow—I'll be in the stable.'

As he retraced his steps, Peter pondered on the remarkable change he'd witnessed in Lizzie as the evening had progressed; it had been a joy to behold but he wondered just how long it would be before the warming effect of the wine and the company wore off. He found Edward busying himself with his horses. 'I'll do that,' he said, relieving his uncle at the bale of hay he was forking out. 'It's been a wonderful evening, just like old times.'

'Well, let us hope that your future plans work out as well as they have done in the past. Do you reckon life has been good to you?'

'The Army was the best career for me,' Peter confessed. 'I just wish things had been better for Lizzie, though. Did you see her tonight? The change in her was remarkable.'

Edward turned to Peter, the oil lamp in his hand illuminating their faces. There was a stern look in his eyes, 'Don't fool with Lizzie, Peter. She seems very disturbed and vulnerable sometimes, and tonight's fun took her back to what she once was. Beneath the exterior though, I think she is very troubled.'

'I wouldn't hurt her for the world,' Peter reassured him. 'What I can't understand, though, is why she has built such a barrier round herself, it's as if she's frightened to get close to anyone.'

Edward frowned, 'I don't think her job helps—working where she does, it's bound to have an effect, no matter what Clara says.'

A puzzled frown crossed Peter's face. 'I've never seen sick people disturb a person mentally before,' he said. 'Clara was a compassionate, caring nurse, but never unduly disturbed. I've not met one yet that was, except Lizzie.'

Edward stopped working. 'It's not normal nursing though is it? That's the point. There must be times when the weird behaviour of some patients disturbs even the best of medical staff.'

'You've got me now,' Peter exclaimed. 'What's so unusual in what Lizzie does?'

Edward paused for a moment. 'You do know where she works, don't you?'

'Well I've passed the place but know nothing about it.'

'She didn't tell you then that for the last three years she's worked at The Royal Bethlem Hospital, not far from where she lives?' As this information drew no comment, Edward stopped work again. 'Surely you've heard of Bedlam as they call it? The mental hospital—it's one and the same.'

As the truth dawned on Peter, he gasped. 'No, she never told me that, I just presumed it was part of St Thomas's. Why on earth would she conceal that from me—is she ashamed of what she does?'

'I really don't know, but I wonder if it has had an effect on her, caring for all those strange people, though she says she understands them and that it's a good place to work.'

'If she likes it so much then why is she so determined to go to China?' Edward was unable to comment on this and didn't reply. 'You don't really think it's unsettling her mind do you? I mean the secrecy, the withdrawal, China?' Peter was obviously and deeply concerned now.

When Edward finally spoke there was a tremor in his voice, 'Surely you could talk to her, see if you can discover what it is all about? Tonight I saw a bit of the old Lizzie and began to think that you might possibly get to the bottom of it. We can't.'

Peter breathed deeply and let out a sigh, 'I'll do my best but I'll have to be cautious or she'll think I'm interfering too much in her affairs.' As they made their way back the house in silence, Peter wondered if his uncle's request was more than he could handle. The fresh air had cleared his head a little and he wasn't prepared to spoil the evening by upsetting Lizzie again. In the sitting room he found Clara sewing and Lizzie reading in a scene of calm domestic simplicity.

Clara looked up and asked, 'Has Edward finished out there? If so, I know he likes a hot drink before going to bed, would you two like one?'

'He's just changing his boots Clara. And yes I would like a drink, thank you.'

Lizzie rose to help Clara, who gestured to her to stay where she was. 'No, Lizzie you can have a chat, I'll do it, I've been seated far too long.' She lifted herself with some effort, a swollen ankle causing some discomfort. 'I feel like a sow about to have piglets,' she said wearily as she made her way slowly to the door.

Taking the chair Clara had vacated, Peter sank into it and stretched out his long legs nonchalantly. 'It's cool out there; misty too; I hope it lifts in time for tomorrow's walk.'

'Every season, all kinds of weather conditions have their own charm,' Lizzie replied, putting her book to one side. 'Or have you forgotten?'

'No I haven't, but the weather is so unpredictable in England compared to India. At least there you know where you stand.'

'How do you cope with the heat?'

'It's very tiring and it dries the moisture from your skin and bakes the earth hard. Then the monsoons come. It pours torrentially for weeks on end so that you never get dry. There's mud everywhere—it's bloody awful...sorry, I beg your pardon.'

'Don't mind me,' she replied. 'I'm not so sheltered you know, I hear bad language regularly.'

'Still, it's not a word to use in front of a lady. I apologise.' Peter wondered if this would be a good opportunity to urge her to be frank, as Edward wanted. His uncle had not joined them, so Peter presumed Clara had waylaid him for some reason or other in the kitchen. 'Where in China will you be going?' He decided that this approach would show his interest in her plans.

'There's to be a new hospital endowed in Hankow soon which will be run by the church Missionary Society. I am to go there when it is built, but first I will stay at any hospital that needs my help.'

'You're going as a nurse then, not as a missionary?' Peter asked, relieved to hear that she wasn't simply fired with religious zeal.

'Oh no,' Lizzie replied patiently, knowing from his questions he was bound to think of some argument to try to stop her. 'I'm not worthy enough to attempt to convert souls. I want to help anyone who needs it and if they accept Christianity as well, then all the better.'

'Hankow, if I recall correctly, is like a furnace in summer, unbearably hot— surely you'll not be able to stand the heat?'

'Then I shall have to learn to cope won't I? You're not trying to change my mind are you? Because, if you are, you may as well stop right now!' Lizzie was adamant and eyed him sternly to be sure he understood her intentions were irrevocable.

'It would take a cleverer man than I, Lizzie, even I know that,' he teased, admiring her steely determination, which was so reminiscent of the old Lizzie. 'I just want to make sure you are aware of the facts—I care enough about you to feel it my duty to inform you.'

'Thank you, but others have done what I intend to, and if they managed, then so shall I!' Her reply was straightforward enough and had a ring of finality about it.

'I'm looking forward to going with your father tomorrow,' he remarked, acknowledging the end of the discussion. 'I shall be sad to leave here not knowing when, or if, I shall ever return.'

'How do you mean, if?'

'Sometimes I think my luck might run out—I know it's stupid, dangerous even to feel this way, but the life of a soldier is a tenuous one. Perhaps it is getting time to call it a day.'

A despondency was settling upon him which Lizzie realised was not drink induced. She was used to observing disturbed people: was sensitive to their mood changes and recognised in Peter symptoms of stress, or even fear. She knew what fear was like. So far she'd managed to control her own, but for how much longer? For some time now she'd realised that if she stayed at the asylum indefinitely her own obsessions could drive her to a nervous breakdown. Peter's presence had deflected some of her inner anxiety at coming home; in fact there had been moments when her dreadful memories had been temporarily obliterated, such that she had not suffered the nightmares which so often disturbed her sleep. Suddenly the prospect of returning to London lost some of its urgency.

'I've enjoyed this visit more than I thought I would,' she said soberly. ' And I shall miss your company when I return alone to help Clara.' The hollowness in her tone did not go unnoticed by her companion, who eyed her with sympathy yet was at a loss as to how to ease her troubles. She knew she could never tell him. A fresh start was needed, away from everything, a chance in fact to work off her guilt. Her work at Bedlam with the tormented souls there was beginning to depress her. So, when the offer to go to China came, it had lifted her spirits and re-awakened some of her old desire for adventure. If she did not grasp the opportunity now, time itself would probably break her. She looked at Peter sitting opposite, clearly uncertain and worried. Oh, why now? Why had he come back at this crucial time in her life? It was not simply a case that she loved him, if he showed that he cared that way for her, she knew she would then be forced to tell him: 'I killed your brother and buried him beneath a pile of rubble. All this time I've known where he was. I could have saved all of you the constant worry over his disappearance.' She could never be her true self with him unless she did one day confess. She tried to suppress the desire to comfort him, and sighed to herself. However, in not speaking out she knew she condemned him to a lifetime of uncertainty and animosity towards his brother.

In their silent contemplations, Peter and Lizzie found that a sense of real distress had developed. Peter's mouth was dry and he had difficulty in swallowing, whilst Lizzie found herself holding back tears which threatened to dissolve her control.

With Edward's heavy footsteps approaching, Lizzie forced a smile as he brought in a tray of drinks. However, Edward was no fool and in seeing their downcast faces he felt a surge of guilt: had he contributed to the unhappiness between them? Nine years ago he'd made it known that a liaison between them was out of the question and that Lizzie would lose her inheritance if ever she married him. The conditions in Abe's Will had been wicked, causing changes in his own life, but had it spoiled their lives too? He placed the drinks on the table with a heavy heart, mumbled a few inconsequential words and retreated back to the kitchen to find solace with Clara.

He closed the door behind him. 'There's something amiss in there,' he told her as he sat heavily on a chair, 'I've never seen such misery in two young people before, you can feel it the minute you enter the room.'

'They're hardly young people any more,' Clara replied, shaking her head. 'There's nothing we can do but leave them to sort it out, and no point in us worrying—we can only try to support them. Here, have your drink then we'll go back in together.'

In the sitting room, Peter coughed to clear his throat as he stood up to get the drinks. He handed one to Lizzie who clasped her hands round the beaker as if seeking warmth. 'Are you cold?' he asked, relieved to have something to talk about.

'A little,' she replied feebly, 'I'm more cold inside than on the surface.'

'I know what you mean. It's as if a blanket of gloom has descended in the room,' Peter found himself admitting. 'What has happened to change you so, Lizzie. Is it that place where you work?' Lizzie bristled at this remark and she eyed him sharply. 'Edward told me that you work at Bedlam, not St Thomas's,' he offered apologetically, 'and I think it is commendable of you: it's a rare thing for someone to understand the workings of the mind—but is it healthy to dedicate your life to it? Doesn't it distress you at times, or get you down?' She would have stopped him there but he held his hand up, commanding that she listened. 'You're still young, you've done a lot for mankind, don't leave it too late to make a life for yourself.'

The sincerity in his plea restrained Lizzie's natural instinct to retort; in fact she was impressed by his deep concern for her and his understanding. 'I am getting away from it, Peter,' she said softly, 'I'm going to China!'

He shook his head, 'That's not what I would like for you. I want to see you happy, to see you sparkle again, like you did tonight. You seem to be carrying a great burden on your shoulders these days.'

'I think I'm past sparkling, and if it takes wine to make me do so then that's not the answer.' She flushed self-consciously and forced a smile. 'I would like to travel, and China has a mysterious culture which draws me. If I can do some good at the same time then so be it. However, I am equally concerned for your safety after what I have heard of the Arabs. You face difficulties and danger every day. Do you like danger?'

Peter's face clouded over. He was tired and the conversation was beginning to go round in circles again. 'Not any more,' he confessed. 'In fact I quite dread going to the Sudan if you must know. I'm fed up with trying to sort out century old disputes and hatreds.'

She was stunned by his admission, having never imagined him anything other than a confident, even fearless, soldier. 'I'm sorry,' she said, seeking to reassure him and boost his morale, 'do you have to go, can't you resign?'

'It's too late now, I am committed. Besides, you heard the conversation the other night; I need to prepare for the future and will do so immediately, when, or if, I return. Perhaps reality is setting in and I'm beginning to realise that I am not invincible.' He realised also that he was talking to Lizzie as he'd never before spoken to anyone other than Edward. Whether this was due to her work with troubled minds or not, he wasn't sure. 'You must see many people who can't cope with life, Lizzie. Does it pass? Or is it this place?' He looked around the room, 'It's tucked away like some secret garden, protectively wrapping its tentacles around us.' He suddenly cared deeply what she thought, and sought direction from her. 'You must have had a great deal of experience with lost souls?'

That he respected her opinions so much pleased her, but whether she could help him was another matter. She too needed help, yet no-one could ever be entrusted with her secret. 'I suppose as we get older we do need our roots, a base to which we can return when all around is in chaos; without that we are lost.' Her tone was wistful, longing almost, and Peter didn't want the conversation to end. At last he felt he could talk to her as an equal and that he could trust her completely. His own loneliness stemmed from not being able to share his hopes and fears without ridicule or misunderstanding. He looked around him fondly, thinking of the many hours he'd spent here as a young man, sparring with Edward, trying to please Hannah, and showing off to Lizzie.

'A penny for them?' Lizzie said, fearing to disturb him, yet knowing that he needed an outlet for his unease.

'I was just remembering how things were; your lovely mother; Edward, and you!' He placed a certain emphasis on the word *you* causing her to redden. 'This was my escape from an unhappy home.'

'Then you decided to join the Army,' Lizzie reminded him, 'you came here one day full of excitement, and no-one could talk you out of it.' Peter laughed at the memory. 'You had such energy then, so many ideals, and I used to sit listening to you in wonderment—you were my hero!'

'I know,' he replied, 'and didn't I play at being one! It was an idyllic world; fortunate, happy and then I suppose we grew up. Well, I grew up. The experience of war leaves scars on the mind and soul, as well as the body, but we can't go back—we can't re-capture that which has gone.' Suddenly he looked young again as if pleasant thoughts had brushed away time. 'Were you a little in love with me, Lizzie?' he asked teasingly, without considering the wisdom of his question, for he had no other motive than to rekindle memories of happier times.

'Yes!' Lizzie said with a chuckle, 'I think I was.'

He became more serious. 'I tormented you and egged you on, didn't I? But I meant no harm, really I didn't, in fact I was very fond of you then.' He saw Lizzie's bemused expression at his last statement and stammered, 'I still am, damn it!' He was flustered now and quite embarrassed.

'Careful,' Lizzie responded playfully, attempting to defuse what had become a confusing situation, 'Whatever will Edward and Clara think if they overhear you.'

He laughed, grateful that she apparently still had a sense of humour. In truth he'd no idea what had prompted his outburst, but it had shaken him. 'We're kindred spirits, you and I,' he said, getting to his feet. 'Now then, it's getting late, and if I'm to go with Edward tomorrow I suppose I'd better make a move towards bed. You know, Lizzie, I've greatly enjoyed this evening; we really mustn't let another nine years go by without meeting. When I get back from Africa and you from China, we must meet regularly.' There was urgency in his voice, almost a plea, which Lizzie knew stemmed from his insecurity and not from the passion of love. This she could accept. In some respects it mirrored her own feelings, and she could not deny that part of her did still love him. 'We must write to each other,' he went on, 'I would like to know how you fare in China, and what you discover there—I'd appreciate that.'

'Yes, of course I'll write, but there is no knowing when our letters will arrive or how long they will take to reach us. I understand they are passed along and some do not always reach their destination. We can but try.'

'Thank you. In my dreariest moments I will look forward to receiving yours no matter how late they are.' He looked quite forlorn as he turned to leave. 'Good night, and sleep well, my dear,' he said, 'good friends are hard to find when one is on the move.' He left the room rather abruptly leaving her baffled and not a little disturbed.

A few moments later Edward joined her, almost as though he'd been waiting for the opportunity. 'I'm off now, Lizzie,' he said, 'an old man needs his sleep. I'll see you in the morning.'

'Has Clara gone up yet?' Lizzie called as he turned to go.

'No, but don't keep her too long, she needs more rest these days.' At that moment Clara also made her way into the room. 'Now don't be long, you two,' he ordered, kissed her on the cheek and left.

Clara lowered herself carefully onto her usual chair. 'Oh, for a bit of peace and quiet. Edward is a dear but he does fuss so.' Then, without waiting for a reply she asked, 'Are things alright between you and Peter? He seems very down sometimes.'

'I think he's worried about Africa—he doesn't seem to have the same fighting spirit anymore.'

'He's getting older and it's not good for a soldier to go to war demoralised; he needs a strong will to survive. In Aldershot I saw many whose killing instincts had gone and I really do believe that Peter will resign when he gets back. Let's just hope things will have quietened down by the time he gets to the Sudan and he can then return safely, that's the important thing. He can sort his future out later.'

'He's asked me to write to him—do you think it will help?'

'Yes, I do. Men need news and reassurance from home. It gives them a sense of purpose and belonging. Why? Do you have some reservations?' Clara prompted, not wanting to pry.

Lizzie thought for a moment. 'Writing would be the easy part, but what worries me...' she fell silent, her thoughts racing ahead. Did she want the responsibility of boosting his morale and his hopes, only to let him down when he returned, if by then he had assumed a greater attachment to her from the letters?

Clara thought she knew exactly what was troubling Lizzie. 'Can't you simply write and let the future take care of itself? If you're thinking what I believe you are, would it matter? Things will have altered here; my child will change the legacy. Besides, I don't think your father is quite so adamant anymore about what happens on his demise. All he wants is my security and your happiness. He knows that if I am left a widow here I couldn't manage the farm alone: I wouldn't want to either. I would simply move back to Aldershot, to the house Father left me which is still rented out. I hope that never happens and that I will have my own family here, but the future is never clear. I knew that in marrying an older man our lives together could be uncertain, but was willing to face that because I loved him. You must do what you think is right— ignore the legacy, it has a taste of evil about it. Your father will come round in the end; he's a very sensitive man and loves you dearly.'

'Oh, Clara, you are so level headed. I can see why my father fell in love with you—I do so admire you.'

The twinkle in Clara's eyes was a reflection of the fondness she felt for her stepdaughter, who she knew was trying hard to find a little happiness. 'And I admire you my dear, with your resilience and determination. Perhaps your work in china will, after all, give you the satisfaction you seek, because you don't seem happy in London. I can quite understand why you don't want to remain here permanently but we miss you very much.'

No, thought Lizzie, you can't understand, how could you? And how could she burden Clara with the truth? 'It's getting late and I am keeping you from your bed,' she said, 'Father won't be pleased if I keep you up.'

'He is probably asleep already,' Clara chuckled, 'snoring contentedly, totally unaware that I'm not there.'

'Still, I'm tired myself. It's been a long day and a lovely evening so it would be a shame to drag it out discussing uncertainties. Do you need anything before I go up?'

'No, dear, you go, we can talk again tomorrow when the men are out.'

Once Lizzie had gone, Clara sat quietly in the firelight, musing on the day. She would be quite happy if Peter and Lizzie became more than good friends, they both deserved better from life. It wasn't her own domestic contentment that prompted these thoughts, more perhaps because she understood the pair of them better than they knew themselves. One thing was clear, however, too much pushing would only drive them apart.

Though clad comfortably against the cold in Edward's old coat, Peter was not in a buoyant mood as the two men climbed higher up onto the moors next morning. He had envisaged a bright brisk walk but the ground was boggy, the view partly concealed by mist and the damp air clung to their clothes. The wet bracken flailed against his legs, and once they were above the tree line he had to step carefully between tufts of heather to maintain his balance.

'You're quiet today,' Edward said as they crossed a swift flowing stream. 'It's a shame about the weather but it does bring out a good smell of the earth, don't you think?'

'You're right as ever Uncle. Still, the walk is good exercise and I like your company.'

'You wouldn't think so; you've hardly spoken a word so far.'

'Sorry, Uncle, it's not your fault,' Peter assured him. 'I'm just contemplating where my life will lead me during the next few years—to be frank, I'm a bit disillusioned. What's the glory of Empire all about if it isn't for wealth and power, and I'm not seeing much of either.'

'Mmm, I seem to recall this conversation from some years back, only it was me complaining then—don't tell me I was right after all, or are you getting older, like me?' Edward wasn't being sarcastic for he understood how Peter's youthful enthusiasm and high ideals had made him join the Army in the first place, and why he'd sought a better future away from his family. 'We take whatever resources these lands have to offer and, in return, give the people new religions, diseases they've never had before, and eventually expectations we can't fulfil. I can't say I'm proud of what we do.' Edward was well read in spite of living in isolation. Newspapers were delivered to the village regularly and if, when he collected his, some were out of date at least he read them from end to end. One of his greatest pleasures was discussing their contents with Clara. 'You need a wife!' he said bluntly. 'And a family to fight for and protect.'

Peter groaned. 'That's what I told Lizzie, that she needed to get married before she becomes an old maid.'

'I don't suppose that went down too well,' Edward retorted grimly. 'And it was a little unfair to state the obvious. Doesn't the Army teach its officers manners any more?'

'I apologised of course, but you know how Lizzie provokes me at times, nevertheless, I shouldn't have said it.'

Edward didn't labour the point; he remembered his own twinge of guilt the night before when observing the gloomy pair before going to bed, instead he asked, 'Did you find out more of her intentions? Is she still determined to go?'

'I'm afraid she is, and there's no more I can say to her without causing trouble. However, I do see that she needs a change in life, especially if she doesn't marry.'

'But why China for God's sake?'

'I think she's well aware that China and its culture is vastly different to all she knows here, but therein lies the challenge. She's been offered work in a hospital being built by the Missionary Society. At least she doesn't intend going off into some savage jungle to preach.'

'No, but there are still mosquitoes and the like. She could even be attacked. The English aren't God's gift to mankind, even if we think we are.' Edward had equally strong views on his government's actions overseas.

'I do believe the best thing is to let her go with good grace,' Peter suggested, 'after all, nursing is different to fighting.'

'You've done well for yourself Peter, don't belittle your achievements. However, perhaps the time has come for you to settle down—only you can be the judge of that.'

They were now surrounded by the mist which clung with cold fingers to their faces and clothes. 'I think we'd better head back,' Edward suggested. 'There's not much point in going on and I can see this lot turning into heavy rain.'

'Fancy, the one day I have free to come up here, and just look at it,' Peter grumbled, 'still, there is a kind of peace in its isolation. At least it will be warm in Africa,' he chuckled.

Having decided to return they quickly descended from the high land and, as Edward had predicted, the mist slowly turned to heavy rain, thus ruling out any opportunity for a pleasant ride with Lizzie.

'Can I do anything around the farm to help you?' Peter asked. 'Once I've dried out I'd be only too willing to help.'

'As a matter of fact there are some logs in the barn that need splitting. It's getting a bit much for Jack and me: do as many as you like, I'll be very grateful.'

'As good as done!' Peter was grateful not to sit idly in the house and for couple of hours he worked his frustration off on the wood with considerable satisfaction.

'You'll ache tomorrow,' Lizzie informed him as she handed him a tankard of beer, noting the enormous pile of stacked wood against the wall. To see him in his shirt-sleeves, bathed in sweat and with his hair dishevelled amused her, as she had never seen him anything other than neat and well turned out before.

'Thanks,' he said, drinking deeply, and savouring the coolness of the beer as it rinsed the dryness from his throat. 'I'm ready for this.' He took a last swig of the dark refreshing liquid and then grinned impishly at her. 'I must look a mess, but it's done me good.' He stepped forward, intending to return the now empty mug but Lizzie appeared to shrink before his eyes. Her face was ashen and she looked shocked, frightened even. 'Whatever's the matter?' he asked with real concern. 'Are you ill?'

Lizzie was transfixed; fighting to regain some semblance of normality, as, in his few steps towards her, she had seen not Peter, but Nathan! The family likeness in their features had wiped out all else and she stood rooted to the spot. 'I'm alright,' she managed to gasp weakly. 'It's something that happens occasionally.'

Peter stepped closer, 'You frightened the life out of me, Lizzie, have you seen a doctor about it?' He was deeply worried by the suddenness of it all and the pallor of her face.

'There is nothing anyone can do,' she whispered, still trying to control her nerves.

'There must be something, Lizzie, surely you know someone who can advise you. What about Clara or Dr McCreary?'

'No!' Lizzie replied firmly. 'Nothing can be done. Please don't tell Father, or Clara, she needs no upset at this time.' Colour was slowly returning to her cheeks as the shock wore off. 'Please, Peter, you mustn't upset either of them, as I do believe the symptoms are not life-threatening.'

'Are you really fit enough to go to China?' he asked.

At this remark, Lizzie took a grip of herself. 'Yes, yes, I am. I can assure you.'

Peter reluctantly accepted her answer. 'Well, if you're certain.'

'I am. But I will go back inside now, if you don't mind. Please don't bother my father about it, will you?'

'I'll come in with you, I've finished here anyway. I won't say a word, but it won't stop me worrying.' He realised then that he was clutching the empty tankard in his hand so tightly that his fingers were white. As he relaxed his grip, Lizzie saw why he had approached her. She could hardly apologise for misconstruing his action without some explanation, so was forced to let the matter drop, albeit with a feeling of great relief.

As they approached the house Lizzie paused. 'I'll go and rest in my room, Peter. Just say that I've gone to do some packing for tomorrow will you? I'll come down when I feel up to it.'

London 1884

Their return journey to London was very different to the one which had brought the two cousins to the valley five days earlier. Peter's attention to Lizzie's needs was almost overwhelming. He was kind and protective and only left her side to buy their tickets and make sure that their luggage was safely installed in the guard's van, as the train was quite crowded.

'It seems as though we've been away ages,' he remarked as the train rattled and swayed, gradually picking up speed for the journey ahead. 'It has been a strange time in many ways, but I wouldn't have missed it for the world. I'm just very worried about you, especially after what happened yesterday.'

'I admit to having enjoyed being home more this time,' Lizzie said, ignoring his reference to the incident in the barn. 'The break has done me good, in spite of everything.' She looked keenly at him, 'You didn't tell them, did you?'

He shook his head. 'I promised, didn't I? Though I was sorely tempted to ask for Clara's advice. I didn't, of course.' He leaned forward and placed a protective hand on hers. 'If ever I can be of help, you will let me know, won't you.'

The mixture of compassion and wistfulness in his eyes and the firm pressure of his hand did not disturb her this time. She nodded and smiled with affection and gratitude, before turning to look out of the carriage window.

Peter sat back and watched also as the train rumbled onwards past green fields and smoky towns, drawing them ever closer to their destination.

'You will write, won't you?' he asked, and took comfort when she agreed with some enthusiasm.

In the capital, Peter first escorted Lizzie home before making his way towards his own lodgings. As they passed the imposing structure of Bethlem Hospital, standing in its own grounds behind iron railings, he expressed curiosity about the place. 'What exactly do you do there, what can anyone do with such people?'

His interest seemed genuine, and this pleased Lizzie. 'Would you like to see for yourself?' she asked, wondering just what his reaction might be when placed in close proximity to some of her patients. 'I could arrange a visit.'

He wasn't sure if he could face a ward of mentally sick people, and hesitated before replying. 'I've seen men lose their minds in battle,' he said, 'and it's not pleasant: very disturbing in fact. I don't know if I'm up to it.'

'The hospital is a very orderly and compassionate place, Peter; the patients don't rant and rave all the time. Most are like children who have lost their way and need to be taken care of. Many of them simply sit there in a private little world of their own. Others react only to certain stresses and are more harmful to themselves than others nearby. We have a few battle-shocked men here, but most are ordinary people, artists, businessmen, and sometimes those who have been ground down by difficult circumstances, or the cruelty of other human beings.'

'Your understanding is praiseworthy Lizzie, but the things I dislike most are those which I don't understand. When you can't reason with someone it perturbs me. I suppose it's similar to speaking a different language to another culture; if you can't converse there is no meeting of minds. If you don't think alike, force won't help; I think you'll find China the same.'

'Perhaps my work here has given me a better understanding and preparation for such events.' Lizzie replied. 'I've been told that the Chinese take their time in all things, are not to be rushed and soon feel humiliated: these things I'm used to. Be that as it may, would you care to visit the hospital, or not? I promise you will be enlightened if not entertained by your experience.'

By this time the hospital had disappeared from view and the carriage had entered Walcott Square. 'Will you stay for supper?' she asked. 'You can decide about tomorrow later.'

'No, I won't if you don't mind, I'll help you with your luggage, then go on to my lodgings, I have so much to do before I leave for Ireland.' Turning to the driver he ordered him to wait, as he would return after escorting Lizzie indoors.

'I've had a wonderful few days,' he said, once she and her luggage were safely inside. 'May I call on you tomorrow evening?'

'Yes, please do,' she replied, relieved that he would not simply part from her without making further contact. 'I won't be back until after seven, will that be too late?'

He was a little disappointed. 'It will be a long day, but no matter. If I come about 7.30 will that be suitable?'

'Yes, I think both Dr and Mrs McCreary enjoy your visits, especially if you talk to them of Clara, and providing you don't stay too late. Mrs McCreary will no doubt invite you to supper.' Then a little shyly, Lizzie added, 'I too have enjoyed the past few days, for which I thank you very much.'

With a flamboyant gesture he took her hand, lifted it to his lips and kissed it gallantly, then with a wave he departed quickly as if embarrassed by what he had done, leaving Lizzie with an empty feeling inside.

Reporting for duty the following morning Lizzie had little enthusiasm for her work, nor could she banish Peter from her thoughts. Her absence had obviously been inconvenient to her colleagues, so she endeavoured to make up for this in spite of her feelings. As the afternoon wore on, however, her steps lightened as she looked forward to seeing Peter once more, and it was with some relief when the harder than usual day's work ended.

Walcott Square lay a mere five minutes walk from the hospital and this was one of the reasons for Lizzie's isolation. In such a short distance, much of it traversed after dark, she encountered few people with whom she could do more than nod in acknowledgement. Understanding this, the Doctor's wife had urged her, almost dragged her to the local Mission as a way of encouraging her to find friends. At first Lizzie had gone simply to please Jane McCreary but, eventually, the distraction and comfort she found there had broadened her outlook. Although she had no keen interest in religion, attending their services somehow eased her conscience and made life more bearable.

The square in which she lived was a neat, triangular area of three-storeyed terraced houses, their frontages giving an appearance of being flat-topped. They were sturdy, respectable dwellings, totally in keeping with Dr McCreary's status, and Lizzie knew she was privileged to be given a home there. Railings protected passers by from the windowed basement area, and as she climbed the five short steps to her front door, she realised how similar the houses were to the one that Clara still owned in Aldershot. Was she a fool to give up such comforts in order to travel into uncertainty? On the other hand, life in Walcott Square very much depended on the tolerance and kindness of Dr and Mrs McCreary, their health and, indeed, her own unmarried status.

With time to spare before Peter's arrival, Lizzie was nervous at the thought of meeting him again and she fastidiously washed and changed, intending to rid herself of the odour of the hospital which she sensed about her person. Taking a final glance in the mirror before leaving her room she was critical of her reflection; she'd never been one to gaze with great interest at herself, aiming simply to be neat and tidy with no desire to impress. It was no longer a pallid, sad face which she saw, but one coloured by the winds from the moors, youthful yet still too thin. When greeting her, Mrs McCreary had declared with some satisfaction that she looked healthier and that the visit had obviously done her good.

Hearing the rattle of the door-knocker below, Lizzie hurried onto the landing and hesitated as she heard Mrs McCreary bustling down the hall. She saw Peter, smartly dressed as ever, shake hands with her friend.

'Come in young man, Lizzie will be down shortly,' Jane offered. 'Let me take your coat and hat. I'm sure she will have heard the knocker, one can you know, it seems to penetrate the whole house.' She led Peter into the parlour, well aware that Lizzie was waiting and watching on the first floor landing. 'Sit down and make yourself comfortable,' she insisted. 'My husband will join us soon, then we will leave you two in peace until supper time—you will stay for supper, won't you?'

'That's very kind of you, Mrs McCreary, I'd like that very much,' Peter replied with enthusiasm, 'but I won't be staying too late.' Then, hearing the rustle of Lizzie's skirt he turned as she entered the room. 'Good Evening, Lizzie,' he said pleasantly. 'The break has done her good, don't you think Mrs McCreary?'

'I certainly do, Peter. I'm afraid Lizzie doesn't go out often enough. Mind you, it won't be long before you're both off on your adventures.' She enjoyed Peter's company, his lively manner and the way he brought Lizzie to life. It was good, having younger people about the house, and she dreaded losing Lizzie who she treated as the daughter she'd never had.

'I'm afraid I shall be leaving London tomorrow,' Peter replied without enthusiasm. Judging by today's papers, the expeditionary force is definitely going to the Sudan, so it is as well that I return to my unit in Ireland tomorrow.'

'Oh dear!' Jane McCreary cried, 'I shall miss your visits.'

'That's very kind of you, Mrs McCreary.'

'And Lizzie will go back into her shell again,' the older woman lamented, noting how Lizzie's face had flushed as these remarks were made. She observed the pair before her with motherly interest, though sad that what she hoped might have developed into an 'interesting situation' could not now do so, as Lizzie would soon be leaving for China.

Dr McCreary joined them and chatted for a while before his wife informed him that she needed his help in the other room. This left Peter and Lizzie slightly bemused by the obvious scheming of their hostess, and a rather stilted conversation followed as each tried to find common ground to discuss whilst avoiding anything too personal.

After a while Peter said dismally, 'It really does seem a pity that we are to part again after such a short time.' He looked lost, even despondent, and Lizzie recalled Clara's words in that he needed moral support if he was to face his immediate future with confidence. The compassion she felt was reflected in her face, softening her features and making her look ten years younger. 'You really are beautiful,' he whispered, as if seeing her fully for the first time. 'Don't change, Lizzie. Please! Wait for me to come back.' He paused, almost pleading for a favourable reply.

Nobody but God could see into the future, so much could happen and Peter needed a source of strength to draw on. Lizzie knew that he saw her as his link and inspiration: what harm would it do if she agreed to wait? She could not explain that because of Nathan she would never be free to love him. She was resolved to go to China as planned, and also genuinely believed that once out of danger, he would re-assess his life and her value to him would diminish. 'I will wait,' she said softly, 'and meanwhile I will write, but from China.'

As if reading her innermost thoughts, he responded 'I will tell you in my letters how much you mean to me, and if we both survive our ordeals, with

God's help we might find happiness.' He deliberately omitted the word 'together', fearing that the very haste of their commitment might frighten Lizzie—but he knew what he wanted, and would give the Dervishes and the Mahdi swift justice so he could return quickly and safely to take up her promise. He squeezed her hand with a gentle reassurance, aware that at any moment their hosts might reappear and be surprised at his and Lizzie's familiarity. 'It's best if we say no more now' Peter advised, 'or the good Doctor might object. We are fortunate as cousins to be allowed to meet without a chaperone.' His consideration pleased Lizzie, who smiled warmly at the thought of the supposed intrigue they shared and, in contrast, the comfortable understanding they had actually arrived at.

A light cough from the hallway heralded the return of their hostess who invited the pair to join her and her husband in the dining room, as supper was ready. The change in Lizzie's demeanour however, was not entirely lost on Jane McCreary but she was determined that her husband should not become aware of her suspicions. In her opinion, any man who could bring genuine happiness to a forlorn soul such as Lizzie was to be held in great esteem. Consequent to these thoughts, she fussed over them both; chatting enthusiastically for some time, thus leaving Dr McCreary at a loss and mystified as to the cause of his wife's excited behaviour. He mused for some time over this, and came to the conclusion that he ought not to neglect her so much, and must take her out more often away from the mundane tasks in the house.

Putting these thoughts to one side, he turned his attention to his guests and asked Lizzie, 'Were you able to arrange a visit to the hospital for Peter?'

'Oh, yes,' she replied, 'I'd almost forgotten. Any morning would be convenient, but Peter leaves tomorrow I'm afraid.'

'It'll be alright tomorrow, Lizzie.' Peter was determined to see her once more before he left. 'I'll catch the afternoon train but will take my luggage to the station earlier in the day, to save time.' He turned to Dr McCreary, 'I'm keen to learn just what Lizzie does there, and to find out what has given her such an understanding of life.' He had now regained his composure fully: no one would have guessed that only a short while before he had been in an emotional disarray.

'People misunderstand the mentally ill,' the Doctor informed him, 'but things are changing for the better I might add, and not all are completely insane or incurable. The genuine insane are to be pitied for being trapped in another world. We don't have them at Bethlem anymore as they were removed to Broadmoor Asylum in the 60's, and the cruel regime here at Bethlem no longer exists.'

'Thank goodness,' his wife interrupted. 'One heard awful tales of the goings on in the past.'

The Doctor nodded his head in agreement. 'I was privileged to know Dr Hood, whose hard work and influence brought humanity and even a little pleasure to the place, with the help of a Dr Help, if you'll pardon the pun.' He laughed heartily, his plump chins and ruddy cheeks wobbling slightly as he did so. He always managed to bring a smile to Lizzie's face, he had a good sense of humour and gentle ways, but Peter had missed the point as he'd never heard of this Dr Help. 'No matter young man, you'll get used to me in time, won't he dear?'

'In time,' his wife replied fondly.

Peter didn't stay late and decided to walk and hail a passing cab when he could. He left the square and eventually the Asylum appeared silhouetted against the moonlit sky, the perimeter railings fronting the gardens casting prison-like bars across his path.

London was a dangerous place at night and eerie shadows caused him to quicken his step in the hope of finding a cab. He wished now that he'd arranged for one to collect him from Walcott Square. Eventually he reached Lambeth Bridge and, much to his relief, the moonlit bridge had few corners behind which a ne'er-do-well could hide and surprise passers-by.

The inky black river below had a foul smell which offended his nostrils and almost overwhelmed him as he waited apprehensively for a cab, pondering all the while on the strange events of his evening with Lizzie. He'd spent the whole day in town looking forward to their meeting yet it had been unexpectedly revealing to both of them.

He gazed down into the water below which seemed to draw him towards it. So many bodies were washed up along the muddy banks of the Thames each year that it made him shudder to think of the river's malignancy. The water was no more than an open sewer and in his contemplative mood the clean deserts of the Sudan appealed more than the prospects of life in this smoky, grimy capital. He seemed to wait forever before a cab finally did appear, and quickly boarding it, he slumped gratefully onto its hard horsehair-filled seat.

It was almost midnight when he arrived home, and too late to light a fire in the grate; instead, he undressed and climbed wearily into bed, seeking warmth and comfort there, whilst reflecting once again on what had occurred in Walcott Square.

Sleep persistently eluded him as memories of the evening flooded back, waking him with a jolt each time his eyes closed. Finally, however, tiredness overcame him but not before he resolved not to let Lizzie escape him again.

In Walcott Square, Lizzie was also preoccupied by the promise she'd made to Peter. In spite of her feelings for him nothing could overcome her inability to be honest with him. She tossed and turned the whole night, relief coming only in the form of an exhausted sleep half an hour before Jane knocked loudly on the door to call her for breakfast. With a heavy heart Lizzie rose from her bed, worried now as to how, under the circumstances, she should behave with Peter.

Peter, similarly, was just as apprehensive as he stood, as arranged, at the hospital's lodge gates. Having delivered his luggage to the station earlier, he'd managed to obtain a single rose for Lizzie which he held self-consciously at his side. He knew he looked dashing in his uniform and waited eagerly for her, and for her greeting.

Lizzie smiled the minute she saw him standing there, for he was a figure to be admired. At first he didn't see her, not knowing from which direction she would come, so she took him by surprise. Flustered, he immediately presented his rose to her, grinning sheepishly. 'It's lovely, thank you,' she cried warmly, 'it has a delightful scent.'

'I'm pleased you like it, although looking at the gardens here you could pick a rose anytime,' he remarked as she led him through the well laid out grounds towards the hospitals entrance steps.

'But you gave it to me, that makes all the difference.' Lizzie's pleasure at the gift gave him immense satisfaction, and he was pleased that instead of turning away the importunate flower-seller he had allowed her to entice him into purchasing the rose. As they passed through the porticoed entrance to the lobby, Lizzie paused. 'Be careful what you say to any of the patients,' she warned, 'a simple word, if the wrong one, can trigger totally unexpected reactions. One woman here is perfectly rational most of the time, but it takes just one remark or comment to bring about delusions.'

Peter was impressed by the fine reception room as they started their tour, though nothing was quite as he'd expected, and in Lizzie's company the hospital looked quite an orderly, comforting place to be. He shook hands with the Medical Officer, Mr Robert Smith, to whom Lizzie introduced Peter as her cousin, and noted the quizzical look the man gave on seeing the rose which she still held. 'Cousin indeed,' Peter whispered as the man left them, 'I wonder if he believes us?'

'Well we are cousins are we not? It's no lie,' she replied teasingly, but her professional manner was to the fore as they entered one of the long galleries in the hospital. 'Come, we have an excellent library at the far end.'

If it hadn't been for the strange attitudes of some of the patients as they shambled along the same passage, heads sunken, hands clasped behind them as if listening or deep in thought, Peter would not have believed what he saw. Chaotic their minds might be, but all around was neatness and order. Along one side were long window casements in which hung baskets filled with plants, there were comfortable chairs, tables and ornaments, even a carpet for the full length of the gallery. All this was beneath an arched ceiling, which helped give an air of light and tranquillity. Only the dull, expressionless faces and lethargic figures of the inmates reminded him that all was not as it seemed. The rooms leading off from the opposite wall to the windows were apparently plain but comfortable sleeping apartments, most of which were locked and rarely needed during the daytime. Seeing them, Peter had to admit that they would be the envy of many a normal person living outside the hospital.

Heeding Lizzie's warning, Peter only smiled and nodded affably when stared at by a patient, and said only 'Good Morning,' where necessary. He was grateful for her protection against things he didn't understand and the incessant ramblings of woe from walking patients, first on the men's gallery then the women's; although there his curiosity was roused by the various activities and handicrafts being practised.

'The women in this gallery are approaching sanity again,' Lizzie explained, 'most are curable. At least these will be released to their families free from the risk of harming themselves or anyone else.'

Seeing a caged canary, Peter stopped and put a finger against the wire. 'Caged within a cage,' he observed, 'but it's not a place for you, Lizzie, freedom becomes you! When I return from the Sudan we must change all this.' His tone was gentle and there was no hiding his sincerity, 'Whilst I'm away I'll be able to remember you here and appreciate the good you are doing.'

Had he forgotten that she was going to China? Lizzie did not remind him that she would not be here on his return, there was no point. The future was uncertain and adversity could play strange tricks with people's lives. Nearby a woman sat in a rocking chair, constantly stroking the cat on her knee. 'Gently now, Martha,' Lizzie remonstrated, though not unkindly. 'Don't rub his fur off!'

'They all appear remarkably well in spite of everything,' Peter commented once they'd reached the end of the gallery and were heading towards the library.

'Our patients are mainly sick in mind only, though we do have a physician and full nursing staff. When the weather is good patients are allowed out into the gardens and in winter there is a covered walkway for taking exercise. We are particularly fortunate in having our own water-well so that keeps us free from cholera and diarrhoea.' She was very proud of her workplace, even though the hours there were long and extremely tiring.

He looked around at the contents of the library with appreciation. 'If the place wasn't what it is, it would be an enviable place to live.' He looked out of the window to the garden below, 'Here they are protected from poverty, disease—and wars...' his voice trailed off with this thought. Suddenly he turned, reached out with his hands and drew her close to him. 'Please don't go to China, Lizzie! At least if you are here I will know that you are safe.'

She was stunned by his action and found herself being held firmly against the jacket of his uniform. She did indeed feel safe in his arms, his whispered words close to her ear. All she had ever wanted was for Peter to love her, now it was too late, and wrong. She had killed his brother. Tears ran down her cheeks as she thought of what might have been. She could never let him hold her this way again, and for this moment only could she allow herself to rejoice in his affection, before sending him away to war. If he never returned, then at least he would die with the knowledge that someone cared for him. Lizzie shuddered at the thought of his possible demise and prayed that God would watch over him. If this man returned safely it would take great courage on her part to disappoint him.

Peter felt her tremble, and slackened his hold, easing her from him so that he could see her face. 'You've been crying,' he murmured, 'but you don't reject me!' His eyes were filled with concern. 'It's my turn now to comfort you.' Peter gently raised her head, then slowly and gently kissed her.

How could she push him away? To do so would only hurt him, yet by not doing, she was slowly allowing herself to be engulfed in a swell of emotion she found impossible to quell. It was no kiss of passion but one of tenderness, it only made matters worse for Lizzie, as she recognised the sincerity with which it was given. She made no effort to pull away but stood savouring the moment, the sensation of which would have to last her a lifetime.

She said nothing when he released her; instead she instinctively touched his face lovingly with her fingers. With the sound of footsteps approaching the library door she stood back: only then did she trust herself to speak, 'I pray God will take care of you.' she whispered, as she reached out for a leather-bound volume from the nearest shelf just as the door opened.

'Martha's getting to be a nuisance Miss Hardy. Can you help?' The voice was rather stern and the doctor eyed Peter with some curiosity. 'Can you come now, please!' he repeated, whilst wondering at the dishevelled rose and petals which lay at her feet, as he turned to leave.

'Of course, I'll come immediately,' Lizzie called out, quickly replacing the book on the shelf. 'I'm sorry, Peter,' she said, 'but I will have to go and I may be some time. Can you find your way back to the waiting room?'

Peter nodded ruefully, 'I haven't time to wait, Lizzie, if I don't see you before I leave, remember this. I love you!'

Lizzie's heart sank, 'Thank you,' she whispered huskily. 'I will be thinking of you constantly.'

On reaching her patient, Lizzie dealt with the problem with less compassion than was normal for her, which only aggravated the unfortunate woman so that it took much longer to calm her down.

'Is he your boyfriend, Miss?' Martha asked impishly, 'don't 'e look smart!'

'No, Martha,' Lizzie tried to explain, 'he's my cousin, and he is going out to Africa to fight a war, so he came to say good-bye.'

'Aw, he's nice, Miss,' Martha cooed. 'Pity your rose has lost its petals.' Lizzie had picked up the bruised rose from the library floor where it had dropped, leaving some of the fallen petals behind in her haste. She hurried back to retrieve them but they were no longer there. Had Peter taken them? She looked sadly at what remained of the precious flower that had been crushed in their embrace, deciding to press what petals were left in her diary.

By the time Lizzie returned to Martha she found the cat once more being almost strangled with affection and removed it for its own safety. With the situation now under control she went in search of Peter, only to find that he had indeed been unable to delay his departure and had left the hospital to catch his train.

Shanghai 1885

In spite of the long tiring sea journey,
often spent being tossed about in bad weather or
lying uncomfortably on her bunk bringing up all she'd eaten, Lizzie could not
now quell her mounting excitement as her destination drew nearer. For weeks
she had suffered indignity after indignity on a voyage that seemed never-
ending, and one which she never wanted to repeat. If returning to England
entailed the same gruelling experience then she doubted that she would ever
return home willingly.

Now, entering the mouth of the mighty Yangtze River, from a sea that
for many miles had been changing from a beautiful blue into a turbid yellow
flood caused by rich soil washed from the land, Lizzie saw nothing but other
vessels and sluggish mud flats.

Amongst this a lightship guided the flotilla of boats into a narrow navi-
gation channel, and soon they were heading into the Huangpu River towards
Shanghai.

Lizzie was unimpressed by the many miles of flat, endless terrain through
which they passed. There was, however, no time to be bored, for all around
them heavily laden junks sailed by, together with smaller sampans almost
submerged by their cargo. Steam ships with hooting sirens, and tacking tea
clippers manoeuvred, seemingly haphazardly, along the watery thoroughfare
and she was fascinated by the hectic movements of dozens of small craft as
they challenged each other for space. As an array of ramshackle buildings and
warehouses came into view, however, it was hard to stifle her disappointment,
for this was not the China she'd imagined. There was much to observe but
little to admire so far and she drew her shawl closer to defy the cold dry wind,
thinking wryly of Peter's warning against soaring high temperatures that he
said would be unbearable.

It was certainly a colourful, dangerous waterway and one that hinted at
mystery and intrigue. Where had all the boats come from, what did they carry
and where were they all heading in such great numbers? Eventually, after miles
of uninteresting scenery, her ship rounded a broad bend in the river bringing
a totally different aspect into view. The waterfront ahead was edged with fine
European villas and mansions. It was a shock, as well as a surprise, to see the
facades and elegant balconies standing proudly there as if to welcome her, in
complete contrast to the monotonous landscape and seedy, built-up outskirts

of the city through which they had just passed. Seeing the impressive array of palatial buildings, including a tall clock tower, the vista stretching for miles, she was affected by many different emotions. Why, if Shanghai was so affluent was it necessary to convert its inhabitants and why were her nursing services required?

By the time their vessel was in a position to dock alongside one of the many projecting landing stages, her puzzlement had dissipated and was replaced with a tremor of excitement. Nothing was quite as she'd expected, yet she was eager now to disembark and see for herself why so many people in England held the Chinese in awe.

Immediately Lizzie stepped onto the landing stage she was importuned by numerous Chinese men offering to transport her wherever she wanted to go. She had been instructed to wait until someone from the Mission arrived to collect her and as she waited was intrigued by the number of European women on the quayside, either awaiting friends or merely curious as to who was arriving. All appeared fashionably and elegantly attired, and in contrast Lizzie felt bedraggled, almost ashamed of her travelling clothes which showed signs of being in need of a good wash and iron. It wasn't long before she was approached by a smartly dressed, if not in high fashion, lady of about fifty years of age.

'Miss Hardy?' A firm and very English voice enquired. Lizzie nodded and smiled. 'Welcome to China, I'm Molly Bradshaw from the Mission.' The woman held out a hand in greeting.

'Thank you,' Lizzie responded with some relief, as she took the hand offered. She was spellbound by the loud fervour of activity around her and quite incapable of conducting a light conversation with the stranger. 'Thank you,' she simply repeated.

'Is all this your luggage?' Molly Bradshaw asked, looking down at Lizzie's trunks and boxes with some concern.

'I'm afraid I may have brought too much,' Lizzie said, finding her voice and apologising. 'I didn't know what to expect in China; I brought everything I thought I might need.'

Mrs Bradshaw smiled broadly and shook her head. 'Don't be fooled by what you find here on the Bund', she said, pointing to the promenade up ahead, 'or in the European settlements. Once you get into the countryside you will see a totally different world.' She turned and indicated to a porter that he should collect Lizzie's belongings and follow them.

Lizzie gasped as the man piled all her possessions onto a handcart, and marvelled as to whether he could possibly push or pull such a weight without losing some items en route.

'They're quite adept at moving large amounts of goods,' Mrs Bradshaw said on seeing Lizzie's consternation. 'Come, I have a buggy waiting for us.' She led Lizzie along the flagged walkway to a horse-drawn buggy that had been secured nearby.

It was soon obvious to Lizzie that she would need to rely heavily on Mrs Bradshaw's knowledge for quite some time before venturing into Shanghai proper. 'I'm glad to be on land again,' she said, once they were seated in the buggy. 'I fear I will never make a sailor.'

'Oh, my dear,' Mrs Bradshaw responded, turning to her, 'was the journey a bad one?'

Lizzie nodded, 'It seemed never ending, and I'm afraid I disgraced myself by being constantly sick. More so than the other passengers.'

'As we all were in our turn,' her companion agreed, 'but you're here now and your help will be most appreciated.' Lizzie was already warming to the lady and pleased to find that she wasn't the stiff, prim spinster that Peter had suggested all single English women became when abroad. She smiled to herself and wondered if his prejudice was uttered more to stop her coming than anything else. Lizzie watched with a traveller's eye as they went. There was so much to see and it was at this point that she was struck by the small stature of the native population, amongst whom a tall English woman would not be able to mingle unobserved as she'd hoped; this was a great disappointment to her.

'Have you been to foreign parts before?' Mrs Bradshaw asked, seeing that Lizzie's eyes were darting here, there and everywhere.

'No, never!' Lizzie replied excitedly. 'I was very disappointed coming up river; the land is so flat and uninteresting, but here there is so much life, so much bustle.'

'Don't be fooled,' Mrs Bradshaw cautioned again. 'Shanghai is half European, half Chinese, and the diversity amongst the Chinese themselves is vast. Different areas have different customs, the Han Chinese and the Manchu speak separate languages, also their food varies, as do their religions. The higher class Chinese in Shanghai try to emulate the 'Foreign Devils', as they call us, they want fine houses and all that goes with them. These are not the people whom we are here to help.'

'Do they still call us Foreign Devils?'

'That and more. Ghosts with long noses, many names I'm afraid.'

'Aren't we liked then?' Lizzie asked, a little disturbed by this news.

'Tolerated, but not liked. Except by those who really know us. We're thought of generally as greedy money-makers. We at the mission try to show a different side, a Christian side, but the Chinese are superstitious, and in many cases ignorant of the wider world.'

'I seem ignorant myself regarding other cultures in spite of the information I have been given in London.'

'There is a lot to learn here before you go on to Hangchow, or Hankow where you will probably be working. We don't expect you to learn everything at once.' Mrs Bradshaw saw Lizzie draw the shawl closer as the buggy sped along, causing the cold wind to bite deeper. 'When the season changes and the heat comes you'll wish this wind back,' she warned. 'At the height of summer Hankow is like a furnace.'

Perhaps Peter was right after all, Lizzie conceded. He was never far from her thoughts these days. Was he well, did he lay in some hospital bed ill or injured, or worse—was he dead? For so many years she had thought of him with love and affection, imagining him to be invincible and enjoying his life as a soldier. Now, when it would have been possible for them to at least be happy together, there were dangers, they were a world apart in distance and there was of course Nathan: he never left her thoughts for long and she worried constantly, fearing that his body might be found. The buggy suddenly shook violently when it hit a pothole as the driver tried to avoid colliding with a coolie who had suddenly dashed across their path. This man was pulling a cart-like contraption on which no less than four people perched precariously, but he carried on as if nothing had happened, leaving the buggy driver to cope with the result of a near disaster. Lizzie gave an involuntary scream, expecting to be flung in a heap onto the road.

'You'll get used to it,' Mrs Bradshaw said calmly, righting herself and smoothing her skirt. 'The Chinese are all rush, or no rush at all, as they can sometimes take forever to do the simplest of jobs. It is better to let them go at their own pace or they will stubbornly take the longer stand, you can't hurry them. Left alone they will work their fingers to the bone—if only to waste what they earn at the end of the day on opium.'

'Is opium such a problem?' Lizzie queried, 'I know that in England many members of Society take opium—it doesn't appear to ruin their lives.'

'Here it's different, particularly for the poor and those doing hard manual jobs. All they have to look forward to in an evening is oblivion. If we Missionaries can convert these people we stand a chance of getting them off opium.'

'I do have much to learn,' Lizzie conceded.

'We also feel we have a duty to convert them from their superstitious ways,' Mrs Bradshaw went on. 'Apart from anything else it is our fault in the first place for making opium available—we imported so much of the dreadful stuff into China as trade that we have gone a long way towards destroying a fine and proud race. We need to be here now to rectify such a wrong.'

The buggy had long since left the main thoroughfare with its impressive gardens and splendid trees still awaiting their spring foliage, and they were now in an area of fine wide streets lined with shops. As a sightseer, Lizzie was extremely impressed, and pleasantly surprised, to find the bustling, crowded streets remarkably clean and sweet smelling, in comparison to those in London. 'Everywhere seems very clean,' she said. 'It must help combat disease.'

Mrs Bradshaw smiled, 'Believe me, beyond the affluent foreign settlements lies another world, and few European women have ever been into the old walled city of Shanghai. I don't want to disillusion you, my dear, but there is much work to be done here and in the interior. Your efforts will be very much appreciated.'

'Will I be allowed out by myself, is it safe?' Lizzie asked solemnly in anticipation of a negative reply.

'Oh, yes, you'll be advised of course as to where you can or should not go. In the settlements here you will be alright, providing you follow that advice.' Then as if reading Lizzie's thoughts she went on, 'In spite of the many Chinese in their fine silk robes and the elegantly dressed Europeans, there are humble coolies, and quite a number of Westerners who have fallen on hard times, one way or another. We have several hard-working charities here specifically to help those people. However, Shanghai is not China. The influence of the West has given it a character of its own, which is totally false and at odds with the rest of the country.'

Lizzie appreciated Mrs Bradshaw's advice; it was such details that would prevent her from appearing ignorant amongst her new colleagues and from making a fool of herself. Mrs Bradshaw did not quiz Lizzie about her background, having learned by experience that she would find out all she needed to know very quickly. Loneliness in a strange place often compelled new arrivals to open up, and she was quite used to being the mother figure to them when things became difficult.

The buggy finally halted before the gates of a walled compound where they waited to be let in to the Mission. This was to be Lizzie's home until she became familiar with her surroundings and could speak sufficient Chinese to make communication easy. Once through the gate they alighted and Mrs Bradshaw said, 'I'll take you to your room and leave you to gather your thoughts and have a rest.' So saying, she led Lizzie to a clean but sparsely furnished room. 'If you come across to the refectory in half an hour there will be some refreshments as you will no doubt be in need of something to eat. I will send someone to fetch you.'

'Thank you,' Lizzie replied, smiling gratefully at the only person she knew in this very strange place. 'I must admit to feeling hungry—it seems a long time since I last ate.'

'Once you've eaten I'll show you around and explain a little more about the work here. By the way, did you manage to learn a little of the language in London?'

Lizzie grimaced and nodded, 'Just a little, but it sounds very strange coming out of my mouth.'

'Good!' Mrs Bradshaw said encouragingly. 'It is important to be able to speak to the patients and servants in good Chinese, otherwise they misconstrue our intentions. Often they laugh and mock us behind our backs when we say what to them are ridiculous things. But I've said enough for now—I'll leave you in peace and see you later.'

She went, leaving Lizzie to take stock of her new surroundings and to ponder on her immediate future. Firstly, Lizzie placed the few bits and pieces she had with her into the top drawer of a large camphor-smelling chest of drawers, then sat waiting for the rest of her luggage to be delivered by a Mission helper. She noticed that a jug of water and basin had been left for her use, so she washed and tidied herself ready for when Mrs Bradshaw sent for her. She could hardly believe that she'd arrived in China, or that the long and tiresome sea-journey was over. Yet, though conscious of Mrs Bradshaw's warnings she was still full of excitement at the thought of exploring what she had already seen of Shanghai. Knowing that the work ahead might be hard and the conditions primitive, the prospect didn't worry her greatly; after all, she'd come to serve and to learn. However, she felt that taking a little time out to explore would not be too much to ask.

Strangely enough, once the ship had set sail from England she had ceased to feel so bound up with the past. The enforced close contact with her fellow passengers had somehow changed her outlook. Together they had, literally, all been in the same boat, in storm and calm, occasionally racked with sea sickness, and no-one knowing the other's background. She was ready to make a fresh start now, taking comfort in the knowledge that she had helped Peter go to war with hope and comfort. With so many miles separating them she was temporarily free of that commitment—and from decisions which could hurt them both. As she had stood on the ship's deck enjoying the invigorating breeze, she had understood his need to travel. Peter was becoming a constant mental companion to her, rather than a prospective husband. They may never meet again but, as kindred spirits, they could at least be a comfort to each other, so she determined that he would be the recipient of her musings and experiences, that is if he were still alive, and this thought chilled her momentarily.

It was within the Mission compound, which was under the protection of the British Legation, that Lizzie came into personal contact with her first 'Chinaman'. He was small, cheerful and polite. He kowtowed with bent head whenever he met her and it wasn't long before Lizzie found herself responding in likewise fashion. Wang Li had become a Christian many years before and now spoke English well. He loyally supported the cause of persuading his fellow-country men to forget their superstitious and heathen beliefs, and was much respected within the British Legation. He lived there in a small cottage with his wife and two daughters, rather than within the old walled city of Shanghai: a place Mrs Bradshaw had warned was unsuitable for unaccompanied western women.

It was Wang Li who collected Lizzie on behalf of Mrs Bradshaw, and it was he who gave her a plate of sandwiches and some tea in the refectory while she waited for Mrs Bradshaw to come. 'The Lady say you are to eat,' he smiled pleasantly, bending his head respectfully, 'she also say she come soon.'

'Thank you,' Lizzie replied, a little unsure of herself but nevertheless returning his smile. His bent head seemed almost submissive and she felt humbled by his action. The man bowed again and withdrew from the room, leaving Lizzie devouring the sandwiches as if she'd not eaten for several days. What a change, she thought from the repetitive diet of the last few weeks.

When Mrs Bradshaw appeared, not a crust remained uneaten and Lizzie flushed, 'I'm afraid I've eaten them all,' she hastily apologised, 'they were so good!'

'Don't worry, my dear,' the older woman chuckled. 'We bake our own bread here but I'm afraid at the Missions in the interior you will need to get used to rice, with whatever else is available at the time. Now let me show you round and introduce you to members of the Mission and household.' She led Lizzie from the refectory, all the while imparting information which she knew would be of use to her later.

'Do many find life here unbearable and return home?' Lizzie asked, suddenly thinking of the enormity of the task she'd undertaken.

'A few, if they're too frail to stand the conditions or they lose heart, but in the main most eventually dedicate their lives to China. You will find moments when it's difficult to accept the heinous beliefs here and this can wear one down. You wouldn't believe that before we came here, sometimes out in the villages if a child died it was cast into the street, or simply left as rubbish by its mother. They really did believe that once it was dead that was the end.'

Lizzie was profoundly shocked. 'But I thought they worshipped their ancestors and the dead?'

'There is more than one belief in China, my dear; they actually place offerings for the ancestors to help them in the afterlife. You can see why our work is so vital. Once convinced that Christianity is a true way of life the Chinese will give their lives in loyalty to Christ. Apart from their superstitions they are a childlike and charming people. However, unless you understand their customs you will be vulnerable to mistrust and attack. False rumours go round that we eat children! You can imagine if a foreign woman appears in the countryside unprotected, then a crowd will gather who, if incited by a rabble rouser, will attack. There is nothing quite so spine chilling as a howling mob of Chinese.'

'I begin to wonder if I am up to all this,' Lizzie replied, her voice shaky and nervous. 'In London such tales seemed unbelievable and I was of the opinion that with patience and understanding I could help to bring about great changes.'

'Oh, my dear, you have a lot to learn, as does everyone else who comes, but it takes time. There are many rewards when a family truly believes. Some pretend to believe in order to get free medicine and treatment, then they go back to their old ways. We don't turn away anyone who needs help though. They can also be very cunning, so learn now, do not believe everything they tell you as they have different scruples to us.'

Passing from the courtyard into the main section of the Mission, Mrs Bradshaw began to introduce Lizzie to people they met of both English and Chinese origin. The warmth of their greetings did much to calm Lizzie's anxieties, but as always she was cautious, afraid of becoming too familiar with strangers lest they asked too many questions. She nodded pleasantly; letting others do the talking as she followed her guide through various buildings, trying to familiarise herself with the layout for when she would be expected to make her own way to them.

'Will I be in Shanghai for any length of time?' Lizzie asked. 'I mean before I go to Hangchow?'

'Usually a month or two to familiarise yourself with Chinese customs and to learn the language as well as you possibly can.'

'I would like to see the old city: why is it frowned upon for European women to go there?'

Mrs Bradshaw paused, they were about to enter a building containing the dispensary. 'In our society here it is unseemly to show too much interest in the place. It is thought that visitors there might bring back smallpox or other infections. It really is a most unhealthy, stinking area, and if for some reason or other the people there take against you they may do you harm.'

'What a sad state of affairs, I had hoped to explore such a place in order to learn and improve my understanding of the Chinese.'

'It takes a lot to understand things which I'm sure half of them do not fully understand either. Blind obedience to religion and the Imperial Family blots out human reasoning. How a clever nation of people could accept such ludicrous ideas baffles us all but this inspires us to carry on in spite of everything. Be patient, my dear,' the older woman advised, 'it won't be long before you go up-river where you will see all the Chinese customs you want.'

By the end of the afternoon, Lizzie had been introduced to so many people and visited such an array of rooms, buildings and houses that she was almost dizzy with exhaustion, but Mrs Bradshaw hadn't finished. 'From today on I want you to try to speak nothing but Chinese to the coolies, house boys and even Wang Li, that way you will learn fast.'

'Oh dear,' Lizzie sighed ruefully, 'my mind is in a whirl already, but I'll try.'

'At least here in the compound you will not be mocked for your mistakes, they know that you have come to help and will be trying your best.'

'Thank you,' Lizzie responded without much enthusiasm.

'You must be very tired,' Mrs Bradshaw remarked in a motherly tone, 'go and rest, sort out your luggage and relax.' She turned to leave, then paused. 'Thank you for coming to China, my dear, we need all the hands we can get, especially nurses. The body needs as much attention as the soul.'

When the kindly woman had gone, Lizzie sat heavily on the bed and lay back against the pillow, her mind racing as she tried to recall the scant amount of Chinese she knew. Then, letting her thoughts mull over the happenings of the day she gradually relaxed. It had been a very long day and one full of new experiences and surprises, yet it was only when fact and fiction began to merge that she realised she was half-asleep. Before long she was indeed in a deep sleep, in which on this occasion she was spared any troublesome dreams.

In the weeks that followed, Lizzie saw leaves form on the trees and the temperatures moderate, so that by the time she was ready to leave Shanghai she'd seen it at its best. Blossoms waved in the breeze and gardens flourished. The fine buildings on the Bund seemed brighter in the sunlight and she had explored as much of the settlement as was advisable without guide or chaperone.

One thing became very clear however, no matter how hard she tried she would never be able to mingle inconspicuously amongst the people she'd come to help. She was simply too tall. Compared with the small-framed Chinese she was an Amazon, and she realised that not even the silk robe she'd purchased disguised her European origins. She enjoyed the busy if sometimes frenetic behaviour of the people, and was in danger of falling in love with Shanghai, but it would soon be time to leave.

She had worked many long hours in the dispensary, all the time improving her knowledge of both the language and understanding of the strange culture of the patients. 'You've done well, my dear,' Mrs Bradshaw said, after calling Lizzie into her office one day. 'We think the time has come to send you on to Hangchow where your talents are needed even more.' Lizzie's face displayed mixed emotions at this, she was happy in the settlement and for the first time in years she was at peace with herself. However, she knew that was not why she was here; she was here to help. 'You have even managed to master a good amount of the language, and will not now be so shocked by what you encounter. Always respect their beliefs, for the only way we can bring them to Christianity is by gaining their confidence and trust.'

Looking at the kindly woman who had been her guide and mentor, Lizzie replied, 'I am a little afraid to move on. Without your help I shall be lost.'

Mrs Bradshaw laughed modestly. 'My dear, there are many more like me, simply going quietly about their work.' She looked appraisingly at Lizzie, 'I think you might quite easily become one of us if you can stand the summer climate and do not succumb to the various sicknesses which prevail here.'

'Nevertheless I am in debt to you for the way you took me under your wing. I shall miss you and the others very much.' Lizzie swallowed hard, a shiver ran through her; she wasn't sure if it stemmed from fear or anticipation at the thought of exploring the unknown.

'That's the reason for moving new arrivals on as quickly as possible, for here a false atmosphere prevails. Too many would stay to the detriment of the cause elsewhere. You will experience both heartache and great satisfaction in your work; often there will seem to be no progress at all but, for each body you heal, your example may just reach the heart of the patient. Our aim is not to force the patient into Christianity but to help them see there are different ways of thinking and reasoning, other than superstition.'

'I'll do my best.' Lizzie promised, eager to please Mrs Bradshaw.

'I know you will dear, and I shall keep a constant eye on your progress.' The older woman's eyes softened, a smile again played on her lips and the tiredness on her face fleetingly disappeared. Lizzie conceded that she must once have been a very handsome woman.

'You will leave tomorrow evening,' Mrs Bradshaw revealed, almost apologetically.

Lizzie's face fell. 'That soon?' she gasped, a little dismayed at the news. 'By myself?'

'No, no! You will travel with a Mr Ward from the Consulate who has to go there on business; he will take you all the way. You will then be met and taken to the hospital on arrival, so there is no risk of you getting lost.'

That evening, Lizzie packed in a flurry of anticipation. It was perhaps better to be moving on, and quickly, before her fondness for Shanghai and its people distorted her reason for coming in the first place. It was no good going to bed early for she was far too excited, instead she sat in the light of the lamp hastily writing to Peter with her news so that she could post the letter before leaving for Hangchow.

The following day she worked in the dispensary until four o'clock and due to the constant stream of patients had no time to dwell on her impending journey. After dining she bade farewell to the friends she'd made in such a short time: Wang Li seemed quieter than usual, and she was sure his silence reflected her own thoughts of parting, perhaps forever, from her new found friends.

With a mixture of sadness and disquiet, Lizzie was transported to the smaller landing stages on Suzhou Creek where she was safely entrusted into the hands of Mr Ward, her temporary companion. Mrs Bradshaw did not remain with her for long and soon, in the red twilight, the steam-powered launch began pulling a long string of smaller vessels from the creek to begin the hundred and fifty mile journey to Hangchow. Lizzie watched Mrs Bradshaw's figure grow smaller in the fading light, just as the sound of exploding firecrackers and crashing gongs diminished too. By now Lizzie was growing accustomed to the frenzy and noise that always accompanied any large activity in China, as if it was a duty to fill the air with a cacophony of sound.

As night descended, Lizzie found herself standing on the deck of the moving launch with Mr Ward, who seemed a quiet man and not at all forthcoming. She felt ill at ease and considered going to bed early in the small cramped compartment provided for her, but did not want to appear rude. The smell of burning incense wafted through the air. 'Heathens,' Mr Ward murmured half to himself, as they watched a man in the boat behind them kowtowing to an idol illuminated by candles in a small shrine. The man carefully lit an opium lamp and slowly passed into his Elysium before their eyes, whilst his family settled down into their quilts and slept soundly.

'I think I should retire too,' Lizzie remarked as they watched similar rituals taking place about them. She drew her shawl closer and thought how dull Mr Ward was, perhaps he too wanted to retire but was afraid of offending her? She waited a while longer, the air becoming increasingly cool over the dark, evil looking water of the river, and made that her excuse for going to her compartment. Mr Ward also seemed relieved to leave the deck and after telling her to send for him if she had any problems, bade her a good night.

Making her way towards what passed as her cabin, instead of undressing in the cold she decided to remain fully clothed, and huddled gratefully beneath the wadded quilt Mrs Bradshaw had insisted she take with her. A simple canvas sheet was all that separated her from the crew who were by now almost out of their minds with opium, but it at least gave a form of privacy. She had endured the cramped sleeping conditions on the long voyage from England, so it was no hardship to make do now for the couple of nights they would be on board. Almost hourly Lizzie woke: aching from stiffness and cold until eventually, with sunrise, she was glad to get up and rub her weary limbs. After a bowl of rice tasting like nothing she'd ever eaten before, she watched the passing countryside which was flat but beautiful in its lushness. Here and there a village, sometimes a temple, appeared and went; the chaotic river traffic miraculously missing each other as they wended their way heavily laden with rice, silk, vegetables and other commodities. She chatted on and off with Mr Ward, who appeared more relaxed, shy even, but his comments about China were sound and his explanations of their surroundings more than interesting.

The day passed quickly as they steamed through village after village, under high-arched picturesque bridges and beneath the overhanging balconies of the small huddled houses lining the canals.

After a second uncomfortable night the steam launch cast off its string of smaller boats and drew into a smaller canal, from which they were raised by the use of a lift into a wide water-street that led towards Hangchow. By this time, the slightly grey-haired Mr Ward was gradually becoming more confidential. He told Lizzie of the twenty years he'd spent working for the Diplomatic Service in China, and of his many frustrations in dealing with the never-ending problems of the settlements, many being engineered by the sly and devious Mandarins. She began to feel sorry for him and hoped she would not be bowed down with as many problems if she remained in China for the same length of time.

Mr Ward was instrumental in informing Lizzie of many more interesting facts during their last day together, for which she was grateful. 'You'll find Hangchow a great centre for silk,' he told her when she remarked on the abundance of certain trees. 'Those are Mulberry trees upon which the silk worm feeds, they are planted on every available spot of land.'

'I love the feel of silk,' she confided to him in a childlike way. 'It's very soothing—almost healing in its touch.'

'Some of the finest, most beautiful silk goods are produced in Hangchow, and in summer the streets are ablaze with coloured silk.' His voice sounded soft and far away and Lizzie looked closely at his bent head as they looked down on a passing sampan. He was not as tall as Lizzie and of slighter build; not handsome, but with pleasant intelligent features, and she wondered what secrets lay beneath his air of propriety. He looked wistfully ahead and straightened to his full height. 'My wife liked silk,' he said, 'but she died many years ago of dysentery. This is a dreadful climate in summer, the heat breeds mosquitoes by the million.' There was no bitterness in his voice, only a resignation from which his reserve probably stemmed.

'I have been warned,' Lizzie replied, not wanting to encroach on his personal tragedy. 'I just hope I can adapt to the way of life.'

'One tip, keep your cupboard doors ajar to let the air get to your clothing, or they'll go green with mould,' he advised. 'Even leather shoes go green.'

'Why do you stay?' Lizzie asked bluntly.

'Why does anyone?' he replied, a smile flickering across his face. 'To tell the truth half of us don't know the reason. Here though, I'm financially better off working for the British Government. I have no family in England and my wife is buried in China, also I do hate the London fog. There is nothing to go back for. As for other people, the motive is either profit or zeal, the latter is admirable if sometimes misplaced.'

Lizzie enjoyed the unexpected confidences and his openness, as it reminded her very much of her relationship with her stepfather and Peter, both of whom had always treated her as an equal. Many times in the past she had been thought stand-offish through her reluctance to speak more than a few words with men who were strangers, but she'd been so because they expected a woman to show no interest in politics or matters of substance. She was not comfortable when talking of trivial things was all that was required.

The emotion in his outburst seemed to release Mr Ward from his earlier restraint, and Lizzie began to enjoy his company more. 'I suppose China is a challenge, as well as a place which needs help,' she said sombrely.

'Is that what brings you here?' he asked, as if doubting her. 'I sense somehow that you have a different temperament to the usual missionary.'

Such frankness flustered Lizzie who was relieved to have an approaching high bridge to study, so she delayed giving an immediate answer, yet he obviously expected one for he was watching her closely. 'I needed a challenge, besides I am a nurse first and a Missionary second. I too came to get away from the fog!' She smiled at him, hoping the small joke would satisfy him.

'Just as long as you're not another woman running away from reality,' he rejoined, hoping he hadn't over stepped the mark by giving his opinion so freely.

His reply stunned Lizzie even further. He was almost a stranger yet obviously astute and wise. Did he suspect she had other motives for coming? 'I don't think so,' she answered with more honesty than intended, her tone almost subdued.

'Which means that you probably are,' was all he said, before pointing to an over-laden vessel in an effort to ease her discomfort. Lizzie couldn't bring herself to speak again for fear she would confess all to the stranger by her side.

'Well,' he said finally, 'I wish you well in your endeavours. If you ever need a friend in China to confide in remember I do come to Hangchow regularly. I'll leave you my address and if I can be of help just write to me at the Consulate in Shanghai. It's good to have someone other than colleagues to talk to, the Missions can be a little claustrophobic at times and it doesn't always pay to reveal too much of oneself. It's a great temptation to do so when you're isolated and away from family and friends.' There was no doubting the sincerity in his voice or the kindness behind his offer, and Lizzie found herself warming to the man. She thanked him for his concern and put his address in her purse, but doubted that there would ever be a need to use it.

Conversation from that point became less personal, though equally companionable, as Lizzie drew repeatedly on his knowledge about everything new they passed. Mr Ward was quite willing to assist and became quite attentive, having once lowered his reserve. It was therefore, a disappointment to Lizzie when they approached a highly decorated bridge ahead of them, and he indicated that their journey was nearly over. 'Don't forget,' he insisted before they disembarked, 'if you need a friend or help, let me know. Good luck and God speed.'

'Thank you for your patience and companionship, you've been very kind,' Lizzie replied, a little reluctant to part with yet another new friend. For many years solitude had been her solace but here, miles from home, she was becoming painfully aware of her vulnerability as new acquaintances came and went like ships in the night. Her sadness at parting from Mr Ward deepened as he waved good-bye after leaving her in the care of yet another stranger, one of the Missions staff.

With his charge in safe hands, Leonard Ward, who had little luggage of his own, walked off briskly hoping to procure one of the waiting chairs. Once installed in the contraption he sat back allowing the bearers to run with their usual efficiency, whilst he watched for any unusual or unexpected changes since his last visit. There was no hostility in the crowded street that he could sense and things appeared to have settled down over the past few months. He knew, however, that beneath the surface lay discontent and unrest amongst the citizens of China against foreigners, particularly the French and Japanese.

During the twenty years he'd been here he'd come to sympathise with the ordinary Chinese whose Imperial rulers were constantly humiliated by greedy foreigners, all fighting to gain territory by treaties not always in China's best interest. He lamented on the mentality of the Manchu Court, living in isolation within the Forbidden City in Peking, totally ignorant of the needs of its people outside. The Imperial Family had no policy and was inconsistent in its behaviour, so that its Court was riddled with suspicion and fear. If he was Chinese and a young man he would probably be just as indignant and resentful of much that took place in his country. In short, he felt that China's progress was hampered by conflicting traditions and customs, as well as the shortage of competent, honest men. These days Len tried to make amends for his own country's failures by acting the mediator.

He thought then about the journey he'd just made and of the young woman he'd met who seemed intent on changing the world. He'd seen so many just like her arrive; some to stay, some to leave, and many to die—like his Mary. He sighed deeply, wondering why this one was strangely different. His intuition went deeper this time, and he was sure she was no dried out spinster, she was still in her prime but below the facade there existed a troubled soul. In spite of what ailed her she was able to converse unselfconsciously with him as an equal, without vanity or coquetry. He wished her well! Then, as always when disturbed, he turned his concentration to the work in hand. He liked Hangchow, considering it to be one of the finest Chinese cities he'd seen in his travels through the Middle Kingdom, despite the still visible damage caused by the Taiping troops during the rebellion years before. This was the real China; Shanghai was not. One day, Hangchow could become a vital port serving the foreign settlements; it would of course take much work and coercion for it to happen and he hoped his influence with the merchants and Mandarins would help pave the way for such an opening.

Lizzie followed the man sent to collect her and was allotted a chair but one that was closed as befitted a woman. This was a disappointment for she could see little of her surroundings, although she could smell the sordid waterfront through which they passed to reach the towering city wall which she could just see through the gap above the bamboo door.

At the city gates the chair passed through the wall via a tunnel at least twenty feet long, before emerging at the other end into the noisy, crowded and bustling city. Within the confines of the chair the clatter outside was sometimes deafening, a little frightening even, yet she longed to be out there mingling with the people.

The hospital lay behind its own wall within the city and it was here that Lizzie met the much respected Dr Main and the staff with whom she was to work. Medical problems were never dull and it was a joy to be associated with dedicated people; this was why she had come to China, and not primarily to convert the Chinese to Christianity. To divert them from superstitious ways yes, the rest she cared little for, though she kept such thoughts to herself. As time went by she found she could cope with the disfigured lepers and the ordinary sick or infirm, but with patients suffering from self-inflicted wounds she could not. She was appalled by the results of tightly bound feet and was almost physically sick each time she had to see them uncovered, withered and infected. How could any parent break and mutilate their daughter's feet, binding them almost double, thus ensuring a life of pain in the name of vanity and a guarantee that a girl would marry? How could any man want a woman to be so crippled for his gratification, such that she had to be constantly carried about? Once bent in this fashion, the feet took on the shape of a lotus flower, but over the years they would suppurate and stink, the leg flesh above the bindings would literally hang in folds over the ankles. It made Lizzie angry, not at the victim, but the madness behind the deed. It wasn't the peasant class that did it, for they needed their daughters to do manual work: neither was it the Manchu leaders, but the middle-class who should have known better. Lizzie was also upset and frustrated by the news of suicides, not by the depressed or love sick, but by those seeking revenge in the belief that by suicide the spirits of the dead would haunt and injure their aggressors. It was after one such incident, when a woman had thrown herself down a well to annoy her husband, that Lizzie sat in the garden, emotionally distraught. For some reason or other this well happened to be empty, leaving the woman with horrendous injuries but still alive. This act had a profound effect on Lizzie who sat grieving, trying to understand it all.

It was at this moment that Leonard Ward chose to visit Lizzie who, because of her distressed state of mind, did not immediately realise he was there.

'Good afternoon, Miss Hardy,' he said respectfully. Lizzie looked up and in her surprise, forgot her woes. 'Remember me?' he asked.

Lizzie hesitated only for a moment to compose herself and collect her thoughts, 'Why, yes of course, Mr Ward,' she replied. 'You must forgive me, I was miles away.'

He seemed younger than before, the summer sun had tanned his face and lightened the colour of his hair. 'How nice to see you,' she said, 'I have often wondered how you were.'

'I'm well,' he replied, 'as I hope you are.' Lizzie smiled warmly, which pleased him. 'There was a letter for you which arrived via the Consul and as I was coming to Hangchow, I thought it a good opportunity to call and see how things were progressing.' There was a shyness about his manner which previously she may have mistaken for dullness, and his eyes were gentle and enquiring.

'How very kind of you to bother,' Lizzie instinctively replied as she took the letter. It was from Peter! 'I'll open it later, when I have time to read it.'

'Would you like me to go so that you can do so now?' he asked. 'I thought it might be important.'

Lizzie shook her head. 'No, the writer is obviously alive, that is the most significant thing. Would you like some tea?' she asked, inviting him to sit on the bench beside her. He looked very hot and a little tired. 'Have you just arrived in Hangchow?' she asked.

'I came yesterday but couldn't call earlier as I had several other visits to make. I don't think the letter would have arrived any quicker by the normal route.' He was very apologetic and Lizzie realised that the letter had given him an excuse to call. 'And yes, if you don't mind I will have that tea.' He dabbed the perspiration from his brow. 'Do you mind if I remove my jacket?' he asked, as she rose to her feet.

'Please do, the heat is almost unbearable today, is it not.' Lizzie hastened away, leaving Mr Ward fanning himself with his hat. On returning she informed him that someone would bring tea shortly.

'I must admit I will enjoy the drink when it arrives, but tell me, how are you finding life in Hangchow?'

'The work is hard, the heat gets me down sometimes, but at least it's free from fog here!' She said the latter with a wry smile.

He beamed at her. 'Good, I see your spirit has not left you. Yet when I arrived I observed you studying the garden with some intensity.'

'Aren't the flowers beautiful, the perfume is almost heady,' she replied, unable to explain her true feelings. Fortunately at this point Lizzie heard the soft patter of feet on the path and turned her head. 'Ah, here comes tea!' she exclaimed as a young woman, pretty in her bright silk tunic arrived with a tray. Mr Ward thanked the woman in Chinese, as Lizzie attended to their needs. When they finished the refreshment he made to put his jacket on as if to go.

'Please,' Lizzie said, 'don't put it on on my account. I come from a farm in the country and am quite used to a less formal life.'

At this Mr Ward paused. 'I sensed that you were different,' he said, 'I find it much easier to converse with you than so many other ladies. Where do you hale from?'

'On the border between Yorkshire and Derbyshire, though I was born in Sheffield. From the age of six I lived in a very wild and beautiful place, but I left for London nine years ago. My father and his wife still run our farm there. Where do you come from?'

'The West Country, Bristol. It must be twenty years since I left and I've never been back.'

'Did you find it hard to settle here when first you came?' Lizzie asked. It was a simple question but one into which he read more than she knew.

Suspecting that Lizzie might be in need of some reassurance, Mr Ward was cautious in his reply. 'Well, I had my wife with me in the beginning and it is so much easier when you can share your hardships and doubts with another. Being alone unfortunately does sometimes allow one to dwell too much on problems. By the time Mary died I had grown to like it here and didn't feel that I could readjust to life in England on my own.'

Sadly he was right. In all her adult life, Lizzie had concealed her fears and feelings because she'd had to; now it was too late. 'You're a very wise man,' Lizzie said, praising him, and she sighed deeply. If only there had been a Mr Ward at the time of Nathan's death, her life could have been so different. She saw that he was slightly embarrassed by her praise and tried to make light of it. 'It's the strange beliefs here that disturb me, I find there is no logic in their harmful thinking.'

He smiled patiently. 'You will find it gets easier as time passes. The Chinese are a likeable race, it is such a pity that they are at the mercy of so many bad influences. Don't lose heart, remember the fog back home!'

She laughed gently. There was no guile in him and Lizzie found herself warming to his kindness. Perhaps he too was lonely and needed someone to talk to, other than his colleagues who had their own affairs at heart. 'I feel better already,' she assured him. 'Your visit has done me good!'

He drank more tea then looked at his watch with dismay. 'My goodness, I've taken up so much of you time,' he said, 'and I too have work to do. Please don't forget, if you need help or advice you have my card,' and he rose to leave.

'Yes,' Lizzie replied, 'I have it safe, and I am most grateful for your delivery of the letter.'

'I couldn't help but notice that it comes from the Sudan, obviously from someone in the Army. Do you have someone there to whom you are very close?'

She had almost forgotten Peter's letter in her pocket. 'A cousin, to whom I write telling him of my encounters here,' she replied. 'He hasn't written for some months but he must be alright.' She touched her pocket, 'I was anxious for his safety.'

'It must have been quite a worry for you, especially when General Gordon was assassinated in January. He was greatly admired here by the Chinese, you know.'

'I had heard of Chinese Gordon, but not the details. I'm told that many here were very shocked when the news filtered through and I've heard a few garbled accounts of his deeds. Do you know the facts?'

Mr Ward sat down again as if forgetting his urgent business. 'Twenty years ago he helped rid this country of what had become a mob of rampaging vandals who, had they stuck to their original ideals might have been good for China. Instead they ravaged the land and left millions in desperate plight. You can see how much damage still remains in Hangchow after twenty years, all caused by the Taiping Rebels.' He was quite animated in his narrative, and Lizzie was touched by the strength of his feelings. 'General Gordon's death was a blow to us all,' he concluded.

'You speak as if you knew him,' Lizzie said with sympathy.

'I met him many years ago and admired him, but he could be a man of contrasts. He was a devout Christian, very temperamental and given to bouts of righteous rage. However, his heart was in the right place, though I think in the end, his judgement failed him.'

'I must tell my cousin of your visit and that you had actually met Gordon. He will be interested.'

'Oh dear, I hope I haven't bored you,' he muttered apologetically, 'and I have taken up so much of your time.' He stood up, took her hand and shook it gently. 'Forgive an older man's ramblings.'

He turned to leave. 'Thank you for coming,' Lizzie said, and touched his arm with her hand. 'Our conversations remind me so much of those I used to have with my father and cousin. That's how I learned so much about the world from being a child. Please do call again if you can spare the time!' The invitation was spontaneous and modestly given, and he could see by her demeanour that his support was genuinely appreciated.

'I'll call whenever I can,' he replied, as she opened the gate in the hospital wall to let him out. 'Enjoy your work, it is always easier if you like what you are doing!'

'I think I will be happier now,' she replied, smiling, and closed the gate after him.

Pleased that his visit had given Lizzie some comfort, Leonard Ward chose to walk to the business premises of one of the many city merchants who had been complaining to him of late. Normally in this heat he would have taken a chair, but as none were available he made his own way. He felt no danger in this part of the city, but even so ensured that he kept to very public places where he could see and be seen. He pondered on his visit to the hospital, and knew it was really no business of his how Lizzie fared; but he felt drawn to her, and therefore wanted to keep a fatherly eye on the situation. The visit cost him nothing, yet in return it gave him an added bonus when coming to Hangchow.

That Mr Ward had taken the trouble to seek her out was a comfort in itself to Lizzie, who retraced her steps to the garden bench intending to take the tea things inside, but the girl had already removed them. Lizzie was reluctant to open Peter's letter as her several letters to him had produced no response, so now she didn't know what to expect, or think. After his declaration of affection in London she'd feared receiving similar affirmations as a result, and hoped that she'd not led him to expect too much in return. She had deliberately written her letters in the form of a daily journal, both to support him and as a way of sublimating her inner fears. The fact that she had always loved him was overshadowed by the circumstances of Nathan's death, and she hoped by writing in such a fashion he would tire of her.

There were several possibilities as to why he hadn't written earlier: one, that he regretted his declaration; two, that his letters were delayed or lost; and finally, that he was dead. Presumably the latter was not now the case. Her hands trembled as she fingered the envelope. At least he was alive and well enough to write in the distinctive style he'd always used when writing to Edward. She was, by now, long overdue for her duty at the opium retreat and with this in mind, she returned the letter to her pocket and went indoors. She would open it in the privacy of her room later, where she need not be afraid to show her feelings.

After Peter had sailed from England it was some time before Lizzie's first communication reached him. He was not dismayed, for he knew that their diverging lives made contact difficult and he was after all in transit with his regiment, relying on Army post. When, eventually, letters did arrive they did so in batches, and he began to depend heavily on the distraction they brought. Due to the pressure and stress the expeditionary force was under to reach

Khartoum quickly to relieve Gordon, he and the men were weary, edgy and insecure, and in no mood for writing romantic letters home. Peter found it difficult, from the tone of Lizzie's letters, to understand precisely what he was supposed to think? They were not the personal, loving letters which he'd hoped to receive, and he now wished that his declaration of love for her had been made earlier, so that Lizzie would have known his true feelings for her. He could almost see her sitting at some table or other trying hard to please him, to inspire and entertain him, but in doing so there were no expressions of love. In believing now that he had rushed her, he could also see that her experiences in China were changing her, and this bothered and bewildered him.

The Sudan expedition was very different to Peter's previous postings, first in Africa against the Ashanti, memories of which were still unpleasant, then latterly in India where half the time soldiers were simply acting as peacekeepers. Britain's aggressive involvement in many other areas of the world was beginning to bother him; the constant acquisition of foreign lands, or the making of treaties to ensure a constant supply of raw materials always ended in conflict or betrayal. In South Africa, Afghanistan, Burma, India, Egypt, and even China, it was always the same. Now there was a scramble going on between European nations for African lands, and he wanted no part in it. He could hear his Uncle Edward's voice in his mind, saying, 'I warned you of this years ago,' but perhaps such wisdom only came with age. He thought of the farm and of Lizzie's good news that Clara had given birth to a son: a reward Edward so richly deserved.

If he couldn't write to Lizzie of love, what should he write about? Without the sure knowledge of her feelings there was only boredom, heat and the occasional skirmish to describe, and at this low ebb he simply did nothing. In his mind he wrote reams of letters to her; in reality he failed to put pen to paper. Had she written saying that she found China unacceptable, too dirty, too hot, too…anything that would cause her to return to England, it would have been different. He should have known Lizzie better. She was a good writer and much that she wrote was amusing, her descriptions were clear and he could almost see the places she wrote about, but to his regret she never mentioned their last meeting or gave a hint of any future together. He began to understand her moods, her frustrations and where her values lay. Was he even worthy of her, he wondered?

He had to get back to England and sort out his future, as unless he did there was nothing to tempt Lizzie to his side. He needed her as he'd never needed anything before, therefore he had to prove that any sacrifice she made allowing them to be together was worth it. None of these thoughts did he communicate to Lizzie, yet she continued to write to him despite his long silence.

Finally, after several months, he wrote. It was a difficult, clumsy letter in which he could not fully explain his tardiness, and it was this letter that now lay in Lizzie's pocket.

With mixed feelings, a tired Lizzie finally opened the letter in the quiet of her room and read by the light of an oil lamp.

Khartoum
May 1885

My dear Lizzie,

How can I thank you enough for the long and interesting letters which have kept me going these past months. As you can see, I did not succumb during the march on Khartoum, but you will have heard the bad news that we were too late. Our steamers got to the junction of the White and Blue Niles behind schedule, and only two days short of relieving the city which was under siege. So the Mahdis army was able to assault the place and capture it: Gordon was killed almost immediately and we lost Khartoum. He should have evacuated the place earlier, though I despair at the decisions made in London sometimes and the inept way they are carried out. All this dithering annoys and depresses me. Now there's a crisis developing in India with the Russians attempt at expansion in Afghanistan, and I do not want to return there: I am sick of war, waste and death.

But enough of this gloominess. I was delighted to hear that Clara has produced a male child, surely there is no reason now why you cannot marry me—is there?

Lizzie, I am just no good at writing personal letters to a female. In truth I don't know of anything in The Sudan worth telling you about and as this missive may take weeks to reach you, the news will then be old. I do hope you will continue to write to me, the contents of your letters are of great interest. I do fear, however, that you will get to prefer China to England if you stay too long.

It is with deep sincerity that I hope you are well and in greater heart than I. What am I to hope for? You give me no indication either way. Did I overstep the mark in the hospital library that day?

Whatever you do, please don't stop writing.

Your devoted,

Peter

A tear ran down Lizzie's cheeks. The letter was obviously written when he was at a low ebb and feeling insecure about his future. She knew that she was partly to blame: she'd deliberately curbed her own feelings, not wanting to give him false hope where there was none. His face came to her for a moment—clear, bright and, as usual, full of life. This caused her sadness to deepen, yet she could not pick up a pen and write the words which she knew would mean so much to him.

Another month passed in which the summer heat nearly exhausted her. She worked on in spite of the flies and the heat and still came to the conclusion that she was happier in China than she'd ever been in London. Peter was right, she would not return to England unless forced to. He had not written again and she acknowledged the fact that she may have deliberately allowed her only chance of marrying to pass by. Nevertheless she continued writing to him and fell into habits of childhood, teasing him but never once answering his question. She couldn't even be sure if he was still in the Sudan, and trusted that the Army would forward her letters to his new location.

Summer was drawing to a close, and the later part of September showed signs of becoming idyllic. An inner calm came to Lizzie and that, combined with the healthy colour she'd acquired, gave her an extremely attractive appearance, so that when Mr Ward again called unexpectedly he was delighted by what he saw.

'You do look well!' he said, as Lizzie's eyes lit up at his approach. 'I need not have worried about you.'

Lizzie laughed pleasantly. 'Was I so gloomy when last you came?' she asked, leading him towards the garden.

He responded with a warm smile. 'I was afraid that China would wear you down as it has done many others. You seemed more than a little lost last time. However, I am delighted to see that you have acclimatised well.'

'It may surprise you to know,' Lizzie responded, 'that your kindness and advice has helped more than you can imagine.' She paused for breath, being a little overcome by his unexpected arrival. 'I'm so pleased to see you—how are you?'

He nodded. 'Better now that most of the heat of summer is past. However, I'm afraid you may be disappointed in my visit because I have no post for you.'

'Don't worry,' Lizzie assured him. 'Now that I am settled here, my letters come directly with other correspondence for the Mission. Not that I get many, an occasional one from my father who is very busy with his new offspring, and one came from the Doctor and his wife with whom I lived in London.'

'And the young man in the Sudan?'

'Not a one! He is tardy in replying, but then perhaps a soldier has better things to do. I write regularly to keep his spirits up but I'm afraid my ramblings bore him.'

'I'm sure that's not true,' he rebuked, sensing her disquiet. 'If he doesn't reply then he's very remiss after the efforts you make on his behalf. Still, I do hope you don't mind my calling again.'

Lizzie was far from disappointed to see him. 'No, no! You are really most welcome, though I have little to give in return for your trouble.'

He shook his head. 'You are a good listener and I'm flattered to have someone so young show an interest in my experiences. I like travelling but it can be a lonely thing. Now I have an added incentive when coming to Hangchow.' He seemed a little flustered by his own enthusiasm, and this caused her to blush. 'Oh, dear,' he sighed, 'have I embarrassed you?'

'No, but I'm happy to think that you will call whenever you come to the city,' Lizzie quickly reassured him. She got the impression he was regretting being so forthright in case he had exposed himself to ridicule. 'However,' she said in a subdued voice, 'I may be sent to Hankow soon.'

· Leonard Ward's face fell at this news; such an occurrence was always a possibility but he hadn't expected it to happen so soon. 'When?' he asked lamely.

'There is talk of extending the hospital there and more help will be needed, but I may have to go before then.'

'It's a horrible place,' he stated bluntly. 'Malaria is rife, it is extremely hot in summer, things go mouldy—I hate the thought of you going so far inland.'

Lizzie was taken aback at the intensity of his feelings. 'I'm strong,' she replied, 'with quinine I should be alright, and I am adjusting to the heat. Have you stayed in Hankow yourself?'

His face paled. 'My wife died there,' he said simply. 'We had been in China five years when suddenly my world collapsed.' He was in some distress by his admission and Lizzie felt moved with compassion for him.

'I'm truly sorry,' she said kindly. 'Would you like to talk about her, or shall I leave you in peace for a while?'

Shaking his head he looked at Lizzie. 'What a kind thing to say,' he said, 'but over the years I have grown accustomed to what happened. Now though, the thought of you also going there has re-kindled my fears.' His earnest grey eyes searched her face, 'And I shall have lost my incentive to come to Hangchow.'

'You do me a great kindness by coming to visit,' Lizzie replied, 'and I have reciprocated by causing you pain, for that I am sorry.'

Realising that he was in danger of spoiling the real reason for his visit Leonard Ward sought to ease Lizzie's discomfort. 'True friendship is bound together with pain as well as laughter,' he offered, 'isn't it true that something shared seems halved?' His face softened as he regained control of his feelings. 'Anyway, I'm afraid I have to go,' he said, to Lizzie's disappointment. 'This was simply a quick visit as I'm here to stay for a couple of days, but I wondered if you would like to accompany me on a sightseeing trip. Do you think you could be spared tomorrow, or the day after—that is if you would like to come?'

Within the space of two minutes Lizzie had unexpectedly experienced several changes of emotion, leaving her both bewildered and slightly light-headed. She was constantly being surprised by Mr Ward, she looked at him with child-like eyes. 'What a wonderful idea,' she cried happily, 'I'm sure the hospital will allow it as I never take time off.'

'In that case, I would advise you to wear oriental clothing,' he suggested. 'Not bright flamboyant silk which will draw attention to you, but something simple in cotton. No fancy hat either, and strong slippers—I think you may find someone will have what you need within the Mission. You see it is essential to blend in and not appear unseemly, otherwise complaints will be made against the Mission.'

When Lizzie asked to be allowed to take time off she was advised that a day's notice would be more reasonable, so Mr Ward had to be content to wait a little longer to see her again. To date she had only walked the paved main streets of Hangchow in the company of a Chinese Bible woman, and had been enthralled by what she'd seen. Displays of rich, elaborately embroidered coloured silks hung everywhere, red banners were suspended above shops, and all manner of goods lay on open display, from fans to choice teas. The streets were remarkably clean, noisy and busy, and she was quite happy standing aside to make way for richly dressed Mandarins in coloured robes as they passed by in their chairs. To go beyond the city walls was a prospect that had Lizzie in a state of heady anticipation.

Having borrowed a plain tunic, trousers and a straw hat from a colleague, Lizzie felt shy as she stood before her mirror. She giggled at the image reflected there and fervently hoped Mr Ward would approve. She waited nervously for his arrival and was surprised to see that he too was dressed in a loose fitting jacket and trousers, which, although blending in did not disguise the fact that he was a European, because of his build.

He looked approvingly at her when they met at the entrance to the main hospital. 'I thought we would go to Si Hu,' he announced. 'It is a beautiful lake and, even if you have already been, there is much to see. What do you think?' He was carrying a canvas bag and a small basket which she later found contained sufficient food and drink to last them all day.

'I haven't been beyond the city walls since I arrived,' Lizzie told him, 'it sounds delightful.'

'I have two chairs waiting,' he said, protectively taking her by the arm and leading her outside. 'I'll be behind all the time,' he reassured her, before climbing into the second vehicle and giving instructions to the runners.

Hers was a closed lady's chair, again preventing her from seeing much without craning her neck, and this was difficult as the contraption swayed to the runners' movements. The outing was all the better for being unexpected, but she would have liked to have seen more of where she was going. Eventually the massive gates of the Western Gateway appeared on her limited horizon and, once through them, because the road descended, she could just see the lake and wooded hills beyond. It didn't take long for them to reach the water's edge which shimmered in the morning sun, yet they did not dismount.

Mr Ward's chair drew alongside Lizzie's, 'Are you alright?' he called, 'it's a bit shaky, I know! If you don't mind I'd like to go on across the causeway to the island.'

'Are we allowed?' Lizzie called back as she peered over the top of the door. 'We won't annoy some Mandarin, will we?'

'I have obtained a pass and as long as we behave no one will object.' Instructing the bearers to proceed once more he sat back out of view.

From within the confines of the chair, Lizzie could see the clear blue sky and a half-concealed pagoda amongst the trees, she wished Mr Ward would halt for a while to answer her many questions.

Once across the causeway the chair came to a sudden halt and she was relieved when he came and handed her down before dismissing the bearers, telling them to come to the city end of the causeway later in the afternoon to collect them. 'We'll have to walk back, I'm afraid,' he said. 'I hope I'm not expecting too much of you?'

'If you saw the rugged paths and steep hills back at the farm you would have no fears,' she replied to the challenge. 'I've walked and ridden all my life.'

'It sounds a wonderful place.'

She looked around, taking in the fresh sweet smell of the lake and allowing the breeze to gently caress her face after the warm confines of the chair. 'It was,' she said abruptly. Then, seeing his reaction she softened her tone, 'But I have so many questions to ask about this area that I prefer to forget about the past if you don't mind.'

In spite of Lizzie's enthusiasm to learn more about her surroundings and her comment, her companion still wanted to know more about her past. Something obviously disturbed her deeply but he tactfully let the matter drop, hoping that one day she would confide in him. For the moment, however, he was quite content to enjoy himself and to see her happy.

All around them the forested hills and ornate pavilions appeared to stand as if in another world and it was hard for Lizzie to conceive that amongst such beauty, heathen beliefs existed. She was spellbound and could almost understand why this ancient land stood still, not wanting to change. The good in its culture was wonderful; the bad was beyond her.

Seeing her bewilderment, Leonard said, 'It is in this kind of place where myths and folklore begin. Today I am happy to let those legends inspire me.' He turned to look back at the city across the lake, perched high on a hill. 'Reality is for tomorrow.'

Standing there beside him, she was glad she had persevered that first night on the steamer to draw him out, for he was quickly becoming the source of all her enjoyment. Their friendship had expanded in response to that encouragement.

'There is another much longer causeway further along the lake,' he explained, unaware of her thoughts. 'This causes an inner lake, man-made I understand, to stop flooding. It's the home of a hot-tempered dragon.' He looked at her attentive face and expectant eyes, and smiled, 'I suppose you want to know why he lives there?'

She nodded playfully, 'I suppose there is some story of a lost love or some such tale.'

'No!' he teased. 'Nothing quite so romantic.' Lizzie feigned disappointment. 'It's quite simple. The tidal bore from the river Ch'ien T'ang can be twenty feet high, and when it roars down it sounds like an angry dragon. Without that noise I suppose he would be a peaceful dragon. All lakes, rivers and clouds in China have dragons as inhabitants, didn't you know?'

'You do love China, don't you?' Lizzie commented, hearing the fondness in his voice as they walked by the lake. 'Do you think we should leave the Chinese alone in their ignorance?' she asked.

He frowned. 'No, not entirely. The whole world is changing around them, getting smaller, and if they don't adapt to some aspects of our ways, they will eventually be worse off. It is already too late to stop the clock or attempt to turn it back. It's sad isn't it, but there is also much wrong with China's obsession with the past.'

So much of Mr Ward's explanations made sense, and Lizzie realised how much, over the years, she'd missed the lengthy discussions she'd once had with her father and Peter when he'd come to visit.

They had walked for some time, chatting, admiring, discussing the many facets of life, when he suggested they sat on the rocks by the lakeside for a while. As they'd walked round the island the scenery had changed; now they faced a thickly wooded hillside. 'It's so peaceful, balm for the soul even, don't you think?' he asked, pleased to see Lizzie relaxing more as they talked.

'I had never thought to feel such peace again,' Lizzie confessed, as she admired the lily pads floating gracefully on the surface of the lake. She didn't realise that she'd spoken her innermost thoughts out loud, nor how momentous her admission could be.

Mr Ward didn't pry, he simply accepted that below the surface a great weight was spoiling things for her. He let her stare out over the water, deep in thought, and was helpless to ease her burden. They sat for some time in quiet companionship, delaying the moment when, inevitably, they would have to leave. Nor were they entirely alone, all sorts of people passed by, some curious, others unaware of the two foreigners sitting amongst them. He had of course been right to insist on dressing as they had, for it gave some privacy and safety.

'Do you come to the lake very often?' Lizzie asked quietly, loath to disturb the moment.

'Not often. I look out over the lake from a part of the city wall sometimes, but when alone there is nothing to encourage me down here; beauty is often poignant when you have no-one with whom to share it. You say you can give me nothing in return for my interest in your welfare—this is what you give. The opportunity to share a thought or two, and to enjoy the tranquillity of the lake in congenial company is reward enough.'

He had an almost poetic turn of phrase sometimes, which in the gentle ambience of the lake-shore, made Lizzie do something unexpected. She leaned over and gently touched his hand. 'I'm pleased at that,' she said, and removed her hand without realising what she'd done.

Leonard knew why Lizzie had touched him so gently, was aware too that she'd done it without thinking, without motive, and it moved him deeply. 'If you're still here when I come again, perhaps we could explore more,' he suggested quietly. 'There is the wonderful Imperial Library here, to which, with luck, I may be able to obtain permission to take you. I've also been meaning to take a boat ride to the Island of Little Oceans where there are countless bays and inlets to see around the lake.' He was full of enthusiasm now. 'You might also like to visit the temples and the giant statues of the Gods of Wind and Thunder which guard the delta.'

'Have you been there?' Lizzie asked, eagerly.

'Once many years ago—it's well worth a visit.'

'How could I refuse such an offer,' she replied laughingly, watching as he extracted several packages from the basket he'd brought. She hadn't realised how hungry she was until that moment, and waited impatiently to see what he had to offer. 'How thoughtful of you,' she said, sipping the cold tea which he poured from a glass bottle. 'I never thought to bring anything to eat, how remiss of me.' Then her curiosity got the better of her. 'Where do you stay when you visit Hangchow, it never really struck me before? How did you manage to obtain a picnic?'

'I stay with a Chinese family, a retired merchant from Shanghai who has a small mansion here. There are many such merchants with homes, or small villas in the city. Hopefully, one day, Hangchow will become a treaty port open to the world and I come here to help pave the way. I also try to sort out any problems the merchants have with their export trade in Shanghai. It was Madame Ling who was kind enough to suggest I brought refreshments, otherwise it would not have entered my head.' With a smile he added, 'I am merely a humble man.'

'I think not,' Lizzie remonstrated. 'However, the meaning of humble is very different here, is it not?'

'Ah, you are learning fast,' Mr Ward replied with a broad grin. 'A man being humbled in China feels disgraced and, as you know, this can lead to ostracism or even suicide. I don't feel that humble!'

Lizzie laughed out loud, the merry sound ringing out across the water. Their lively banter went on for some time as they ate Madame Ling's kind offerings, and when they had eaten sufficiently he suggested they should stroll slowly back over the causeway towards the city shoreline. He pointed out many things of interest as they went, Lizzie was enthralled and began to dread the day ending. 'This has been a day I shall not forget,' she told him. 'When I despair at the idiosyncrasies of the people, I will remember the beauty here which inspires their legends—then I think I will see them more as children needing guidance.'

'A word of caution, Lizzie, they can be crafty too and extremely cruel if misguided.'

She sighed, 'I have noticed that, particularly when they want medication, or don't want to follow advice.'

They walked on, 'Did you know that from the wall of the city you can actually see the ocean?' he asked, as she paused to admire the peach trees overhanging the path.

'No I didn't. You are full of surprises, Mr Ward. I'm sure that but for you I would miss many wonderful aspects of China.'

'Next time I come, providing you are still here, the weather may not be good enough to come to the lake, but I could take you to the vantage point so that you can see the ocean for yourself.'

'I do hope I will still be here,' Lizzie lamented. 'If you could give me warning I would try to re-schedule my duties so as not to inconvenience anyone else. I must not neglect my work too frequently or people might think I am not dedicated enough.'

'I will write if I can, although I often don't know definitely until a couple of days beforehand.' He was so absorbed with ideas over what to show Lizzie next time he called, that he didn't notice that she was now quite subdued.

Contemplating his departure depressed Lizzie, as she knew that on her return to the hospital she would again be obliged to remain there, unless accompanied by an elderly Chinese female as an escort. She tried to remind herself that she was not here for light-hearted pleasure but to work, yet deep down the old Lizzie still lurked and, encouraged by the ease of Mr Ward's company, she was beginning to resent the restrictions.

As he turned to help her into the chair as it arrived, he caught sight of her face. 'What on earth is the matter?' he asked impulsively, then immediately regretted his haste.

'I'm having doubts about my dedication to the cause,' Lizzie admitted sadly. 'Today has been unforgettable, and now I must return to a form of isolation that I don't think I'm up to.'

Her companion was lost for words. Had he unintentionally and selfishly spoilt things for her? He looked back across the lake, aware that the mood had changed. 'I do apologise,' he muttered. 'Perhaps it was unwise of me to interfere when I know how constricting life can be for some within the Missions. I thought it would help.'

'No, No!' Lizzie protested, thinking that she may have forfeited any further chance of seeing him. 'It is I who should be sorry, after all you have done for me. I can't help it but I do feel sad: my heart is heavy and I don't understand why. I feel I no longer have the strength of my convictions, and ask myself, why am I here?' She was near to tears and the bearers were becoming curious.

'We must move,' he said. 'We are beginning to attract attention. Just remember that you are human, not a machine, and there is no disgrace in needing support.' Reluctantly he left her and climbed into his own chair, ordering the runners to take them to the hospital.

Swiftly they were carried through the enormous gateway into the town, the men hoping for a good tip as reward for their efforts. They were not disappointed for Leonard Ward was known to be generous if their work was well done.

Due to what had just transpired, Len was far from happy at leaving Lizzie immediately they arrived at the compound. There was so much that he wished to say to her, yet he didn't want to attract the attention of the others at the Mission: nor did he want to leave Lizzie in such a low state of mind. 'I'd better be going,' he said with some reluctance. 'I hope that today has helped you to see China from a different perspective.' He glanced round, knowing that several pairs of eyes might be watching, and lowered his voice to say, 'I'll write to you when I get to Madame Ling's. Dwelling too long on problems is no good to anyone but remember, I'm here to help if I can.' He looked directly into Lizzie's sombre eyes in an effort to impress on her his sympathy and concern for her plight.

Appreciating this, Lizzie nodded miserably and lowered her eyes to conceal the emptiness she felt. 'Thank you for a lovely day,' she replied, matching his caution, 'I have learned so much.'

He shook hands, gripping hers tightly as if in reassurance. 'Au revoir,' he said softly, before taking leave of her.

Fearing that she hadn't expressed her gratitude properly for his kindness, Lizzie called after him, 'Thank you for taking me!'

When he'd gone she returned to her small, tidy but sparse room. 'Oh dear,' she sighed, 'it is I who need help, as much as any Chinese.' She hadn't intended to speak out loud, but the words once uttered made her feel guilty. How could she have marred the end of such an enjoyable day by disturbing Mr Ward so? Just because one man had ruined her life, when many others had enhanced it; she owed it to the latter to continue with her work. She sighed again as she changed into her uniform, then returned to the wards determined to make an effort to dispel the gloom that had settled upon her.

When, weeks later, Peter received the letter written by Lizzie later that particular night, he sensed a change in her and realised that if he didn't act sooner rather than later, he could risk losing her completely. He cursed the time it took for the exchange of their letters, and wrote back immediately to inform her of his plans.

After their outing to the lake a letter arrived for Lizzie from Mr Ward. He thanked her for the pleasure she'd given him, and expressed his sorrow at having to leave her in a dispirited mood, for which he felt responsible. He repeated his concern over her feeling of isolation and encouraged her to spread wider her circle of friends within the Mission. He regretted that he would not be able to return for several weeks, but hoped that he would still be welcome when he did. The letter had obviously been written at Madame Ling's before he left for Shanghai. Lizzie replied via the Consulate service, assuring him that she was trying hard to fulfil her duties, that she very much appreciated his help and looked forward to him visiting her again when next he came.

Winter settled over Hangchow, bringing cold dark evenings in which Lizzie struggled by the light of the fire and her lantern to write to Peter. Whereas before she'd been able to describe what she'd seen and done, now the gloomy long evenings were reflected in her letters. She knew he would have seen and heard enough of sickness and inhumanity, yet there were so few entertaining incidents worth relating. Even the garden was bare of all leaves and flowers, in fact had she not taken the trip to the lake with Mr Ward, she might never have known of the beauty lying beyond the city walls.

Life and work went on, and occasionally, in the company of another nurse or with an old Chinese woman from the Mission as her escort, Lizzie went into the busy streets to shop. The winds often bit harshly into her, despite the heavily padded coat, so that there was little pleasure to be found in hurrying to-and-fro in search of respite from the cold.

Christmas came and went, and the small Christian community celebrated it in a modest way, although the steady daily queue of patients with their problems did not ease. With the English New Year over and winter still bitter and unforgiving, Lizzie huddled round her small stove each evening, remembering with nostalgia the roaring fires that would now be blazing back home at the farm in Bradfield. It wouldn't be long there before the hoarfrost and snow disappeared and the lambs fought their way bravely into the world. Her memories were sharp and deep. She felt much as the lapwing must have done, seeing the valley from above: an observer, yet of a different world. These thoughts stirred emotions in her which she thought were long since gone. But there was no going back, only a future of uncertainty lay ahead. She would just have to be content now, looking forward to feeling the warmth of the sun on her limbs, seeing the different greens of spring, then to smell the flowers of summer.

At this time, when Lizzie's despondency was acute, two letters arrived. With shaking hands she took them to her room, the familiar handwriting of each left no mystery as to the senders, though the contents excited her imagination equally. Would Mr Ward be keeping his promise to call again? Was Peter well and happy? Selfishly she opened Mr Ward's letter first in the hope that he might be coming to provide distraction from the humdrum of winter. She tore it open and saw in his usual polite and diplomatic style that he enquired after her health; commented on the weather and absence of fog;

looked forward to the prospect of spring, and the coming Chinese New Year. He went on, keeping the news of his intended visit until last. Providing the canal wasn't frozen he was hoping to travel to Hangchow shortly, and if it so pleased her he would take her to Madame Ling's house for tea. Lizzie gasped at his kindness, her eyes clouding with tears of relief and emotion. She closed her eyes, trying to imagine what Madame Ling would be like, and wondered what powers Mr Ward had, to enable him to do the things he did. She was indeed fortunate to have him as a friend, realising also that it was an honour to be invited into the home of a wealthy Chinese family—she would also now have the opportunity to wear the silk robe she'd bought in Shanghai!

Suddenly she felt quite guilty, for she'd almost forgotten her second letter. There was now a reluctance in Lizzie preventing her from thinking of Peter as anything more than a friend. However, due to her new understanding of life, her feeling was that what he didn't know about Nathan's death was less harmful to him than if he knew the truth. Now, she realised that Nathan fully deserved what had happened, and that she'd behaved foolishly to allow him, in death, to blight hers and Peter's lives. It was too late now to rectify many things, but it was still possible to bring about a semblance of order out of chaos.

That Peter's letter came directly from London pleased her, at least he was safely in England and out of harms way. She scanned the pages with mixed feelings, would there be news of a fresh posting to some other troubled spot in the world?

Much to her surprise, however, he announced his intention to resign his commission and possibly enter diplomatic service. She brightened at this news as she would no longer have to worry about him. Yes, he was well, he wrote, but he passed lightly over those matters of which previously he'd unburdened himself constantly, at her expense. She was perturbed however, when the tone of the letter became more personal and there were hints at his rescuing her from her fate. This was completely unexpected and sent her into a tizzy. There had seemed to be a cooling off of his ardour, or so she thought, which had made life easier because it asked little of her in return. Now, unfortunately, she could see that a challenge might lay ahead. She smiled to herself, two letters in one day! The spring in her step as she left her room to go to the dispensary did not pass unnoticed by Dr West with whom she was working that day.

A smile played on Lizzie's face as she worked and Dr West couldn't resist commenting on it. He knew life in the Mission and hospital wasn't easy, particularly in the bitter cold of winter, and often the hard work and disillusion could cause depression: he'd recently seen Lizzie slowly succumbing to both. 'How do you find your work here?' he asked, thus carefully edging his way towards the source of her up-lift in spirits.

Coming out of a reverie, Lizzie started. She looked directly at him and smiled. 'It's not quite what I expected,' she replied frankly, 'although I really didn't know what it would be like. So much more needs doing here than in England, but I'm beginning to understand a little of how the Chinese see things.'

'Understand, but not agree with their sentiments, I hope!' There was a smile on his face which invited an air of camaraderie which Lizzie enjoyed. 'You know, Miss Hardy, that smile on your lips brings a sparkle to your eyes. Have you a secret about which we are ignorant?'

Lizzie was amused by his curiosity. 'No! No...well, yes! It's just that I have received two letters today, both bringing good news of a sort.'

Dr West laughed, 'I wish we could all receive such letters,' he replied. 'We all work hard but it's not easy to relax and enjoy oneself when huddled round a fire of an evening. We did our best to enjoy Christmas, but until spring comes it is rather a gloomy existence.'

'It's the Chinese New Year soon, isn't it?' Lizzie asked, 'How do we Christians view this?'

'It's a very noisy affair. Actually it is also a very serious festival for the Chinese, as you will find out. They see it as a time for a cleansing of mind and spirit. All debts must be settled, and property spring-cleaned, though sadly there are many suicides by those who cannot pay up. It's all to do with losing face.'

This was the first lengthy conversation Lizzie had had with Dr West and she concluded that she herself had been at fault in this. With much always on her mind and her usual way of holding people at arms length, she had inhibited close relationships from the start. Today, however, things were different. The letters from Mr Ward and Peter had boosted her confidence and now with Dr West treating her almost as an equal she felt that she was making headway in her life.

'Liu Yu will explain, if you ask her,' Dr West suggested. 'Befriend her and she may even take you shopping at their New Year.' Seeing Lizzie's eyes light up he smiled again. 'You need a change,' he said, not unkindly. 'Liu Yu has been with us for years and is very respected both in the hospital and the city. You'll be safe with her.'

So far there had been no further mention of her being transferred to Hankow and the longer she remained where she was the harder it would be to move on yet again. 'You are all very kind,' Lizzie said, 'I dread moving to Hankow and starting afresh there.'

'Oh, I shouldn't worry about that,' Dr West advised, lowering his eyes to check the medicine he was dispensing. 'The extensions have come to halt there, so it may not be for some time yet, and in China anything can happen. God forbid, there could be more riots, it doesn't take much, especially with an unstable and contrary Imperial Ruler like the Dowager Empress in charge. Life here doesn't go on in a rational fashion as it does in England. You've not been here long enough to see just how volatile things can be.'

His remarks set Lizzie's mind at rest and back to the impending visit of Mr Ward. She intended cultivating further her acquaintance with Liu Yu and seeking her advice. This lady had been a Christian for many years in the face of much opposition from her family, in fact she'd been ostracised by her village years ago for her faith and had sought shelter in the nearby Mission. Her daily help at the hospital was invaluable: she calmed and reassured patients without forcing her beliefs on them, so that many lost their fear of the 'foreign devils'.

Shyly at first, then, as their friendship grew Liu Yu instructed Lizzie on what was expected of a woman in Chinese society. If Lizzie did not follow this advice her conduct would appear unseemly and attract abuse and possibly the violent attention of the mudslingers. Lizzie was grateful for Liu Yu's help, as she didn't want to let Mr Ward down. She never doubted that he would keep his promise to come even if the weather delayed his visit and she wanted to be prepared, to surprise him. In the event he sent her a message to say he would collect her.

Allowing Liu Yu to assist, Lizzie arranged her hair to suit the style of the loose silk dress she'd bought in Shanghai. 'I feel strange,' she remarked, eyeing herself in the mirror. 'I'll never pass as a Chinese woman.'

'You too big for Chinese woman,' Liu Yu giggled, 'but pretty enough. Pity about the round eyes and big nose.' There was no malice, only teasing on Liu Yu's part. 'You make too big movement! Keep legs closer together when walking, take short steps along street.'

'I don't want to shame Mr Ward,' Lizzie protested, 'and Madame Ling must be kind to invite a stranger into her house, and a 'foreign devil' at that.' The two women laughed together as they fussed over Lizzie's outfit.

'You marry Mr Ward?' Liu Yu asked bluntly. 'All this fuss for him, not Madame Ling!'

Lizzie was speechless; her face grew crimson as she tried to protest. 'No, Liu Yu! Please don't say that or Mr Ward may stop coming to see me. He has been very kind, we are only friends.'

Liu Yu snorted. 'You think Englishman has no feelings? All men the same— you see.'

These remarks flustered Lizzie who didn't want to spoil her friendship with Liu Yu, neither did she want Mr Ward to be the butt of hospital gossip. 'You must not say such things, Liu Yu,' she repeated firmly but kindly. 'Mr Ward is a good man—he had a wife whom he loved very much. He is lonely and knows that I need a little help in adjusting to life in China, so he was asked to accompany me here, that is all.' She spoke slowly making sure that Liu Yu understood.

Liu Yu mumbled something under her breath and a sly smile flashed across her face. 'We see!' she said out loud in her sing-song way as she looked at the clock. 'Get coat on quick, is time,' she urged, helping Lizzie into her heavily quilted coat. Lizzie felt that she must look enormous in the bulky garment, but followed Liu Yu to the reception room to await Mr Ward who, when he arrived, was accompanied by a serious faced middle aged Chinese woman.

'This is Chung Shi,' he said, introducing the woman: 'she is Madame Ling's amah, and looks after the children.' Lizzie formally returned the woman's kowtow and waited nervously for Mr Ward to finish speaking to Liu Yu. 'I'm pleased you could come,' he said, smiling directly at Lizzie.

'It is good of you to ask me,' Lizzie replied shyly. 'Do I look fit to meet your friends?'

Although he himself was in a European suit he appreciated Lizzie's efforts to please the Lings. 'Thank you for such a respectful gesture,' he said. 'As a diplomat I am excused the courtesy, but even so I have brought Chung Shi as an escort to protect your reputation. I have the chairs waiting outside, so shall we go?'

That he'd mentioned the Lings having children was a relief to Lizzie. She had imagined Madame Ling to be a beautiful and aristocratic hostess, but now she saw her as a wife and mother, with hopes and fears like anyone else.

The journey was a short one and soon their bearers lowered the three chairs, suspended on long bamboo poles, outside the high whitewashed wall which surrounded the Lings' house. At the amah's knock the heavy wooden gates were opened to admit them to the inner yard. The house was large though only of single storey, its corner roof tiles curved and supported by protruding bamboo poles that were painted and decorated, creating a picture to behold.

Until this moment Lizzie had had little opportunity to speak with Mr Ward and she walked obediently behind him with the amah. There was no reason to think him overly quiet, but not having seen him for several weeks, she was a little perplexed over how to behave. Just before reaching the house steps he paused and waited for her to catch up. 'I'm so glad you could come,' he said, repeating his earlier greeting, 'You'll like Madame Ling and her father-in-law Ling Jen I'm sure, also because they're used to westerners you can relax a little. Ling Jen retired here from Shanghai, bringing his son and daughter-in-law with him. They speak English moderately well so don't worry,' he reassured her as the door opened. The amah immediately bowed and disappeared somewhere within the grounds, leaving them in the care of a house-boy who led them into a reception room where they were greeted by their host Ling Jen who bowed courteously.

He was a slightly built old man with gaps in his teeth, and as he stood there in his heavily embroidered silk robe he evoked the image of an honourable and proud race. Even though his movements were graceful, Lizzie felt that in his youth he must have been a powerful man in spite of his small stature, and she knew it was an honour to respond to his kowtow.

The reception room in which they stood was spacious but sparsely furnished and quite cool, so Lizzie was relieved when they were led into a cosier room with fretwork windows and richly carved blackwood furniture.

Madame Ling was waiting there with her three children. She was beautiful: her small exquisite features were almost doll-like, but there Lizzie's preconceived image ceased, for the young woman gave an almost subservient attention to her guests. Her welcome was warm and friendly, but as Lizzie had noticed with the women who came to the hospital, Madame Ling seemed to cower obsequiously beneath the responsibility of showing respect. It therefore came as a surprise when, in slightly accented English, she said to Lizzie, 'You perhaps keep your jacket on if you are cold, we are used to it not so hot, but in the house it can be windy.'

She saw Lizzie start, and as if reading her thoughts, added, 'I learn English in Shanghai as child, and mix with many foreign children, this is best way to learn, I think. Unfortunately my father-in-law does not speak it so well.' Madame Ling paid homage to her father-in-law, and once the children had paid their respects to the visitors they were shepherded from the room by their amah.

This was a great disappointment to Lizzie for they were shy, extremely polite and had the sweetest of faces and she would have liked to have seen more of them. Whatever Madame Ling had said to them seemed to placate their demands, for they had left the room obediently enough. She turned to Lizzie and explained, 'Later, before they go to bed they will come and see you.' It was obvious by her easy movements that her feet had not been bound as a child and this pleased Lizzie greatly. However, she was disappointed when her hostess asked to be excused and left her alone with the two men.

As Lizzie had expected, Mr Ward behaved more formally in the company of their host, which was just as well as there were so many questions she had for him. Her curiosity had been aroused as they entered the house by a family shrine in the reception room. Lizzie would dearly have liked to study it more closely. Instead, she now sat quietly as Ling Jen and Mr Ward chatted on, this giving her the opportunity to observe the room they were in. Lizzie was well aware that as an unmarried Englishwoman in China, she had to be very cautious lest she unwittingly committed some impropriety, yet she hadn't expected her companion to be quite so observant of the rules.

Later, when Madame Ling returned, they sat for supper at a heavy blackwood table and Lizzie struggled more with the chopsticks than with the conversation. As she had suspected, Ling Jen understood far more English than was intimated at first, and between mouthfuls of rice and fish he began to question her. She found him pleasant to talk to and, in responding, quite forgot Mr Ward who was listening intently. When the conversation turned to business, Lizzie relaxed and watched Mr Ward deftly using the ivory chopsticks without mishap as the two men talked; so much of his background was still a mystery to her. He noticed her watching him once and smiled, his grey eyes twinkling mischievously. How could she ever have thought him dull? She felt a little guilty at having even considered him so, then suddenly her reverie was broken when she realised he was watching her with a strange look on his face.

She lowered her eyes quickly, shyly, Liu Yu's words ringing in her ears. This moment however, reminded her of her resolve to tell him more about Peter and his ideas involving her future, but the thought of losing Mr Ward's friendship frightened her.

Then she realised he was talking about her. 'May I show Miss Hardy the garden, Madame Ling?' he asked, as they rose from the table, 'would you mind?'

'Please. Yes,' Madame Ling smiled, 'I get Li Pai to light lanterns first. Now is almost dark out there.'

It was a strange request, Lizzie thought, there would be little to see on a cold, winter evening, so she waited apprehensively until Madame Ling returned. She came with their coats and took them towards the door leading to what Lizzie presumed would be the courtyard and garden.

When the door was opened, Lizzie was intrigued to see an ornate covered wooden walkway leading towards a large inky-black pool of water that stretched onwards towards yet another walkway. All was illuminated by twinkling lanterns which cast rays of light on the water. Lizzie stood mesmerised, this was an incredibly beautiful and secret world, she drew her breath in sharply causing Mr Ward to laugh.

'This is the China I love,' he murmured softly, as he stood to one side to allow her to take in the scene fully before gently taking her elbow and leading her further along to some steps.

These led down onto a path of cleverly laid pebbles forming small mosaics. It was not at all like an English garden of grass and beds of flowers: instead it was one of strangely-shaped and strategically placed rocks round which the path twisted and turned. These rocks were large and heavily eroded, giving the impression that the pool was far larger than it actually was. The lanterns gave it a ghostly air and, where the path seemed to disappear completely, it merely rounded a bend, beyond which a tiny ornate bridge crossed the pool to a small island on which stood a beautiful tiny pavilion. 'I can quite see why you find China so attractive,' Lizzie said as she fingered the surface of one of the nearest rocks. 'How strange, it's perforated with small holes, almost like limestone at home.'

'It is limestone, and many stones have been dredged from Lake Taihu and brought to gardens of the wealthy in the past.'

'Is the house very old? It's so beautiful and peaceful.'

'I believe it is—I'm so pleased you like it.'

'Where is Madame Ling's husband?' Lizzie asked. 'You never mention him.'

'Ling Li is in Shanghai seeing to his family affairs, he comes home as often as he can. I bring messages and parcels for the family when I come on business and in return they allow me to stay here. I've known Jen and his son for many years, long before Ling Li married. Ling Jen likes to hear the gossip I bring from Shanghai.'

'Is Ling Jen a widower?'

They were standing in the tiny pavilion, looking back across the illuminated pool towards the house. 'Yes, I'm sorry to say. Like me he's been a widower many years, but it gives Madame Ling a greater position in the household: mothers-in-law in China have a bad reputation for being unkind to their daughters-in-law, so in this case Madame Ling can rule the roost without fear.

'Why do you call her Madame Ling,' Lizzie asked, 'is there a French connection?'

He chuckled. 'It's just a whim on my part I'm afraid. One day I called her Madame Ling by mistake and she laughed. Since that time I have always referred to her in that way when I'm here, and to you. She admires much about the French and can speak the language too, which I do not. It's just a foible of mine.'

Suddenly Lizzie shivered. 'You're cold,' he said softly, 'we'd better go indoors. I so wanted you to see this place, especially at night. This may have been our only opportunity, one never knows.' He hesitated as if about to confide something to her, then, thinking better of it, he continued, 'Perhaps you could write about it in that journal of yours.' Taken aback by this remark Lizzie turned away and in doing so stumbled, almost falling into the dark water which at that moment seemed ominous in its stillness. Seizing her arm, he gasped, 'Are you alright?' His face showed real concern.

The shock of his reference to the journal, followed by her near accident, unnerved Lizzie and she could have wept at his kindness. Why had she not been honest with him? She had never told him that the 'journal' was in fact the style of her letters to Peter, that all she had learned and experienced through Mr Ward, she had used to amuse and comfort Peter. In the moment before the fall she had in fact been contemplating the best way to tell him. Now, in the light of the lantern she saw the look on his face and realised that he could be falling in love with her! The tender concern in his eyes forbade her telling him the truth. She smiled weakly, 'I'm not hurt, thanks to you. I would have been terrified had I landed in the water.'

He hesitated before walking on. 'May I ask you a question? Would you mind if I called you Lizzie, in private?' He quickly went on, as if expecting her to refuse. 'Please say if you prefer that I didn't.'

'Why of course!' she replied, now more composed, 'It has become such a habit between us to use formal names, that I never thought anything about it.'

'Would you like to call me Leonard or Len in return?' he ventured. Lizzie smiled and nodded her approval, and at this he continued, 'It's difficult to find an opportunity to speak to you in private these days. Now that winter is upon us it is obviously too cold to sit in the garden, and protocol makes meeting in private almost impossible, but I would like to talk with you as we have done before. I enjoy your company very much.'

This frank revelation left Lizzie at a loss for words. Had she really been so naïve as to think Mr Ward wanted nothing more than an occasional meeting?

Even now he'd said nothing that asked for more, yet she'd seen the look on his face moments before and heard the tenderness in his voice. Had he deliberately planned tonight's walk in the garden? She needed time to think, needed his company and the pleasure and hopes that his visits brought, but in no way could she hurt him.

The cold was beginning to bite into her and this muddled her thoughts, causing her to shiver again. 'How thoughtless of me,' Leonard said, looking at her with consternation. 'We must go in before you catch a chill.' As the path was narrow, Len followed closely behind her cursing himself for having exposed Lizzie to the night air, the magic spell of the garden diminishing as his anxiety grew. 'I had forgotten how low the temperature can get,' he apologised, 'and your slippers can't offer much protection for your feet.'

Through chattering teeth, Lizzie tried to reassure him that it had all been worthwhile and that he was not to blame himself. She could hardly admit that it wasn't so much the cold that was affecting her but the impact of what she'd heard.

When Madame Ling saw the state Lizzie was in she admonished Len severely. 'She is shaking and very pale, Len; you should not keep her out so long.' She ushered Lizzie towards the stove and brought a chair for her to sit on. 'Rub hands, they are stiff and have no blood. Get blood flowing again Len, I fetch hot tea!'

Obeying her orders, Len drew a chair closer and held Lizzie's stiff fingers in his own, gently massaging them until she slowly began to feel them again. She was mortified to realise that he was getting the blame after all his troubles; he was a kind man and had meant no harm. As he concentrated on her hands she suddenly became aware that he was quite still and that he no longer rubbed them with purpose; instead he was cupping them tenderly, allowing their growing warmth to fuse their hands together.

What was he thinking? What was she thinking of? 'Thank you,' she whispered shyly, 'they don't hurt any more.'

'I hadn't realised how cold my own were,' he replied, still holding them protectively around Lizzie's.

How long he might have held them in this fashion she would never know, for Madame Ling came back with a house-boy bearing two bowls of hot tea. 'Hold these close and heat will do good,' she said. 'You not shaking but still pale.'

Lizzie was grateful in more ways than one, and smiled up at her. 'I will be alright now,' she replied. 'I hadn't realised how sharp the evening air can be. At the hospital I usually stay indoors all evening huddled close to my fire.' Reluctantly Len released her fingers and took one of the bowls himself, it seemed lost in his large hands. Lizzie was confused: all her adult life she'd shunned close physical contact with any other human, except her patients, or when embracing her father or Clara, yet Leonard's touch had not repulsed her. He had even brought a kind of peace to her existence. She gripped her tea-bowl tightly, enjoying its heat on her fingers. What was she to do? It was obvious that Len cared for her, yet she was more or less committed to Peter. She didn't wish to hurt either of them! Perhaps after all it would be better not to see Len again; better to slowly and gently let distance and time divide them, even if she too was the loser.

Once the colour had returned to Lizzie's face and the warmth to her body, she felt more at ease. Shortly the children were allowed in to see her before going to bed: shyly at first, they approached their visitor, staring with barely unconcealed curiosity at her face. Lizzie smiled broadly at them, encouragingly, and this brought giggles to the smallest, a boy of about three years old. Madame Ling immediately murmured something in Chinese bringing the giggles to an abrupt end.

'It's mainly our eyes and noses that fascinate them,' Len Ward spoke up in the children's defence.

After the children had gone, Madame Ling said, 'They like you, I can tell. My father-in-law he pay his respects to ancestors now, then he will come.' She looked closely at Lizzie, 'Do you feel better now that you warm up?'

'Yes, thank you—I think we stayed outside too long admiring the splendour of your garden,' Lizzie replied, quietly admiring the pale smooth skin of the woman before her. She judged her to be of similar age to herself though very petite and of slight build, like so many of her race.

'You are nurse?' Madame Ling asked, 'or Missionary?' The question was abrupt but without animosity, and Lizzie perceived that her host assumed there was a definite distinction between the two.

'A nurse. I came to China to help the sick and perhaps learn a little about Chinese medicine.' Lizzie spoke so quickly that Len Ward found it necessary to interpret the less familiar words to Madame Ling.

'Ah!' she exclaimed, turning as her father-in-law entered the room. She proceeded to talk to him so rapidly that Lizzie in turn was unable to follow, yet she realised the discussion was about herself, as Ling Jen kept looking at her in a studious way. He had the appearance of an old sage with his wrinkled face and thin, plaited pigtail hanging limply onto the collar of his jacket. He nodded, and then smiled.

'Chinese medicine good,' he said, 'but Western surgeon good also. Put two together, very good!' He nodded vigorously, seemingly very pleased. 'Here we have herbs and cures for many things. But Western religion not so good for respect of ancestors.'

Being a guest, Lizzie thought it best to avoid any controversy, and chose to overlook the latter part of his statement for the sake of harmony and peace. She had seen Len Ward tense in his chair at the mention of religion, no doubt fearing that such a discussion might be awkward. As Lizzie apparently showed no intention of commenting on Ling Jen's remarks he sat back and listened to their further conversation with interest.

'With herbs you have the natural way of curing many sicknesses,' Lizzie replied respectfully. 'In olden times in England, we too used many herbs but new discoveries are being made which can be used to enhance that kind of medicine.' She waited patiently whilst Len translated the more difficult words then, finally, Ling Jen nodded and smiled at her.

'You understand Qi. Very important!' the old man said.

'Energy,' Len interpreted.

'Yin and Yang most important too!'

'Cold and heat—opposing forces,' Len again broke in.

Seeing Lizzie's absorption with his statements, Ling Jen nodded again, vigorously. 'Tongue tell many things, where trouble is, then cure can be made.'

Lizzie was aware of some aspects of traditional Chinese medicine, having heard the Doctors in the hospital discussing it, but as a nurse she was often expected simply to obey orders and tend to her patients. 'I find much of this very interesting,' she said, looking first at Ling Jen and then Len Ward. 'I would like to learn more but I don't want to bore everyone, especially as you have been so kind to me.'

'Very welcome,' Ling Jen said, bowing his head. 'I too am interested in your medicine, operations cutting things out, very clever. Not everyone in China accept it a good thing.'

Len Ward glanced at his fob watch. Surprisingly time had passed very quickly and he realised that Lizzie ought to get back to the hospital soon if she was not to compromise her reputation. She noticed his action and felt sad, for not only had she enjoyed the evening but had found it enlightening in more ways than one. That the invitation had ever been given was in itself a privilege and she was reluctant to leave. Len rose, explaining that he must return Lizzie to the hospital, and at this Ling Jen bowed deeply, his face wreathed in smiling satisfaction.

'I will send Li Pai to look for chairs,' Madame Ling offered, 'amah will accompany you. You will be coming back with amah, Mr Ward?'

'Yes, it is getting late. Once I have seen Miss Hardy home I will return.'

Ling Jen thanked Lizzie for coming to his home and begged to be excused. He bowed and left the room.

'My father-in-law enjoys good discussion,' Madame Ling said, 'perhaps Mr Ward bring you again some time?'

Thrilled at the idea, Lizzie's eyes lit up and she smiled with gratitude. 'Yes, I would very much like to come again, you have been very kind.' Having spoken spontaneously she then remembered her earlier vow to distance herself from Len Ward, something she was now going to find almost impossible.

At the hospital Len saw Lizzie safely into the building but departed immediately so as not to keep the amah and the chairs waiting. Before doing so, however, he said, 'I must see you tomorrow if possible before I leave— could you spare ten minutes at about two o'clock?'

Realising that this was of some importance to him, she agreed. 'Yes, I think I can arrange it.' However, once he had gone she was perplexed as to why it was so urgent that he saw her before he left for Shanghai. That he wanted to continue their friendship she had no doubt. After all, he had merely asked that they should use their first names when addressing each other in private instead of the stilted and impersonal Mister and Miss. Had she in fact read too much into what had transpired, or indeed the look on his face? Had she been fanciful under exceedingly pleasant circumstances? The evening had certainly been happy and enlightening, spoilt only by the severity of the cold and possibly her overactive imagination. Len Ward had done nothing wrong.

Sleep, however, did not come quickly to Lizzie that night as she mused over all that had transpired. Her mind was too active and she tossed and turned, thinking that sleep would never come. Over and over, little things came to the fore, pleasant thoughts mainly, but they also confused her. Mr Ward (she had great difficulty in thinking of him as Len or Leonard) was a kind and gentle man, very much like her stepfather, both were reliable and made her feel secure. He had rubbed her hands so tenderly because he cared; to hurt him by ending their friendship would be cruel and unwarranted. After all, what need had she to tell him about Peter who she might never see again? Certain aspects of the evening plagued her more than others but, finally, sleep overcame her.

As her morning work proceeded, Lizzie's mind was never quite on the task in front of her and by lunchtime the anticipation of seeing Len Ward was becoming almost unbearable. She had asked permission to take him into a small room away from prying eyes, explaining to members of staff that he had some personal business to discuss and that she did not want him to be embarrassed by constant interruptions.

Promptly, at two o'clock, he arrived; his face showing no sign of stress. This afforded Lizzie much relief as she was hoping there would be nothing too serious about which he wished to speak. He shook hands and she immediately led him to the side room, leaving the door slightly ajar to suit convention.

'Thank you for agreeing to see me,' he said pleasantly, 'I do hope I haven't inconvenienced you too much?'

Lizzie shook her head reassuringly. 'No, not at all, and it does give me a chance to thank you again for such a really interesting and pleasant evening. I'm sorry if I spoilt part of it, I really should have worn gloves.'

'Madame Ling expressed her happiness at your visit, especially the respect you showed to her father-in-law. Sometimes European women forget how important it is to the Chinese that proper homage is shown.'

'I found him extremely interesting,' Lizzie said. 'I feel honoured to have been allowed to talk to him.'

'That is what I want to discuss with you. Madame Ling and Ling Jen wonder if you would like to go to their home at the Chinese New Year. He feels that your sympathetic approach could be useful in bringing a greater understanding of China amongst your colleagues.'

Lizzie was immensely pleased with Ling Jen's approval of her. 'That would be wonderful, I gladly accept the invitation,' she replied without hesitation. 'Will you be there?'

'It depends on the weather,' he said with a note of regret in his voice. 'I will try though.' At this Lizzie's face fell, for how could she cope without him? As if reading her thoughts, he added, 'Between you all, I'm sure you'll manage well enough.'

She didn't want to go alone, nor did she want to let him down. 'I will go, but I do hope you can come as well,' she confessed with some apprehension.

Len hastened to reassure her. 'I know you're quite capable of conducting yourself in a way which will please the Ling family and I will endeavour to come—but the weather will be the master of events.'

Lizzie looked at him quizzically. 'We are the best of friends, are we not?' she asked. 'And I agree with you we should not address each other as Mister and Miss in letters and in private, but I do find it difficult to think of you as anything other than Mr Ward!' She laughed out loud, 'It is a complement really, you have become my 'Mr Ward', just as you have your 'Madame Ling,' Lizzie said, teasing him.

He had seen many changes in her over the months, including a growing sense of fun. 'Call me what you will,' he said pleasantly, 'but I take it that I can call you Lizzie?' She nodded approvingly. 'However, I'm afraid I have to go now, but I promise to be here by the twenty-third of January if possible, in time for their New Year. Failing that I'm sure the Lings will send a messenger to explain the arrangements.'

When he left, Lizzie felt an emptiness: a hollow gnawing sensation which made her sigh deeply. She looked out of the window and saw the garden in its winter mantle looking as forlorn as she felt. It was a sensation she had experienced years before whenever Peter had gone away from the farm. In the intervening period she'd learned to shut her mind to the pain of separation from those close to her. Now, having allowed Mr Ward into her life, she felt vulnerable and alone. Foolishly she wanted to call him back; instead she did as always when in time of stress: she took up her pen and wrote. It did occur to her that Leonard may have deliberately avoided mentioning something of importance to her, and wondered if he would have done had the circumstances and their surroundings been more conducive.

London 1886

The foggy chill of London ate into Peter's bones as he walked away from the offices of Jardine Matheson in Whitehall, where he'd successfully obtained a post giving him a reasonable salary and some security. He was not short of money, caution having always been his maxim as a result of seeing the thriftlessness of his own family over the years. Peter wasn't an ambitious man in the sense that he sought wealth, but he always acknowledged that without money he could be reduced to a level in society that would not please him. As it was, he had saved regularly for when the time came for him to resign his commission in the Army, and that time had now arrived. His experience of commerce was limited of course, and it would take him some time to learn, but there were many other qualities he had as an officer which would be of use in the business world. However he did not wish to be alone in this venture, and needed a woman by his side to share the life he wanted to build. He knew he could achieve this with Lizzie, but she had taken herself off to the other side of the world; including her in his plans now would make them more difficult to achieve. Why, oh why hadn't he proposed to and married her before he'd left with Wolsley for the Sudan? That would have been the most sensible thing to have done, but doubts had made a coward of him.

Peter knew Lizzie's stubbornness well enough; had he rushed her she would almost certainly have turned him down. Now, he had the task of enticing her back. He was more nervous at the thought of facing her than he was of confronting the enemies of his Queen and country. Any wounds inflicted by Lizzie would be harder to bear than those made by gun or spear. He had no way of knowing how she would accept his present proposals and no choice other than to go out to China to find out. Fortunately the position he had just accepted would take him to Shanghai and, hopefully, to Lizzie also.

Hangchow 1886

The Chinese New Year of the Pig was
fast approaching, as was obvious by the change in
everyday habits of the inhabitants of Hangchow. Bright red flags and streamers festooned the city, and for several days families had been displaying and selling any items not wanted, cherished things even, in order to pay off their debts. This was a sacred obligation before the New Year. All guilt and evil spirits had to be expelled if the future was to be a joyous one. The contents of houses were scrubbed clean, also the shutters and doors which were then strung with firecrackers whose noise, when detonated, was intended to rid the house of evil spirits and prevent new ones entering. There was hectic commotion everywhere, the din of gongs was deafening, so much so that this frenzy and noise roused Lizzie's sense of excitement.

Unfortunately, her invitation to spend time with the Lings did not entirely please some of her colleagues, who saw it as condoning the Pagan rites of the festival. Notwithstanding their comments and faithful to her intentions, she convinced them that it would give her a greater understanding of things Chinese and, at the same time, this would foster good relations with the Mission. She explained also that there was no chance of her believing in myths and legends, so what harm could her visit do? She got her own way and with almost child-like excitement she waited in the hope of Len appearing.

With every firecracker explosion Lizzie jumped. 'For goodness sake, Miss Hardy,' the Doctor she was assisting said irritably, 'you're no good to anyone today, forget the New Year and concentrate on your work! I also fear Mr Ward is becoming too much of a distraction to you and think it would be best all round if he didn't call quite so frequently.'

These remarks troubled Lizzie who had never before been reprimanded for poor work or lack of discretion. To challenge the Doctor would only cause discord. 'I'm sorry Doctor,' she said respectfully, 'I'm behaving like a child but it has nothing to do with Mr Ward,' she lied, hoping to end the matter, and got on quietly with her work. However, the spirit of rebellion long suppressed in Lizzie was coming to the fore: she was determined to see Len Ward no matter what anyone thought. If her work wasn't good enough then they would have to manage without her!

The weather was not as harsh as expected, thus allowing Len to make his promised journey to Hangchow. It was with great excitement that Lizzie greeted him, her eyes sparkling. 'Something has happened in my absence,' he said with a smile, 'you look defiant, I am most intrigued.'

'I am so glad to see you!' she said with such force that he laughed. 'Oh, dear, do I sound exasperated?' she asked in a more subdued tone.

He shook his head smiling. 'You sounded more like a firecracker. Someone or something must have upset you?'

'I'm not a nun you know, and must have a life of my own.' Her simmering anger at the Doctor had found some release by now and she felt better for it.

'Ah, I suspect someone has said something about my visits. Have I caused you some embarrassment?' Len looked at her enquiringly, troubled at the possibility that his attentions might have become a problem. 'I suppose your seniors would like to have you completely under their control—it's easier that way.'

'But why? It isn't necessary; people can work for a cause without sacrificing everything else.' She was flushed by the strength of her feelings.

'Can they? Can they really, Lizzie? Whatever brought you here was not religion, I know that. Can you honestly say that you want to spend every day, every year in a closed community?' He had lowered his voice in case anyone should hear him, but there was an earnestness in his words which shook her, for they held a great deal of truth. 'Look at me,' he insisted, 'and tell me, do you want this forever?'

'No, Leonard, I have to admit that,' Lizzie replied truthfully. 'Yet I'm not ready to go home until I have fulfilled something within me!'

You're halfway there, Lizzie, he thought, although you don't know it. He admired her frankness and determination. 'Good for you!' he replied, still amused by her strength of feeling. He heard the sound of approaching footsteps and reverted to simple everyday conversation. 'I'll call to collect you tomorrow at six,' he said, 'and will look forward to it.' He was loath to leave but there was nowhere private where prying eyes wouldn't make more of the situation than in fact there was.

Lizzie's anger was already subsiding; the chance to get things off her chest had relieved the pressure. 'I'm pleased that the weather has been kind enough to let you come,' she told him, 'I wish...' but before she could continue someone came to talk to her and she found herself reduced to simply bidding him farewell.

When he came to collect her as promised, she was again dressed in silk beneath the quilted coat, but her hands were now concealed in a pair of gloves she'd brought with her from England. 'I'm taking no chances,' she said shaking his outstretched hand. He smiled knowingly. 'Do you feel happier today?' he asked as he led her to the door and the waiting amah. 'I thought we would stroll. It will give us a chance to talk and you'll see that everyone is in a gay mood and dressed in their finest clothes.' After exchanging greetings, the Ling's amah proceeded to follow them at a polite distance as was the custom. Lizzie took the first opportunity then to apologise for her behaviour the day before. 'I felt a little guilty after you'd gone. I never really asked how you were or if you'd had a good journey from Shanghai?'

'It took much longer than I expected due to all the New Year preparations, and as there will be no boat going back for two days, I may as well earn myself a bad name on your behalf by calling yet again.'

This pleased Lizzie. 'I'd like that.' She lowered her voice almost to a whisper, 'They can think what they like, I work hard enough and have no other indulgences except to receive you occasionally.'

'It is as much discipline as jealousy I believe. Your safety, welfare and, most of all, your reputation, lies in their hands.'

She laughed. 'Then I shall have no reputation at all if you continue to call.'

'Would that matter, or shall I stop calling?' His question, although spoken lightly, belied his inner concern that their friendship might be curtailed by protocol.

She might have squeezed his arm reassuringly had it been acceptable in Chinese society, and not misconstrued by Len. 'How could I have survived without your support,' she said simply and let the matter drop.

All around them, brightly clad families jostled politely along the streets, many on their return from the temples after taking gifts to their gods and ancestors. Occasionally someone greeted Len respectfully as they walked towards their destination and Lizzie was exhilarated by the carnival atmosphere. Heathen beliefs might have been at the root of it all; it was un-Christian, certainly, but Lizzie would never willingly have missed the atmosphere—it made her feel so alive. She felt a great affection for these people who were making so much noise that it became difficult to continue any conversation for long. Suddenly they were pushed aside to make way for an arrogant Mandarin seated in his gilded chair, but this again was the custom.

By the time they arrived at the Ling's address it was getting dark but lanterns lit the streets adding a magical touch to the already colourful scene. Firecrackers exploded constantly in all directions and Lizzie marvelled that children could grow up sanely in such ear-splitting cacophony. Once Lizzie and Len were inside the walls surrounding the house, the sounds diminished so that conversation could resume with some normality.

'Why is it the Chinese love noise so much?' she asked. 'They seem incapable of doing anything quietly.'

'They believe themselves to be surrounded by demons and spirits which must be constantly frightened away or appeased. Of course the noise is always much worse on special occasions: today being the most important of all. We Europeans never quite get used to it.' Saying this he gave her a small parcel. 'By the way, I've brought some ornate wax candles for you to give Madame Ling,' he said, 'its pagan I know, but it will please Ling Jen who will offer them to the spirits.'

Lizzie was shocked by his remark. 'I can't do that, not as a Christian,' she protested. 'Shouldn't we set an example?'

'We don't have to believe their reasons for burning them. After all, Catholics burn candles, if I'm not mistaken?' He wasn't rebuking her, but merely explaining his own point of view. 'We've been invited to a Chinese family celebration and are taking a gift for the family, if they want to share it with their ancestors how can we object?' He looked at her patiently, hoping she understood. 'This is China, not England.'

He was right, of course, and he had gone to the trouble of bringing a gift whereas she hadn't; at least not for the adults. Indeed, she had put a great deal of thought into producing three small paintings of animals, one for each child, with words in both English and Chinese characters to celebrate the coming Year of the Pig. Sounds of merriment came from within the house, and while they waited Lizzie wondered if she would have had the courage to come alone. At last, Li Pai opened the door and Len gently urged Lizzie into the house. A strange silence followed when Lizzie ceremoniously bowed and handed over Len's parcel, leaving him to explain that the candles were a gift for the ancestors.

Once the offering had been humbly accepted with as many bows as protocol dictated, the curiosity their arrival had aroused died down, and noise and chatter erupted once more.

A young man about Lizzie's age made his way towards them. 'This is Ling Li, Madame Ling's husband,' Len said, introducing her to a younger version of Ling Jen. Although taller he was still obviously Ling Jen's son.

'Welcome to my house,' he said with grave dignity. 'My friend Len tells me of your presence in Hangchow. Hangchow a very beautiful city.'

'Yes, it is,' Lizzie reassured him, 'very beautiful! Thank you for asking me to join you for your New Year.' Then very hesitantly in Chinese she added, 'May the new joy be yours.'

'You speak Chinese already,' he said, praising her. 'Please be happy in my home, my father will be most satisfied that you have come. I go to fetch him if you excuse me, I will speak with you again later.' He had obviously been occupied at the time of their arrival and was now needed elsewhere. 'Take care of Miss Hardy, Len, I will be back as soon as I can.' He left his guests in the reception hall giving Lizzie an opportunity to observe the family shrine without appearing too inquisitive. It was festooned with gold and silver tinsel, and with gifts; the smell from the accompanying burning candles and incense created an ambience that was almost hypnotic. Pagan it was, and shocking perhaps to her colleagues, yet it indicated a family unity that she could appreciate. For Lizzie, who had only turned to religion because of her guilt, this glimpse into the family lifestyle of a Chinese gentleman was a step towards her further understanding.

Len saw the fascinated expression on her face. 'If you'll stay here for a while, I'll just get something from my room; I'll not be long,' he murmured. 'Most of the other guests here can't speak English, so try your Chinese when they approach, they'll appreciate that. I won't leave you alone much tonight and no-one will comment if I stay close by you. I'll help explain any misunderstandings that may occur.'

Lizzie thanked him. 'How would I have managed alone? I don't think I would have had the courage to come on my own.'

He laughed. 'I always intended being here, it was only the state of the weather that worried me. I would not have accepted the invitation if I could not have accompanied you. As it happens, this evening has worked out well so far—and you will have a feast like no other.'

When he returned he found her deep in conversation with Ling Jen who, after a while, excused himself and left her alone with Len once more. 'I'll introduce you to the people I know,' he offered, 'but frankly most of them are strangers to me as well. We're going to eat soon, that will help break the ice for you.'

'I shall probably make a fool of myself using chopsticks.'

'Remember to hold the bowl close to your face and half scoop the food into your mouth with the sticks, but don't expect to pick up every grain of rice separately. Watch me do it.'

Lizzie looked at him shyly, 'I've brought a spoon and fork in my pocket,' she lied, and waited for his reaction.

'No! You mustn't use those!' he interrupted hastily. 'Don't show me up; I would lose face if you did that.' He looked at her in disbelief, 'You won't, will you?'

She shook her head and laughed. 'No, of course not, I didn't really bring them, although it might have been a good idea to do so.'

Occasionally throughout the evening she found herself being observed by one party or another across the room and realised that to them she was an oddity, a wonder. Unlike Len who was a man, she was an unmarried English woman who could only live within the settlements or Missions, and then under great restrictions. To someone like Lizzie who was not totally dedicated to the cause, these were closed societies. Once summer returned there would, of course, be the rounds of tea-parties and tennis for the Europeans, all held within their walled compounds when time permitted. Hangchow was unlike Shanghai with its racecourse and other Western pastimes.

'You look deep in thought,' Len said, seeing her distraction, 'Is there a problem?'

Turning to him, Lizzie realised just how often he seemed to have an uncanny knack of reading her mind or mood. 'Am I so transparent?' she asked, with a smile. 'Have I no secrets without you being able to sense them?'

'I'm sorry if it disturbs you,' he said in a low voice, 'but I can't be unaware of your worries or anxieties. I like to think that it is because you trust me that you lower that reserve of yours. I get a great deal of satisfaction in being able to help you; my one intention is to see you happy.' His voice had softened and, beneath his words, Lizzie sensed something deeper. Was it tenderness, simple fatherly care, or did it go deeper? She wished she knew. The more she saw of him, the more she realised how difficult it would be to halt any growing affection that might be there. Would she ever find peace? She had set herself on a career which offered a life of dedication to her fellow men, only to have it flounder, first with Peter's return from India and all that entailed, and now with her growing friendship with Len Ward.

'You have not been at ease tonight,' Len said wistfully as they arrived back at the Mission at the end of the evening. 'I can tell there is something troubling you: perhaps it was a mistake to go after all? Will life in the Mission be harder to bear now?'

'What an ungrateful wretch you must think me,' Lizzie replied, 'I have spoilt your evening. I don't understand why you have so much patience with me; all I ever do is ruin things.'

Such was the despair in her voice that Len instinctively took her hand in his and said, 'Whatever has hurt you in the past must be pushed from your mind, you have so much to give, it mustn't prevent you from being happy. If it was a man, then I apologise on behalf of all men; if not, then let me share your troubles.' He pressed her hand tighter and only then was Lizzie aware that he actually held it. To draw away would be churlish and hurtful. However, by not doing so she was encouraging him to speak freely.

'I take it there was a man involved, your silence speaks for itself. If it is any comfort to you I will speak out.' He looked about them and was relieved to see that the amah was occupied in chatting to the chair-bearers leaving the entrance unoccupied. He continued, 'You must know by now that I am very fond of you; whenever I return to Shanghai suspecting that you are troubled, I want to help, but the distance separating us brings even greater disquiet. I'm aware that your feelings are not as deep as mine, and ask nothing of you but friendship, but I would that it were different.' He was embarrassed by his declaration and let go of her hand in a gesture of futility.

Lizzie felt a surge of bewilderment. What had she done to encourage him? Whatever it was she had done the same to Peter. She acknowledged the courage it had taken to confess his feelings, even when suspecting that it was probably useless. What was she to do?

'I must go,' he muttered, 'this is not the time or place for such a conversation and I have probably made a fool of myself.' He moved to leave, avoiding her eyes, but his steps were hesitant and Lizzie knew she couldn't let him go in that state of mind.

'I didn't dare to presume such a depth of feeling,' she murmured, stepping towards him, 'and don't want to lose your friendship.' Her mind was in a whirl from the shock of his revelation.

He turned to her. 'I cannot go on returning to Shanghai with an emptiness in my heart that is difficult to bear,' he admitted, knowing that he had nothing to lose. Having already spoilt his chances she may as well know the truth. 'It gets harder with each parting.'

158

'I didn't realise,' Lizzie whispered softly. 'I didn't seek to take advantage of your kindness. I like your company very much and look forward to your visits.' She was at a loss as to what she could do or say to him that would help.

Accepting that it was impossible to retract his words, he said, 'If friendship is all you desire then I will make do with that. I won't mention what has passed between us again.'

There was no doubting the sincerity in his voice but it did not lessen Lizzie's dilemma. 'I am not so wicked as to want to hurt you,' she said lamely, 'nor do I want to lose your friendship, but I am overwhelmed by the suddenness of it all.'

He looked directly at her, his eyes sombre. 'I cannot take back my declaration, but please don't let it ruin everything. Unfortunately I must go now, before tongues start to wag: think kindly of me, Lizzie, I will be on hand if you need me.'

After closing the door behind him, Lizzie sat on the hard wooden bench in the hall and stared at the whitewashed walls about her. She was only too aware of the empty feeling Len had described, she had known it most of her adult life.

If only she had explained about her real situation with Peter earlier as, by not doing so, she had now made things worse. Of course she'd been preoccupied tonight, Peter's latest letter hinted at his growing impatience to see her again, and even suggested the possibility that he might come to China!

She was in no state to think clearly. She didn't want to return to England, nor did she want to lose Len's friendship, but it would never be quite the same again, and she was afraid of what she would do if Peter came halfway round the world to see her.

Sheffield 1985

'Oh what a shame!' Mark exclaimed
as he put Mimi's manuscript down.

This outburst woke Mimi who was still sleeping on the sofa after several hours' work amending the text. 'What? Is it that bad?' She responded gloomily as she sat up in a daze. 'Is it my interpretation or is the story too feeble?' She was alarmed at his apparent disappointment and nearly ready to shed tears. The idea of writing Lizzie's life story had fermented in her mind for so long and she had put her heart and soul into the project over the past months. This had involved hours of research as she strove to ensure the basic facts were accurate. Coming to England had been the last stage in her effort to confirm her findings. However, with Lizzie's secret now revealed she felt this added dimension would make it an even worthier biography. Mark's sudden announcement was like a shower of icy cold water, dashing her hopes.

'No! No, it's good.' Mark quickly reassured her, 'There is the odd spelling mistake here and there, and perhaps some rephrasing needed where appropriate, but the situation Lizzie finds herself in after all she's been through is quite disturbing. I think this could be a great book.'

Mimi's eyes lit up. 'For one moment I thought you were going to say it was rubbish. I've worked hard to get the facts right, in spite of being puzzled by some of the mysterious innuendos in Lizzie's letters and diaries: now I've been able to fill them out it's made all the difference.'

'Without a doubt it has! It's the type of story Catherine Cookson would love to get her hands on.' He saw a puzzled look on Mimi's face. 'She's one of England's great modern novelists, haven't you heard of her?' Mimi shook her head. 'She's more of a lady's writer,' Mark went on, 'but very popular and worth a fortune.'

'So you really think it's worth pressing on with?' Mimi repeated, hoping he would say an emphatic yes'.

'Of course, but I am intrigued to see what happens next.' He glanced at the clock. 'Good heavens,' he exclaimed, 'it's gone midnight—I've been reading for three hours! Come on, I'd best get you home or Eileen will be thinking the worst.'

'You will finish the manuscript before I go home next week won't you?' Mimi pleaded. She was now fully awake, 'Can't I sleep here? It's quite comfortable on the sofa and it will save you going all that way. Eileen will probably be thinking the worst already, so can't we ring her and explain?'

Mark was in two minds what to do. He was surprisingly drained by the emotional ups and downs in Mimi's well-written story and didn't fancy driving her all the way home. Besides, Eileen would have gone to bed long before now, and wouldn't appreciate being disturbed at such a late hour. Perhaps, after all, it would be better to take Mimi back in the morning and work out a good excuse before they went. 'Maybe you're right. Either way we'll disturb them, providing you don't mind being seen as a compromised woman!' Mimi laughed at the thought. 'You can have my bed, I'll take the sofa,' he offered.

'No, I've already had three hours sleep and you have to go to work tomorrow. I'll be fine here.'

'I'll not argue, if you're sure you can manage. I've got some pyjamas you can borrow and at least you can have lie in if you're tired. I'll ring Eileen from work to explain and you could meet me at lunchtime, you've only got to catch the bus across the road and it goes right into the city centre.'

'OK, why not,' Mimi exclaimed, 'and if you don't mind providing me with some paper and a pen I could amend the final chapters for when you get back.'

Mark disappeared into the bedroom and returned with a clean pair of pyjamas and sufficient bedding to make Mimi comfortable. 'I'll be off to bed now, if you don't mind, I really am whacked,' he said. 'I'll try not to wake you in the morning before I go. There's food in the cupboards and some paper in the desk drawer over there. Let's meet at ten past twelve in the basement of Lyn's café. Will that be alright?'

After he'd gone, Mimi realised that her long sleep had in fact refreshed her, so she set about writing the adjustments needed to the last chapters of the book.

The following morning when Mark arose, he found her curled up beneath the blankets, fast asleep on the sofa. It was obvious from the papers on the desk that she had spent some considerable time working there. On closer inspection he realised that she must have been up half the night. The misspelling of one word caught his eye, and he couldn't resist underlining it in red ink, before adjusting the blanket to cover her feet which were sticking out from beneath the covers. He left the flat musing on her enthusiasm and determination.

Although Mark had originally seen Mimi's request for his help simply as an aid to her research into her families history, he had slowly become more deeply involved with the case. Lizzie's story, because it was true, intrigued him and today his mind constantly wandered, causing him to make one mistake after another in his work. He was tired and irritable and finally asked for the rest of the day off. It wasn't something he did very often but in the circumstances he justified his action against the mistakes he'd made so far that morning.

When he reached the café, Mimi was already downstairs enjoying a coffee. 'I've not been here long,' she said as he joined her. 'Shall I order the same as before?'

'Please, I'm starving; I didn't like making a noise before I left the flat so I only had a cup of tea.'

Mimi smiled teasingly at him. 'Red pens don't make a noise, do they?'

He looked a little sheepish, 'Sorry about that, I couldn't resist it. Were you up all night?'

'Mm, several hours, however I made up for it this morning and now I feel refreshed. How about you?'

'I feel groggy; in fact I've taken the afternoon off before I make an expensive blunder at work. My concentration wasn't what it should be.'

'Oh dear, that's my fault and I'm sorry. I guess you'll be glad to see the back of me.'

'Strangely enough I'm not too worried. I don't usually take time off unnecessarily but with the lack of sleep and constantly thinking about Lizzie, I thought—to hell with it.'

'Did you remember to ring Eileen? Does she think the worst?'

'I told her the truth and trust that she knows me well enough to believe me. I also told her that I would take you back early tonight.'

'Do you think she believed you? I dread going back to face her.' Mimi grimaced at the thought.

'She was alright about it, but did add that I wasn't to let you lead me astray!' Mimi's mouth fell open at this. 'I'm only joking,' he hastily reassured her.

Relieved, Mimi finished her coffee just as their order arrived. 'I do love English chips,' she said, sticking her fork firmly into one. 'What are you going to do this afternoon now that you're not working?'

'I thought we might go to a museum, and then I'm going back to the flat to read the rest of the manuscript. After that we're going to Eileen's,' he said decisively as he got on with his meal.

'Do you think the book will have an appeal over here, when it's finished?' Mimi asked, hoping for some kind of approval.

'I'm sure, particularly if you could include more local history. The Sheffield Flood for example. I'll help you in that respect and do some editing, if you like.' Suddenly the chips and quiche became less attractive as the pair once again became engrossed in Lizzie's affairs, and they didn't realise that time was slipping by until the staff in the café began clearing round them. Sensing that they would probably be asked to leave Mark stood up and helped Mimi with her coat.

'I'm really looking forward to this afternoon,' Mark said as they climbed the stairs to street level. 'I feel quite liberated at taking the afternoon off.'

'It doesn't take much to give you pleasure then,' Mimi teased. 'A good book and a good woman's company.'

'I don't know about the latter, but I'm determined to get to the end of the book if it kills me!'

Hangchow 1886

Anger soon replaced the panic Lizzie had experienced at the thought of the situation she was now in. Was there no end to her dilemma, no peace to be found anywhere? Rising from the seat in the hall, she went to her room with Len Ward's words ringing in her ears. He had virtually declared himself to her then gone away unhappy and depressed. She felt mentally exhausted and, instead of writing in her journal, she went straight to bed and promptly fell asleep.

It was not, however, a peaceful sleep. A nightmare kept recurring in which a serpent with two heads, those of Len Ward and Peter, bore down on her. She woke bathed in sweat, and tried to rationalise what was troubling her. In the end she realised that it was her struggle between the serpent China, Len and Peter all combined. She was going to have to make a choice, and soon.

To add to her discomfort and misery, next day there seemed to be a conspiracy of strange looks in her direction from some of her colleagues and she realised that someone must have been in the vicinity of the hall the night before. How much they had actually overheard or witnessed was not apparent, but Lizzie felt alienated by the atmosphere around her. Perhaps Len's visits were becoming a bone of contention and if Peter turned up too, she had a feeling she would be disciplined severely. As a result she found the day long and tiresome. Len did not visit even though she knew he would still be in the city. The weather was foul, it rained frequently and there was a sharp lazy wind that cut through the body rather than passing around it. After tea she was tempted to climb into bed simply to keep warm, rather than sit shivering in the cold, but if she fell asleep the serpent might reappear in her dreams. She wondered why Len hadn't called to see her, yet could hardly expect him to after laying bare his feelings, without receiving some encouragement from her.

Perhaps it would be better after all if she moved on somewhere where neither man could find her. No, Len Ward was an honourable man and would not embarrass her by pursuing her: Peter would though, and she could hardly be a coward and hide from him if he came so far. Here she was, at the age of twenty-eight, seemingly with all the cares of the world on her shoulders when she should be flattered by the attentions of two men who actually cared about her.

There was a little improvement in the weather when she woke the following morning, and Lizzie knew that nothing would prevent Len from travelling on to Shanghai that day.

'You see much of Mr Ward,' Liu Yu said accusingly as she swept out Lizzie's room. 'You going to marry Mr Ward?'

'No, Liu Yu! As I told you, he is just a good friend,' Lizzie replied firmly.

'Everyone say yes.' Liu Yu persisted. There was a touch of mischief in the woman's face now. 'Miss Wells say you go to Hankow soon, it good for you!'

Although this sudden announcement shook Lizzie, she managed to remain calm. 'Perhaps everyone knows more than I do, Liu Yu,' she said. 'Tell them I will go where I am sent. Now finish sweeping and go—I have letters to write.' With a sour face Liu Yu quickly finished her work and left Lizzie to ponder the woman's remarks.

So, she hadn't imagined the coolness in her colleagues' attitudes recently: perhaps, after all, a move from Hangchow to Hankow might solve her problems! She would write to Peter immediately suggesting he delay his trip to China for a while; as for Len she would write a friendly note, taking care not to give him any encouragement.

Hankow was reported to be a boiling hot cauldron in summer and rumours abounded of rebellion and unrest amongst the inhabitants against foreigners. Would Hankow be bearable without the support of Len Ward?

In all this, within the walled confines of Madame Ling's house another tortured soul sat listlessly in his chair, the spark of expectation which had accompanied him from Shanghai having been extinguished completely.

'You are not happy my friend,' Madame Ling said softly as she handed him a bowl of tea. 'I see it in body, see it in face. Can I help?'

Len shook his head. 'I don't think so, Madame.'

'It is Miss Hardy! Before you happy, now like lost dog. Why you not tell her?' He sighed. 'I think she not happy too: why do you not tell her today before you leave?'

'It is no good Madame Ling; she likes me but does not love me.'

The hopelessness in his voice irritated Madame Ling. 'Love, Bah!' she exclaimed. 'She not know it—I see it. You like children!'

'You make it sound so simple,' Len protested. 'Miss Hardy is a good woman with a fine mind, but I think someone has hurt her very much in the past. I fear she may not want to love anyone, let alone me.'

'I think you too kind. You fetch her here before you leave. If not, it will be too late, I think.'

'No, you cannot make someone love you,' Len said firmly. He smiled kindly at her, 'You are very kind and mean well, but this is something I have to accept and live with.'

'Then I go and talk to ancestors and spirits, maybe they help.' She turned and swept from the room defiantly, leaving him to wonder at her perception of the situation and his own inability to solve it. He would be leaving for

Shanghai later in the day where no-one would know his secret, but returning to Hangchow again when business required would be a hard thing to do.

The hospital was busier than ever after the New Year celebrations, as if the sick had supplanted the festivities with their ills, and Lizzie buried herself in work, refusing to contemplate anything beyond the care of her patients.

It was whilst she was dressing a wound that one of the administration staff approached. 'When you've finished there, Nurse Hardy, you are to go to the office,' she said, giving no indication as to the reason.

It was an unusual request under the circumstances and Lizzie was puzzled. 'I'll not be long,' she replied, wondering why she had been summoned. Had she done something wrong? To be sent for usually meant a reprimand or some urgent matter of great importance. She tied off the bandage, gently patted the patient's leg and made her way apprehensively to the office, where, to her surprise, Madame Ling stood with an agitated look on her face. She had obviously been exchanging a few strong words with the administrator before Lizzie's arrival because neither received her with any grace.

Seeing Lizzie, Madame Ling immediately grasped her arm. 'You come quickly,' she said. 'My father-in-law Ling Jen is unwell—he asks for you, only you!' Lizzie was startled to hear this, and looked apprehensively at her senior officer who was standing behind the desk in a none-too-calm frame of mind.

'I keep telling her you are *not* a doctor,' he said emphatically, almost ignoring Madame Ling.

Lizzie flushed. 'I'm sorry; I don't understand why I specifically have been asked to go. I know the Ling family, but that is all.'

'He like you, you talk with respect for Chinese medicine—he wants only you!' Madame Ling's voice rose higher and higher, almost to a shrill squeak.

The administrator's face was flushed with annoyance and he shook his head. 'You must go then, but this is most irregular. When you return I will need to speak to you again. And take that apron off before you go.' There was no disguising his disapproval and Lizzie thankfully followed Madame Ling from the room.

After carefully shutting the door, she asked, 'Is your father-in-law very ill?'

'It is the heart,' Madame Ling replied. 'It is heavy, very down.'

'But I have no knowledge of the problems of the heart,' Lizzie protested; she was greatly concerned for the welfare of the old man, 'You must see a doctor!'

Madame Ling took no notice and pointed to the chairs waiting outside the wall. 'You please get in.'

Bewildered, Lizzie did exactly as ordered. If Ling Jen was so very sick she doubted there was much she could do, except to fetch help. She tapped her fingers continually on the bamboo side of the chair as they went: what if Ling Jen died through her lack of skill? This would cause an immense amount of trouble. She should have refused to come without being accompanied by a doctor, but Madame Ling was a powerful woman it seemed and had they not complied with her request, it could have caused ill feeling against the Mission amongst the inhabitants of the city.

The house-boy was waiting dutifully at the gate in the wall when they arrived and before Lizzie could pass through Madame Ling caught her arm. 'I do this for Len,' she said in a quiet, secretive voice, 'he know nothing—not his fault.' Lizzie had no idea what Madame Ling was talking about and presumed she was simply in a distressed state of mind. However, at the mention of Len Ward's name, Lizzie realised that he may not have left yet and she would be forced to meet him again. Nevertheless she hastened forward, prepared for the worst, with Madame Ling hot on her heels chattering wildly in Chinese.

At the sound of their scurrying feet and Madame's voice, several members of the household appeared in the entrance hall to see what might be needed. Amongst them, looking as fit as a fiddle was Ling Jen. Lizzie turned and saw the sheepish look on Madame Ling's face. She stared at her in disbelief, baffled, 'But your father-in-law looks well enough!' She then remembered her manners and bowed to Ling Jen, asking, 'Are you sick?'

He grinned innocently back at Lizzie. 'I not sick, why you ask?'

'Not him!' Madame Ling quickly intervened in a timid voice. 'Mr Ward sick in heart, he need you!' Then she went on in Chinese to those about them, intimating that Lizzie had misunderstood something: with that, her servants disappeared obediently, leaving Ling Jen waiting impatiently for an answer.

'Is Len Ward sick?' he enquired oblivious to Lizzie's concern for his own person. In a very respectful and subdued voice Madame Ling replied in Chinese, again excluding Lizzie who was getting a little exasperated herself by such inexplicable behaviour. She suspected that Ling Jen was not being told the truth. 'Ah!' he said suddenly as if beginning to understand: then, turning to Lizzie, he smiled and nodded. 'Before you go I show you something,' he said, and bowed leaving the two women alone.

Immediately he'd left the room Lizzie faced Madame Ling, 'What is going on?' she asked. 'You have brought me here, all this way, and Ling Jen is not sick at all! Why have you fetched me? Is Mr Ward sick?'

'I not understand what you say,' Madame Ling unashamedly lied. 'I ask Mr Ward to translate.' She walked swiftly away towards the back of the house, again followed by Lizzie, who by this time was becoming annoyed at what was taking place. 'Mr Ward know nothing,' Madame Ling repeated the strange statement made on their arrival. Pausing at a door she knocked timidly. 'Mr Ward sick in heart,' she said, pressing a hand against her chest. 'You mend it!'

'Come in,' Len called out, startling Lizzie who was desperately trying to make sense of the situation. It was obvious that he was certainly just as surprised to see her, as she was to see him. He got up to greet her. 'How very pleasant,' he exclaimed warmly, 'I hesitated to come to the Mission in case my visit might be an embarrassment.'

She looked at him quizzically as Madame Ling made to leave the room, but Lizzie stopped her. 'It was Madame Ling who fetched me; she told us at the hospital that Ling Jen was sick and would only see me! Now I find that there is nothing wrong with him and I cannot understand what is going on?'

Madame Ling's face was a picture of guilt. 'I fetch her to mend broken heart,' she stammered pointing at Len's chest. 'You mend it please,' she said to Lizzie with such feeling that Lizzie felt sorry for her.

As the truth began to dawn on Len, he realised that in her good hearted and simple way Madame Ling was trying to help him. 'Madame Ling,' he said sternly, 'I know you meant well but it was wrong of you to fetch Miss Hardy like this. She will get into trouble now.' Lizzie had never seen him anything other than patient and kind, she was shaken by the severity of his tone. 'I will sort this out so that you won't lose face, but I do not need help!' He was quite aware that he was a guest in her house and that the Ling family friendship was important to him: he could also see that she was near to tears. 'You meant only to be helpful!' Lizzie was convinced that Len had nothing to do with what had happened, and that Madame Ling had deliberately lied as an excuse to execute her plan.

'But I make you happy now?' Madame Ling implored, looking from Len to Lizzie with such childlike trust that Lizzie found it difficult to be angry with her. 'I go, leave you alone!' And before either of them could speak she slipped away, closing the door behind her.

'I do apologise for Madame Ling,' Len said once she'd gone. 'It is difficult to understand the Chinese mind sometimes. Simplicity is often at the root of their thinking.' He looked at Lizzie, attempting to establish her reaction to the farce that had just taken place. 'I do assure you that this had nothing to do with me.'

'I can see that,' Lizzie admitted ruefully. 'I am beginning to understand that there is often no logic to Chinese thinking. You should see the lengths to which they will go in order to obtain our medicines and drugs; it is often quite unbelievable. Nor will they obey the instructions given, so that afterwards some undo all the good we've tried to do.' She sighed, still baffled by the events which had just unfolded.

'It does need a lot of patience sometimes. However, I am so pleased to see you. I wanted to apologise for my behaviour when last we met. I was afraid I had ruined your evening, and maybe our friendship.' He hesitated before going on; had she arrived of her own volition he could have judged her mood more accurately, as it was he had nothing to base his hopes on.

'I would not like to lose your friendship either.' Lizzie confessed with a candour that surprised even her. 'I have done nothing but think about the situation, in fact my work is suffering because of my inattention and it is becoming noticeable.'

'Madame Ling's actions won't have helped either. What exactly did she say?'

'She said Ling Jen was very ill and that he would see only me—no-one else! The administrator was not very pleased but in order not to upset the local Mandarins and population in general he reluctantly agreed.'

'That was very wrong of her,' Len replied, 'it puts the Mission in a difficult position, you even more so. I think she mistakenly thought she was helping me.'

'It makes it look as though I am involving myself in local affairs behind their backs,' Lizzie said, 'I can see that, but what made her do such a thing?' For all the incident was not of Lizzie's making, she knew that it would most probably sour her relationship with the Mission. Yet another problem to be faced!

'Oh dear,' Len sighed. 'Madame Ling is a very perceptive person; she must have thought I was subdued and unhappy after the other night. Unfortunately she blames it on you, believing that if you married me then all would be well!' Lizzie's mind was in a whirl, and she found it difficult to reply, especially as she could see by the look on his face that it was equally sensitive to him.

'I doubt that any excuse I give on my return to the hospital will suffice,' she said, lowering her voice. 'They will believe I have become too involved with the Lings: I also think that there are rumours linking you and me; all I can hope for is to be transferred elsewhere.'

He did not miss the wistfulness in her tone or the fear in her eyes. 'Is that what your really want?' he asked, blaming himself for her predicament. 'I do promise not to call again if that would help.'

She sat down helplessly on a nearby chair. 'I don't know if that would help at all, besides I like to see you! It would be quite painful to know that you were here yet not be able meet you.'

'I don't have to tell you when I'm coming,' he offered. There was a catch in his voice that belied the calm appearance of his features.

'How unnatural this is!' she cried despairingly. 'I know we are restricted severely as foreigners, that I can accept, it is the close confines of the Mission I cannot.'

'What did you expect?' he asked quietly, and watched her carefully.

Lizzie's face was unreadable. How could she tell him what he really wanted to hear? Yet if she was truly honest she could not return to the hospital knowing that he would never call again. What use would simple letters be to anyone? Her letters to Peter were a façade: he was a stranger, not a real person any more. Len didn't push her into answering his question, he merely watched patiently, seeing in her face the struggle within.

Suddenly she lowered her face. 'Had I known how unsuitable I was for the work I would not have come. I mistakenly believed that I could put my heart and soul into helping. I am not even a committed enough Christian to want to spread the word; I thought helping the sick would be sufficient.'

'But you were doing that at home,' Len gently pointed out. 'Can't you tell me what it is that you're running away from?' Her eyes opened wildly, filling with panic. 'Can't you trust me?' he asked, hurt by her inability to confide in him.

'I can't!' she sobbed. 'There is nowhere for me, no peace. I don't want to go back to the hospital; I don't want to return to England. If I tell you what troubles me you will think ill of me and I shall have lost you too.' Her voice had risen with agitation. So confusing were her babbled words that Len himself found it difficult to think clearly. All he could do was let her go on in the hope that the relief at speaking out would help. 'Nobody could ever understand or forgive me!' she cried.

'Lizzie, you will always have my friendship, of that I can assure you. No matter what the problem is—if you wish to unburden yourself I promise I will never speak of it to any living soul, under any circumstances.' Although his voice was calm, his heart ached with sadness but he intended to get to the bottom of the matter even if it destroyed all his hopes. 'Perhaps you need to talk instead of bottling up your fears. You are allowing them to ruin your life.'

'I have never spoken of it—it is too dreadful a burden to saddle anyone with,' Lizzie confessed tearfully. 'My life is already ruined by it!' Beneath the tears the bitterness was undisguised, the years of torment had taken their toll, unless she found release soon she could not go on—she could no longer live with the lies. If Peter came she was afraid she might tell him everything that had transpired all those years ago. 'Even in death there will be no release.' She was totally drained emotionally by these thoughts: her face had no colour and her eyes were dull with pain as if her life was already ebbing away.

The intensity of Lizzie's anguish alarmed Len who began to believe that she would harm herself. 'You are not returning to the hospital in this state,' he stated emphatically. 'I shall go myself and make it my responsibility to straighten things out. When you are fit to return I shall go with you.' Lizzie started to protest but there was no certainty or conviction in her voice, and he realised that she was past caring. 'Nor shall I return to Shanghai until we have somehow eased your burden. I will send a message by the next boat with some explanation for my delay, and will return there only when I feel the time is right. Meanwhile, I want you to rest while I go and arrange things with Ling Jen so that you can stay here.'

She had no power to resist or will to protest. She had carried the guilt for Nathan's death for too long and now Len Ward's strength of mind was overriding her own.

'Just sit and think of nothing: empty your mind. I'll be back as soon as I can,' he ordered. He could have taken her in his arms and comforted her at this point, he doubted that she would have had the will to protest; but it would have achieved nothing. When eventually he returned, Lizzie looked at him with a sad lost air about her, and he knew he'd been right to control his momentary impulse. Unless he could get to the bottom of her problems, there could be no future for them together, nor for that matter, one for Lizzie on her own.

'Ling Jen and Madame Ling are only too willing to let you stay here, at least until I return to Shanghai,' he informed her. 'He is very angry with Madame Ling for her behaviour and asks that we do not tell Ling Li or the hospital of her foolishness, or they will lose face. Ling Jen will not go out for a few days and will pretend that he did indeed feel unwell.'

'Thank you,' she said meekly, 'I'm so sorry for all the trouble I've caused and am grateful simply to leave everything to you.'

'I think,' he replied with caution, 'that you now have to face your inner demons and tell someone just what bothers you. Surely whatever it is you have done has been more than paid for in pain— and you have so much good to give others. Surely it could not have been something you chose to do, for I see no wickedness in you and life itself can often put terrible strains upon us.' He knew that she was listening, despite the fact that she'd lowered her head again, yet she said nothing, as though still fighting her inner battle. 'I am not in any position to judge you. I see a young woman torn apart. By opening up your heart you may find it eases the pain. Won't you trust me?'

Lizzie was crying softly to herself: what had she to lose by telling him, she was too tired to go on alone. She swallowed hard, her whole body shaking with nerves as she fought the desire to unburden herself. What did it matter any more, death would be preferable to a living hell. Then, as if compelled by an unseen power, she heard the words leave her, 'I killed a man!' she cried, lifting her hands to cover her face. 'There is no escape from that!' She sobbed uncontrollably as her awful burden was finally shared with someone else.

Unable to speak as the truth sank in, Len struggled to know what to say or do. He bit his lip and stared at her. He could never have imagined such a terrible possibility.

As Len had remained silent, Lizzie could only believe that he was thinking ill of her. She made to rise, accepting that it would be better to leave and return to the Mission rather than face his condemnation. She felt sick, her limbs were heavy and her mind anguished. 'If you don't mind,' she whispered, 'I will go back to the Mission. Try not to hate me too much, I couldn't bear it.'

Seeing the state she was in, Len knew he had to say something. 'Don't go,' he pleaded. 'I am having difficulty coming to terms with what you have just told me. I know you wouldn't have cold-heartedly killed someone—few people could. Won't you tell me what happened? You might as well. If I know the circumstances I'm sure that I will understand. I promise to keep my word and never repeat anything that you tell me. Do you believe me?'

'I shouldn't have blurted it out like that,' Lizzie apologised lamely. 'It would have been better to have prepared you by telling you the story from the beginning.' She sank back into the chair as if in a dream. 'I have endured with this on my conscience for over ten years and find it hard to live with myself. I never intended to kill him, yet the final blow was one of rage and fear. Do you really want to hear? Because by telling you what I have done I will have burdened you with my guilt and this, in law, makes you as guilty as I.' She looked up; searching his features for the disdain which he should rightly feel but saw only pity.

On his part he could see only terrible remorse and deep misery etched on her tear-stained face. 'If I don't hear your side of the story I will never know what drove you to such a thing, the question would fester at the back of my mind forever. At least by telling me, I will be able to judge for myself—you owe me that much for having already moved some of the burden onto my shoulders.' He was always a fair-minded man: a man of principles, but he was disturbed—wondering what his feelings for Lizzie would be when he was in full receipt of the facts.

'It's not a long story,' Lizzie said in a flat, lifeless voice. 'You know so little about me that I will begin at the beginning.' She told him of her removal from the slums of Sheffield with her mother, who became housekeeper to and then the wife of Edward who was now her stepfather. She described the dreadful flood that had destroyed his original farm before roaring down the valleys and through the town, killing at least 240 people on that fateful night. How her mother had married Edward and how happy their lives had been. Only briefly did she mention Peter, Edward's nephew, who had joined the Army in a bid to escape the clutches of his worthless family. She did not have to tell him that she was fond of Peter; it was etched on her face. 'My mother then died, and half of me died too!' she cried. 'My stepfather brought me up, he spoilt me, I'm afraid. When I was seventeen, Peter's mother died, and he came with his intended bride, Clara, to stay with us in order to go to the funeral. During that visit Peter was drawn into a fight with his bullying brother Nathan, who, without provocation had slighted my reputation. Bruised but satisfied, Peter returned to Aldershot with Clara only hours before Nathan came in search of him for revenge.'

Here Lizzie paused, afraid to go on.

'Did you love Peter?' Len asked with some sympathy, encouraging her to proceed.

'I believe I did, but Edward would have forbidden it because there was a clause in a Will prohibiting anyone connected with Peter's family inheriting the farm.' This puzzled Len somewhat but he didn't ask for an explanation, he simply wanted Lizzie to come to the crucial point of her story. 'Besides, Peter was only interested in India, and Clara.' To Lizzie it was as if she were a stranger telling the story to another stranger, yet the effort was draining her strength. 'I remember waving Peter and Clara good-bye on that fateful day. I remember the call of the lapwing as it soared above; its plaintive cry must have been heralding my coming fate.' She could hear the bird even now, the high-pitched call ringing in her ears.

Len waited quietly, well aware that Lizzie was reliving every second of the past, aware too that when she had finished she would either have benefited from the relief of telling, or be cursed with the torment for the rest of her life.

'Later in the day I went riding on the moors and Nathan jumped out at me. He was drunk and looking to settle the score with his brother. Hearing that Peter had already left for Aldershot he became bitter and insulted me as he tried to pull me from my horse. I struck him across the face with my crop and galloped away. I was terrified and hoped never to meet him again—he'd come a long way for his revenge. Some time later in the afternoon, when Father was away from the farm, I was stabling my horse when Nathan surprised and attacked me!' Lizzie shivered violently, her body trembling with distress. 'He intended to violate me, and when I couldn't fight him off I managed to reach something heavy and hit him. He struggled to his feet and came towards me with a vicious hatred in his eyes.' Lizzie's drained white face shocked Len. 'At that moment I had to stop him, I wanted him dead,' she cried. 'Something took over, that is what I cannot forgive, that feeling which made me hit him so hard and so deliberately. If I had not, he would have had his revenge on Peter by using me! But I stopped him by killing him. He deserved what he got but I cannot forgive myself for taking such drastic action.' Lizzie paused for a while before continuing, 'Our old farmhand helped me bury him in the ruins of the old house—and he's still there!' she cried helplessly, appalled yet again at the enormity of what she had done.

This revelation shook Len deeply: it was something almost beyond his capability of solving. He could clearly visualise what she had been through and how it must have been a nightmare to live with. What else could he do but try to comfort her? 'Why on earth didn't you tell the truth at the time?' he asked. 'Surely people would have understood?'

Miserably, Lizzie continued. 'I thought they would say I encouraged him, or even blame Peter because they had been fighting a few days before. I thought of the shame it would bring on my father; that Clara wouldn't marry him if she found out, and that Peter would despise me for killing his brother. All I wanted to do was to hide Nathan—to cover everything up—and I have lived ever since with the thought that, one day, he would be found. Neither should I have involved our farmhand and his son who helped hide the body, for they too will be seen as guilty. There is not a day goes by when I don't see Nathan's face coming towards me, and wish I too was dead.'

It was as if a stranger sat before him. 'I can understand that,' he said. 'However, by shielding everyone the way you have, you've created a living hell for yourself, for one day he surely will be found. Let's just hope that it won't be in our lifetime.'

'I suppose you think I was stupid, if not wicked. God knows I never wanted it to happen, nor do I fully understand why it did—do you think He will ever forgive me?' She looked at Len, beseeching him to somehow lift the burden. 'Is it possible?'

No-one had the power to play God. No-one was above the law either and Len Ward acknowledged this to himself before he replied. 'I am not a religious man and cannot speak for God but, if He is all we believe Him to be, then He must be capable of understanding, of seeing things as they really are. If not, then there is no justice and humans may as well behave as they will, without fear of retribution. Men in positions of power often have to make terrible decisions which they then have to live with for the rest of their lives.' There was silence for a moment before Len continued. 'But tell me about Peter, the man who writes to you: do you still love him?'

Lizzie did not want to think about Peter, let alone discuss him with Len Ward. However, having gone this far there was nothing to lose, his good opinion of her must by now have completely evaporated. 'I don't know,' she confessed, averting her eyes. 'Just before I came to China he returned from India after nine years abroad, and asked me to meet him in London. His regiment had been put on standby to go with the relief force to the Sudan. We got on very well: but as for love? How could I let myself fall in love with him again—I could never marry him after killing his brother. I couldn't live with him and hide that knowledge.'

'I see your dilemma,' Len said, holding his own emotions in check, yet he had to know, 'but do you love him otherwise?'

'That's a question I often ask myself, and now he intends coming to China to find me! He believes we could be happy together.'

'But do *you* think so?' Len persisted. He knew he was forcing her to face facts and that this was surely a selfish act on his part. He needed to know where he stood and whether he was fighting a losing battle for her affections. It never occurred to him at this point that her revelations might destroy his own feelings. He was simply anxious to help her in any way possible.

For Lizzie, it was a relief to tell him of her troubles, and he knew too much about her now: if she wanted help then she must trust him. 'What is love?' she pleaded. 'I loved my mother, and I love my stepfather and his family but I don't know what love between a man and a woman is. I see jealousy and disharmony, I see young people displaying their feelings but I don't understand it.'

'Then you don't love Peter or you would understand,' Len said gently, trying to guide her through the maze of emotions besetting her. 'Love is working together for a common purpose, wanting what is best for each other, but not everyone marries for such reasons. Too many do so for position and money, sometimes even in desperation; these are the reasons that usually bring unhappiness in the end.'

'You must have been very fortunate,' Lizzie lamented. 'Were you very happy?'

Len nodded and for the first time since they met that day, he smiled, reflectively. 'Yes, if there is a God then he blessed me. But it was a long time ago and I miss that kind of union; to be able to share thoughts with someone, happy or otherwise. All I can do is be thankful that I did once have such a love, to have it twice would perhaps be asking too much.' He looked wistfully at Lizzie's sad face. 'I hope you will find such a companion one day,' he added so tenderly that Lizzie mentally winced. 'Don't give up too soon, but think carefully about remaining in China. Life in the Missions is very limiting and I feel you need to live a little, to try the happier things in life before it is too late. Don't end up like a bird fastened in a cage, the world is too beautiful for that.'

Looking at him, Lizzie saw a wise man, one who had come to terms with a great loss in his life, yet it hadn't soured him. She felt pain at his loneliness and knew she was fortunate to have met him when she did, at a crossroads in her life. 'I cannot turn back the clock,' she said, 'but you have spoken words of wisdom which I will never forget and could have done with earlier in my life: neither will I forget your kindness to me today. Thank you for not condemning me out of hand, the shock must be great I know but please don't let it stop us being friends; without you I should be lost.' She heaved a sigh. 'Oh dear, I do feel tired, my mind is whirling and I feel quite sick.'

'You must be mentally exhausted, and I'm not surprised. Would you take a further piece of advice and let Ling Jen give you something to make you sleep? A herbal drink that has no side effects but will help you sleep peacefully?' He paused a moment, to contemplate another problem. 'I'm afraid until Madame Ling sorts out the sleeping arrangements you will have to use my bed but no-one will disturb you, I promise.'

'Whatever you think best,' she replied. She was beyond making any decisions and the thought of blotting out the world around her was a relief, nothing would please her more than not having to think for a while.

'I'll be back shortly,' Len said, and left without waiting for her to protest.

When he'd gone Lizzie wrung her hands helplessly. What on earth could he be thinking of her? Not once had he condemned her or shown any sign of rejection, in fact he'd been almost clinical in his comfort and advice. She had put her life in his hands, yet couldn't be sure whether he still cared for her or not. Hearing his footsteps, she wiped her face quickly on her sleeve and tried to compose herself.

'You'll not be surprised to learn that Madame Ling has already prepared a bed for you. Here, drink this, it won't harm you,' Len said. 'Whilst you're sleeping I will go to the hospital and try to sort things out. I'm going to tell them that you're involved here and trying to help, so will stay awhile to look after Ling Jen.'

'Thank you!' Lizzie took the bowl and drank carefully. 'You won't go back to Shanghai yet, will you?' she pleaded. 'I would like to speak to you again when I can think straight, and when you have had time to consider what I have done.'

'Don't worry, I will still be here when you wake up,' Len reassured her, 'now go and rest.'

Many hours later it took Lizzie several seconds on waking to orientate herself with her surroundings. She had no idea how long she'd been asleep and was embarrassed to see that she no longer wore her heavy European clothes:

instead someone had substituted them with a soothing cotton robe. She was surprisingly warm beneath a heavy quilt and, as she lay reflecting on why she was there, realised she was lying on a K'ang, a bed built on bricks with a small stove beneath, producing a comforting heat. She cringed to think of the last time she'd spoken to Len, and wondered why she had risked everything by confiding in him. She buried her head beneath the quilt in an effort to hide from the world, dreading the moment when she would have to face it, and him, again.

She realised that it was late and that she couldn't lie there much longer, besides, the call of nature was overriding the need to stay hidden. Lizzie dressed quickly, noted the position of the sun through the window, and realised she must have slept for at least twelve hours. She blushed: who had removed her clothes, and unfastened her restricting stays? More than likely it had been the amah, but whoever it was must have wondered about the strange attire of this English woman, and no doubt laughed as she described it to her female friends.

Peering into the corridor, Lizzie saw a house-boy on duty there, who promptly went off in search of his Mistress.

'You better now!' Madame Ling said with some satisfaction as she entered the room. There was no hint of guilt stemming from her behaviour the day before and Lizzie realised that Madame Ling had probably rationalised her actions with the spirits, and that was that. 'I get boy to bring water for wash?' she offered politely.

'Yes please,' Lizzie replied, amazed by the woman's total lack of artlessness. 'You have gone to much trouble on my behalf,' she continued, although unable to forget whose fault it was that she was there in the first place. 'Ling Jen's medicine worked very well, I must thank him when I have made myself more presentable.'

'You wash, make pretty and I tell Mr Ward you awake.' There was a hint of glee in her eyes which she had difficulty in concealing.

Trying to delay the meeting with Len, Lizzie did not rush her toilette, but in the end knew it was impossible to put it off any longer. Would he feel it his duty to tell the authorities of her crime? With a great deal of apprehension, she finally made her way back to the hall, wishing unjustly that he had gone back to Shanghai after all, so that she wouldn't have to face him.

Her stomach knotted with nerves when she heard his voice. He was speaking in Chinese and Lizzie marvelled that he mixed so freely with Ling Jen and his family when most foreigners were eyed suspiciously and with disdain, even in Hangchow. His frequent comings and goings amongst the Chinese seemed to irk the Mission staff, or was it only since his attention to her had grown?

Whilst waiting for him to finish speaking, she had time to observe him, and she wondered what had prompted him to develop his acquaintance with her in the first place. She drew in a short breath at the memory of her earlier judgement of him; it was that he was dull. How wrong she had been! Sensing her presence he broke off his conversation and turned, smiling broadly at her, something he rarely did, before resuming his attention to his host. Finally he and Ling Li came towards her, greeting her warmly and drawing a quiet smile from her in return. Sensing that his guests needed to be alone, Ling Li soon excused himself and left the room.

Len looked at her carefully, 'Good Afternoon! You look much improved on yesterday, are you feeling better now?'

This friendly reception was a relief to her. 'Yes,' she responded, 'I do feel stronger and everyone has been so kind. I have Ling Jen to thank for that—and you of course.' She looked quizzically at him, wondering what was in his mind now that he knew what she had done. She needed to know, even to talk about it, because having broken her silence after so many years she yearned for someone to understand. 'What did they say at the Mission, are they very angry?'

'Not now, not after my explanation.' He smiled, 'I'm not a diplomat for nothing, I will tell you about it later. Ah, here comes the house-boy with the hot fish soup Madame Ling suggested. There'll be something more substantial later, when you need it.'

In her concern she hadn't realised just how hungry she was. 'I am very hungry, it is good of Madame Ling to think about everything, but what does Ling Jen say about it all?' Len waited for the house-boy to leave then lowered his voice so that he could not be overheard, and answered, 'He expects her to make up for her silliness by making sure no-one outside the family knows about it, so that the family won't lose face. Now, for the time being I'll leave you alone to enjoy your soup, and come back when you've eaten as I have a plan.'

Lizzie quickly finished the soup together with the rice and vegetables that followed, then she waited quietly for Len to return.

Before long Madame Ling appeared. 'You eat good?' she enthused. 'I sorry for trouble yesterday—you forgive?' The wry smile did not convince Lizzie that her hostess was repentant. 'Mr Ward happier now,' she grinned.

Forcing a smile in return, Lizzie thanked her for her kindness, and asked meaningfully, 'Is your father-in-law well?'

Sheepishly Madame Ling replied, 'better than in temper!'

'Where are the children today?' Lizzie queried, 'everywhere is so quiet, I do hope it's not because of me being here?'

'Children very good, make no noise while you sleep. Not always like this.' She shrugged her shoulders. 'Mr Ward likes children, makes them happy with games. When you ready he see you for talking. Then I take children away. Come!'

'I do forgive you, Madame Ling,' Lizzie couldn't help saying, trying to put her hostess at ease as she followed her, 'but my people at the Mission don't always understand. They're too busy making the sick well again, and they need me to help.'

They had reached Len's room and Madame Ling knocked before entering. To Lizzie's surprise the children were sitting behind a low table, their traditional writing brushes poised as if frozen in time. The sudden appearance of their mother and Lizzie distracted them completely, resulting in an excited outburst of giggles.

'I'm afraid I'm not a very good tutor,' Len exclaimed with some embarrassment. 'I'm trying to teach them to write in English, a mistake I think, when using brushes instead of pens.'

Looking down at the papers, Lizzie could see what he meant and agreed he might be wasting his time, though judging by the bright eyes and enthusiasm which the children displayed he certainly knew how to amuse them. She praised their efforts and was sorry when their mother removed the loudly protesting children from the room, leaving her alone with Len.

Had he chosen to wash his hands of her she wondered? She had no idea what might be forthcoming.

'Don't stand there as if I were judge and jury,' he said gently, 'I can see you quaking before my eyes.'

'What am I to think after what I told you? Sometimes I can't believe what took place that day; it's a nightmare that never goes away.'

To calm her down he replied, 'I don't mind you talking to me about it. The more you do then perhaps, eventually, the pain may ease. It is such a shame that your life has been spoilt in this way.' He paused as if considering what might have been. 'I've thought long and hard about your predicament, and have come to the conclusion that, as a young girl of seventeen, you must have been at your wits end not knowing what to do. It must have been inconceivable that anyone would understand and it's such a pity that the man who helped you wasn't wise enough to give better advice. I really do think that at this late stage it wouldn't help to tell anyone, and we must just hope and pray that body remains hidden long enough so as to do you no more harm.'

His words, though well meant, did little to ease Lizzie's conscience. 'The harm is done, I can never wipe away the memories of that day, nor forgive myself,' she said firmly. 'My father is getting old, he has found happiness and for his and Clara's sakes I dared not unburden myself to anyone. Indeed I must not!'

'You have tortured yourself all this time, not without reason, and I agree that no good would come from confessing the truth now. If the body were discovered, then that would be a different matter.'

'But God knows,' Lizzie said solemnly, 'I can never hide it from Him!'

'No. Just let us hope He is an understanding God and forgiving.' Her face was pale, her eyes misty with tears and Len was at a loss as what else to say. 'I think it is not God we have to fear but the justice of man, if ever the truth be known.'

'How do you know that I'm telling the truth?' Lizzie asked, her eyes searching his face for signs of doubt. 'And how did you know that something momentous was troubling me?'

'Simply because I believe that the eyes mirror the soul, the pain, and the doubts. When someone refuses to meet your eyes with theirs it's difficult to trust them. Some people are open and candid which makes it easier to understand them.'

'Do I betray my inner feelings so much?' She flushed, wishing she hadn't asked him such a personal question.

'Sometimes,' he replied with a twinkle in his eyes. 'I don't have the power to read your mind but there is much to be seen by simply watching. On long journeys, in lonely places, I pass the time observing people; you can learn much about someone without even speaking to them.'

'You are very wise,' she sighed.

'Perhaps it comes with age,' he suggested lightly. Lizzie then realised that he was watching her closely as he spoke and she deliberately lowered her eyes. He laughed, 'I cannot read your every thought you know, but I do often see inquisitiveness as well as trust in you: I hope no-one will ever take advantage of this.'

Changing the subject, Lizzie said, 'Perhaps now you can see why I never really encouraged my cousin Peter. I couldn't live with him and not tell him about Nathan; neither could he live with me knowing that I'd killed his brother. It would be impossible, intolerable.'

'But do you love him? Does he love you? Surely he might just understand, knowing his brothers character?' Len held his breath hoping that Lizzie wouldn't lie to him.

Knowing that only the truth would do, Lizzie shook her head. 'I don't know, I see only the young man he was. In ten years the gulf has become so wide between us that now he is really a stranger. I have left him thinking the worst of his brother for apparently deserting their father. I allowed myself to become promised to him out of compassion, because he was depressed at going to war. I don't know if that is really what I wanted.'

'Do you think he will come to China looking for you?'

'He said as much in his last letter and I fear it may be too late to write and put him off.'

'It's a long way to come without reason,' Len said a little sharply, 'have you given him false hope?'

The edge in his voice did not go unnoticed by Lizzie, who could quite understand that he must be weary of her problems by now. 'I never imagined he would follow me: I believed he would grow away from me once the fear of battle had subsided. He had convinced himself that he had participated in one skirmish too many and that his luck had run out, so I tried to give him moral support. I was determined to come to China, though really I suspect I was hiding my head in the sand again.'

'I think,' Len advised, 'that under the present circumstances you should ask to return to Shanghai on a sabbatical, to work out your feelings in a more normal setting. Give yourself time; many women question their callings after their first bad winter and hot summer in China. If you were asked to go deeper inland, to Hankow for instance, then you should be convinced that you want the hardship and the sacrifice that this would entail.'

Lizzie thought for a moment. 'Where would I stay in Shanghai if not at the Mission—what would the hospital say to my leaving?'

'You've been in China nearly a year now; your request shouldn't be refused. I took the liberty of explaining that you had been worrying about your cousin in the Sudan and over your father who was becoming frail; also, that for all you didn't speak about your problems, you had let them get you down. I suggested that a furlough in Shanghai might help; otherwise they might lose a good nurse. I also explained that although Ling Jen's condition was not in anyway serious, he felt in need of reassurance, and having discussed medicine with you during your visits, he wanted your opinion: that really the old man wanted comfort and understanding, nothing more. I did also point out that his asking for you, a Christian, is a sign that his respect for the Mission is growing. I hope you didn't mind my bending the facts a little.'

Len had certainly gone to great lengths on her behalf, even as far as twisting the truth: he was a good diplomat and she was happy to take his advice. 'You seem to have a good understanding of life, and people,' she said, praising Len without patronising him, 'I do believe you are right, a break may help me to think more clearly. You see until I met you I confided in no-one, I refused to let friendships develop because I believed I was unworthy and dishonest by not telling them the truth. I received a form of satisfaction from working hard but it never eased the pain.'

'Don't you see,' Len responded gently, 'that you need the help close friendship brings? I can see why you couldn't divulge the cause of your problem and why what happened affected you so deeply. Now however, you have to move on. There is no going back. A soldier has no choice but to kill, if he considered the other man's goodness, family, the consequences even, his own life might be forfeited. Try to let only good come out of this. Take the furlough; it will give you a chance to re-assess your life.'

'I tried to help Peter for those very reasons, knowing he was tired of killing. Perhaps I gave him cause to think that I would welcome a deeper friendship, but in reality I never could have—in that I was foolish. Neither do I have the faith that most missionaries have. I simply wanted to help the sick. I can see the need to teach the virtues of Christianity in a heathen culture but I lack their dedication.'

'I don't think you were foolish: naive perhaps and certainly in need of help. Now we must put all this into perspective. Come to Shanghai with me: I have friends with accommodation and we can spend time together when you can discuss anything you want. Have a bit of pleasure this time. I will show you a life in Shanghai you have not previously seen. How about it?' Lizzie felt a tremor of awakened anticipation at his suggestion, which Len saw as he watched her. 'Whatever you decide, you must go to the hospital as soon as you can to explain, or they will no doubt come looking for you thinking I'm up to no good.' He smiled, lightening the atmosphere, which Lizzie responded to with a faint smile. 'That's better,' he conceded. 'Let's enjoy life while we can.'

Shanghai 1886

In spite of the sharpness of the late
January weather, Lizzie waited by Len Ward's side,
enjoying a frisson of anticipation as their boat came towards the bridge to collect them for their journey to Shanghai. After much deliberation she had taken Len's advice and asked for a furlough, confiding in part to the Administrator some of her doubts and fears. He wisely accepted the idea of a sabbatical, assuring her that she was greatly valued and needed at the hospital, and that he would welcome her back if she chose to return. She was immensely cheered by the many good wishes she received, and knew if she did return, life would be easier to bear because of this support. On her last day she left with a strange twinge of regret, not knowing if she would indeed come back.

With a lump in her throat, Lizzie looked back at the city walls as the vessel drew away from the quay where they'd boarded. Was this to be her last view of the city and its inhabitants whom she had grown to like so much? If she did return it must not simply be from a sense of duty, but from an inner desire to serve these people who needed her.

'I'm always a little sad to leave Hangchow,' Len said, as if reading her mind, 'and very happy to return.' They were leaning against the handrail, wrapped up against the chill wind. 'It's going to be a long cold journey I'm afraid: if you take my advice you'll huddle round the stove as long as you can. I've bribed the captain to give you the cabin near the boiler; it's the warmest place on board, so don't feel that you have to spend time with me when you could be more comfortable there.'

There was little to do as the miles passed by, except to read or sew in the ill-lit cabin which stank of kerosene, opium and old canvas, so when she could Lizzie sat with Len in the crowded area under a cover by the wheelhouse. Periodically they ventured around the deck to stretch their legs and take in fresh air, only to find on their return that some other passengers had taken their seats.

To help pass the time Len asked Lizzie about her childhood on the farm. She told him about her year away at school in Worksop, of her training as a nurse and the long lonely years in London. In return, he told her of his upbringing in the bustling port of Bristol, and of how working in the offices of a shipping agent as a youth had eventually led to him to coming to Shanghai, where he met his wife. Mary Ward had been the daughter of another shipping agent: they'd fallen in love and married quite quickly, but their happiness was short lived as, after only five years, Mary caught dysentery and died. There was nothing then for him to go back to England for; his parents were dead, his job in China was secure and he'd grown to love the country and its people.

Not once during the long journey did Len hint at having any special feelings for Lizzie and she began to wonder if her shocking revelation had, in fact, changed his thoughts about her? She couldn't blame him of course if this was so, it was only to be expected, but at least he had promised to remain a close and valued friend.

The boat finally docked at its jetty in Shanghai, and as usual the landing stage was alive with people and chairs. As usual, Lizzie was quite content to allow Len to organise the transport that would take them to the lodging house of his friend.

'I will not be able to take you home with me,' he'd said during the voyage. 'If I did you would have no reputation left at all! I also advise that you stay away from the Mission until you're sure of what you intend to do. I have a colleague whose wife takes in English boarders and travellers, so I'll take you there first.'

'I don't have a lot of money,' Lizzie quickly reminded him, 'especially as my leave had not been planned in advance. I have some savings in the Hong Kong and Shanghai Bank, but there is a limit how far those will stretch. It's there in case I needed to return to England at some point.'

'We'll try not to plunder it too much,' Len assured her. 'I'll gladly lend you some money until you can get to the bank, then you must do some planning.'

'When will I see you again?' Lizzie asked, knowing he had to catch up with the work he had neglected on her behalf. 'Will you be able to spend a little time with me or have you a busy time ahead?' Having enjoyed the last five days in his company she was loath to see him go.

'Once I've got you settled I must report to the Consulate. I expect there will be a mountain of paperwork to sort out and probably some visits to make tomorrow. I'll make a point of calling in during the evening if you like. Meanwhile, consider your options and go out and about. Providing you stay within the British settlement and on the main thoroughfares you should be safe enough.' Lizzie felt quite despondent as their carriage rolled on. 'You're quiet all of a sudden,' Len commented. 'Are you regretting the decision to come?'

She smiled weakly. 'I'm not sure. I feel lost somehow. Having had all my routines and responsibilities taken from me it is quite unnerving. I don't know anyone here. Do you really think it unwise for me to stay at the Mission? Mrs Bradshaw was always very kind to me; she seemed to be a very understanding woman.'

'Go and see her by all means, and ask for advice, but I recommend that you wait a day or two before doing so.' The carriage stopped before a modest house which had a strong iron gate at the front. 'Here we are. I should warn you that Mrs Gough can be a bit bossy at times, but you won't be here long enough for it to worry you. Just humour her and all will be well.'

Len didn't stay long once he'd introduced Lizzie to the lady and had acquired a room for her. 'I'm leaving you in good hands,' he said before leaving, 'and I'll call in after tea tomorrow.'

'A good man that,' Mrs Gough remarked, once Len had gone and she showed Lizzie to her room. 'I'll get someone to help you with your luggage later. The Consulate knows I take in boarders and they often send me customers.' She showed Lizzie where everything was, told her when supper would be ready and left her to settle in.

The room was well furnished and comfortable, the likes of which Lizzie hadn't seen since leaving England. She looked nostalgically at the small things that make an English gentlewoman's home: a rug on the floor, ornaments, pictures, linens and lace. She knew that some of the families within the Missions had brought their treasured belongings with them but she hadn't yet been invited to view them.

After attending to her toilette Lizzie awaited supper with a growing appetite. To her relief Mrs Gough had two other temporary boarders taking supper at the same time, a mother and daughter en-route to Peking where the husband worked in the British Consulate. Both women showed a genuine interest in Lizzie's experiences in China as this was their first visit to the country. By the time supper was over, all three had arranged to go out together the following day, exploring those parts of the settlement Lizzie thought it safe to see. This chance encounter thrilled Lizzie for it gave her a freedom which would otherwise have been denied her had she been alone— and it made up for the separation from Len.

As the three women strolled along the Bund the following day watching the comings and goings of the countless vessels, Lizzie recalled just how busy a port Shanghai was. All day a very excited Miss Turner kept her mother and Lizzie on the move, exploring and shopping, until Lizzie feared she would lose her voice as she continually had to raise it above the noise to explain what little she knew of the place.

To shop for shopping's sake had never been one of Lizzie's habits, yet in the eager company of this mother and daughter she found the experience quite breathtaking. Many of the shops they visited dealt solely in goods designed to please the foreigner who wanted to take something of China home with them. Miss Turner bought a fan of filigree ivory, delicately painted but completely useless for the heat of Peking, whilst Mrs Turner purchased an ornament of jade which Lizzie considered to be more suitable for taking back to England, rather than on to Peking. Finally, in a light-headed moment, Lizzie chose for herself a colourful pair of embroidered slippers, simply because it was the first time she'd seen any big enough to fit her European feet. She had of course haggled the price down, and was admired for doing so by her companions.

When the three of them returned to the boarding house, they were completely worn out and in need of a rest. Even the young and vibrant Lucy Turner looked jaded by their outing. However, when Len called after work he found Lizzie refreshed and flushed from the sharp cold wind, eager to tell him of her day. He was mystified as to what had transpired in the previous twenty-four hours to so energise Lizzie and bring about such a change in her spirits.

'You haven't stayed in all day reading then?' He said with a hint of amusement. 'I expected to find you bored and as a result, pleased to see me.'

'Oh, but I am!' Lizzie quickly assured him, 'pleased to see you I mean. I have made friends with two ladies here, and together we have explored Shanghai until we could walk no further.'

It was obvious that Lizzie had thoroughly enjoyed herself, and this pleased Len, although he wasn't sure she'd given much thought to her predicament, or future.

Seeing his expression, she sobered a little, exclaiming, 'Oh dear, and you have had to catch up with a backlog of work!' He nodded in agreement. 'I did, however, manage to get to the bank to sort out my finances,' Lizzie babbled on. 'Tomorrow will be the Turner's last full day free before going on to Peking, so I thought we might explore a bit further.'

'You will be careful, won't you? Shanghai has its rogues too,' he warned, concerned that Lizzie's growing confidence might make her reckless.

It was plain to see that he was slightly bewildered by her exuberance and she tried to calm down. However, at that moment the Turner ladies made an unexpected appearance and a wide smile came to Lizzie's face. 'Do meet Mrs and Miss Turner,' she said, drawing the ladies toward him. 'This is my dear friend Mr Ward who also works for the British Consulate but here in Shanghai, not Peking.' Len shook hands, at the same time recognising the qualities in the women which had brightened Lizzie so much. Both were charming, well attired ladies whom he doubted would lead Lizzie astray, though he surmised that being in China would eventually temper their buoyant spirits.

'I suppose you have things to discuss,' Mrs Turner said. 'Would you like us to retire?' The small sitting room that Mrs Gough had provided for her guests was adequate enough but offered little privacy, and Mrs Turner quite rightly felt it better to politely withdraw.

'There's no need,' Len assured her, 'besides, you have obviously enjoyed your day together and wish to plan for tomorrow.'

'Miss. Hardy has opened our eyes, Mr Ward,' the mother replied, 'and it is hard to believe she's been here less than a year. I'm afraid I speak no word of the language so will have to learn of course, and once I reach Peking it will be easier because my husband has been here for some time.'

After half an hour or so of general conversation Mrs Turner touched her daughter's arm, 'Come, my dear,' she urged, 'we've had a rather hectic day and must begin our packing if we are to spend most of tomorrow sightseeing. If I get as exhausted again I shall not last the course.'

'Must we, mother?' Lucy protested. 'I'm not tired now.' She was a young woman of perhaps twenty-two or three, Len estimated, with pleasantly rounded features made prettier by clear blue eyes which danced merrily as she spoke. She was also a mirror image of her more forceful, but nevertheless attractive, mother, and Len approved of Lizzie's choice of companions.

As he rose to shake hands, Len asked, almost shyly, 'I wonder, would the three of you like to come to supper at my home tomorrow evening? I could arrange for a carriage to fetch you.' He watched for Lizzie's reaction, hoping that she wouldn't mind his invitation, or in him including the Turners,

'That is very generous of you; it won't be too much trouble will it?' Mrs Turner replied, 'it's such short notice?'

'It will be my pleasure: I have a Chinese housekeeper who I'm sure can be persuaded to prepare a simple meal.'

'Then we had better go and pack, Lucy, tomorrow we shall be very busy.' She turned to Lizzie, 'We shall be ready at ten as arranged, Miss Hardy, and thank you again for an unforgettable day.'

When both had left the room, Len sat down. The place seemed strangely empty now, he turned to Lizzie, 'Did you mind me asking them to supper tomorrow? It seemed a golden opportunity.'

'Of course not, and I must admit to being curious about that part of your life,' Lizzie confessed, hoping she didn't appear too forward.

He appeared not to notice. 'Do you think this furlough was a good idea, or haven't you had time to consider it?' he asked with a touch of humour.

Lizzie's mood changed, her previous light-hearted demeanour being replaced by more sombre thoughts. 'Believe it or not it has been constantly on my mind, although in the presence of those two ladies I have been able to temporarily forget my problems. I thought that for these two days I would allow myself the pretence of being normal. Is that so very wrong?'

He appeared satisfied and not in the least annoyed by her answer. 'Lizzie, it is something you should have done years ago: had you been allowed to, you could have enjoyed life. Now is the time to sample it, then to decide which path you want to take.'

Looking wistfully at him, Lizzie thought again how shrewd he was. She did not regret her decision to come, yet perhaps the break brought with it more questions than it could solve. 'I think I will visit Mrs Bradshaw when the Turners have gone. I feel she could help and guide me; she intimated that she'd given advice to many who have found China too much of a challenge.'

'Just be careful, try to sort your needs out first; that's all I ask. If you were to go back to Hangchow and then were sent further up the Yangtze to Hankow or even Chunking, there is more to consider. Those places are alive with mosquitoes; the summer temperatures are very high and sultry, followed by icy cold winds in February. The Consul is also worried right now about unrest in the area, it may not be safe.' He advised her as gently as he could, knowing that if he pushed too hard she might resent it. He had just seen what the spirit of freedom had given her when he arrived earlier. 'I will not be able to come beyond Hangchow to see you either,' he said in a matter of fact way, as if dealing with some client.

There was something in his manner when he said this that startled Lizzie; it was almost as if he was warning her that by going further into China, this could put an end to their friendship. She recalled that since leaving Hangchow he had spoken hardly any words of affection, had his opinion changed because of her terrible disclosure? His companionship was becoming precious to her: to lose it would be to destroy the very foundation on which she now stood. She sighed, 'You must think me very fickle to have come all this way only to have doubts, and I really have no desire to go back to England. I am in a complete muddle.'

'I am very pleased that you don't want to leave China—at least I'm not guilty of driving you away. But will you be able to convince the Missionary Society that your heart is still in the work—will they allow you to stay and nurse the sick in Shanghai or Hangchow? Perhaps there may be no compromise. Also, what would happen if Peter suddenly arrived here?' Lizzie's face clouded over. 'Go and see Mrs Bradshaw by all means but, unless you are frank with her, the problems will not go away.' He knew he was pushing her, and in order to soften his firmness he added, calmly and deliberately, 'If it is any help to you in your decision making, there is one other alternative. Would you marry me?' He sat watching in silence as she struggled to grasp the significance of this moment, realising that she couldn't be expected to reply without giving the matter a deal of thought. Then he went on, 'Well, at least you haven't turned me down flat, I would far prefer that you came to me because you cared, rather than out of desperation.' He had been frank, leaving himself open to the pain a refusal would bring, but it was a risk he was prepared to take.

'How can you want me, knowing what I've done?' she gasped finally. 'Think of the consequences should Nathan be found! I could not stand by and let someone else take the blame; I would be compelled to go back to England.'

'I want you because I believe in you; in your integrity, and for those reasons I am willing to take that risk—I would not let you return alone. I'm not a fool; I'm just a man wanting to take care of you. Don't give me your answer now, take your time.' He paused as if unable to continue, 'I'm afraid I have a secret to confess as well.' he said, somewhat embarrassed. Lizzie held her breath not knowing what to expect. 'I've intercepted a letter for you that came to the Consulate from a ship which arrived yesterday. I believe I recognised the handwriting.' He handed the letter over. 'It was childish of me I know, but I wanted to tell you where I stood before you read it. In my own defence, I could have let it go on to Hangchow and it would then have been a further week before you received it.' He looked quite sheepish as he sat there. 'I was going to give it to you before I left tonight.'

186

Hesitatingly she took the letter; it was of course from Peter. She could have been annoyed, for Len had concealed the letter for almost an hour. Yet it was hardly a crime and his motive signified the importance of his feelings. 'I have much to consider,' she replied. 'Although I think I know what I must do. If you will be patient with me for a day or two I will give you my answer then.' She deliberately kept her emotions in check; much depended on her not making a mistake now. 'I am honoured to know your feelings and for that reason I must be sure of my own. You have become very dear to me,' she admitted, 'I must deliberate carefully for I don't want to hurt you—or anyone else for that matter.'

'You will still come tomorrow, won't you?' he asked, as he prepared to leave.

'Of course I will. And I look forward to it very much,' Lizzie said softly, wondering if by keeping him waiting for her answer she was unwittingly tormenting him.

'May I make a suggestion for the three of you tomorrow if the weather is dry? Hire a carriage and go for a ride down Bubbling Well Road towards the race course—it's very pleasant that way, especially if the sun is out.'

Once Len had departed, Lizzie hurried to her room and tore open the letter. Had Peter made up his mind about following her, and how would she feel if he did? She quickly scanned the contents; it was in affectionate terms and left her in no doubt of his intentions. He had resigned his commission and left the Army; he'd been successful in obtaining a position with a shipping agent and last but not least, would follow his letter on the next Jardine, Matheson & Co. ship bound for China. Lizzie was stunned, staring blankly at the paper in her hand. Peter could arrive at any time in Shanghai as Jardine's vessels sailed frequently and speedily in order to be competitive. What on earth was she to do?

Sheffield 1985

At this apparently critical point in Mimi's manuscript Mark groaned, 'You're tearing me to pieces, is there no end to Lizzie's predicament? I hope there's a happy ending after all this, I feel like telling her what to do!'

Laughing, Mimi put her pen down, 'I think I'll start making tea,' she replied as she rose from the desk where she was putting the last brush strokes of refinement to the biography.

'Come on, put me out of my misery—how does it end?'

Mimi shook her head adamantly. 'No, read on. Though remember that her life wasn't fiction and I can't change its ending.'

'You'll be the death of me,' Mark laughed. He watched her go into the kitchen, her short hair shining in the sunlight as she went near the window. She had turned his normally quiet existence upside down, with her bubbly personality and, sometimes, impetuous behaviour; he liked having her around the flat and he would miss her when she left. 'I feel lazy sitting here reading instead of working,' he called out unconvincingly. 'Please, put me out of my misery and tell me what happens.'

A sharp emphatic, 'No!' reverberated round the flat. Mark seized the manuscript once more, determined to find the answers before tea.

Shanghai 1886

The following day dawned bright but
cold for the trio, although dark clouds could be
seen on the horizon threatening rain later on. Heeding Len's suggestion, the
ladies hired a carriage and rode down towards the racecourse.

'What a good idea that was of Mr Ward's,' Mrs Turner exclaimed as they left
the more crowded parts of town, 'I didn't realise that China was so advanced!'
Lizzie was also impressed by the extensive developments of European-style
houses which were new or under construction along the route, each being set
in its own grounds, an indication of the wealth and success of the merchants
of Shanghai.

'I agree, China is not as backward as I'd imagined,' Lucy said as she
admired the properties. I think I will enjoy it here.'

Not wanting to spoil their illusions of the day's outing, nevertheless Lizzie
felt obliged to warn them yet again that Shanghai, with its Western developments, in no way represented the real China. Their freedom would be
exceedingly curtailed in Peking, and the dangers very real. To someone as
lively as Lucy the social rounds within the settlements would soon pall.

After a pleasant hour they returned to the city and once more strolled
along the Bund, mingling with the multitude of western and oriental sight-
seers, all hoping for news, business, sights and sounds from the outside world.
Being in the company of the Turners allowed Lizzie to see Shanghai from a
different perspective, and after months of seclusion in Hangchow she could
understand the fever of curiosity that drew exiles to the wharf-sides to greet
each arriving ship. Unlike Lucy, who had been in Shanghai less than a week,
Lizzie was starved of news from Europe: even her clothing seemed tired and
unfashionable after only a year away. Accordingly she decided to look for a
more suitable outfit in the many shops that catered for consular and
businessmen's wives.

Later that day with this aim in mind, a sense of excitement filled the three
ladies as they searched avidly for something Lizzie could wear that night at
Len's supper party. She did eventually select a gown which would have
multipurpose uses; this was not quite what the Turners had in mind for her,
but anything too fancy or frilly would get little use if she returned to
Hangchow. Protesting firmly, Lizzie finally compromised by choosing an
elegant and tasteful gown which fitted her perfectly.

'There!' Mrs Turner said later, when Lizzie joined them in the sitting room to await their carriage. 'You look wonderful, my dear. It always brightens the spirit to have a new outfit, don't you think?' She fussed about; straightening the lace on Lizzie's fitted bodice and smoothing the folds of her skirt in a motherly fashion. 'There, doesn't she look perfect, Lucy? But why must you have your hair up in that severe way? Still, it's too late too change it now, perhaps tomorrow we could try a different style, if you like?'

'But you're leaving tomorrow,' Lizzie replied, smiling inwardly for she was very pleased with her purchase—and her hair if it came to that.

'No, No! A note has been delivered to us, and we are to be delayed a further two days, apparently the ship's captain has taken it upon himself to wait for more cargo, and no amount of persuasion has made him change his mind. Is everything so lackadaisical here?' Mrs Turner asked with no little irritation.

'I'm afraid so,' Lizzie explained, 'it's best not to rely on anything, just take things as they come. You will often find your patience tried to the limit, but accept it and you will find life much less of a strain.'

Mrs Turner tut-tutted. 'I do like things to be orderly,' she complained, 'however Arthur stands it I just can't imagine.'

'Two whole days!' Lucy exclaimed. 'I quite like the idea—what shall we do tomorrow?'

'It is wintertime, I'm afraid,' Lizzie commiserated, 'and I don't know Shanghai sufficiently well to have joined any of the ladies clubs here where I might have taken you. I do have some business to attend to as well, but if you like I'll go with you to the Bund in the morning and watch the vessels come in. We might also take a ride in a rickshaw; I've never done that myself.'

Lucy's eyes lit up at this, but Mrs Turner sighed. 'If you don't mind I'll take a rest tomorrow, I really have had enough of this gadding about. I was so looking forward to setting off to see Arthur after all this time apart.' She suddenly looked older and wearier than before, and Lizzie wondered if the woman knew just what she was letting herself in for by coming to China. 'Time will quickly pass, I suppose,' she added. 'Ah, I do believe I can hear the carriage. Mr Ward will be waiting, we'd best go!'

All day Lizzie had tried to suppress her curiosity over the coming visit to Len's home, but with the Turners constantly referring to it, it had been very difficult. Tonight she would see a new side to Len but at least she would not have to face him alone. What would he think of her extravagance in buying a new gown, especially as she had talked of having little money to spare? Breaking the habit of a lifetime had been partly due to the refreshing exuberance of the Turners, and she felt a quiver of excitement at the result.

The carriage when it came was empty, Len having decided there would be more room for the ladies if he remained at home, ready to welcome his guests when they arrived. The journey was not a long one, and soon he came out to greet them. He seemed relaxed and very smart in his well-tailored suit with his white shirt immaculately starched; Lizzie was immediately glad she'd taken the trouble to buy a new gown. Once inside, the house-boy took their cloaks and Len led them into a large, airy sitting room which, for a single man, was remarkably comfortable.

'Supper won't be long,' he announced, once formalities were over. 'I'm pleased you could all come,' he went on, being careful to include Mrs Turner in his conversation. 'Did you enjoy today? It was a pity it rained so heavily this afternoon.'

Mrs Turner took no time in replying, thus giving Lizzie and Lucy an opportunity to glance at their surroundings. Lizzie was particularly delighted to find that he obviously enjoyed reading, for he had several shelves filled with books on a range of subjects.

'We took your suggestion and went to the racecourse before lunch,' Mrs Turner was saying. 'It was a very pleasant excursion, thank you. But I was very despondent on returning to Mrs Gough's because we've been told we will have to remain in Shanghai for two more days.'

'I'm sorry about that,' Len commiserated politely, 'unfortunately it is quite normal for such delays to take place here.'

Seeing that Len Ward's attention was constantly being drawn towards Lizzie and Lucy, Mrs Turner couldn't help remarking, ' We managed to persuade Miss Hardy into buying a new outfit whilst it was raining. She looks very well in it don't you think?'

Lizzie flushed, for although she'd been enjoying browsing through the titles of Len's books, she had in fact been surreptitiously listening to their conversation.

'Yes, an admirable choice,' he replied warmly, causing Lizzie's colour to deepen even further. 'I'm honoured. To have three such charming visitors in one evening is indeed a pleasure.' A gong suddenly sounded from beyond the room and Lizzie breathed a sigh of relief. 'Ah, supper is ready—would you like to go through? I suppose you will be hungry after all your exertions.' He turned to Lizzie, 'No chopsticks tonight, Lizzie!' he said with a knowing smile.

'I will never eat with those things,' Mrs Turner said adamantly. 'I shall take cutlery with me wherever I go!'

'Most Westerners here have knives and forks, Mrs Turner, but you will be in danger of insulting your Chinese host if you insist on taking your own utensils with you,' Len pointed out. 'It's not difficult when you get the hang of it—is it Lizzie?'

'I don't know about that,' she grinned at him, 'it can get a little messy and long-winded if you don't get it right.'

She looked round the dining room; it was not as she'd imagined, she had half-expected him to have adopted some Chinese customs, but no, they might well have been in a middle-class house in England.

Once they were seated, Len said, 'I try to eat the local produce, but for tonight I thought a mixture of dishes would make an interesting experience for you.' The cook brought in several dishes which she placed in the centre of the table. 'Please do help yourselves; try a little of everything first, eat what you like, leave what you don't.' He had provided a feast of vegetables, fruit, fish and rice cooked and prepared in differing ways, there was something for everyone.

'Oh, I do like the crab,' Mrs Turner exclaimed, taking a second helping.

'Try the salted shrimps, Mama,' Lucy advised.

'Not salt, my dear, not for me! Though what I have tried I have enjoyed but goodness knows how I would cope with chopsticks, I really don't know.'

Lizzie ate on, well aware that Len was watching her. He had gone to a great deal of trouble to ensure that his guests were enjoying themselves, but Lizzie could sense from his glances that this evening was for her. The Turners, although welcome, were the excuse he'd been waiting for.

'Do you think I will like Peking Mr Ward?' Lucy asked. 'Lizzie has painted a dull picture of isolation and inward thinking in the settlements.' Lizzie tried to protest; she had never meant to disillusion Lucy, only to give advice. 'What do you think?' Lucy persisted.

'I don't think she meant the advice unkindly. Peking is very different to Shanghai and Hangchow. If you are good at mixing socially you may find it a round of activity, but sadly this can soon pall in the heat of summer or the icy winds of April.'

'I'm sorry if I gave the wrong impression,' Lizzie protested. 'You are younger than I and will make friends more easily. The only problem is that the older children are often sent home to school out of the heat and disease; it's a pity but is thought to be necessary.'

'I suppose I will manage,' Lucy said confidently, 'I have only come to see Papa, then I shall return to England without Mama. If I don't see him soon I shall forget what he looks like.'

'Then you will enjoy your stay. It is the long-term isolation that requires a special constitution.'

'Your father's work is out here,' Mrs Turner admonished her daughter, 'and I do miss him; I will simply have to adapt unless I want to remain alone in England.'

'I think you will cope quite well,' Len said, although he wondered if she would. 'Do you play tennis or sing, or play cards?' If you do, life won't be so bad.'

'Cards, yes, tennis no!' Mrs Turner's voice had a touch of horror in it. 'I never could stand strenuous activity, as for my voice, the least said about that the better.' Lucy laughed. 'Now, my girl, just because you have your Papa's talent for singing that is no reason to mock my poor feeble attempts.' Lucy smiled wryly at Lizzie but said no more.

'Would you like a game of cards now? What do you play?' Len asked, looking from one guest to another. All nodded approvingly, prompting him to bring a pack of cards from the nearby drawer. 'I'm a bit stale,' he confessed, 'but a good-natured game will suit me very well.'

The good-natured game lasted two hours until suddenly Len looked at the clock. 'Oh, my word!' I'm afraid the carriage will arrive to collect you in fifteen minutes,' he said in amazement. 'I hadn't realised how quickly the time was passing.'

'It has been a splendid evening, Mr Ward, I cannot thank you enough. I just wish I could offer you such hospitality in return, and a chance to beat me at this game next time perhaps. If ever you are in Peking you must let Arthur and me know, you will be most welcome.' She turned to Lucy, 'Come dear, help me with my cloak.' She led her daughter out into the hall, leaving Lizzie alone with Len.

'I think she's arranged this,' Len said softly, a smile hovering on his lips. Then, lowering his voice even further, he continued. 'Thank you for coming, Lizzie, I don't have time now to show you the rest of the house, but it is yours if you want it!' He took her hand gently and pressed his lips against it.

'You are too good to me, Mr Ward, I don't deserve such kindness,' Lizzie said softly, teasing him.

'For God's sake Lizzie, call me Len, people will think we're strangers.'

A lump rose in Lizzie's throat and she touched him gently on the cheek with her hand. 'Thank you for tonight,' she whispered, 'the day after tomorrow I will give you my answer.' Before he could respond, Lizzie slipped out into the hall just as the house-boy came to announce the arrival of the carriage.

'I feel a strange optimism in the air, for all of us,' Len said as he closed the carriage door. 'I think we will meet again some day!'

As they rode on Lucy remarked, 'What a nice man. I know what he means; there is a kind of inevitability in that having got on so well, we will remain friends. I do hope so, I felt very comfortable there.'

This frank appraisal of Len Ward amused Lizzie who never expected such a remark from the lively Lucy. 'Mr Ward has been a great support to me since I arrived in China,' Lizzie confessed, 'he is very patient and understanding.'

'Why has he no wife?' Lucy asked, 'You could do very well there, Lizzie.'

'Don't be so rude; asking such questions, Lucy,' Mrs Turner snapped. 'I really do believe it's time you found a man who could control you!'

Lucy fell silent at her mother's admonition and Lizzie felt a pang of sympathy for the girl.

Arriving back at Mrs Gough's house, the three women parted company on the assumption that Lucy and Lizzie would go down to the Bund the following morning. Lizzie really had more to do than go there again, but Lucy was pleasant enough company to be with and it gave her another chance to procrastinate over her visit to the Mission.

'I'd never tire of watching all this activity,' Lucy cried as she watched large sea-going vessels slide menacingly between the smaller sampans, night-soil boats, junks and fishing boats, heading for their berths.

So much noise, so much bustle! Lizzie's mind was not on the Bund however but elsewhere, with Mrs Bradshaw and the advice she would hopefully give. A sleek clipper had been eased through, swiftly docked and was disembarking its passengers onto the Bund. 'You seem very far away, today,' Lucy commented, 'do you want to go back?'

'No, it's just that I have much to think about, that's all. I have a lot of decisions to make, and soon, before my furlough is up. I wasn't due for a break for some time and I do believe I was suffering from nervous exhaustion, that's why I came here.' Lizzie gazed idly over the jetty as another vessel was mooring alongside. It was a Jardine Matheson vessel and judging by the number of spectators it drew, had come directly from England. Lizzie would have moved if Lucy hadn't pleaded and persuaded her to stay and watch the disembarkation of the many men, women and children on board.

Having suffered a long and tedious voyage, the passengers slowly spilled down onto the jetty, some bewildered with the feel of firm ground beneath their feet once more, others determined to stretch their limbs without restrictions.

Twenty minutes must have passed before Lizzie decided the time had come to leave. 'I'm sorry Lucy,' she said firmly, 'we have to go I'm afraid.' Reluctantly, Lucy agreed and they headed down the Bund away from the crowd. Something, instinct maybe, caused Lizzie to look back to the jetty. A figure stood out against the backdrop of the white vessel, tall, familiar, causing her to stop abruptly.

'What is it?' Lucy queried. 'I thought we had to go?' She looked closer, seeing the shock on Lizzie's face, 'Are you ill? You seem distressed.'

Gathering her wits and striving to sound pleased, Lizzie replied, 'I do believe that's my cousin Peter, over there! I thought it would be at least another week before he arrived in China.'

So the matter was being brought to a head faster than she had anticipated. Had she been alone at this moment, or had not disclosed her discovery to Lucy, she might well have been a coward and waited to meet him after he had tracked her down.

'Come, we had better go and greet him before he disappears into the crowd,' Lizzie said, resigned to the fact.

'Are you sure?' Lucy cried. 'Just think, if we had left earlier we would have missed him.'

If only that were so, Lizzie thought, as they hurried down onto the jetty. Once there, surrounded by boxes and trunks being off-loaded onto the landing-stage it was not easy to spot her cousin. 'I do hope we haven't missed him,' she complained, feeling very apprehensive at what lay ahead.

'There! Over there! Is that him?' Lucy waved her hand in the direction of a tall man not unlike Peter.

Lizzie looked. 'No, he's very similar, but that's not the man I saw. It was definitely Peter.' Lizzie was annoyed with herself now for losing sight of him; if it hadn't been for her present situation she might well have been delighted to see him. 'There! There he is!' she cried, catching sight of him as he bent over an assortment of luggage, trying to extract a trunk from the pile. Lucy would have had them rush forward but Lizzie stayed her, pressing a hand on her arm. 'Give him a chance to get the trunk,' she cautioned, stalling for time in which to gather her thoughts. She waited, watching. Dear Peter, as handsome as ever. Oh, how many times in the past her heart had fluttered with excitement at the mere sight of him.

'Come on,' Lucy cried, 'before he goes.' She looked at Lizzie questioningly, 'Don't you want to see him?'

'Of course,' laughed Lizzie, 'it's just such a shock seeing him standing there like this.' She moved towards him, calling his name. 'Peter! Peter, welcome to China.'

Peter swung round. 'My God, Lizzie,' he cried. 'How did you know I'd be arriving today?' He smiled broadly, and looked at her closely. 'You've lost a bit of weight m'dear, and look different somehow.' He threw his arms around her and gave her a squeeze. 'I thought I was going to have a job finding you.'

Embarrassed by his open show of affection, Lizzie remembered Lucy by her side. 'Peter,' she remonstrated, 'it isn't done here to be so openly affectionate, besides, I have someone with me whom I would like you to meet.' Letting Lizzie go, Peter grinned and waited to be introduced. 'This is Miss Lucy Turner; it is she you have to thank for us being here: she so enjoys watching the boats come in to port. Lucy, this gentleman is my cousin, Mr Peter Martin.'

'Pleased to meet you,' he said holding out his hand. 'An English rose in China,' he joked, causing Lucy to blush deeply.

'We came out of curiosity to see who was arriving, to watch the different boats come and go and while away the time,' she replied, trying to hide her confusion.

'Don't let him tease you,' Lizzie warned, 'he really is a torment.'

Turning back to Lizzie, Peter looked at her carefully. 'Is it really eighteen months since we parted? I thought you were in Hangchow anyway, what are you doing here?'

'I should be, instead I'm here on furlough sorting out a few problems that have cropped up. I'm glad you're well after the Sudan—have you really left the Army?'

'Free at last, Lizzie! Resigning my commission took some doing but I've got a job here in Shanghai just to be near you!' The words struck Lizzie hard as she realised that his plans still revolved around her.

'But I have to go back to Hangchow in a week's time,' she stated lamely.

He laughed, ever the optimist. 'Then it's a good job I came when I did. You'd best write down your address here so that I can contact you; I'm supposed to be met here on the quayside by a member of the firm.' He reached in his pocket for a pencil and a card, 'Here, write it on this.' As she did so, Peter chatted amiably to Lucy who, by this time had regained her composure.

'If I'm not in when you call, leave a message to tell me where you're staying,' Lizzie said. 'Only I have to go to the Mission this afternoon on business, but will be in tonight.' She turned to Lucy, 'We will have to go now, Peter will be alright on his own, he's used to foreign parts and it won't be long before he's collected. They will know by now that the ship has docked.'

Peter's face fell. 'Deserted as soon as I land,' he quipped. 'But you're right. I'll make contact as soon as I can—it is good to see you though!' He stood with a mock hangdog expression on his face, making Lizzie feel quite guilty.

As the two women made their way back to Mrs Gough's, Lucy asked Lizzie, 'Your cousin seems a good sort, is he bringing his wife to China?'

The question surprised Lizzie somewhat, 'He's never been married, well, only to the Army,' she replied.

'Papa was in the Army, before he met Mama that is. About three years ago he began to hanker for foreign parts again, then last year he got a job in Peking,' Lucy revealed with an air of confidentiality.

After reaching the lodging house, Lizzie ate a quick meal which Mrs Gough had prepared earlier, then set off to find a rickshaw to take her to the Mission. Fortunately, Peter's arrival would make her explanation to Mrs Bradshaw much easier and believable, but it made her dilemma more acute. Mrs Bradshaw was delighted to see her. 'I'm so pleased you've decided to come to me with your problems, my dear,' she said. 'I received a message from Hangchow regarding your furlough, and the longer you stayed away from us the more I worried that you had decided to abandon us completely.

'No,' Lizzie replied emphatically, 'I haven't forsaken my duties altogether, but my problems built up until I think I must have been on the verge of a breakdown.'

'From your experiences at Bethlem, you are in a position to recognise such stresses. You seem bright enough now, so the break was probably the best thing to do, it is the future we must sort out.' She gave a motherly smile. Over the years she'd had many women approach her with their troubles and she recognised the value of listening and remaining calm. Usually she was able to come up with a solution, one way or another. 'Now, dear, tell me what I can do to help?'

Hesitatingly at first, Lizzie described the pressure she was under regarding her work, Peter and Len. When she had finished, Mrs Bradshaw smiled broadly. 'My dear, having two men after your favours must indeed be a distraction, especially when you've set your course on an independent road. I will do my best to explain matters to the powers that be, and will contact you as soon as I can. Meanwhile, do try to relax and enjoy your leave, I will let Hangchow know—I'm sure they will be delighted by your decision.'

'I do appreciate your understanding, Mrs Bradshaw. I never envisaged that such problems would occur when I first agreed to come to China. I know I have caused a lot of inconvenience, especially in Hangchow, I never meant to!'

'No, I can see that. But I wonder if while you are here you could spare me an hour or so to help out. One of the nurses has caught an infection and is ill, so we are very short handed.'

Hiding her reluctance to delay what she had to do at her lodgings, Lizzie agreed. She could hardly refuse after Mrs Bradshaw had been so understanding. As a consequence she arrived back at Mrs Gough's just as everyone was finishing supper.

'We were beginning to worry,' Mrs Turner admonished. 'What would we have done in order to find you?'

It had been a very long and exacting day, and Lizzie was far from pleased at being thought a nuisance. 'I intended to be back a couple of hours ago, but Mrs Bradshaw had an emergency on her hands at the hospital and asked me to help out—I could not refuse.'

At this point Mrs Gough entered the room. 'You've had us all anxious, Miss Hardy,' she said, 'and both your cousin and Mr Ward called, I really thought I was never going to get supper prepared. The sitting room was quite crowded I might add.'

'Oh, dear, I am sorry I'm late, it won't happen again. As for my visitors I had no idea they would cause such inconvenience. Did either leave a message?' It had never occurred to her that Len would arrive before supper, before she could explain to him that Peter had arrived. He, quite reasonably, must be wondering what her reaction to Peter's arrival had been.

'You must ask Miss Turner here if there are any messages, she managed to keep both entertained, though what she could think to say for so long quite intrigued me. Anyway, I'll go and warm up your supper.'

'What did Mr Ward say?' Lizzie asked Lucy who was taken aback by Mrs Gough's comments. 'Is he coming back?'

'It was all very confusing,' Lucy stammered. 'They were both in the room when I came down and it was some time before either knew who the other was. I eventually tried to explain to Mr Ward how we came to see Mr Martin on the quayside, and that you were expected back earlier. Mrs Gough gave them both a cup of tea and we chatted for some time. Mr Ward seemed very worried at your lateness. Peter says he will call again later this evening.' Conscious that she'd called Peter by his Christian name, Lucy blushed.

'But what about Mr Ward? Did he leave a message?' Lizzie's tone was sharper than she had intended. This only served to fluster Lucy even more and she shook her head, admitting that she didn't remember him leaving one.

'Oh dear,' Lizzie sighed, 'he will never understand. I so wanted to speak to him about something important, Peter's arrival has made everything much more urgent.' She knew she'd said enough already to arouse Lucy's curiosity, 'I'm afraid I'm a bit bad tempered, Lucy,' she admitted. 'I'm sorry if I sounded cross, it's just that I am feeling so confused.' She let the matter drop for fear of saying too much, and was grateful when Mrs Gough returned.

'Rice doesn't re-heat like potatoes do,' the landlady complained.

'Please don't worry, Mrs Gough, it is entirely my fault. I didn't expect to be away so long or I would have warned you. Nor did I expect my cousin to call.' Lizzie ate her meal wondering what to do next. If the men returned together a conversation both false and strained would take place. She pushed her empty plate away. 'I really do feel strange, Lucy, would you mind if I retired to my room? If anyone calls for me, please would you explain that I don't feel well. I'll write a note for Mr Ward and for my cousin in case either should return.'

She rose clumsily from the chair and went towards the door. 'Would you be kind enough Lucy, to come to my room in ten minutes to fetch the notes? It would be very helpful to me.' With hesitating steps Lizzie made to leave the room.

'Can you manage?' Mrs Gough asked, seeing that Lizzie was in some difficulty.

'You're very kind, but if I take my time I shall be alright.'

Once in the privacy of her room Lizzie sat at the small occasional table pondering what to write to whom. She was actually perfectly well, though tired, and now feeling guilty at her performance downstairs which had been her way of avoiding what could have been a very awkward and hurtful situation.

Sheffield 1985

'Dinner's ready!' Mimi called cheerfully from the kitchen, 'come and get it!'

Won't it wait?' Mark called out, refusing to put the manuscript down. 'I'm nearly at the end.'

'Nope!' Mimi shouted, putting the plates on the table with more than a little glee. She then went to the sitting room and resolutely took the papers from Mark's hand. 'Eat first—read later.'

'You're enjoying this aren't you! You could put me out of my misery and tell me what happens, I promise I will still read it.'

'Nope!' Mimi repeated. 'And if you don't say you enjoy my cooking I'll hide the papers so you'll have to wait even longer.' She ran from the room into the bedroom and hid what was left to read, before coming out with her face wreathed in smiles.

'This is good,' Mark said with genuine admiration as he ate. 'I must confess I've not had a Korma before, it's not American is it?'

'It's Indian—done Mimi's way. Good old Uncle Ben's and chicken. It's easy to do!'

Mark sat back and looked at her, 'I shall miss you when you go home,' he said. 'I feel as if I've known you for years. Working together has been something special.'

'Don't remind me about going home,' Mimi moaned, 'time has simply flown by. When I arrived I wondered if I was going to be able to fill my time usefully; now there is so much I want to do that I just won't get through it all.'

'Come again sometime soon,' Mark suggested, 'you'll always be welcome.'

'I simply can't afford it,' she had to admit. 'I've been saving a long time for this trip.' She fell silent; the thought of leaving had spoilt the moment. 'What do you really think about the story, do you think it will sell?' She asked this without any great enthusiasm, its value suddenly seemed unimportant.

Mark's evening had also been marred by the fact that Mimi's return to the States could possibly mean the end of their friendship.

'The book's great, but it's such a pity it costs so much to fly, I somehow feel that writing to each other won't be the same now we've met in person. We'll just have to hope the book sells well enough to allow you to come back.'

'Why don't you come out to Chicago, Mark? It's a great city, on the lake, has good cheap food—and me of course!' Mimi looked straight at him, 'I mean it, why don't you come?'

'I haven't really thought about it, would you like me to?'

'Mmm, you bet!' Mimi replied with a smile. 'I wouldn't have suggested it otherwise.' She stood up and gathered the dirty plates. 'Right now though, you've got work to do—I'll fetch the manuscript.'

Watching her disappear into the bedroom he realised he'd grown to like her company and the thought of her winging her way back to America, and out of his life, gave him a hollow feeling. 'Thanks,' he said moodily, as she handed him Lizzie's story. 'I'll be finished soon, then I suppose I'd better get you back to Eileen's.' He moved to the sofa and sat down with little enthusiasm.

'Go on then—get reading,' Mimi called out, as she peered round the door, 'I want your honest opinion!'

Mark opened the ring binder slowly, reluctant now to face Lizzie's problems when he had several of his own to think about.

Shanghai 1886

There was a knock at the door.
'It's Lucy.' a voice called out.

'Come in,' Lizzie quickly replied.

'Are you feeling any better? Have you managed to do the notes?' Lucy enquired gently.

'Yes thank you, I'll be alright now if I just lie down for a while.' Lizzie said. 'Do tell Mr Ward and Peter if they call, that I am sorry to let them down again, but what I really need is a good night's sleep.' She yawned, hoping that Lucy would take the hint and leave.

'You will let someone know if you want anything, won't you?' Lucy responded, as she closed the door.

'I will.' Lizzie called after her, 'I really will.'

When she met Lucy in the dining room for breakfast the following morning, Lizzie was disappointed to hear that only Peter had returned to see her. 'So Mr Ward didn't get my message,' she said, trying to hide her dismay.

'No, only Mr Martin did. He was concerned and hopes you will be well by tonight when he intends coming back. At the moment he's having to arrange suitable accommodation as well as trying to understand the work they are giving him. It's all new to him you know.' This last remark was said with such compassion that Lizzie wondered just how long Peter had stayed talking to Lucy.

Throughout breakfast Lizzie fretted about Len's absence; was he becoming weary of the whole situation? She was desperate to see him before her meeting with Peter, and decided to find him, if possible, at the Consulate that morning.

'I must go out,' she informed Mrs Gough. 'If Mr Ward calls, could you be so kind as to tell him that I need to see him with some urgency before this evening? I will be in all afternoon.'

Without explaining where she was going, she then made her way to the Consulate on the Bund. This low building, with its long façade, commanded a view of the river where the Suzhou Creek joined the Huangpu River. With some trepidation, Lizzie asked an official in the foyer if she could see Mr Ward. Eventually she was informed that he would be with her in twenty minutes time and would she please wait?'

When he arrived he was pleased to see her, although his manner was somewhat restrained. Lizzie put this down to them being where they were, 'I apologise for coming,' she said, 'but I desperately wanted to see you before tonight. Would it be possible for us to meet somewhere soon?' She felt uneasy in the large waiting room and their meeting was not going with the smoothness she had hoped for. 'I was asked to help out at the hospital yesterday afternoon which made me very late back,' she went on, 'and I did so want to tell you of Peter's arrival before you found out for yourself!'

'It doesn't matter,' Len replied, 'he seems to be a likeable fellow and Miss Turner kept us entertained whilst we waited. I took the liberty of going to the Mission afterwards because I was concerned over your lateness, and they told me what had occurred. When I knew you were safe and probably tired, I went home.'

'But I did so want to see you, to explain,' Lizzie lamented.

'I also thought you might want to see Peter alone after so long?' It was difficult for Lizzie to interpret his feelings from the tone of his voice. 'However, you're right, we can't talk here. If you don't mind waiting half-an-hour we'll take a cab back to my house, even at the risk of being misunderstood.' He showed no emotion whatsoever, and Lizzie wished she'd never come to the Consulate in the first place. 'Have you managed to speak to Peter alone yet?' She shook her head. 'Are you sure you don't want to see him first? Don't you think you should?' He was quite decisive in his remark, leaving Lizzie a bit taken aback.

'I have made up my mind already and wanted to discuss it with you,' she said flatly. 'I would prefer to wait here, if you don't mind.'

'Look, whatever you have decided I think it only fair to talk to Peter about it without delay. After all, he's come a long way for his answer, and no doubt presumes you will marry him; you may have decided to do so. Either way you should see him first.'

This was a side to Len Ward that Lizzie had only encountered when he was negotiating with the Chinese. Perhaps she had been foolish not to have given him her answer earlier. 'Go back now,' Len's voice had softened a little, 'see Peter, and then I will be available if you need me! Wait until tomorrow night and then come to the house.'

'But...' Lizzie felt that Len was pre-judging the result of her decision.

'No, Lizzie,' he said interrupting her. 'Take my advice, see him. He's a handsome fellow and you haven't had the chance to properly assess the possibilities for or against. I'll bring a cab to collect you at seven, does that suit you?'

It didn't, but Lizzie accepted his advice with seeming good grace. 'Yes, but I have already made up my mind, though what others will make of it is another matter!' She sighed and prepared to leave, 'I will go now, I have much to do.'

Don't lose heart, Lizzie,' Len said softly. 'You have your whole future before you. Think carefully.'

As she left the Consulate, Lizzie had the feeling that he was watching her from somewhere inside the building. She lifted her head in a dignified manner, but her eyes were misty with tears.

On returning to the lodging house, she was met by an exuberant Lucy. 'He's been,' she cried. 'Peter's been!'

'I thought I told him in the note to come this evening!' Lizzie was annoyed to find her plans disrupted once more.

'Oh, he is coming this evening; he simply called to see how you were. Wasn't that thoughtful of him?'

'Yes, I suppose it was, but it doesn't help me when people keep bobbing in and out like this.' Lizzie was also mildly irritated to realise that Lucy was responding to Peter's charms.

'Are you angry with him, or Mr Ward for not returning?' Lucy asked, slightly put out by Lizzie's attitude. 'Or are you still feeling unwell?'

Lizzie shook her head. 'It's the situation that annoys me, and I have a decision to make which is confounded by circumstances.' Lucy looked bewildered. 'It's not your fault, Lucy! In fact it is nobody's fault but my own.'

For the rest of the day Lizzie occupied herself by writing a long letter to her father and Clara, explaining her whereabouts, telling of Peter's arrival, and finally of her decision. She had no intention, however, of posting it until all was concluded. Whenever she left the room she was aware of Lucy hovering in the background, until in the end she became very annoyed with her. 'Please, Lucy,' she finally managed to pluck up courage to say, 'I do need a little time alone with Peter tonight.'

Lucy blushed self-consciously and stammered, 'Why, of course. Do tell me when to go!'

Lizzie looked at her keenly. 'You've not done anything wrong; it's simply that I have family matters to discuss with him.'

'Can I join you afterwards?' Lucy asked timidly. 'Do you think Mr Martin would mind?'

It was obvious that Lucy was bent on joining them and as they were both lodgers in Mrs Gough's house they were equally entitled to use the room. 'Of course you can join us, but I am going to ask Mrs Gough for her indulgence in allowing me to see Peter in private first.'

'Thank you, Lizzie,' Lucy cried, the smile returning to her face. 'I do think he's very handsome, don't you?' She blushed again.

Laughing, Lizzie agreed. 'Well, yes I suppose he is.' As the young woman returned to her room Lizzie pondered on her behaviour, and it struck her that therein perhaps lay another problem. Lucy of course saw Peter merely as Lizzie's cousin and not someone who had come halfway round the world with marriage in mind. Lizzie would certainly be glad when this particular day was over.

Yes, Lizzie thought to herself as she met Peter in the hall later, you've always been handsome, perhaps dashing was a better description. She greeted him with a hug. 'I'm sorry I was unwell yesterday, and out when you called today,' Lizzie said fondly, 'but you always did turn up unexpectedly and turn our worlds upside down.'

He searched her face, 'You've changed again, Lizzie, you seem to be a woman of many parts. Obviously China suits you.' He did not seek to embrace her in return for which she was grateful. 'Hello, Miss Turner,' he called out as Lucy hurried past on her way to her room. 'How's the packing?'

'Nearly done, thank you, ' Lucy smilingly replied.

'What's the matter with Lucy?' he asked, bewildered by her haste, as he followed Lizzie into the sitting room.

'I asked her to give us half an hour alone so that we could talk—she may join us later. In fact you should be careful, I do believe she is half in love with you.'

'Which is something you are not, I gather?'

'How...?' Lizzie gasped, 'what makes you think that?' she stammered.

'But it's true isn't it, Lizzie? Your letters, welcome and life-saving though they were, never hinted of love.' Peter sighed deeply, 'Oh, Lizzie, I think we missed our chance years ago. What if I had not gone to India, would things have been different?'

'You loved Clara at that time, don't forget!'

He laughed, with a slight bitterness. 'At the end of the day I suppose I am a selfish man and have got what I deserve.'

'Oh, Peter, I've always loved you, in a dreamlike very impractical way.' This admission made her feel sad and remorseful. 'I have dragged you all this way only to let you down!'

A slow smile of acceptance crossed his face. 'Lizzie, I knew the truth from your letters: I just needed to confirm my fears, but I also needed to start a new life. England, beautiful though it is, does not bind me to it. I still like adventure but not with the Army, and you gave me an incentive to make the break. Besides, now I have a part of my family with me in China! I knew when you met me on the quayside that my intuition was right. There was no joy, no lovers greeting, only apprehension.'

'I am so sorry,' Lizzie cried, a tear running down her cheek as she studied his dear face. 'We are a strange pair, are we not? I am so happy to see you and I think we can share happy times together, but in a different way to that as man and wife.'

Peter gave a wry smile. 'Like we always have. You've outgrown your obsession for me I know; perhaps at last you have found something deeper than I could ever have given you. However, you are not getting away lightly; I want you to teach me as much about China as you can: teach me Mandarin for example, so that I will be more useful in my work.'

Lizzie was overjoyed by his perception of what their relationship could be. 'I'm glad that you've left the Army,' she admitted with genuine relief. 'I could tell that in your state of mind it wouldn't be long before you became ill or, even worse, careless and lost the keen sharpness that a soldier needs to stay alive. You've done your duty; let others take their share of that kind of responsibility.'

'I was becoming very disillusioned with my life as a soldier. You gave me the strength of mind to do what had to be done, there was no longer any sense of achievement, no desire to conquer; I began to question too much and that for a soldier is dangerous. You helped me through it all, Lizzie.'

'You don't know what a relief it is to hear you say that. Then all was not wasted?'

'By no means, but will you do one more thing for me? Please—give me another hug, even if it is only a motherly one!' As he held her, Lizzie enjoyed the warm comfort of his arms, but there was no surge of excitement, simply the love of a cousin. 'That's more like it,' he said. 'So, what does life hold for you?'

When, after an hour, Lucy finally knocked timidly on the sitting room door, Lizzie and Peter were discussing Edward's son William, who would take over the farm when he grew up. 'Come in, Lucy,' Lizzie called out, 'come and keep Peter company whilst I find Mrs Gough to arrange for him to have something to eat with us. Would you like a cup of tea, too, we're parched?'

'Yes, please!' Lucy quickly replied. 'I would like that.' Her normal bubbly self was suppressed now by self-consciousness, and she modestly refrained from looking directly at Peter.

'Please, do sit down,' Peter invited her. 'Is everything finished in preparation for tomorrow?'

Nodding, she sat down, suddenly lost for words, making a sad little figure.

'What's the matter—I thought you were looking forward to Peking?'

'I'm not sure any more, I like it here. I know I can't stay, Mama couldn't afford it anyway, but I feel as though I am going to lose all my new friends. Once I leave it will be the end. Lizzie, Mr Ward and Mrs Gough have all been very kind.'

'Look,' Peter said, 'why not come out with Lizzie and me to a theatre tonight, if we can get tickets that is. Wait until Lizzie comes back and I'll ask her—what about it?'

At this Lucy came to life, 'Oh, could I—I'd like that—could we take Mama as well?'

Hesitating before re-entering the sitting room, Lizzie saw Lucy and Peter in lively conversation, totally unaware of her presence. It pleased her to see them enjoying each other's company and she knew that, with a little help, Peter might find his new life in China quite rewarding.

When Lucy and Mrs Turner were finally packed and ready to leave the following day, Lizzie accompanied them to the steamer that would take them on the long journey to Peking.

'Don't lose touch,' Mrs Turner admonished Lizzie. 'We must keep in contact, it's good to know there are friends not too far away.'

'I'm afraid I'm not a good letter writer,' Lizzie replied, 'and you'll soon tire of my travelogues, but no doubt I will hear of your news from Peter, as Lucy intends to correspond with him, I understand.' She turned to Lucy. 'He's not the best of communicators either, so don't expect too much!'

'Men never are,' Mrs Turner commiserated. 'Now, do take care of yourself and Mr Ward. Perhaps Lucy could call in when she returns on her way to England—depending where you are of course. Oh, and please do thank Mr Martin again for taking us to the theatre last night, even if it was an amateur production.'

This last remark caused Lizzie to smile in agreement with her, for having seen professional productions in the past the comparison left a lot to be desired.

'Well, I enjoyed it immensely,' Lucy spoke up in defence.

'You would,' Mrs Turner retorted, 'now hurry along, won't you?'

Leaning over, Lucy gave Lizzie an affectionate peck on the cheek. 'I shall miss you all,' she whispered, before following her Mama onto the steamer. Lizzie quite liked Lucy and her outspoken Mama, and wondered if she would see them again some day.

'The cab is here, my dear!' Mrs Gough called out to Lizzie, who sat nervously in the sitting room. 'Doesn't it seem quiet without the Turners; I wonder what they will make of Peking?'

'You must see so many people come and go, never to meet them again—don't you find it upsetting?'

Mrs Gough laughed. 'Mostly I'm ready for a break when they're gone. Sometimes when they've mixed in well I do feel a twinge of sadness, but one gets used to it. Now, don't keep Mr Ward waiting, off you go!' Then, as an afterthought she added, 'I don't suppose Mr Peter will be dropping in quite so often, not now Miss Turner's gone.' Lizzie chose to say nothing in response, but made her way to the door just as the bell rang. 'Go on, open it! You know who it is,' Mrs Gough called out.

'I'm ready,' Lizzie informed Len without inviting him in, 'shall we go?' He handed her into the carriage politely, but she felt uncomfortable throughout the journey so made light conversation by telling him of the Turner's departure.

As they neared the house he explained that his housekeeper was there so there could be no reason for any gossip over her visit. He handed her down, took her cape after entering the house, and shepherded her into the sitting room. 'You're very quiet tonight,' he said. 'Are you angry because I asked you to wait until now to talk?'

'No, but it has been a traumatic twenty-four hours. Firstly there was my discussion with Peter and then the Turners' departure—I shall miss Lucy very much.'

'I must admit I was surprised to see Peter at Mrs Gough's,' Len said, with no emotion or sign that could give Lizzie a clue as to his thoughts. What was she to make of it? 'And I gather you were no less shocked when you saw him on the jetty! He seems to be an agreeable fellow, so I hope he makes a go of it in Shanghai.'

'He is, and has always been so,' Lizzie conceded. 'I could not believe it when I saw him standing there amongst the luggage. I had Lucy with me at the time and I'm afraid I did not give him the welcome he deserved.' Len raised his eyebrows at this, but said nothing. Lizzie realised that he was leaving it to her to tell him exactly where he stood with her. 'I have now had a long talk with Peter and have told him that I couldn't possibly marry him—though he seemed to have already reached that conclusion before I even opened my mouth to speak. Dear Peter, I do hope he finds his feet here in China; it's a long way to come, only to fail. Mind you, I have a feeling that he and Lucy may eventually become good friends. I do hope so, as Lucy is a little in love with him already!'

'What prompted you to reject him? Is it still Nathan, or simply that you don't love him?'

'I will always love Peter,' she cried defensively, 'but only as a cousin. Circumstances have changed things, and I have changed too. I could never have been what he would want, what a wife should be to him. Perhaps it was Nathan who caused it. Perhaps I was too young to even understand love.'

Len asked gently, 'Do you think you would feel like this with all men?'

'I don't know,' Lizzie cried, distraught. 'I am inexperienced with men.' She lowered her eyes, 'Peter kissed me the day we parted in England but it left me cold, and because of that I had hoped with the passing of time his ardour would cool too.' Lizzie had now admitted to Len yet another of her failings, she wished desperately for something to hold, to occupy her trembling hands. She dare not lift her eyes in case he saw the confusion in them.

Fearing that he had lost her, he moved closer, slowly, hoping to show her that she had much to lose by being fearful. It was a risk he felt worth taking. 'Before you tell me your decision,' he said, 'look at me! I will not take advantage of you by trying to change your mind by argument; simply let me hold you for a moment so that you will not forever wonder what it is like to be loved.' Without waiting for a reply, he reached out and drew Lizzie closer to him. 'Not everyone feels love in the same way; love can be many things to many people. Comfort, understanding and companionship, all are just as important as passion and the pain of physical love,' he whispered gently. 'Then, if eventually these come together, there can be joy.' He held her as a father would a child, whispering his words of comfort. 'You have suffered a great deal and now have to find yourself.' He lowered his head to hers and was silent, allowing her to feel the warmth of his face against her hair, trying to protect her from her innermost fears. 'You have so many feelings, it's not right to suppress them. Even if it is not me, at least let someone share your life. Without happiness it can be a very lonely journey.'

For a long time he held her in his embrace, pleased simply that she did not struggle to escape. Slowly she softened and relaxed, her head nestling against his.

A surge of emotion flooded through Lizzie, and it was she who spoke next. 'I don't deserve your love,' she said softly. 'How can I, with all my faults, make you happy? I am moody, untutored in wifely things, and most of all independently minded.'

He laughed, 'Good grief, I'm not looking for a perfect wife, as that would necessitate me being perfect too! I think,' he said with a touch of humour, 'that I could suffer your many failings, if you could put up with my odd one or two!' His face was wreathed in smiles now, which Lizzie could sense from his tone of voice.

The things Lizzie liked most about him were his way of making her feel at ease, his saying that which made her problems appear smaller than they were, and his infinite patience. No doubt he too had his faults, the main one possibly being that he saw only good in everyone. 'I can be very demanding,' she told him, 'of myself as well as of others.'

'I know,' he agreed, much to her surprise, laughing gently at her.

She pushed him from her. 'I'm very serious; I may not make a very good wife!'

'Do I take it then that you are accepting my proposal?' he asked. 'Or are you simply saying I have a poor choice of wives?' His eyes twinkled, a grin barely suppressed.

'Please, be serious! There are things that I have to discuss before I tell you my answer.'

Feigning despair Len nodded, saying, 'Then for goodness sake get on with it and put me out of my misery.' He sat down heavily on a chair. 'I may as well rest my legs if you mean to take all day!' Lizzie was, however, determined to have her say.

She sat primly opposite him as if conducting an interview, but it was difficult not to smile at the impish look on his face. He would be fun to live with! She took a deep breath. 'I saw Mrs Bradshaw today and discussed with her the possibility of me working here in Shanghai simply as a part-time nurse. I told her of your proposal and that I could not accept it if it meant me doing nothing all day except cleaning and cooking, or idling my day away on frivolous things. Indeed I would not be capable of making you happy if all I did was potter about on my own. Did you know that for years before Florence Nightingale found her vocation in life, she hovered constantly between depression and guilt at having nothing useful in her existence? I too would need to keep my mind occupied, but in all other ways I would try to be a good wife.'

'Do I take it then that your answer is yes?' he asked, determined not to prolong the agony any longer.

The speed at which the discussion had taken place had taken Lizzie by surprise. 'Would you allow me to work some of the time at the hospital?' she asked, knowing that if he refused she would still accept his proposal.

'Of course. There is, however, one aspect I feel I must make demands over.' There was a serious expression on his face and she could read nothing in his eyes. 'Just a small foible of mine, I'm afraid.'

Wondering nervously what it could be, she asked, 'What is it?'

He got to his feet. 'Considering that by kissing Peter, you then changed your mind about him, I suggest you put me to that same test and give me your honest opinion.'

He was teasing her, yet she knew that there was more behind the jest than fun. Her face was crimson with embarrassment as he stood waiting for her to make the first move. Slowly she went forward and kissed him gently on the lips.

'Mmm, not bad for a sisterly one,' he said, then slid his arms round her waist, drawing her to him and kissing her fully but firmly on the mouth. 'There,' he laughed. 'Now tell me in all seriousness how I fared?'

'Mr Ward,' Lizzie replied with a straight face, 'you strike a hard bargain. I will willingly become your wife; you have crept into my affections and leave me with no choice if I am to be happy.'

'One more thing,' he said looking into her eyes, 'tell me that you love me!'

As he stood patiently waiting, Lizzie realised that she did indeed love him. He had helped her to come to terms with her life. There would be times when memories would still haunt her, but she no longer had to face them alone. 'I do love you, Leonard,' she whispered. 'Very much indeed!'

The following morning Lizzie posted the letter she had written the previous day to Edward and Clara, and now she was faced with the task of breaking the news to Peter. How would he take it, coming so soon after discovering that she didn't want *him*? She called on Mrs Bradshaw who greeted the news guardedly. It was always unfortunate to lose a Missionary in the field and one with medical training was much harder to replace.

'I can't help being disappointed, my dear,' she admitted, 'but if your heart is elsewhere then there is no point in fretting. You have certainly given the matter a great deal of thought; we wish you well. I had a word with the hospital management who appreciated your situation, they would welcome any voluntary assistance you are willing to offer. When do you intend getting married?'

'Shortly, but as you know, Consular rules state that we must give three week's notice of our intentions, and I do want to return in the meanwhile to

Hangchow to explain matters in person. Hopefully, Mr Ward and I plan to marry in about six weeks, but I will keep you informed.'

'I am sure you will, even though you are going to be very busy. Good luck and thank you for the work you have already done,' Mrs Bradshaw declared.

'I would especially like to thank you too Mrs Bradshaw, for your kindness and advice ever since the day you met me off the boat. Without someone like you, who has knowledge of China and is willing to share it with a novice, the experience could have been very frightening.' Lizzie tried to convey her feelings without succumbing to a display of emotion.

The wealthy shipping firm of Jardine Matheson was situated near to the British Consulate on the Bund, and Lizzie left a message there asking Peter to call on her that evening after work.

She recognised his voice immediately Mrs Gough let him into the house. 'You'll not be disturbed,' she informed them, as Lizzie led Peter into the sitting room. 'Nobody has replaced the Turners so you can relax without fear of interruption.'

'What is it, Lizzie, that required you to leave a letter at work for me? I've been quite worried since getting it.'

'Oh, I am sorry, there is nothing wrong,' she assured him, 'but I have some news and I wanted you to hear it from me before anyone else informs you. Shanghai has a large but close English community, and you never quite know who knows who!'

'That's true of any community living abroad—I know. But don't keep me in suspense, what is the problem and can I help?'

'Oh, Peter,' Lizzie cried, 'it is so good to have you here in China and I do hope we keep contact with each other. However, I hope what I have to say won't upset you. Len Ward has asked me to marry him. Do you mind?'

'I hope you said yes!' Peter replied emphatically, with no anger or hurt. 'I've had my suspicions for some time that Len Ward was becoming more than just a friend. He has been good to you, I know, and I've seen a change in you that is for the better, you look much happier now.'

'But do you mind?'

He sighed. 'No, Lizzie, I really don't! Even had you not met him I don't think you would have married me.' He smiled ruefully. 'It's ironical really. Twice in my life now older men, your father with Clara, and Len Ward with you, have stolen my brides to be! I've learned my lesson, I'll not be thwarted again, I shall not let another man get the same opportunity.'

Lizzie laughed. 'Perhaps if you wanted a woman sufficiently you would not hesitate in the first place.'

He thought for a moment. 'I really am a selfish blighter, I suppose, but life is passing me by. My days of adventure seeking have begun to pall, but not, I'm pleased to say, my appetite for an attractive woman.'

'Like Lucy?' Lizzie dared to intervene.

He looked sheepish. 'Do you think she's interested in me? Am I too old do you think?'

Giggling, Lizzie replied, 'I've told you, I think she is more than a little in love with you already. She's lively and will keep you on your toes. Don't tell me you weren't flattered by her attentions! The other night at the theatre, no-one seeing you together would have thought that I had just given you the biggest disappointment in your life!'

Peter threw his head back and laughed. 'You're too wise for me, Lizzie. You and Len Ward are as suited as any two people could be. I wish you luck!' There was no doubting his sincerity and Lizzie was relieved that he wasn't in anyway bitter at her news. 'Lucy's going to write, you know,' he added, almost as an afterthought.

'Treat her kindly, Peter. Don't lead her on then hurt her. If you're not really interested then don't encourage her, she and her mother have become my friends.'

He grinned. 'I think,' he said, 'that coming to China was, after all, an inspiration—and just think, if I did marry Lucy and we all lived in Shanghai, we would never be without a family around us.' He paused and added, 'To tell the truth Lizzie, I like the idea enormously!'

Sheffield 1985

Putting down the manuscript for the
last time, Mark sat for a while in thought, until Mimi
looked at him expectantly, wanting to draw him out.

'I'm glad the endings are happy ones,' he remarked, 'I must admit that having done so much of the research for you, I feel I really know the characters now. I've found some of it quite moving and think you've done well. Will you publish it as a true story or fiction?'

'But it is a true story. I've used all her letters and diaries, the Will, deeds and newspaper cuttings, to check the facts. All I've done is link these together with some brush strokes in between.'

'And a little licence, I suspect,' Mark chuckled.

'Well, I must admit I did try to read between the lines, but the bonus came when they found Nathan's body and we, sorry I, opened the sealed part of Lizzie's diary.'

Ignoring Mimi's small slip, Mark queried, 'Do you think she intended that in the long run, someone should know the truth? I mean, wasn't it a bit dangerous simply stitching such incriminating evidence together instead of destroying it? I know my mother would have unpicked it years ago.'

'I believe she wanted it to be discovered long before this, and deliberately left the diary at the farm before she went to China in case anything happened to her. I think she feared the body would be found and that Edward or Peter would get the blame.' As Mark made no comment, she went on, 'One of the entries in a later diary did puzzle and disturb me however, and now I know why. Lizzie wrote:

> *If any action of mine should ever come to light that could cause serious trouble for my family, I will go back to England immediately—Len supports me in this. The diary I left at the farm will explain it all if I die first.*

'But it didn't, did it? Not until I read the hidden section.'

'She must have been a very remarkable woman,' Mark said, 'and it would have taken a lot of courage to come back. It would certainly have ruined their lives!'

'I've always felt drawn to her, Mark—though I really don't know why.'

'You haven't told me yet how she fared in China after she married. Did they have any children?'

'No, at least none were ever mentioned.'

'How about Peter then, did he marry Lucy? What happened to them?'

Mimi laughed mischievously. 'I sure hope they got married, they were my Great Great Grandparents!' She was amused as the light suddenly dawned in Mark's eyes. 'They married in Shanghai and had four children.'

'Oh, of course!' He exclaimed, 'Lizzie was your Great Great Aunt. But who then, went to America?'

'Actually, if you recall, Lizzie wasn't a blood relative at all, and not even Peter's cousin, except by adoption. Peter, it seemed, always considered her as such, but in 1898 at the time of the Boxer Rebellion he believed it would be safer to take his own family to America, which he did. Lizzie and Len stayed behind, eventually died of old age, and are buried in Shanghai. She always kept in touch with Peter, and Lucy, then just before she died she sent her diaries to Lucy in America, all but the one you found in the Archives.' When you wrote telling me of its existence and offered to transcribe it for me, I could have kissed you!' Seeing him grin at this remark Mimi blushed furiously.

'Really?' Mark said, his eyes sparkling with amusement. Losing all interest in Lizzie's story he stood up. 'Am I to understand that you still owe me that kiss?' he asked with a laugh.

'I didn't say that!' Mimi protested, backing away in feigned horror.

As if coming to his senses Mark stopped teasing her and sat down again. The happy atmosphere disappeared and he flicked the pages moodily, his thoughts confused. 'I think the book's great,' he said, eventually breaking the silence. 'You will send me a signed copy, won't you?'

He was withdrawn, and pensive now, leaving Mimi puzzled and unsure how best to respond. 'Of course I will!' she replied hastily, then asked, 'I wonder, if it does get published, would you come over to the States—to Chicago, to the launch I mean, and share some of the success? I'd really like that!'

He thought for a moment. 'I don't know,' he said, frowning, 'it's a lot of money, and a long way to go just for a book signing. You're sure you'll get it published then?'

'My publisher was already interested before I left home and now I think he'll be even more so. Besides, I'd be disappointed if I never saw you again.' She looked at Mark solemnly. They had become good friends in the ten days since her arrival and with just two days left before her departure, the thought of returning home was losing its appeal. She was having difficulty in keeping conversation going; something had changed between them and she couldn't fathom out what it could be. Mark seemed withdrawn and gloomy; had the book depressed him or was her presence beginning to disturb his routine too much? 'I think we'd better go,' she said quietly. 'Eileen will think me ungrateful, staying out all hours. Besides I feel a bit apprehensive about the flight back.' She began gathering her belongings which were scattered about the flat. As Mark said nothing, she continued, 'You know, you don't have to drive me all the way to Gatwick if you're very busy, it's such a long way, and I could easily go by bus or train?'

'I've got it all arranged now,' he answered stiffly. 'What makes you think it's any trouble?'

She was bewildered at the change in him, and that he'd apparently misconstrued her suggestion. 'It was just a thought to save you a long tiresome journey, that's all.' She bit her lip nervously, concealing her disquiet. 'Please can we go,' she repeated, 'I think we're both over tired, neither of us slept well last night, so perhaps we need an early night.'

Mark got up with a sigh, found the car keys, seized his coat and offered to carry Mimi's bag, 'I'm sorry if I'm a bit crabby,' he said. 'Maybe I've become too involved with Lizzie's story, and now it's over things seem flat.'

'Has the book depressed you, is it too disturbing? Be honest,' Mimi pleaded. 'Only all of a sudden I could cry! After all the work we've done and the excitement of the discoveries we've made, I feel lost.'

'Things will change once you get home, you'll have all the excitement of your book launch. Believe me there's nothing wrong with the book, I've just got too involved that's all,' he said, trying to reassure her. He put her bag on the rear seat of the car and asked, 'What plans have you got for tomorrow?'

'Well, I thought I might spend the day walking round Totley, I'd like to explore its nooks and crannies, or maybe walk up on the moors again to blow the cobwebs from my mind. Solitude sometimes helps to clear ones thoughts.'

He glanced up at the sky. 'I hope it's good weather, but take a raincoat, conditions can change quite quickly up there. One minute it's sunny, then ten minutes later there can be a thundery shower,' he advised with some concern, 'I quite envy you having the opportunity to go.'

'Hey, you can go any time you want! This will be my last chance as I must do some shopping on Friday, and start packing.' Mimi looked out of the window, yet not really seeing what was there; so many things needed to be discussed with Mark and she wished she'd not been so hasty in suggesting they left the flat. 'I've had a wonderful time, Mark, thanks to you! I'll never forget your kindness, or the time you've given up taking me around. Somehow this place has grown on me; there's so much history and so many beautiful places to see. You'd like Lake Michigan back home, it's vast and you can't see anything but boats and water to the horizon. I could show you so much in Chicago—it really is a wonderful place.'

'I promise to think about it,' Mark replied absent-mindedly as he drove, not wanting to commit himself to something so important without very careful consideration first. 'Shall I call for you tomorrow evening?' he asked, changing the subject.

'Yes, I would like that,' Mimi agreed, 'that's if you haven't had enough of my company already.'

'On the contrary,' he reassured her, and was sorry he'd let his depression spoil the evening earlier. He parked the car and got out. The damp evening air was bringing out the smell of the moors; it was evocative and never ceased to make him grateful for the ease with which he could access the nearby hills. He never quite knew why such moments played tricks with his emotions, and tonight was no exception. 'Can you smell the moors and the gardens?' he asked. 'This is my favourite time of day.'

Mimi nodded, 'It's almost hypnotic—like a heady perfume.'

'Don't overdo it tomorrow,' he advised. 'I'd like to take you for a final walk if you'll come, it would be nice to spend our last evening out in the open air.'

At the house, Eileen greeted them sarcastically, 'Ah, the wanderers return!'

'I'm sorry we're late, and you'll not believe it, Sis, but we've been working on Mimi's book. When it's published I'll get you a signed copy, and you'll see how hard Mimi's worked on it.'

'Just so long as I do get a copy,' Eileen conceded, relenting over her disapproval of her brother's uncharacteristic behaviour. 'I suppose you'd like some supper then?'

'Just a quick drink for me, please,' he replied, 'I must get off and…catch up!' He caught Eileen's suspicious glance, 'And before you think evil of us,' he said, 'I slept on the sofa last night!'

'It's none of my business what you did, but I should hope so! Mimi has her reputation to protect.' She winked at Mimi as if blaming Mark for everything.

As luck would have it, the following day dawned bright allowing Mimi to do what she'd planned. She strolled about the village taking photographs and making notes, with an idea for another novel forming in her mind; one which would be set amidst the stone walls, moorland streams and banks of bracken to be seen all around. She soon lost all sense of time and distance, so that when eventually she climbed the steep hill back to the main road, her legs were aching. Remembering that Mark expected her to be fresh for their evening walk, she rested in her room after lunch until called down for tea. The fresh wind had deepened the colour in her cheeks and she could quite see how Lizzie's return to the moors from a foggy London had soon removed the pallor from her face.

'You look a picture of health,' Eileen commented as she handed Mimi a cup of coffee. 'Did you go far?'

'Yes, onto the moors; they're lovely, so near to the city yet so isolated. I sat on a bench high on the hill and looked back towards Sheffield: I could have stayed there all day but I wanted to refresh myself for tonight, so I came back for a rest. Thank you for leaving the sandwiches out for me.'

'I thought you might need something to eat before I got back,' Eileen replied, 'and you were right to rest. I just hope you've got enough energy to keep up with Mark, he likes his walks.' She turned at the sound of a movement at the door. 'Ah, here he is,' she said with some satisfaction, 'always on time.'

Joining them in the dining room he sneaked a biscuit off the table. 'I hope you've not eaten too much,' he said. 'I've an idea where we can go for a meal later!'

'I guess I could find a corner somewhere,' Mimi assured him.

As the car headed out into the countryside once more, Mimi realised how fond she had become of the beauty surrounding her, especially the long sweep of the moors stretching out into the distance. 'This place inspires me,' she said softly, 'I can understand why painters, writers and photographers strive to capture what they see and feel.'

Mark knew exactly what she meant, though his powers of expression failed to match hers. 'I'm going to take you to my favourite spot,' he said, 'before the light fails and the sun sets.' He turned off the main road and drove slowly along the moorland route until they passed through a gap in the rocks where he pulled in and parked.

'What a splendid valley,' Mimi cried, surprised by what she saw. 'Round every bend, over every hill there's always something spectacular.'

They left the car, climbed a wooden stile and headed for an outcrop of rocks looming above them. The track was rugged, but Mimi valiantly followed Mark, trying to keep up. After a while he stopped and waited for her. 'I enjoy the feeling of the solid earth beneath my feet, with the bracken brushing against my legs. I don't think I could live anywhere far from the Peak District,' he said poignantly. 'I can fully understand the pull that the farm had on Lizzie; it must have been a soul destroying wrench for her to leave it behind.'

'That's strange, I felt exactly the same earlier today when up on the moors,' Mimi replied. 'I just wish I'd seen a lapwing in flight, as she did!' They climbed higher to reach the top of the escarpment. 'I do admire the animals,' she said between sharp gasps of breath, 'they obviously come this way, judging by the droppings left behind.'

'The sheep make tracks all over; they have surer feet than we do,' Mark replied, offering a hand to help her the last few yards up through a gap in the gritstone rocks. At the top he was disinclined to release her and did so reluctantly, disturbed by his emotions. Was he foolish to have brought her here to share his private Utopia? Nothing would be the same again, and for this reason he'd hesitated to bring her earlier.

Mimi stood beside him, admiring the view. 'I can see why you love this place so much,' she said. 'I wish I had a panoramic camera to capture the whole wide sweep of it.'

He nodded in agreement, then pointed in the direction of a small hamlet, saying, 'That's the village of Curbar down there, where my grandmother was born.' There was a catch in his voice and Mimi glanced at him, wondering why this place disturbed him so much. His quietness was due to the knowledge that the vibrant colours caused by the setting sun would soon disappear, leaving them alone in the dusk of evening, just as Mimi's imminent departure to Chicago would soon leave an emptiness in his life.

'I shall miss all this, and you, when I leave,' she said softly, turning away so that he couldn't see her face or, more importantly, the expression in her eyes. The view had now lost its glory and she stood still, expectantly by his side.

When he didn't reply she felt shut out and cold. 'Please, let's go,' she said, and started to walk along the ridge towards the car.

Suddenly Mark came to life. 'Mimi,' he called, 'don't go!' She hesitated and waited for him to catch up. 'Please,' he said as he approached her, 'you must think me an idiot, getting all moody like this, but can't you see how despondent I am, and how hopeless things are?'

'What is it, Mark?' she asked. 'What has made you so unhappy?'

'The thought of your leaving distresses me, but there's nothing we can do about it. I shall miss being with you and the future seems barren.' Confronted by the suddenness of the situation he had spoken spontaneously and now felt embarrassed.

So this explained why he had been withdrawn, even moody during the last twenty-four hours, and she too was experiencing a hollow feeling at the thought of going home. 'Don't you see that I feel like that, as well,' she murmured, trying to control her emotions.

As if talking to himself, he said dejectedly, 'What's the point in starting something we can't finish?'

'I think it's already too late, Mark,' she whispered. 'Far too late, something has happened to change things for us. We can't simply walk away from each other!'

'But it can't last, can it? You'll go back to America and I'll stay here in this confined little world with few prospects. America has everything, it's bigger, more modern—what could I offer? Look at me,' he said disparagingly, 'I'm only a lab technician, and poorly paid at that!'

'I am looking at you, Mark! I've tried American men. My husband was handsome, clever and charming, but he didn't make me happy. The time I've spent with you has been different. We seem to think alike, enjoy doing things together—that's worth so much more.'

'In two days it'll all be over, why torture ourselves?' he said bitterly. 'Besides, even if you loved me you'd soon miss your friends, your family, a better way of life, and for what?' Mark was adamant. He wanted to touch Mimi, yet knew that if he did he could raise emotions to a point of no return. The light was now fading fast, taking with it all warmth from the sun. 'Come on, let's get back whilst we can still see where we're going,' he said flatly, as if in a daze.

Mimi followed, trying to suppress her feelings, whilst half accepting that there was a lot of truth in what he'd said.

As they sat in the car, each of them deep in thought, neither knew what to do. Mark cursed himself for telling her how he felt, believing it might have been better to have spent a different sort of evening together and then get the next forty-eight hours over with in some sort of peace. He wasn't normally a moody man, but the situation in which he'd found himself and the thought of the long, lonely months ahead without Mimi had begun to dishearten him. Nevertheless he should have pretended a little longer, and kept silent.

In the end it was Mimi who spoke out first. 'Mark, can't we just go and have that meal you promised? Anything would be better than sitting here like this. When we get into the company of other people we may be able to cope better with our problems.'

Agreeing, Mark turned the key in the ignition and drove off. After a while he pulled into the car park of a public house with a reputation for good food, though that no longer interested him, he was so disappointed at the way things had turned out.

'Thank goodness they've not modernised this place,' he remarked, as they sat down at a table in the restaurant. A log fire burned in the grate and the low lighting cast a warm glow over the diners. Suddenly he spoke. 'I really am sorry,' he said, 'I seem to have ruined everything. I never realised that someone could come to mean so much to me—I don't know what to do.' He shrugged his shoulders. 'Pathetic, isn't it?'

'Mark, listen to me. I've loved being with you, neither of us wanted or expected this to happen, but it has! Do you think I'm looking forward to leaving you? It's going to be hard for me too—you say we mustn't start anything—isn't it too late? Something special has already happened—we can't just ignore it. We're not children, we know there will be pain but that's better than turning away, only to regret it later. If what we have doesn't last, then at least we will have been honest with ourselves instead of forever wondering 'if only'.' She waited a moment for him to reply, then leaned across and covered his hand with hers. 'Please don't shut me out.' She clasped his hand tightly so that if he tried to draw it back he would attract attention from the other diners. Slowly, she felt the tension in him slacken, and only then did she loosen her grip, hoping he would respond to her touch. For several seconds she waited, wondering what made him so reserved and insecure. She knew he was fighting some inner battle with himself, and having experienced similar problems in the past, she was quite prepared to let him take his time.

Slowly at first he moved his fingers until finally they entwined with hers. He raised his head enquiringly and Mimi smiled encouragingly until he smiled back. His shyness was so obvious to her, she knew that he would always be as gentle as he was reliable. 'If it worked out,' she whispered, 'I could be happy in England: I would not expect you to move to America. But will you try to come to Chicago, to see my home and meet my folk—that's all I ask?' She liked the clasp of his fingers on hers and a feeling of happiness crept over her. 'This is our last night together, can't we just enjoy it?' she pleaded.

Before he could reply, the waiter arrived to take their order. His cheeky banter broke the ice and, as Mark smiled, Mimi laughed out loud in response. 'You're incorrigible,' he admonished when the man had gone but the fondness in his eyes belied any criticism.

It seemed the longest meal Mark had ever eaten. Between every mouthful of food they shared ideas and repartee, and the longer Mark gazed at Mimi the greater was his desire to hold and kiss her. 'Did you really mean it when you said you could have kissed me when you got my letter?' he asked, teasing her. When Mimi chuckled, he said, 'I might just take you up on that offer!'

'That's when things started to go wrong, wasn't it,' Mimi remarked in a more serious tone. 'I realise now that when I said that, you jumped up full of joy, and as suddenly sat down again in a strange mood. I should have had the sense to see it, but how was I to know that you cared for me?'

'All week I've been deeply affected by Lizzie's story, and eventually I think my own feelings became so mixed up with hers, that in the end I didn't appreciate what was happening to me,' he confessed, his face flushed with emotion. 'I've never been in love before.'

This simple announcement made her realise the strength of his feelings, and her own reluctance to leave him. 'I don't want to go home,' she responded glumly, all traces of flippancy gone, 'not now.'

'Come on,' Mark said softly, 'it's time we went.' He took Mimi's hand firmly in his and led her to the car. He'd had several girlfriends over the years but none had such a profound effect on him as Mimi. She was different, her bubbly nature and irrepressible laugh, together with her determination to see things through, these qualities had slowly endeared her to him. He was conscious that she was the more experienced in life, and it was this, rather than shyness that had held him back. The thought of a future without her was too bleak to consider. 'I've grown used to having you near me,' he said softly, 'and I shall be utterly miserable when you've gone. I never dreamt that you could feel anything but friendship for me.' In the darkness of the vehicle he put his arm gently round her shoulder and drew her to him. 'I'll claim that kiss now, if you don't mind,' he said with a sudden surge of confidence.

Later, Mimi rested her head against him, listening to his heart beating, and she smiled to herself. 'To tell the truth,' she confessed, 'I quite fancied you the first day we met, but you're so typically English, reserved and gentlemanly, that I thought you saw me simply as a loud and brash American.'

He laughed. 'I suppose I am exactly that, and you're right, I do think you're a brash American. A lovely, bubbly, brash American!'

She drew back and shook her head. 'You know, you English do have a weird sense of humour sometimes,' she protested. 'I don't know whether that was a back-handed compliment, or not!'

He squeezed her gently, his face half hidden in her hair and sighed. 'I don't know either,' he laughed.

Chicago 1985

The long flight home had been a poignant one for Mimi, and was lengthened by a delay when, on landing in New York in order to change planes, she was compelled to wait a couple of hours due to an electrical storm over Indiana. She couldn't wait to reach home and telephone Mark to reassure him that she loved him. Memories of the last precious hours spent with him had prevented her dozing during the flight, but now that euphoria was being replaced with impatience. However, by the time her plane eventually took off she was fast asleep.

It was well past midnight when they finally approached O'Hare Airport where her parents had already been waiting several frustrating hours to collect their daughter. Looking down as the plane circled over the city, Mimi was enchanted. The sight of a myriad coloured twinkling lights below outlining the grid-patterned streets, contrasted sharply against the black mass of the lake, it was a wonderful experience.

Mimi was happy enough to be home and looked forward to her comfortable bed, though her heart and deeper emotions remained in England. In just two short weeks she had discovered Lizzie's secret, completed her book—and fallen in love with an Englishman! She smiled happily to herself, the future seemed bright; there was a lot to do and Mark had agreed to visit her in September.

Later, with her own belongings about her once more, she relaxed contentedly in her familiar surroundings, thinking. There would be much to miss if she moved to England but also much to gain, and if Lizzie and Peter could travel the world all those years ago and find happiness, then why shouldn't she?

Suddenly the familiar wail of a nearby railroad engine broke the silence of the night as it moved on its long journey towards the plains. Perhaps, just as Lizzie recalled the cry of the Lapwing over the farm, so might she in years to come, remember fondly the sound of the trains calling out brazenly as they passed through her home town.

Marjorie Dunn

The T'alli Stone

The T'alli Stone is a gentle but compelling love story set in South Yorkshire around the the time of the end of the Napoleonic Wars, when the starving lower classes were ready to rise against oppression.

Fanny Garnett is a respectable but rebellious girl, she becomes infatuated with John, an idealistic reformer who is the victim of a vicious revenge plot. The third character in this romantic triangle is Gervase, a shy, respectable business man, who has known Fanny since she was a child.

Although a work of fiction, many of the incidents cited in the book have been drawn and adapted from actual events and from local newspapers of the time, giving the book a fascinating insight into life in Sheffield and the surrounding area at the turn of the nineteenth century.

ISBN: 1-874718-16-4   £5.95

The Hallamshire Press

Marjorie Dunn

The Maggie Kelly

Carefully researched, and written with a touch of humour and sympathetic understanding, the Maggie Kelly takes us on a journey along the canals and rivers between Sheffield and Kingston-upon-Hull, in 1851. The story is set partly in these two towns and tells of Michael, who, after the death of his father, struggles to take over the running of the keel with the help of his sister. Their future looks bleak because of the gradual decline in trade on the canals until help comes from an unusual man and his family. This has far-reaching consequences for them all. The trials, tribulations, loves and adventures of these characters will keep the reader intrigued to the last page.

ISBN: 1-874718-58-X   £7.95

The Hallamshire Press